HOPES & DREAMS

Claudia Carroll is a number one best-selling author in Ireland and a top ten bestseller in the UK, selling over 700,000 copies of her paperbacks alone. She was born in Dublin where she still lives and where she has worked extensively both as a theatre and stage actress. She now writes full-time.

Also by Claudia Carroll

Meet Me in Manhattan
Love Me or Leave Me
Me & You
Will You Still Love Me Tomorrow?
A Very Accidental Love Story
Always & Forever
Do You Want to Know a Secret?

HOPES & DREAMS

Claudia Carroll

First published in 2010 by Avon,
a division of HarperCollins*Publishers*

This edition first published in the United States in 2019
by Aria, an imprint of Head of Zeus Ltd

Copyright © Claudia Carroll, 2010

The moral right of Claudia Carroll to be identified as the author
of this work has been asserted in accordance with the
Copyright, Designs and Patents Act of 1988.

All rights reserved. No part of this publication may be reproduced,
stored in a retrieval system, or transmitted, in any form or by any
means, electronic, mechanical, photocopying, recording,
or otherwise, without the prior permission of both the
copyright owner and the above publisher of this book.

This is a work of fiction. All characters, organizations and events
portrayed in this novel are either products of the author's imagination
or are used fictitiously.

A CIP catalogue record for this book is available from the British
Library.

ISBN 9781788548557

Aria
an imprint of Head of Zeus
First Floor East
5–8 Hardwick Street
London EC1R 4RG

HOPES & DREAMS

*For my great friend, Weldon Costelloe.
With love and thanks.*

'Only when the tide goes out, do you discover who's been swimming naked.'

Warren Buffet

'They say that when you ask God for your heart's desire, he'll give you one of three possible answers. The first is yes. The second is, not yet. And the third is, I have something far, far better in mind.

Answer three is kind of where this story starts . . .'

Jessie Woods

Prologue

Once upon a time, there was a little girl whose favourite fairytale character was Cinderella. It was easy for her to relate to her heroine because, you see, they'd so much in common. Just like Cinderella, her mum had died when she was three years old, leaving only herself and her dad. Course, she was too young to remember; all she was aware of was that everyone – neighbours, distant relations she'd never met before or since – was suddenly an awful lot nicer to her. Money was tight and her dad had to slave away all the hours he could to support them. But no matter how busy he was, he'd always rush home and snatch time to read his little princess her favourite fairy story.

And so this child, whose name was Jessie by the way, grew up dreaming. But never about fairy godmothers or pumpkins magically changing into glass coaches with mice to drive them, which frankly she thought was all a bit daft and OTT. No, what Jessie really loved most about Cinderella's story was the very last sentence, 'And they all lived happily ever after.' Because that's what she wanted more than anything else. To live happily ever after in a huge big castle, far from where she came, where she could make sure her dad never had to work so hard or fret about money ever again. Somewhere she could feed him more than just spaghetti hoops on toast for dinner night after night, which was pretty much all she knew how to cook. Somewhere miles from the corporation house they lived in, where they'd be able to afford a glittery tree and presents at Christmas and maybe where they could even take a holiday to the seaside, just like all the other girls in her class did. And most of all, somewhere she wouldn't have to worry about her dad any more. A place where he'd be happy; so happy, that never again would she have to listen through the paper-thin walls to the muffled sound of him softly crying to himself alone in his room at night, when he thought she was sound asleep.

Then, when she turned ten years old, a life-altering event happened that suddenly turned Jessie's whole little world upside down. Something which made her feel even more Cinderella-like than ever. If she'd been in a hurry to get out and make her dreams come true before, now she was in a race against the clock. But all the odds in life's lottery seemed to be stacked against her. Because how could a girl from the wrong side of the tracks ever hope to live a life of wealth and security? She wasn't brainy enough to be a successful doctor or sharp enough to be a rich lawyer, even if they could have afforded the college fees. And that's when Jessie realised exactly how she could unlock the low door in the wall that would lead her to this magical wonderland.

Fame, she decided, would be her key. Her escape.

Celebrity. Because nobody minded where stars came from or how little they had growing up, did they? She'd work hard, shake off her past, haul herself up and become a real-life rags-to-riches success story, with all the trappings, just like the presenters she loved watching on TV. And their job seemed so, so easy. Talking into a microphone. Asking questions to interviewees, then nodding and listening. Sure any eejit could do that! And if there was anything Jessie was good at, it was asking questions and listening. It would be a doddle. She could do it in her sleep. She'd get paid a fortune, be able to afford beautiful things, be recognised everywhere she went and, most of all, be able to get far away from where she came and take proper care of her dad in a house so big you could nearly sign a peace treaty in it.

And of course if she just happened to meet Prince Charming along the way, then whoop-di-do . . .

NINETEEN YEARS LATER

Chapter One

'Once upon a time, there lived a stunning, modern-day princess whose life was so perfect, it was like a beautiful dream. And here she lives, in her very own fabulous palazzo, with real-life Prince Charming, successful entrepreneur Sam Hughes. I'm speaking, of course, about the nation's favourite TV girl, who's kindly invited me into her breathtaking home today, the one and only Jessie Woods!'

'And . . . . . . CUT!'

Oh God, I knew this was a bad idea. In fact, there's so much wrong with that last statement, I don't even know where to begin. For starters, my house is definitely *not* a 'palazzo', that's just what pushy estate agents call it, just because there happens to be a lot of pink marble going on. Which looks great in photos but, take it from me, is like living inside an ice rink in winter. Well, either an ice rink or a mausoleum. It isn't mine either, I'm only renting it from a couple who are away for a few years. If it was properly mine, I'd have to do a major rethink on all the pink; from certain angles, it's like something Jordan vomited up. Oh, and I don't live with Sam either, not officially anyway. He still has his own place down in the country because, get this, he thinks here is too small for a couple. His home, by the way, is the approximate size of Versailles.

'Jessie, do you think we could get a shot of you over here at the grand piano?' Katie, the interviewer, trills across the room at me, to where I'm perched up on a bar stool, still getting make-up slapped on and nowhere near camera-ready. For the record, Katie's absolutely lovely; young and spray-tanned and skinny, hungry for work and only delighted to be in front of a TV camera. Just like I was at her age. In fact, give her another two years and she could very well end up doing my job. She's also bouncy and energetic and, when there's a microphone in her hand, talks in exactly the same sing-song cadences that air hostesses do. Honest to God, she'll be doing seat-belt demonstrations next. Plus, like most TV presenters, she talks in exclamation marks and uses the word 'fabulous' a lot.

'Oooh, Jessie, I've just had a fabulous idea. Maybe we could film you actually tinkling away at the piano? Would that be OK, do you think?'

She beams at me, brightly, expectantly, and I haven't the heart to tell her that the only thing I could possibly manage to bash out would be 'Chopsticks'. The piano, like so much in this house, is kind of just for show, really. I mean, no one actually plays these things outside of concerts in Carnegie Hall, do they?

'Oh, no, hold on, wait now . . . I've a far more fabulous idea,' Katie thankfully changes her mind, but still somehow manages to sound like cabin crew cheerily telling you to clip up the tray in front of you, that there's only fifteen minutes to landing. 'Instead, how about a shot of you standing just here by the piano and talking us through all the amazing photos you've displayed on it? Yeah? Wouldn't that just be, emmmmm . . . what's the word? Fabulous!'

'Yes, Katie. That would be . . . fabulous.'

I am such a moron. When will I learn that it's a really crappy idea to let a film crew into your house to shoot an 'at-home-with, day-in-the-life-of' piece when a) I'm as hung over as a dog, b) on account of point a), I've had exactly seventeen minutes' sleep, c) I only barely managed to haul myself out of bed in time to clean up the living room for this lot arriving, so if they ask to see any other room, I'm finished. In this house, the law of mess transference applies; i.e., no sooner do I tidy one room than an equal and corresponding amount of clutter appears somewhere else. Plus, because the downstairs loo has been blocked for about three weeks now, the entire house is beginning to smell like low tide in Calcutta and I can't afford to get a plumber out. Ahhh, plumbers. God's way of telling you that you make too little money. Worst of all, though, is point d) in what's become something of a monthly nightmare in this house: my Visa bill has just arrived in a worryingly thick envelope and is now plonked on the fireplace looking accusingly at me, almost daring me to open it.

I'll come back to that last point later. What's immediately bothering me now is that the poor unfortunate make-up artist is having a right job of it trying to disguise the purpley bits under my saggy, baggy, bloodshot eyes, to make me look even halfway human. Because I'm supposed to be all glowing and healthy and radiant for this shoot, not pasty and washed out, with a tongue that feels like carpet tiles and a cement mixer churning round inside my brain.

Then another horrible tacked-on worry; my agent would put me up against a wall and shoot me if he could see the minging state of me right now. In fact, it was his idea that I take part in this whole, lunatic *A Day in the Life* documentary, on the grounds that the TV show that I present is coming up to its season finale, which means my contract is up for renewal, which means, in his sage words, it's time to 'Beef up your profile and hope for the best.'

The show I front, you see, is a light, fluffy, tea-time, family-friendly programme called *Jessie Would*, where people text in mad, wacky ideas for dares and then I have to do them. Yes, all of them; the good, the bad and the downright unprintable. So basically, my job is whipped cream and as said agent is constantly reminding me, this is not a good economy to be whipped cream in. Particularly not when you're in debt up to your oxters, desperately trying to keep up this lifestyle with friends who insist on partying like it's the last days of Rome.

'Late one last night, was it Jessie?' the lovely make-up artist whispers sympathetically to me, brandishing a mascara wand in the same, skilled way that a surgeon holds a scalpel. I manage a guilty nod back. Wasn't even my fault either. In fact, if it were up to me, I'd have been in bed by half ten with a cup of milky Horlicks and two cucumbers on my eyes. Honest. But then you see Sam, that's my boyfriend, got a last-minute invitation to a launch party that a sort of rival-frenemy-business contact of his was having and we had no choice but to go along. Long story, but basically Sam's got wind of the fact that there's a vacancy coming up as a panellist on one of those entrepreneurial TV programmes where people pitch business ideas, some terrific, some crap, to a terrifying gang of business experts, who subsequently either rip them apart or else rob their ideas and claim them as their own. Sorry, I meant to say invest in these wonderful commercial opportunities, *ahem, ahem*. Anyway, the guy who was hosting the launch party last night is already a regular panellist on this particular show, and Sam figured it would be the perfect way for him to network and get his spoke in early, as it were. And I'm not just saying it because I adore him, but he really would be wonderful on the show; Sam is young, charming, successful, has a finger in just about every corporate pie you can think of and genuinely believes that being good in business is a shamanistic power bestowed on the few. Plus, because he's a high-profile economist by trade, with an occasional column in *The Times* and everything, he's already done loads of bits and pieces on telly and one commentator even hailed him as something of a poster boy for the world of finance, 'who manages the not inconsiderable feat of making economics accessible to the man on the street'. Blah, blah, blah. In fact, pretty much every time there's either an interest rate hike or a bank collapse, some news show on Channel Six will be sure to wheel Sam out for keen yet insightful commentary on said crisis. Mind you, it helps that he's outrageously good-looking, in a clean-cut, sharply tailored, chiselled, TV-friendly kind of way. Darcy-licious. Conventionally tall, dark and handsome, like one of the junior Kennedy cousins, right down to the thick bouffey hair, the toothiness and the tan. The kind of fella that even gay men drool over. He's also incredibly hard-working, with about twenty different business interests on the go and basically hasn't slept for about the last five years or so. Oh, and as if all that wasn't enough, in his spare time he's written a soon to be published autobiography entitled, and I swear I'm NOT making this up, *If Business is the New Rock & Roll, then I'm Elvis Presley.*

Don't ask me why he wants this particular TV gig so desperately, although he often jokes and says that you're never closer to God than when you're on television. I think for a high-achiever like Sam it's just the next logical rung on the ladder, the jewel in the crown. Although, knowing him and his Type A personality, no sooner will he get what he wants, than he'll stop wanting it and start chasing some other rainbow. Politics, maybe. He's one of those guys that could basically turn his hand to anything and it wouldn't surprise me a bit if he ended up running the country in a few years' time. But for now, his one goal is to be a panellist on this investment show for budding entrepreneurs and knowing him, he'll basically drill his way through concrete to make it happen.

Anyway, I could talk about Sam all day, but I won't. Suffice to say that like a good little Super Couple (the tabloids' mortifying tag, not mine) I went along to the party with him, intending to only stay for just the one and somehow it ended up being 5 a.m. by the time we crawled out of there ...

The funny thing is, people think that Sam and I have this glittering, red carpet, party lifestyle; what they don't realise is that it's actually work. Honestly. OK, so it may look like our lives are one big, long bank holiday weekend, but trust me, it takes it out of you. It is also costing me a bloody fortune.

'Stop looking over at the fireplace, keep your eyes to me, Jessie,' whispers lovely make-up girl as she gamely dabs concealer into eye sockets which still haven't properly opened up yet.

'Oops, sorry,' I mutter.

Shit. She caught me staring up at the Visa bill. Which,

now that I come to think of it, mightn't be too bad this month, I desperately try to convince myself. Because I really did try my best to be good, cut back and live within my means, as my accountant put it during one particularly stern phone call which I'd quite frankly prefer to blank out, after she discovered that the interest on my credit card was more than half what I pay in rent for this house. And that's only the credit card she knows about; I've another secret one, also maxed out, that I'm too scared to even mention to her, for fear the woman will have an anxiety stroke.

'You don't understand,' I hotly defended myself to her. 'Anyone who lives and works in the public eye has a lot of unavoidable day-to-day expenses.'

'And what exactly would these "unavoidable expenses" be?' she politely asked. The business-class flights for a trip to New York that I forked out for? The clothes and blow-dries and manicures and spending money which I needed for said trip? Not to even get started on the hotel we stayed in, which only cost about five times more than I could afford.

Sam's unstoppable drive and my chronic over-spending, you'll see, are pretty much the twin kernels of my life right now. Tell you something else too; toxic debt-related anxiety and a thumping hangover make for one helluva lethal cocktail. As the sainted make-up girl lashes on more bronzing powder than you'd normally see on the whole of Girls Aloud, I do a few quick mental sums.

OK. I'm three full months behind on rent. I can't even remember the last time I wasn't overdrawn. All I know is that the letters I keep getting from my bank manager are becoming progressively snottier and snottier. Phrases such as, 'Central debt recovery agencies,' and 'You realise this will affect your credit rating for a period of XXX . . .' have even been invoked. Shudder.

And there's worse. Far worse. Up until last week, I was the proud owner of a flashy, zippy little BMW Z4 sports car, cherry red with bright lemon-yellow seats, which I know makes it sound like a packet of Opal Fruits on wheels, but trust me, the colour scheme did actually work. Anyway, I got it on one of those car-leasing HP deals, where the idea is you drive off in a brand, spanking new set of wheels immediately, then pay it off by the month. Perfect deal for someone like me; live now, pay later. Trouble is, I got so scarily far behind in repayments that, one night last week after way too many glasses of wine at some art gallery do, I crawled home at all hours in a taxi to find the car gone from my driveway. Just gone. Disappeared. So I thought it was stolen, natch, and was on the verge of ringing the police when I found a letter on my doorstep telling me it had actually been repossessed. Course I was way too morto to tell anyone the actual truth, so I decided the best humiliation-avoidance tactic was to stick to my original 'stolen car' story. Which I would have got away with too, only Emma Sheridan, my best friend and co-presenter at work, bounced into the production office a few days later and told me she'd just seen my 'stolen' car in the forecourt of Maxwell Motors with a big 'For Sale' sign stuck on it. Definitely mine, she insisted, sure how many other bright red Z4s are there on the road with lemon-yellow leather seats?

So I was rightly rumbled and had to confess all, but the thing about Emma is that she's not just a showbiz pal, she's a genuine pal. In all the years I've known her, there are two things I've never, ever seen her do; repeat gossip or eat chocolate. As discreet as a nun in a silent order about her own private life and yet the only woman I know who's honest enough to admit to Botox. Bless her, when I came clean about my money woes, she even offered me a cash loan to tide me over. So now, whenever anyone asks me when I'm getting a new car, lovely, loyal Emma laughs and waves it aside and tells me it's nearly cheaper for me to get cabs all the time.

Whereas the actual truth is, the way things are going, I'll probably end up walking everywhere from now on. Barefoot. In the lashing rain. With newspaper tied with twine around my feet and bloodhounds baying at my heels. Singing the orphans' chorus from *Annie*, 'It's the Hard Knock Life.'

Worse, though, I think, as a fresh wash of anxiety comes over me, is that there doesn't seem to be any end to my money troubles. Ever. You see, with myself and Sam, there's always the next night out, the next weekend away, the next trip abroad. Easter is only round the corner and we've already booked to go down to Marbella which I can't afford and yet at the same time, can't get out of.

Honest to God, I sometimes feel like I'm stuck on a never-ending financial hamster wheel where I'm constantly stretching my almost-melted credit cards just to keep pace with him. I'm not even certain how it happened, but somehow I've got sucked into a world where appearances are everything and it's like I've no choice but to spend big just to hold my own against all my new, posher, wealthier friends.

This house being the perfect example. The logical part of my brain, which let's face it, I don't hear from all that often, tells me that it's completely mental; the place is ridiculously expensive and way too big for me, but when it first came on the market . . . hard to put into words, but it was like all my childhood fantasies finally coming true. I just had to have it, simple as that. So now I'm a lone, single person renting a five-bedroomed mansion which I can't even afford to get the downstairs toilet unblocked in. Christ alive, let it be engraved on my tombstone. 'Here lies Jessie Woods. Fur coat and no knickers.'

On the plus side though, I really have made a heroic effort to economise this month. In fact, I distinctly remember suggesting to Sam last weekend that there was no need for us to bother eating out in Shanahan's on the Green, where the starters are so tiny, they'd leave a fruit fly gagging for more. Instead, let's stay in and I'll cook, I gamely volunteered. Well, the man nearly had to pick himself up off the floor he was laughing so hard. Honest to God, he was still sniggering two full days later. I'm the world's worst cook and have the burn tissue to prove it. And for some unfathomable reason, no matter what I do to food, it always ends up tasting like wood. Wood, or else feet.

But the point is that I'm *trying*.

Take last month's New York trip for instance. It wasn't even my fault. Well, not really. You see, Sam and I are really matey with this other couple, Nathaniel and Eva, who are old buddies of his, dating back to his school days, and we always pal around in a foursome with them. They're lovely, gorgeous people, but . . . the thing is, they just have so much more money at their disposal than I have. Nathaniel is chief executive of his family's recession-proof beef export business and basically keeps himself on a Premiership footballer's salary. He and Eva have been married for years and have two perfect twin boys, with an army of nannies to take care of them, leaving Eva with a lot of free time on her hands for weekends away, charity lunches and shopping trips abroad. Which is actually how that New York trip came about in the first place; it was their wedding anniversary and nothing would do them but to organise this lavish trip to stay at the Plaza, where they got married. And of course, Sam and I, as their closest friends, were invited along. Now I know Sam would gladly have offered to pay for me if I'd asked, but he knows me well and knows I'd die rather than do that; I'm so much happier paying my own way. OK, I may be up to my armpits in debt, but at least I have my independence.

There's a fair chance I could end up in the bankruptcy courts, but I have my pride, which as my dear departed dad always used to say, is beyond price. Poor darling Dad. The best friend I ever had. There's not a day that goes by where I don't think of him and miss him so much that it physically hurts. But at the same time, half of me is glad he's not around to see the insolvent, overstretched financial disaster that I've become. 'Neither a borrower nor a lender be,' he always used to say and every time I hear his soft voice repeating those wise words in my head, honest to God, the guilt feels like heartburn.

But can I just add this? In my defence, on said New York trip I did suggest we stay in a cheaper hotel, or even rent an apartment between us all, but Sam just laughed at me and I didn't want everyone to think I was some tight-fisted ol' cheapskate, so, instead, I did what I always do. Put it on the Visa card and decided to worry about it later. Because the very, very worst brush you could possibly tar any Irish person with is to inflict them with the Curse of the Meany. You know, someone who doesn't stand their round. Who goes out with no cash, then expects everyone else to subsidise them. Or, worst of all, someone who hangs around with rich people and automatically assumes they'll just bankroll evenings out and expensive dinners and weekends away, etc. And correct me if I'm wrong, but isn't that why credit cards were invented? To help people like me who may have . . . cash flow issues. In fact, now that I'm thinking about it a bit more logically, if my accountant is going to get arsy about this month's Visa bill, then I'll just remind her that I have a job. My lovely, lovely job, that I adore so much that I actually look forward to going into work. A really good, well-paid, telly job too. And these days, sure that's like the Holy Grail.

Come to think of it, I don't even know what the big deal is. I mean, it's not like the bubble is about to burst or anything, now is it?

I just need a new accountant, that's all.

Chapter Two

Twenty minutes, one strong Americano, two Solpadene and three Berocca tablets later and I'm standing beside Katie, feeling an awful lot sparkier and up-for-it. More like myself. Even if on days like this, I almost feel like my nickname could be Solpachina.

'Oooh, look at you! You look fabulous!' Katie squeals in my ear. Which we both know is just a well-meant but polite lie. However, I will say this, the make-up girl deserves a BAFTA for at least managing to make me look like I didn't sleep the night up a tree, before being savaged by werewolves on the way home; the only thing which might possibly account for the nesty, Russell Brand-esque state of my hair when I first opened the door to the camera crew earlier this morning.

'Right then,' says Katie, lining herself up in front of the camera, with a load of framed photos strategically dotted on the piano between us. 'Ready to go?'

'I've been ready for the last two hours, actually,' the cameraman growls impatiently back at us, coughing and spluttering like a Lada.

Lovely. It's going to be one of those days.

'Well, as you can imagine, we're all so excited about this

very special edition of *A Day in the Life* and here's the reason why... Presenting our fabulous hostess, Jessie Woods herself!'

So off Katie riffs in the air-hostess voice and I find myself wondering if anyone's ever told her that there are, in fact, other adjectives than fabulous.

'Oooh, isn't she just like a little girl's idea of what a princess should be?' she says straight to camera and not actually looking at me. 'With her beautiful, blonde hair and fabulous, trim, toned figure! It's like skinny jeans were designed especially with this woman in mind!'

She giggles and I resist the urge to a) vomit, b) remind her that this is, in fact, TV, not radio, so viewers presumably can see for themselves and besides, you should never ever, EVER talk down to an audience. Instead, I just grin inanely and do a false TV laugh back. You know, head thrown back, jaw fish-wired into a grin: ha, ha, HA!

'So, Jessie, we're loving, loving, LOVING your fabulous home, but maybe you could tell us a little about some of the photos you have on display here?'

The camera does an obliging panning shot of some recent pics and just for a split second, I get to see my own life from the outside. It's weird but somehow every single snap manages to look like a posed photo opportunity. Sam and I at the Derby with Nathaniel and Eva; me wearing what appears to be three table napkins strategically sewn together to cover up my girlie bits. The four of us on a ski trip, me in the centre; laughing, messing around, having great craic, the life and soul of the party. Two things strike me. One is that Sam is on his mobile in every single shot. The other is, our lives look so stunningly, dazzlingly perfect... Christ alive, no wonder we piss people off.

'Ooh, here's a terrific one!' Katie sing-songs. 'Just look at you! Like a classier version of Paris Hilton! What a stunning dress! So, tell us, where was this taken?'

OK. The real answer to that question is, *Are you kidding me, Katie? The only thing I have in common with Paris Hilton is dyed blonde hair and a credit card. And the dress isn't a bit stunning; it's more like a big, flowery shower curtain from a Bed, Bath and Beyond sale bin.* Lesson: if you are eejit enough to listen to stylists, then you deserve everything that's coming to you. As long as these people garner column inches, believe me, they're not bothered if you end up beaten into a skinny size zero pant suit, looking like a boiler that's too big for its lagging jacket.

However, I go with the interview answer instead. 'Why thanks, Katie. That photo was taken at the National TV awards, where *Jessie Would* was nominated for best TV show, can you believe it, for the second year running?!' I omit to mention that we lost out to a home video programme where people send in clips of their dogs playing musical instruments, that kind of thing. It sticks in my mind because next day there was a pap shot of me rubbing my eyelid to try and get a bit of fluff out, with a headline, *Who Let The Dogs Out? Jessie's Tears At Being Upstaged By Mutt.*

'Oooh, look at this one, you brave girl, you!' says Katie, picking up a still shot from the show of me skydiving. 'Tell me, is that the hardest dare you ever had to do on *Jessie Would?*'

Real answer: *Funnily no. Sure any eejit can skydive; you just hold your breath and jump. What was weird about that one though, was that some pervert actually texted in a suggestion that I do it in a bikini.*

Interview answer: 'Ha, ha, HA. Not at all, Katie. As a matter of fact, I'm often asked that question . . .'

'Oooh, or what about the time you had to spend the night alone in a haunted house?'

Real answer: *Are you off your head? Best night's sleep I ever had.*

Interview answer: 'Ha, ha, HA. Yes, that one did put years on me, but by far the most challenging dare I've ever had to do on the show was the time I had to work as head chef in a restaurant. Sixty covers in a single night. Nearly killed me.' I might add that fifty-eight out of the sixty customers demanded their money back after they were kept waiting for almost two hours with nothing but the bread sticks in front of them to nibble at. And that was after I had to announce to the whole, starving dining room that if anyone happened to find my earring inside the fish pie, would they please mind letting me know? Oh and for the record, the two people in the restaurant who didn't complain were Sam's parents; God love them, they desperately wanted to be on the show and were just being kind. What people don't realise though, when they're texting in all their wacky dare ideas, is that the extreme stuff doesn't knock a feather out of me. It's normal everyday, bread-and-butter things that make me want to lie down in a darkened room listening to dolphin music and taking tablets. Like bank statements. Or Visa bills. Or anything with 'Final Notice' stamped in red across it.

'Oooh, and look at this fabulous shot of you and the sexy Sam Hughes! Tell us, Jessie, how did you two first meet?'

I glow a bit, the way I always do whenever I get a chance to talk about Sam. OK, the real answer to this question is:

we met at Channel Six when I first started working there, God, almost nine years ago now. I was just twenty-one years old, straight off a media training course and working as a runner on *News Time*, which Sam seemed to appear on every other week, talking about GNPs and PPIs and whatever you're having yourself. 'Runner', though, as everyone knows, is a glorified word for 'dogsbody', so my job basically involved getting the tea, emptying bins in dressing rooms and on more than one occasion, having to blow-dry under one newsreader's armpits with a hair dryer, so her couture dress wouldn't get deodorant stains on it. I'll never forget it; her name was Diane Daly so all the floor staff, myself included, used to call her Diva Di. A nasty nickname I know, but she'd really earned it; this was a woman who'd regularly ring me at 6 a.m. before work, to order me to the fruit and veg market so I could buy supplies of sprouted beans for her, the time she was doing her whole wheat-free, gluten-free, lactose-intolerant thing. And who would think absolutely nothing of getting me to drop her kids to school, while she skipped off to get her Restylane injections. All of which I did happily, gratefully and without whinging because I was just so overjoyed to be working in TV. This, as far as I was concerned, was It, the Big Break, which could only lead on to bigger and better things.

Two things came out of that whole experience for me. One is that to this day, I always treat the runners on *Jessie Would* like royalty: iPods for their birthdays, posh spa treatments at Christmas; toxic debt or no toxic debt, the way I look on it is, they've earned it, the hard way. The other thing is . . . that's where I first met Sam. Vivid memory; it was just before a live broadcast and there he was, patiently waiting behind the scenes to take part in a panel discussion piece about debt to profit ratios or something equally boring. Radiating confidence, not a nerve in his body. He ordered a coffee from me and I was so petrified, my shaking hands accidentally spilled some of it onto the lap of his good suit, but instead of ranting and raving about it, he couldn't have been sweeter. Just laughed it off, said it was an accident, that he'd be sitting down behind a desk anyway so he could be naked from the waist down and sure no one would even know the difference. Then he smiled that smile; so dazzling it should nearly come with a *ping!* sound effect, and I was a complete goner.

Course it turned out every female on *News Time* fancied him, but he was dating some famous, leggy, modelly one back then, so it went without saying that we all knew none of us had a snowball's chance in hell of getting near him. But just for a bit of devilment, myself and the make-up girls used to invent all kinds of imaginary sex scenarios about him, like he was the ultimate Prince Charming; utterly unattainable, but great craic to fantasise about.

'Me and Sam Hughes, on a sun lounger, at sunset, looking out over the Caribbean . . .'

'No, I've a better one, me and Sam Hughes in a dressing room, just before the show . . .'

'No, NO. My go: me and Sam in a log cabin during a power cut with only a king-sized double bed for our entertainment centre . . .'

. . . was all you could hear along the corridors of Channel Six on the days we knew he'd be in. We even had a 'hottie alert' system, whereby the minute one of us saw his car in the car park, we were duty bound to text the others IMMEDIATELY, so everyone had a fair and equal chance to get their make-up on.

Anyway, whenever I did see Sam after the whole, mortifying coffee-on-the-crotch episode, which was maybe about once a month or so, he always made a point of asking me how I was getting on in the new job. Always friendly, always playfully nicknaming me Woodsie, always encouraging, always respectful and never, ever someone who looked down on me as just a humble gofer with Pot Noodle for brains.

Then, one day about three months later, he found me in the staff canteen, hysterically trying to babysit Diva Di's bratty eight- and ten-year-old boys, who were running riot around the place and ambushing me with lumpy cartons of strawberry-flavoured yoghurt. The pair of them had completely doused me in it; clothes, hair, jeans, everything, soaked right through to my knickers. And, of course, life being what it is, at that very moment, in sauntered Sam, as Darcy-licious as ever. He let out a yell at the kids, which did actually manage to shut them up, then sat me down and helped dry me off with a load of paper napkins. I'll never forget it; he x-rayed me with jet-black eyes, laughed and said, 'To think they say working in TV is glamorous.' I gamely managed a grin, suddenly aware that he dated famous models and here I was, stinking of sticky, strawberry yoghurt-y crap.

'So, tell me. Is this really what you signed up for, Woodsie?'

Now the thing about Sam is that he can be a bit like those motivational speakers you'd normally see on *Oprah*; you know, the ones who convince you that you can turn your life around in seven days, that kind of thing. It's like he comes with a double dose of drive and it can be infectious.

So I told him everything. Out it all came; about how I wanted to work for Channel Six so desperately that I really was prepared to do anything without question. Including letting Diva Di take complete and utter advantage of me. I was so terrified of losing my job, I explained, that I just hadn't the guts to point out that babysitting her horrible children and blow-drying under her armpits with a hair dryer, was well above and beyond my job description.

'And where do you see yourself in five years' time?' I remember him asking, a favourite question of his.

'In front of the camera,' I told him without even having to pause for thought. That's all I'd ever wanted or dreamed about. I can even remember the exact phrase I used, 'I'd ring the Angelus bell if I had to.' But then back came all the old insecurities; would someone like me ever be given a shot, would I even be good enough or would I fall flat on my face and make a roaring eejit of myself?

'Are you kidding me, Woodsie?' he grinned, wiping a bit of strawberry yoghurt off my hair with a napkin. 'A knockout like you? They'd be bloody lucky to have you. And always remember that.'

Anyway, I think right there and then he must have seen some spark of ambition in me that mirrored his own, because any time I'd bump into him after that, he'd always make a point of asking me who exactly I'd sent my CV off to, what contacts I'd made, did I know what internal jobs were coming up? Kind of like a career guidance officer with a grinding work ethic, except one that I fancied the knickers off.

Then, by the end of that year, through an awful lot of grovelling/hassling/pounding down doors, etc., I eventually managed to land a proper front-of-camera gig. It was only doing the weekend late-night weather report (at 10 p.m., midnight, then again at 2 a.m.) but to me, it was the stuff of dreams. It was there I first met the lovely Emma, in fact; she used to do the news report, I'd do the weather, then the two of us would skite off to some nightclub and laugh the rest of the night away. We were exactly the same age, we'd both started working at Channel Six at the same time and what can I say? From day one, we just bonded.

The only downside was, I never bumped into Sam any more. In fact, apart from Emma, the only person I ever saw regularly was the nightwatchman at the security hut on my way to and from work. I kept up with Sam through the papers, but of course the only thing I was ever really interested in was who he was dating. An ultra-successful, Alpha female type usually; his identikit women always seemed to be groomed, glossy, gorgeous and it went without saying, high achievers. It was like his minimum dating requirement was that you had to work an eighty-hour week and earn a minimum six-figure annual salary. So I put him to the back of my mind and for the next few years just kept my head down and got on with it. Funny thing was though, the harder I worked, the luckier I seemed to get. It was miraculous; as though the planets had aligned for me and, even more amazingly, I seemed to be able to do no wrong. Job followed job at Channel Six, until eventually, hallelujah be praised, the *Jessie Would* show came about.

Then, flash forward to about two years ago, when I was at the Channel Six Christmas party with Emma, both of us pissed out of our heads. She was celebrating the show being commissioned for a second series, I was drowning my sorrows having just found out that my then boyfriend was seeing someone else behind my back. During Christmas week too, the worthless, faithless bastard. Everyone kept coming over to say congratulations on the show and I was obliged to beam and act all delighted. All whilst sending Cheater Man about thirty text messages, ranging in tone from disbelief to accusation by way of pleading. Waste of time though; every one of them was completely ignored. It was beyond awful; Christmas is when I lost my darling dad and God knows, given the highly dysfunctional background I come from, it's a hard enough time of year to get through without adding 'serially single man-repeller' into the mix as well. And then I saw Sam. Also alone, also dateless. My heart stopped; I'd forgotten how uncomfortably handsome he was. He came straight over, congratulated me on the show's success and then, sensing something was amiss, asked me what was up. Now it takes an awful lot for me to start snivelling or bawling, but the combination of too much Pinot Grigio and being dumped and missing Dad was all just too much for me. I knew if I didn't get the hell out of there immediately, I was in danger of making a complete and utter holy show of myself in front of him and everyone else, so I blushed scarlet, mumbled some lame excuse about having another party to go to and bolted for the door.

But when I replay it back in my head now, it seems almost like a scene from a French movie, complete with mood-enhancing smoke machines and violins playing as a soundtrack in the background. There I was on the road outside Channel Six, in the lashing rain, holding back the tears and frantically trying to wave down a cab; next thing a sleek black Mercedes pulls up beside me on the kerb and the window elegantly glides down. It's Sam. Who knew I was upset and who followed me, bless him. He coaxed me out of the icy rain and into the warmth of his car, gently asking me what the problem was and how he could help fix it. And so, not for the first time, I ended up pouring out my whole tale of woe to him. All about Cheater Man and how he actually broke up with me . . . via text message, the cowardly gobshite. Didn't even have the manners to dump me for someone younger or thinner either.

Sam flashed his Hollywood smile at that, then turned to me. 'Woodsie,' he said, strong, clear and firm as ever, 'any guy that would treat a gorgeous girl like you that way is an idiot and why would you want to be with an idiot? Get rid of him.' Then the scorching black eyes gave me the sexiest up/down look before he cheekily added, 'So then . . .'

'So then . . .?' I swear, I could physically feel my heart thumping off my ribcage.

A long pause while we looked at each other, exchanging souls.

'So then . . . you can go out with me.'

Well, it was like something religious people must experience. Could this really be happening to me? Sam was too rich, too cool, too out of my league. I couldn't get my head around it. Then when we sailed through our first few magical dates and when it became obvious he was slowly morphing from fantasy fling to proper boyfriend, I worried so much about what he'd see in someone like me. Turned out the answer was the very thing that I thought would turn him off me; the fact that I'd never had any of the luxuries he took for granted and was now acting like a kid in a sweetshop, loving every second of the high life he introduced me to. Until he met me, he'd often say, he was becoming jaded with his fabulous lifestyle, but seeing it all fresh through my excited eyes somehow kept it all real for him. Every time he'd see me bouncing up and down on the bed in some posh hotel or gasping in awe at some view he'd long since tired of, like the Eiffel Tower or the Empire State Building, he said it made him fall in love with life all over again.

And in love with me too, I'd silently hope.

'Jessie?'

Oh shit. The interview. I almost forgot.

'You'd drifted off there for a moment,' Katie sing-songs. 'We were asking you about how you first met Sam?'

I go with the standard interview answer. Of course. 'Through work, Katie. You might say Channel Six brought us together. Ha, ha, HA.'

'And, tell us the truth now, any wedding plans?'

Real answer: *Ehhh . . . no. Mainly because he hasn't asked. At least, not yet, he hasn't. But then, with Sam you never know what's around the corner, so I live in hope. I mean, this is a guy who's big on spontaneity and we have been together for just over two years now, my longest relationship by a mile.*

'Jessie?'

Yet again, out comes the interview answer: 'Well, you know how it is, we're both so busy at the moment; honestly, it's just something that's never come up. But if it does, you'll be the first to know. Ha, ha, HA!'

'Oooh, but, look what I found here; what are you hiding from us?' says Katie, waving at the camera to pan right to the very back of the piano.

My heart skips a beat; something embarrassing I forgot to clean up? A pair of knickers from the last party I had? An empty tin of beer stuffed with cigarette butts? A final notice bill from the gas board? It's OK, I think, breathing normally again. Nothing too offensive, thank Christ; just an old photo of me when I first started out as a weather girl, with a horrible mousey brown bob, which kind of gave me a look of Julie Andrews from certain angles. Then another one of me in studio with Emma, my hair as spiky as a toilet brush and far, far blonder, taken when we first started working together, all of five years ago. Emma looks neat, be-suited and pristine, with her chestnut hair elegantly groomed as always, like she's ready to start reading the nine o'clock news at the drop of a hat.

Actually, at the time that photo was taken, I only had a tiny little five-minute feature-ette on what was then Emma's chat show; the wacky sidekick to her more sober, grounded TV persona. The balance of personalities seemed to work though; me wild and scatty, her cool and ordered. Then by some miracle (and a lot of encouragement from the mobile phone companies, who made a fortune out of all the texts people bombarded us with) my mad dare piece took off, and got so big that now the whole show is about me making an eejit of myself out on location, while Emma acts as anchor back in studio. Lesser women than Emma may have been slightly peeved at me stealing her thunder, but like I say, the girl is a walking saint and has never been anything but super-cool and encouraging about the whole thing. If there are angels masquerading as people wandering round this earth then Emma Sheridan most definitely is one.

Back to the interview and by now the camera is panning in on a photo of me with a broken leg, which I got after a bungee jump dare. But no, it was nothing as dramatic as whacking it off a bridge while suspended upside down by knicker elastic or anything; just a piece of camera equipment fell on me as I was clambering back into the van on our way back to base. My hair is longer in that shot and still blonder again; in fact, it flashes through my mind that the more successful I got on TV, the brighter the highlights got, right now the hair is almost platinum, the exact colour of Cillit Bang.

Then, out of nowhere, eagle-eyes Katie grabs up a photo which I'd forgotten all about. 'And here you are as a teenager. So pretty, even then! Tell us, Jessie, who are your two friends in the photo with you?'

Oh God, I'd completely forgotten. That's the trouble with airbrushing your past; the people you knew back then can sometimes seem like ghosts from a bygone age. OK, so the real answer to her question is that yes, that's me, aged about fourteen, with my then best friend Hannah and her older brother Steve, who lived across the road from us and who were amazingly kind to me during a very rough time in my life. We were thick as thieves, Hannah and I; after we left school, we even shared a flat for a few years, which suited both of us down to the ground. We were both eighteen and she wanted her independence, while I had just lost my darling dad and had to get the hell out of our house for . . . well, let's just say for personal reasons. Anyway, Hannah and I had a ball together. My life was slowly starting to turn a corner; I was working as a lounge girl in a bar at night so I could put myself through a media training course during the day, right up until I landed my first gig as a runner at Channel Six. Meanwhile Hannah was doing an apprenticeship in hairdressing and it seems like we just spent the whole time laughing and messing and getting on with our young lives. Steve worked as a handyman doing odd jobs wherever he could, but was always hanging out with us too, and it was just such a happy, joyful time all round. But then Hannah got married, I moved from behind the camera to in front of it and the last I heard of him, Steve had upped sticks and moved to the States. And so the three amigos drifted apart a bit. The way you do.

It's no one's fault or anything, these things just happen. You know how it is; you try meeting up whenever you can, but then realise that actually you don't have all that much in common any more. And in an alarmingly short time, old pals become shadowy people who you exchange Christmas cards with and scrawl across them, 'We must meet up sometime, it's been too long!!' But you never do.

God, I wonder what Hannah would say if she could see me now, given that this is exactly the type of show that we used to crack ourselves up laughing at, slagging off the D-list celebs desperate enough to go on them. 'For feck's sake, Jessie, what are you doing, dressed up like a dog's dinner and throwing your home open to these eejits?' most likely. 'You look like a right gobshite.' Hannah was never one to pull her punches.

I don't get a chance to go with the interview answer though. Because by then Katie has snatched on another, even older photo that brings a whole new set of memories flooding back.

This time it's an ancient, grainy shot of me aged about four, up a tree in our back garden at home, with my dad standing proudly at the bottom, arm rested against the tree-trunk, like he's just planted it all by himself. I'm in a pair of shorts, with a dirty face, scraped knees and a plaster on my arm.

'Oooh, look at little Jessie . . . such a cute little tomboy!! I think you must have been a daredevil even from a young age!'

Real answer: *Funny thing is I can remember that photo being taken so clearly. It wasn't long after my mum died and*

I remember spending all day every day up that tree. Coaxing me down was a daily ritual for my poor dad. He used to call me his little firecracker and would proudly tell neighbours and aunties that I was afraid of nothing. But then, losing your mum young makes you fearless. Because the worst thing that can possibly happen has already happened, so what's there left to be afraid of? I can't say that though, because, even after all these years, there's a good chance I might start sniffling.

Interview answer: 'Yes, Katie, that's me with my darling dad, who passed away almost twelve years ago now.'

A pause, while Katie fingers the old photo frame thoughtfully.

'And you're an only child?'

'Yup, certainly am.'

When I was younger, during interviews I used to do a wistful look into the middle distance whenever it came up about my being orphaned. I stopped though, when it was pointed out to me that actually, I just looked constipated.

'But your father remarried, didn't he?'

Shit. How does she know that?

'Emm . . . well, I suppose he did, yes, but . . .'

'And in actual fact, you grew up with your stepmother and two stepsisters, didn't you?'

'Well . . . the thing is . . .'

'She's called Joan, and her daughters are Maggie and Sharon. Isn't that right?'

Sweet baby Jesus and the orphans, she even knows their names? OK, now the saliva in my mouth has said, 'I'm outta here, see you!' Come on Jessie, think straight. Right then. Nothing to do but brush it off. I mean, everyone has family skeletons in the closet they don't necessarily want to talk about, don't they? And believe me, this is something I never talk about. *Ever.* In fact the only person in my new life who knows is Sam and that's only because he was giving me the third degree about my deep background and I'd no choice but to 'fess up and tell all.

'Well, you've certainly done your research, haven't you Katie?' is what I manage to come out with. Perfect answer. I even tag on the false TV laugh for good measure, because that's how cool I am talking about this. 'Ha, ha, HA!' Then I go into distraction mode; anything just to get off this highly uncomfortable subject. 'So, em, anyone fancy a coffee then? I've a lovely new espresso maker in the kitchen that I'm only dying to try out.'

No such luck though, it's as if Katie smells blood here and isn't budging.

'Yes,' she nods slowly and for the first time I can see steel in her eyes. Bloody hell, is all I can think, this one will make a brilliant investigative reporter in years to come. 'In fact, I've done an awful lot of research on you, Jessie. For starters, your Wikipedia entry said that you went to school at the Holy Faith School in Killiney, but when I called them, they had absolutely no record of you at all. So they suggested I try their sister school on the Northside, who did have a Jessie Woods on file. Yes, they said, you'd been a pupil there right the way through secondary school. They were incredibly forthcoming with information, you know; they even had your old address on file. Which is how I eventually tracked down your family.'

No, no, no, please don't use the F word. You don't understand, I have NO family, I had nothing to do with those people and they have nothing to do with me . . .

'Emm . . . or we could shoot out in the back garden if

you like?' I'm gabbling now, panicking a bit, while thinking, *Curse you, Wikipedia.* 'Ehh . . . there's a gorgeous water feature out there that looks lovely when it's switched on. I mean, it's a bit clogged up with dead leaves at the moment, but apart from that, it could make a great shot for you . . .'

'In fact, as it happens, Jessie, I've already spoken to your stepfamily. We interviewed all three of them only yesterday. For the full afternoon. Fabulous interviews. And you know, they were all so generous with their time, we couldn't have been more grateful. So, it's in the can, as you might say!'

Oh no no no no no no no no no no no . . .

Chapter Three

I should fill you in a bit. Relations between me and my stepfamily are as follows: they can't abide the sight of me and for my part... just when I think I've come to the very bottom of their meanness, turns out there's a whole underground garage of mean to discover as well.

First up there's Maggie; eldest stepsister, thirty-three years of age and still living at home. Honest to God, if you handed this one a winning lottery ticket in the morning, she'd still whinge and moan about having to drive all the way into town to collect the oversized novelty cheque. A woman with all the charm of an undertaker and the allure of a corpse, her philosophy of life can be summarised thus: ambition leads to expectation which inevitably leads to failure which ultimately leads to disappointment, so the best thing you can possibly do with yourself is not try. Just get up, go to work, come home, then spend all your free time, nights, weekends, bank holidays, the whole shebang, crashed out on the sofa in front of the telly, with the remote control balanced on your belly. Low expectations = a happy life.

Don't ask me how she does it, but the woman actually manages to radiate sourness. In fact, as a teenager, I used to reckon that the ninth circle of hell would be like a fortnight in Lanzarote compared with a bare ten minutes in Maggie's company. And that the only reason she didn't actually worship the devil was because she didn't need to; more than likely, he worshipped her.

Oh, and just as an aside, in all my years, I've only ever seen her wearing one of two things; either a polyester navy suit for work or else a succession of slobby tracksuits for maximum comfort while watching TV. Which for some reason, permanently seem to have egg stains on them, but I digress.

She works for the Inland Revenue as a tax commissioner; probably the only career I can think of where a horrible personality like hers would be a bonus. In fact, I was hauled in last year for a 'random' tax audit; all deeply unpleasant and I'd nearly take my oath that she had something to do with it. Wouldn't put it past her. Be exactly the kind of thing she'd do just for the laugh.

I also happen to know for a fact that behind my back she calls me Cinderella Rockefeller, which is absolutely fine by me. Behind her back, I call her Queen Kong. Then there's Sharon, thirty-two years of age and also still living at home. Works as a 'Food Preparation and Hygiene Manager' at Smiley Burger (don't ask). Honestly, it's like the pair of them just settled down without bothering to find anyone to actually settle down with. Like, God forbid, actual boyfriends. The best way to describe Sharon is that she's PRO *Coronation Street*/eating TV microwave dinners straight off the plastic tray and ANTI exercise/non-smokers/anyone who dares speak to her during her favourite soaps. For this girl, every day is a bad hair day. Plus her weight problem is so permanently out of hand that I often think she must be terrified to go near water, in case she's clobbered by a bottle of champagne and officially launched by the Minister for the Marine. Nor, I might add, are any of the tensions in that house helped by my stepmother Joan, who refers to the pair of them as 'the elder disappointment' and 'the younger disappointment'. To their faces.

I don't even blame Dad for remarrying and allowing a whole new stepfamily to torpedo into our lives; I knew how desperately lonely he was, how much he missed Mum and how worried he was about me growing up without a stable female presence at home. When Mum died I was too young to remember her and for years didn't fully understand the enormity of her loss. Even now, I find it hard to accept; come on, dead of ovarian cancer at the age of thirty-eight? But back then, as a scraped-faced, grubby tomboy, permanently up a tree, all I knew was that suddenly it was me and Dad against the world. And, in my childish, innocent way, I thought he and I were rubbing along just fine; we were happy, we were holding it together. OK, so maybe a ten-year-old shouldn't necessarily be cooking spaghetti hoops on toast for her dad's dinner five nights a week, or doing all the cleaning while all her pals were out on the road playing, but it didn't bother me. I'd have done anything to make Dad happy and stop him from missing Mum. I can even see what attracted him to Joan, to begin with at least. Years later, he told me it was a combination of aching loneliness and heartbreak at seeing a little child desperately struggling to step into her mum's shoes and somehow keep the show on the road. Then along came this attractive widow; glamorous in a blonde, brassy, busty sort of way, with two daughters just a few years older than me.

Joan, I should tell you, is one of those women with the hair permanently set, the nails always done and never off a sun bed, even in the depths of winter. She looks a bit like how you'd imagine Barbie's granny might look and can't even put out bins without lipstick on (by the way, I'm NOT making that up).

With a chronic habit of talking everything up as well. Like when she first met Dad, she'd introduce him as 'Senior Manager of a Drinking Emporium'. Whereas, in actual fact, he was a humble barman. How they first met in fact: she used to go into the Swiss Cottage pub where he worked for the Tuesday poker night games, only she'd insist on telling everyone she played 'bridge, not poker'.

I'm not even sure how long Dad was seeing her for before they got married; all I knew was that one miserable, wet day, when I was about ten, he took me to the zoo for a treat, to meet his new 'friend' Joan and her two daughters. That in itself was unusual and immediately set alarm bells ringing; because he never took a day off work, ever. Poor guileless Dad, thinking we'd all get along famously and would end up one big happy family.

I was the only one who actually enjoyed the zoo; to the twelve- and thirteen-year-old Sharon and Maggie everything was either 'stupid' or else 'babyish'. By which of course, they meant that I was stupid and babyish. I can still remember the two of them ganging up on me behind the reptile house to slag me off for not wearing a bra. Then, in that snide, psychological way of bullying that girls have, they said I was so immature, I probably still believed in Santa Claus.

Which, right up until that moment, I had.

I can date my childhood ending back to that very day.

Nor did things improve after Dad remarried. Turned out Joan's first husband had been a chronic alcoholic who'd left her with even less money than we had, which of course meant that right after the wedding, she and the Banger sisters all came to live with us in our tiny corporation house. Me, Sharon and Maggie all under the one roof? A recipe for nuclear fission if ever there was one.

So Christ alone knows what tales they've told the film crew about me. In fact, I wouldn't be surprised if they've got a Jessie doll somewhere in the house with pins and needles stuck in it. But if it comes to it, I've a few choice anecdotes I could regale them with myself. The innumerable petty tortures they'd inflict on me were worthy of the Gestapo; like using my maths homework as a litter tray for their cat, or else, a particular favourite of theirs, hiding my underwear so I'd have to go to school either wearing swimming togs underneath my uniform or else nothing. Then the two of them would gleefully tell the other kids in the playground, so they'd all point at me, roar laughing and call me Panti-free. I'm not kidding, the nickname stuck right up until sixth year.

And there was never anyone to defend me, only myself, as Dad was always off working morning, noon and night, seven days a week, to support the whole lot of us. Bless him; in the days after he remarried I think he honestly believed we were a reasonably happy, if slightly dysfunctional family. Mainly because I didn't tell him a quarter of what went on behind his back, on the grounds that it would only upset him. It wouldn't be fair and hadn't the poor man been through enough already?

Then one fateful day, not long after they first moved in, Maggie made a devastating discovery: we had no cable TV in the house. I'll never forget her turning round to me and sneering, 'So, what did your mother die of anyway? Boredom?'

Well, that was it. Break point. I lunged at her, punched her smack in the jaw and even managed to pull out a fistful of her wiry hair before Joan pulled us apart. There was murder, but I was actually quite proud of my scrappy behaviour, considering that Maggie was then and is now about four stone heavier than me.

Then, the same year I turned eighteen, three life-altering events happened in quick succession. I finally left school, got a place on a media training course in college and, just when I thought my life was finally turning a corner for the better, my darling dad, my wonderful, loving, long-suffering dad, suffered a massive coronary attack when he was in work and died instantly. It was Christmas Eve and he was only fifty-two years old.

So that was it for me. Toughened and hardened, I got the hell out of that house, or the Sandhurst of emotional emptiness, as I like to call it, moved into a flat with Hannah and now only ever see my stepfamily on 24 December, at Dad's anniversary mass in our old, local parish church, purely for the sake of his memory and nothing else.

I try to get through it as best I can by treating it as a penance for all my sins throughout the year. I've even tried my best to drag Sam along with me for moral support/ back-up in case a catfight breaks out, but he always seems to have something else on. Mind you, I think the real reason is that he's too terrified to leave his Bentley parked outside the church in case it gets stolen. Our corporation estate = not posh and I happen to know for a fact that Sam refers to it as 'the land of the ten-year-old Toyota'.

It's astonishing; even ten short minutes of tortuous small talk with my stepfamily on the church steps inevitably descends into a row. Honest to God, it's like Christmas Eve with the Sopranos. It's eleven years now since Dad passed away and they've never as much as invited me back to the house – to *my* house – for a cup of tea and a Hob Nob after the anniversary mass.

Well, you know what? Good luck to them. Whatever crap they've told the TV crew about me, I'll do what I always do: laugh, smile and deal with it. And in the meantime, I choose to take the mature, adult approach; complete and utter denial of their very existence. Those people are firmly part of my past and I have nothing whatsoever to do with any of them. End of story.

The 'At home' part of the interview thankfully wraps up as soon as Katie cops that there's just no drawing me out on the painful subject of my stepfamily, so the documentary crew pack up and get ready to tail me for the day's feature presentation . . . me actually doing a bit of work for a change. Now, technically, I'm not really supposed to know what each week's dare is; the idea is that when I'm told live on camera, the audience see me react looking shocked/terrified/ready to bolt for the hills/whatever. But the thing is, half the time you'd need to be a right eejit not to cop on to what's coming your way.

So when the production office call me and tell me to be at the Mondello Park racing track in an hour, I'm guessing the dare won't involve tightrope walking over the River Liffey. Which, by the way, I did have to do once and of course, much to everyone's amusement fell into the gakky, slimy, rat-infested water below.

Anyway, my point is, working in TV is brilliant, but glamorous it ain't.

'Are you driving yourself, Jessie?' Katie calls over to me

as the crew clamber into the unit minivan, just as we're all getting ready to leave my front garden and hit the road. Next thing, I can physically see her getting a 'light bulb over the head' eureka moment. 'Oh, wait now, I've a fabulous idea! Why don't we get a shot of you driving through the gates on your way to work? Where do you keep your car anyway? Do you park it in the garage? I'm sure you must drive something zippy and fabulous!'

Please, please, please dear lovely God, please don't let them ask me to open up the garage door and see that it's empty.

'Actually... emmmm... I'm afraid... the thing is... well, you see, there's a bit of a problem with my car...' *Stolen car story, remember the stolen car story...*

'In for a service, is it?'

Oh wait now, that's miles better.

'Yes, that's right. It's, emm, in for a service.'

Phew.

So *Jessie Would* goes out live on Saturday at 7 p.m. for thirty minutes with one commercial break; classic family-friendly, tea-time TV. The format is simple. Emma is in studio in front of a live audience, and does a lot of interacting with them, getting them to bet on whether I'll actually manage to do the dare or whether I'll fall flat on my face, then giving out sponsored prizes if they guess right. It can be pretty tricky to predict; my success rate would be about fifty-fifty. But then in the sage words of Liz Walsh, Head of Television and, I think, a fan of the show, seeing as how she's the one who keeps on recommissioning it, it's not about my succeeding or failing on each weekly dare, it's about making a complete tit of myself every week, live to the nation. She reckons the secret of lowest common denominator TV is that it should always appeal to a kid of about twelve and then you're laughing.

There's not a day goes by that I don't thank God for Liz Walsh. She's an incredible woman and has been almost like a Simon Cowell-esque figure in my life. Tough as an old boot but with solid gold instincts that can't be bought or sold. In fact, when I graduated from doing the late-night weather report, then spent the next few years doing random reporting from places where no one else could be arsed going, she was the one who first spotted me and decided I was ripe to groom for bigger and better things. Like so much else in my life though, this was as a result of pure chance and not being afraid to make an eejit of myself on a regular basis. Example: one time I was sent to cover the winter solstice at Newgrange and a giant granite crater, which had happily held up for thousands of years, chose that exact moment to fall on top of me, knocking me to the ground to much hilarity and sniggering from the background crew. I was fine, just a bit concussed, but did what I always do: got back on my feet, brushed myself down and laughed it off. Course, three days later, the clip had nearly eight thousand hits on YouTube and when I saw it back I had to admit, it was one of those laugh-in-spite-of-yourself, slapstick Buster Keaton-type moments. It even made it onto the annual Channel Six blooper show.

Funny thing was, the audience seemed to get a big kick out of the hapless, accident-prone side of me, so from those humble origins, Liz moved me to a 'dare' slot on Emma's talk show and it all snowballed from there. But no matter what challenge *Jessie Would* throws up at me week after week, her wise words are forever ringing in my ears. 'Fall on your face and get covered in as much shite as you possibly can, then haul yourself up and laugh it all off. Remember, that's all they really want to see.'

And so we pull into the Mondello Park race track and, as it's only a few hours to transmission time, hit the ground running. The Channel Six location crew are all here to set up for the live show while Katie and the *A Day in the Life* crew are still trailing me, so we've the surreal situation of one film unit filming another. Anyway, I get busy with the training instructor who fills me in on what's ahead.

The gist of it is as follows: their resident Jeremy Clarkson will do four laps of the circuit in one of those Formula Sheane cars where you sit uncomfortably in a single-seat racer with your bum approximately three inches away from the ground, then I have to try and beat his time. All with not one, but two cameras pointing at me. It's all very Monaco Grand Prix looking, chequered flags, the whole works and everyone here keeps referring to it as a 'time attack'. Anyway, that's the doddley part. The high blood pressure bit right after any dare is when I'm biked back into Channel Six at speed, clinging on to the driver for dear life, then race into studio while the commercial break is being aired, still panting and dripping with sweat. Whereupon a graceful, elegant Emma will interview me about the whole experience, the highs, the lows etc. Then we show footage of me doing the dare, looking petrified and to keep Liz happy, hopefully all caked in mud and crap. Then the ta-daa moment when Emma reveals how many of the audience thought I'd actually make it versus how many thought I'd end up in the A&E. Cue everyone going home with a prize, roll credits and administer Valium to myself and Emma. All done and dusted just in time for the Lotto draw.

Before we go through the safety instructions, I slip off into a locker room to change into the scarlet red jumpsuit and safety helmet they've kitted me out with, but just as I'm standing semi-naked in my bra and knickers, the door behind me opens.

'Jessie?'

I look up to see Katie, microphone in hand, camera at her shoulder, peering around the door.

'Oooh, don't you look fabulous! Just wondered if you could tell us what's going through your head right now?'

I think it's at this point of the day, that she officially starts to grate on my nerves.

Mercedes is sponsoring the whole stunt, so there's a couple of be-suited bigwigs grouped formally on the track behind me, looking tense and nervous and I wouldn't blame them either. The stake for them is high; according to the instructor, there's a fifty per cent chance that I'll crash, in which case they're looking at writing off two hundred and fifty grand worth of car as it literally goes up in smoke in front of their eyes. There's also the slightly lesser concern that I could end up hospitalised, paralysed or worse, but to be honest, judging by the tense, fraught looks on their faces, I'm guessing the car is worth far, far more to them than I am.

Seven p.m. Show time. A hand signal from the floor manager and we're off. The professional driver, who I think has done stunts on movies and everything, takes to the track first and, in a nano second, is off and away, four frenzied laps at a breakneck, dizzying speed. I nearly get whiplash on my neck just following him. His time recorded, he's out of the race car in a single leap and then it's over to me.

Much waving and thumbs up from the crew as I lock the helmet on then clamber in through the window, giving the crew a delightful shot of my big, scarlet arse. Then, I'm not joking, Katie's over, microphone in hand, 'So tell us, Jessie, how are you feeling right now?'

Like smacking you across the head, is what I want to say, but lucky for her, I can't talk properly with the crash helmet on. A second later, a chequered flag is waved in front of the dashboard, a few people start cheering and I'm away.

Now, I'll let you in on a little secret. I've been doing this lark for almost three years now and my survival mechanism is this: when doing anything extreme or life-threatening, the trick is to completely focus your thoughts elsewhere and just let your body take over on auto-pilot. Never fails me. Because there's something about extreme situations which provides solace and absolutely concentrates the mind.

Lap one whooshes by but my thoughts are miles away. In fact, all I'm thinking about is the shagging Visa bill, still lying unopened on the fireplace at home, like an undetonated time bomb. And so I make a firm decision right here and right now . . . I will reform my spendthrift ways and go on an economy drive . . . no more ridiculously expensive nights out, Sam will just have to get used to sitting on the sofa watching DVDs with me at home . . . Lap two comes round and now I'm thinking I'll ban all trips to fancy hair salons as well, I'll just do a Nice and Easy home colour instead. Lap three rockets past . . . hmmmmmm . . . brainwave . . . I could just buy a bike and cycle everywhere and hide my shame by telling everyone I'm being eco friendly . . . and by the final lap I'm wondering if I could be really cheeky and maybe talk to my agent about getting some kind of endorsement or sponsorship deal that might supplement my income a bit ... hmmmm ... worth a try ...

In what feels like the blink of an eye, it's all over. Suddenly, I'm being helped out of the car, dizzy and disorientated, with legs like jelly.

'Amazing, bloody fantastic, good girl, Jessie!' says the floor manager, steadying me on my feet and guiding me towards the camera, so all of this can be relayed back to studio, live. I'm not joking, I'm so woozy and light-headed from the whole thing, he actually has to prop me up.

The next few seconds are a blur; I'm desperately trying to catch my breath while Katie's shoving a microphone under my nose to ask, 'What was going through your mind on the course?' and in the background, the mafia guys from Mercedes are rushing over, shaking my hand and congratulating me. Apparently I was doing 140 miles per hour at one stage. What's weird is that I never even felt a thing.

And that's when it happens. Out from the ranks of people swarming around me, a chunky-looking, balding guy steps out, aged about sixty-plus and built like a rugby player with a neck about the same width as his head. In a honeyed northern accent, he introduces himself as the head of Mercedes Ireland then grabs me by the shoulders to steady me.

'Jessie, we're all very proud of you . . .'

I nod and manage a watery smile but I'm actually praying the floor manager will cut him off and let me outta here. We're under massive time pressure here, so whatever he wants to say, he has approximately four seconds to say it in. It's not unusual for the sponsors to step in after a dare to plug their wares, but what they never think about is that there's a motorbike driver standing by waiting to whisk me into studio for the rest of the show.

'And to congratulate you on completing the course successfully and in such a fantastic time, we have a wee surprise for you,' says baldie man. 'Bring her round here, boys.'

Camera rolling, everyone looking at him, suddenly the roaring in my ears has stopped.

I can't believe what I'm seeing. Being driven around the edge of the track is the most stunning, most amazing sports car I have ever seen. A two-seater hard-top Mercedes convertible, brand new, showroom condition, in a sleek black metallic colour with the softest-looking cream leather seats. So, so sexy and gorgeous and fab that I want to fall down on my knees, to howl and weep at its beauty.

That's when my eye falls in disbelief down to the registration plate: Jessie 1.

'Yes, Jessie, it's your lucky day!' says baldie man. 'We would like to invite you to be a brand ambassador for Mercedes and are offering you full use of this car, free, gratis, for one year! Absolutely no strings attached. Tax and insurance included; sure we'll even throw in free petrol for you! Now whaddya say to that, you jammy wee girl?'

Ohmygodohmygodohmygodohmygod. All at once, I'm gobsmacked, stunned and . . . interested. Well, it's a no-brainer really, isn't it? This is incredible. This is the nicest thing that's happened to me in a very long time. OK, so it mightn't solve all my financial woes, but it's a bloody good start. I mean, come on, a free car for a whole year?

I think it must have been all the adrenaline pumping through my body after the stunt, but before I know what

I'm doing, I've thrown my arms around baldie man, squealing, 'Yes, yes, yes! Thank you, thank you, thank you!'

I think I may have even kissed him but I can't be too sure.

First sign that something's amiss: Are the looks the crew semaphore to each other as I'm helped up onto the motorbike and get ready to leave. Normally there's cheering and messing from the camera and sound guys as I'm biked back to the industrial estate where the Channel Six studio is, especially when a dare has gone well. But this time, there's total silence from them, to a man. Which is, to say the least, a bit weird.

I clamber up onto the back of the bike, clinging to the driver so tightly I might crack one of his ribs, and we're off. As we zoom back to studio, which takes all of about three minutes at the speed we're going at, I do my best to put it out of my head. Come on, I just got offered the use of a free Merc for a year. Chances are the lads are just a bit jealous, that's all. I mean, come on, who wouldn't be? So why are they acting like I just ran over a small child? I can't quite put my finger on how to describe their expressions. Disbelief? Shock? No. It was actually disgust.

Second sign that something's amiss: Normally, when we get back into studio, the stage manager already has the doors open for me so I can race through, leg it into studio, then plonk down on the sofa beside Emma for the post-mortem chat and to get the official 'result' of the dare. All in the space of time it takes for the commercial break to go out. But this time, something's wrong. I sense it immediately. Instead of the usual high-octane panic, the stage manager meets me at the studio door, and in a low, flustered voice, says into her walkie-talkie, 'Yes, she's just arrived. OK, I understand. I'll tell her now.'

'Tell me what?' I manage to pant, breathlessly.

'You're not going back into the studio. Emma will handle the rest of the show. You're to go straight up to Liz Walsh's office. Now. She's says it's urgent.'

'But that's ridiculous, I have a show to finish . . .'

'Come on, Jessie, don't make this hard on yourself . . .' She looks red-faced, mortified and is actually blushing to her hairline. As though I'm some kind of embarrassment that it's fallen to her lot to deal with.

'For God's sake, will you let me past? There's no time for this; I have to get to the studio, they're all waiting in there . . .'

'I'm afraid it's a no,' she insists a bit more firmly this time. 'I'm sorry but my instructions are very clear; I'm not to let you in, under any circumstances. Now will you please just go? Liz is already in her office waiting for you.' As if to ram the point home, she even stands legs astride, blocking the studio door. Like a bouncer in a nightclub.

Third sign that something's amiss: I'm completely winded and now my head's reeling. As I stagger down the deserted corridor to Liz's office I can see a TV monitor on in the background, with the show just coming out from the ad break. Emma's looking a bit frazzled, which is most unusual for her, and she announces in a wobbly voice that there's been a slight technical hitch and that I won't be coming back into studio after all.

A slight technical hitch? But there's no technical hitch! 'No! No, I'm here, just outside the door, ready to finish the gig! Why the fuck won't they let me in?!' I scream at the

TV monitor with sheer frustration, can't help myself. I'd kick the shagging thing only it's hanging about three feet from the ceiling. Right now, I'm starting to feel like I'm stuck in a horror movie, where I'm screeching away and no one can hear. What the hell is happening? Why won't they let me finish the gig?

I can hear Emma telling the audience that I did actually manage to beat the professional driver's time and the good news is that everyone in the audience who bet on me to win is going home tonight with a voucher for two people to the Multiplex cinema in Dundrum, valid for three whole months of free movies. Her voice is reverberating loud and clear the whole way down the empty corridor and it's beyond weird to be hearing it from outside of the studio. Then I hear the audience cheering and stomping their feet, deafening and thunderous, all while I continue to stumble on, head pounding, sweat sticking to me, still in my racing gear with a helmet tucked under my arm.

This is turning into a nightmare. The door to Liz's office is open and she's already standing there, waiting for me, hands on hips, like in a western. Unheard of. Normally, on the rare occasions when you're summoned to this office, you're left outside making small talk with her assistant for at least a good twenty minutes.

So in I reel, nauseous with tension, almost ready to pass out. Liz is tiny, smart, sassy and I'd ordinarily describe her as the coolest, calmest woman I know. But right now, the look on her face would stop a clock.

'Close the door and sit down,' she all but barks at me.

'Liz, I don't know what's going on, but whatever it is . . .' Bloody hell, I'm actually stammering. Heart pounding, mouth dry as a bone. Doing 140 miles an hour around a race track was a breeze compared to this. My heart is twisting with the worry and I swear to God, I've lost the feeling in my legs.

Mercifully, there's never a preamble with Liz. 'Correct me if I'm wrong, but did you or didn't you just accept the use of a free sports car? Live on air? In front of six hundred and fifty thousand viewers?'

'Well . . . yes, but . . .'

'You are presumably aware that it's an unwritten rule and an absolute no-no for a presenter to accept a freebie of any kind whatsoever?'

'Emm . . . as a matter of fact, no, I wasn't. But . . .'

'I'm afraid I can't accept your ignorance of the basics as any kind of excuse, Jessie,' she barks, snapping open a bottle of water and knocking back a gulp. 'After all your years of working here, you're honestly telling me you didn't realise you can't just shamelessly use your profile to go around accepting free commercial handouts? Have you the slightest idea how it looks? How compromising it is for you and for the show? And, by extension, for me?'

'But Liz, that guy just sprang it on me!' I almost yell at her, my chest about to burst with anxiety. 'I found myself saying yes before I barely knew what I was doing . . .'

'In the last fifteen minutes, the phone lines have not stopped hopping, with a lot of people understandably furious about a national TV personality accepting such an extravagant gift while the rest of the country is in the throes of recession. The press department is in meltdown and the director general has just been on to read me the riot act about your stupid, thoughtless, selfish behaviour.'

'But I didn't know!'

Now, there's a horrible pause and suddenly I feel like I'm locked into a death dance.

'I've championed this show,' Liz eventually says, more sorrowfully now which is actually far, far worse than if she yelled at me. 'And God knows, I've championed you. Because no matter what we throw at you, you do it and come up trumps. You're a looker, you're virtually unembarrassable which is a huge asset in this game and you're completely at ease in front of a camera. Most of all though, you've got something that can't be bought or sold; the likeability factor. In spite of crap reviews saying that this programme has all the tension of an ancient piece of knicker elastic. In spite of my bosses saying *Jessie Would* was a carnival of frivolities that had had its day. That's the exact phrase they used, you know. I fought like hell for this show and this is how you repay me.'

'But . . . but . . . Come on, Liz, surely to God we can fix this! Can't I just put out a press release saying it was a horrible, stupid mistake and that I'm really mortified and then . . . just give them their car back?' I'm feeling a tiny bud of hope now. Because there's no problem that's unfixable, is there? And it's not like I've ever messed up before. Never. Not once.

'Jessie, you don't realise. They're lusting for blood like barbarians out there. I can't be seen not to take immediate and decisive action over this.'

'Come on, Liz . . . Everyone's allowed to slip up once, aren't they?'

'Not on live TV they're not.'

And like that, hope is guillotined. Now it's like despair is circulating instead of air.

'But I didn't know I was doing anything wrong! Please

Liz, please. Let's just consider my wrists slapped . . .' I'm actually begging her now, my voice faint and croaky with tension.

'I'm afraid it's not that simple.'

'So I took a risk on this one and it blew up in my face. But you're always encouraging me to take risks. I mean, that's what makes me good!'

'No, Jessie. That's what makes you fired.'

Chapter Four

This feels like a bereavement. And believe me, if there's one thing I know all about, it's bereavement. In fact, if it wasn't for Sam, I don't know what I'd do. It took me ten years to build up my career and ten minutes to bring the whole thing crashing down in flames.

It's sometime on Sunday afternoon, couldn't tell you when exactly, and I'm still in bed. Can't move. Don't want to either. At least here, in the safety of my own home, I'm not a national laughing stock. I'm doing my best to block out most of last night, but horrible fragments keep coming back to me in painful, disconnected shards. Word spread like a raging forest fire and before I barely had time to digest the news myself everyone, absolutely *everyone*, seemed to know. But then that's typical of Channel Six; there's times when it's more like a colander than a TV station.

I remember bumping into a few of the audience streaming out after the broadcast and a middle-aged couple being very kind and concerned and saying they were relieved to see me alive and well. They thought something terrible must have happened to me and that's why I never came back to finish the end of the show. I wish. Right now I'd kill to be lying on a hospital trolley with a few cracked ribs, but with my job and reputation still intact. Physical pain would be a doddle compared with this.

I can remember standing in the freezing cold outside the studio, frantically trying to call Sam on his mobile and not being able to get him. Then, just as I was howling hysterically into his voicemail, some of the studio crew came up to me and commiserated. Nice of them. Said it was an honest mistake which could have happened to anyone. Cheryl, the lovely make-up girl, even said sure, it's only a storm in a tea cup, which would all blow over, Liz's bark being famously worse than her bite. Which was kindly. Untrue, but still well-meant.

But a lot of the crew blanked me. A scary amount of them. The director just walked past me like I was yesterday's news. Which I know I am, but still, it was bloody hurtful. Then, when I finally did get hold of Sam and was begging him to come and pick me up, one of the sound engineers who I'm really pally with, I've even got his family tickets for the show on more than one occasion, brushed right past me. Not only that, but then he flung a scorching look back over his shoulder that might as well have said, 'Selfish, greedy, stupid, idiotic moron.'

I was probably only waiting about half an hour for Sam, but I can honestly say it was the longest thirty minutes of my entire life. Then of course Katie nearly danced over, beside herself with excitement, shoving her microphone into my face and asking me if I'd any comment to make about this 'shocking new development'. I don't even blame her; one minute she's doing a run of the mill job trailing round after me, next thing a hot, juicy story just unexpectedly plops right into her lap.

Can't tell you what the hell I said to her, but I do know it involved a lot of bawling, snivelling and gratefully accepting bunches of Kleenex from the cameraman hovering at her shoulder. Then, thank Jaysus, Sam zoomed up like my knight in a shining Bentley and I collapsed into the seat beside him, completely falling apart and heaving with sobs for all I was worth.

And now it's Sunday afternoon, and I'm still in bed, surrounded by snotty tissues and with a thumping headache from crying all night long. I can't sleep; every time I try, all I can hear is the whooshing sound of my career flushing down the toilet. I physically can't move either. Like a butterfly that's pinned down to a card. It just keeps playing in a loop inside my head, over and over again. *I'm fired, I'm fired, I messed up and got fired and have no money and no job and what the hell am I supposed to do with the rest of my life?*

The only person who's keeping me remotely sane is Sam, who's just being incredible. Sainted. He'd seen last night's show of course, and instantly realised something was majorly wrong when I didn't come back on for the second part. So the minute he got my hysterical messages, he didn't even think; just jumped into his car and drove straight into the studio. He's been brilliant ever since too. Normally after a broadcast we'd go into Bentleys, a posh restaurant and boutique hotel in town, which Sam is never out of, then we'd hook up with Nathaniel and Eva. Usually we'd all unwind with a few drinks (ridiculously expensive champagne, what else?) followed by a late dinner and then at stupid o'clock everyone would pile back here for yet more ridiculously expensive champagne, etc. But I was in no condition to show my face anywhere last night, not even with good friends in tow to support me. Sam took one look at the state I was in, called to make our excuses, then brought me straight back here, where he's been minding me like an invalid with consumption ever since.

Then, this morning, after yet another bout of me howling into his chest, 'But my job! My lovely, lovely job!' he gave me one of his motivational speeches, which I was no more in the mood for, but I suppose he meant well. His pep talk fell into three distinct categories; first the inspirational ('In the words of Barack Obama, yes you can get over this') followed by a classic ('When God opens a door...'), all rounded off with the good old-fashioned ('plenty more jobs out there, etc.').

You see, to Sam, the world is clearly delineated into winners and losers and, as he's never done saying, winners are winners long before they win. One of the qualities he says he likes best about me is the fact that I was born into an underprivileged background with a highly dysfunctional family set-up and yet still went on to become a winner. His theory is that everyone gets their fair and equal share of knocks in life, but what sets the winners apart is that they pick themselves up, dust themselves off and start over. Whereas losers just concentrate on the coulda, woulda, shouldas, blaming everyone except themselves, before ultimately sinking under. Which is exactly what I want to do. Now and forever.

Anyway, on his way out to get the Sunday papers, he bounds up to me in the bedroom, all full of positive energy. 'Get up, get dressed and come with me. Do you good to get out of the house for a bit.'

'Let's stick to attainable goals,' I moan. 'Maybe, just maybe, in a few hours, with a bit of luck, I might just be able to crawl as far as the bathroom.'

'Is there anything I can do to get you out of that bed?' he says, starting to sound a bit exasperated with me now, unsurprisingly.

'You could tie Prozac to the end of some string.'

Sam doesn't react, just runs his hands through his thick, bouffey hair, the way he does whenever he's deeply frustrated, and orders me not to even think about turning on the TV when he goes out.

Shit. I never thought of that. There couldn't be anything on telly about what happened, could there? Hardly a news story, is it?

'Now you promise you won't go anywhere near that remote control?' he calls up from the bottom of the stairs, on his way out. 'Remember it's for your own good!'

'Promise,' I mutter feebly.

But the minute he's out the door I switch it on. Just to be sure. No, at first glance it looks like I'm OK. Everything's fine, I'm worrying over nothing. Just your typical, normal Sunday afternoon TV, *Antiques Roadshow*, soap opera omnibuses that start today and don't finish until next Tuesday morning, that kind of thing. I keep flicking and flicking but there's nothing strange. Then I get to Channel Six, where it's just coming up to the afternoon news bulletin.

Sweet baby Jesus and the orphans, I do not believe this. I'm the second news item. The *second*. I sit up bolt upright in the bed, like someone who's just been electrocuted. But no, there it is, in full Blu-ray high definition. There's even a photo of me on the screen right behind the newsreader; a still shot from last night's show of me kissing the guy from Mercedes who offered me the shagging car and looking like a total gobshite. A wave of nausea sweeps over me and I can feel myself breaking out in a clammy cold sweat. I want to switch if off but somehow can't find the strength to.

'In a surprise move last night, Channel Six has ended the contract of TV presenter Jessie Woods, after an on-air incident involving what was seen as a major breach of broadcasting ethics. In a statement released last night, the station announced that Jessie Woods' position at the centre of their schedule was now untenable, in light of her accepting free use of a luxury sports car during the live broadcast of her top-rated show, *Jessie Would*. Sources close to Liz Walsh, Head of Television, have said the station had no choice but to take swift and immediate action in response to an unprecedented volume of complaints during the broadcast of last night's show. And now over to our entertainment correspondent who reports live . . .'

I switch it off and fling the remote control as far from the bed as I can. I think I might be sick. That's it; I've just been given the kiss of death. Because in TV land, when you hear your name used in the same sentence as 'unprecedented volume of complaints', it basically means hell will freeze over before you cross the threshold of said station ever again.

Then my mobile rings. It's been ringing all bloody morning, but I've been ignoring it. I just don't feel able for a conversation with another human being, apart from Sam, that is; my one link to the outside world. But then the name flashes up on the screen. It's Emma.

'Jessie, are you OK?'

All I can do is just stifle a sob.

'Oh, sweetheart. I've been trying to call you ever since last night. I can't tell you how sorry I am. How are you holding up?'

'I'm . . . I'm . . .' then instead of finishing the sentence, I just start bawling.

Emma is completely fabulous, as you'd expect. Which is all the more amazing when you consider that my fuck-up has meant that now she's out of a job too. She fills me in on the whole horrible story from her side of the fence; how she hadn't a breeze what was happening during the show until it got to the commercial break, when an urgent message filtered to the studio floor from the director up in the production box, saying I wasn't coming back for the second half of the show and that she'd have to carry it all alone. God love the girl, she was completely numb and shell-shocked, but like the pro that she is, somehow she staggered through it, then was summoned into Liz's office the minute we wrapped. The show has been pulled from the schedule, she was brusquely told, but in the meantime you stay on full salary while we find another vehicle for you. Which is actually the best news I've heard so far during this whole miserable day. Because at least my brainless, witless behaviour hasn't entirely left Emma in the lurch. In time, she'll get her own show and no one deserves it more.

'I'm just so sorry,' I keep howling over and over. 'You have to believe me when I tell you I didn't know I was doing anything wrong. I just reacted on the spur of the moment. Yes I was stupid and greedy but with my own car repossessed and on top of all my other money worries, this just . . . looked like the greatest bonus I could ever have asked for, being handed to me on a plate . . .'

'I know, sweetie, I know. They made it hard for you to refuse.'

Then something strikes me. 'Emma, did you know?'

'Know what?'

'This, like unwritten rule or whatever it is, that we can't accept freebies? I mean, what would you have done in my shoes?'

She doesn't even need to think about it. Of course not. Emma is always perfectly behaved and instinctively knows the right thing to say. 'I'd probably have thanked them, but said it was unlikely the station bosses would allow me to accept.'

Flawless answer. Gracious and dignified yet utterly resolute.

'Oh God, Emma,' I sniffle. 'Why are you such a perfect human being? Why can't I be like you?' Another bout of wailing and another fresh handful of Kleenex.

'Jessie, you have to stop beating yourself up,' she says firmly. 'It was only one mistake and I'm sure you'll bounce back from it. When all this unpleasantness dies down, I mean.'

There's a horrible unspoken thought between us. The thought that dare not speak its name. Channel Six will never look at me again and, well, suppose no one else will either? Presenting gigs are hard enough to come by, particularly for women, without being a national disgrace who buggered up a primetime job on live telly. But Emma means well. She's trying to offer me a grain of comfort, so I let her. Even though I don't really believe her. Yes of course, we both chime, lots of other jobs, will see my agent tomorrow, something's bound to come in, etc., etc. In fact, by the end of the phone call, I'm actually starting to believe her.

'Oh, just one more thing before I let you go, hon,' she adds warily. 'Whatever you do, do not turn on the TV and do NOT read today's papers.'

'Ta love. I did see the Channel Six headline and had to switch it off before I vomited.'

'No, sweetie, you don't understand.'

'Understand what?'

'Oh Jess, there's no easy way to tell you this. But forewarned is forearmed, just remember that . . .'

'Tell me what? Jaysus, it's not like things can be much worse than they already are, now is it?'

'Sweetie, the news unit from Channel Six are right outside your front gate.'

Just when I think the nightmare can't get worse, ta-da, fate decides, yes Jessie Woods, you're not off any hooks yet, there's yet another few hundred feet of crap for you to fall through before we're done with you. Wa-ha-haaa, thunderclap, background sound effect of bloodhounds baying at the moon, etc., etc.

So I thank Emma, faithfully swear not to look at the news, hang up the phone then stumble out of bed to root for wherever I flung the remote control. I eventually find it and with trembling hands, switch the news back on. And almost fall over. She's right. There it is, live on national TV, a clear shot of the security gates right at the very front of my house. They're staking me out. In fact, if I went over to my bedroom window and jumped up and down waving like a presenter on a kids' TV show, you'd end up seeing me in the background of the shot.

I slump down with my back against the wall taking short, sharp breaths like a hostage in a bank raid drama. This is so ridiculous; I mean, isn't this the kind of harassment they give to politicians who are found with rent boys in public toilets? The whole thing is completely surreal. Here I am, watching the outside of my own house live on TV. Even through the security gates from the outside, I can still see everything, right down to the overstuffed bins that I forgot to put out last week and a few crisp bags that are billowing round the front drive.

Next thing on the screen, Sam's big posh Bentley pulls up at the gates on his way back from getting the papers. He has a remote for them, but is still forced to slow down while they open up. Cue one of the reporters, a big guy built like a sumo wrestler, nearly having a heart attack with the excitement.

'Mr Hughes, Sam Hughes? Don't drive past us this time, we only want a few words with you!' he shouts at the car, nearly impaling himself on the front bonnet, so Sam has no choice but to stay put.

'Any comment to make?' sumo guy yells through the driver's window.

No, Sam, no, don't do this, not now, just keep on driving, maybe even mow a few of them down if you can manage to get a clear run at them . . . But I'd forgotten, if there's one thing Sam has a weakness for, it's media attention. I see it happening almost in slow motion. The electronic window of his car sliding gracefully down and him flashing his brightest, toothiest smile straight to camera.

'Afternoon gentlemen, how are you all this fine day?' Cool as a fish's fart, not a bother on him.

'Thanks so much for talking to us this time. Anything to say? How is Jessie feeling right now? Is it fair to say she's devastated and hiding away from the world?'

'Gentlemen,' Sam answers smoothly, 'while Jessie has no comment to make at this distressing time . . .'

'Shut up and just drive!' I'm screeching at the TV, before clamping my hand over my fat gob. If they're that close to the house, there's a good chance the bastards might hear me.

'... I would just like to say that in an otherwise stellar career, she made one simple error of judgement, which I'm quite confident she'll recover from in no time. Now, if you'll excuse me.' He swishes off as the security gates open leaving me open mouthed at how practised and almost rehearsed he sounded. A minute later, he's in the front door and bounding up the stairs to me.

The frightening thing though, is that the cool show of strength he put on for the press not two minutes ago has just completely evaporated. Now he looks pale (which rarely happens, Sam is one of those people who's always permatanned, even in winter), rattled (again atypical, Sam lets nothing, absolutely nothing faze him), and dazed. Actually *dazed*.

'OK, Woodsie, I won't lie to you,' he says. 'It's bad. There's three camera crews down there, one from Channel Six, one from RTE and another one I don't recognise. And that's not even counting all the photographers. Christ alive, surely this can't be that big a story?!'

'What . . . what will we do?' My voice is tiny, barely audible.

He thinks for a minute. 'Stay put. They can't get a clear shot of the bedroom. I'll bring up the papers and we'll go through them together . . .'

'No, no, I can't.' It's the firmest I've sounded all day. 'Please, no.'

In the end, he takes one look at me and realises that I'm in no fit state to read horrible things about myself. So he heads down to the kitchen, mercifully at the back of the house where no one can see in, to read them for himself.

'Don't worry, I'll censor them all for you,' he says reassuringly on his way out the door. 'And I'll bring up any that have anything positive to say. Whatever you do, do NOT turn on the news.'

This, no messing, takes a full hour. I try to pass the time by a) watching a documentary about Princess Diana on the Biography Channel, but I have to switch off as the bit about her being harassed by the paparazzi is just that bit too close to the bone today, b) somehow getting the strength to crawl on my hands and knees to the bathroom but I have to crawl straight back to bed again after the shock of seeing my face in the mirror. Honest to God, I look like someone gouged out my eyes and replaced them with flint. Besides, all the crawling around is starting to give me carpet burn. Then there's point c). Like eating a Pot Noodle, I know it's bad for me, I know it'll make me feel worse afterwards, but I can't help myself, I switch Channel Six on again as it's coming up to the six o'clock news and, whoop-di-doo, I'm still there. Still the second bloody news item, which makes me wonder what the hell the third news item could possibly be; ants in a straight line crossing a road?

Next thing Sam's back in my room, so I snap off the TV and pretend to have been just lying there all along, innocently whinging. Then I notice that he's empty handed. Which can only mean one thing.

'Well, I've read them all cover to cover,' he begins.

'And . . .?'

He doesn't answer the question. Which instantly makes me fear the very worst.

'The *Sunday Indo* had an OK-ish piece . . .'

'Tell me.'

'Well, when I say OK, I mean there was one fairly sympathetic article, called "What Next for Jessie Woods?"'

'What's next for me? A gunshot, if I've anything to do with it.'

'Come on, Woodsie, you've got to face this head on,' he says, his huge rugby player's frame hulking in the doorway, eyes distractedly darting towards the window every thirty seconds or so, even though the curtains are drawn. 'Damage limitation, that's key right now. And showing your face in public again. They're having a field day knowing you've locked yourself up in here. You're a sitting target. You're front page in everything but the *Sunday Sport* and that's only because there's some glamour model with thirty-eight double-D cups on the cover. But you made page two. With a picture of the house and a banner headline saying "Hiding out in The Chateau de Shame".'

'Shut up, please! Enough!!' I screech, sticking my two fingers in my ears.

'Look, Woodsie, the absolute worst thing you can do is nothing. In your shoes I'd go straight in to see my agent in the morning and release a statement clarifying your position and above all apologising. Best way to get rid of them is to grovel for a bit, say you're sorry and pray it'll all die down.' Then he sits down on the edge of the bed beside me and for a while we're both silent. I know he's right; just the thought of having to face the world tomorrow is crucifying me. Next thing, he springs up, running his hands through his hair again, so it looks even bouffier.. 'Anyway, speaking of damage limitation, I better go.'

'What? You're leaving? You can't leave!'

'We were due to have dinner at Nathaniel and Eva's, remember? I think at least one of us should go.'

'But . . . Sam, please, no. Can't you cancel? They'll understand. Especially when they see we're holed up like hostages here.'

He's firm though, the way Sam always is whenever he's made his mind up about something. 'No,' he insists. 'We already cancelled on them last night. It would be rude.'

I don't want to be left here by myself, but I know I've no choice. I've royally buggered up his weekend, the least I can do is let him out from under house arrest for a few hours. After all, it's not like he did anything wrong. I look at him and suddenly a huge surge of love comes over me. I mean, just look at him, for God's sake; protecting me, checking through the papers for me, trying to fix me and make everything all better again. My rock. My Prince Charming.

'But you'll come back here later, won't you?' I ask, aware of how pathetically weak and clingy I sound and not even caring.

'Course I will. Now try to sleep,' he says gently on his way out. I just nod and manage a watery half-smile.

Then, from the bottom of the stairs, he calls up, 'By the way? You really need to get the downstairs loo fixed. Smells like a Victorian sewer down here.'

Oh yeah, that's another thing about Sam. He's surprisingly intolerant of lax household maintenance.

Ten p.m. and I'm still awake and staring at the ceiling. Sleep won't come so to pass the time I make out a list of all the crap things in my life right now versus all the good things.

Crap things:
-No job
-No money and I doubt if even Bob Geldof with all his

experience in dealing with Third World debt could bail me out of the financial black hole I'm in. Have a lot of grovelling ahead of me before I can be deemed employable again. If I can ever be deemed employable again. Because it'll take great good luck, plus Liz Walsh having a mild stroke which will completely black out her entire memory bank for the last twenty-four hours
-Prisoner in own home

What a rubbish idea this was, I think, flinging the pen away from me after only a few minutes. Just when I thought I was all cried out, this is only bringing on a fresh batch of hot, stinging tears. So instead, I focus on the positives in my life right now. But it's a far shorter list. Scarily short. Because the only good, rock solid, dependable thing in my life right now is Sam. That's it. He's the one person who's there for me through thick and thin and after the way he's stood by me this weekend, I think I love him even more. If that were even possible.

It's just a bit odd that by 2 a.m., he still hasn't come back.

Chapter Five

He hasn't come back by the following morning either. I hardly slept a wink; just kept dozing fitfully and at about 8 a.m., eventually abandoned that as a bad job. So then I started frantically phoning and texting Sam instead. Twenty-five calls and seventeen texts. Like the demented lunatic I've turned into, I actually counted. No answer to any of the phone calls and no reply to my manic text messages either. Now, just to give you an idea of just how utterly unheard of this is, Sam always, *always* has his phone on his person at all times. He's one of those people who even brings it into the bathroom with him whenever he has a shower, and by the way, I am NOT making that up. Communication is like oxygen to him.

So now I've spiralled off into a sickening flurry of panic. The love of my life has probably been in some tragic car accident and at this very moment could be lying comatose in a hospital bed in plaster from the neck down, unable to say or do anything except move the tip of his little finger, so none of the nurses in the intensive care unit know to call and tell me what's happened.

Suddenly, the lethargy and depression of yesterday are gone and now I'm wired by this whole new world of worry that's just opened up. I try calling Nathaniel and Eva's home number, my hands sweaty with tension, but no answer. Which means this *must* be bad. Frantically, I ring Eva's mobile. She answers immediately, sounding half asleep and groggy. No, she yawns sleepily, she hasn't heard from Sam either, not since he left their house early, about tenish last night after they'd all had dinner. But, here comes the killer, she lets it slip that Sam did call Nathaniel earlier this morning to, wait for it, arrange drinks and dinner with some clients at Bentleys swanky restaurant later on tonight.

Right. So that's the coma worry eliminated then. It never occurred to me that he just . . . didn't bother calling me. So, in other words, he went home last night, as normal, got up for work as normal and even found the time to book dinner and drinks with his best friend.

I have to slump back against a pillow to digest his.

'OK, so maybe Sam hasn't been in touch with you yet,' Eva goes on, calmly, so calmly that it's making me want to scream. 'But it's still early; he'll call you later on. Funny, I assumed he was going straight back to yours last night, but I suppose he must have just gone home instead.'

'But why the hell would he just go home instead? He knew the state I was in and he faithfully promised he'd come straight back here! Eva, you've no idea what it's been like for me. Yesterday was a bloody nightmare.' My voice sounds weak now, croaky and panicky.

'Oh yeah, I meant to say how sorry I am. About . . . emm, you know, everything. How are you doing?'

'I . . . I'm . . .' I can't finish my sentence though. So I just opt for bawling my eyes out instead, which in fairness, I haven't done for at least half an hour.

'Well, never mind. I mean, it's only a job, isn't it?' she says airily and for a split second, her flippancy silences me out of my hysteria. The exact same shock you'd get if you're crying and someone responds by smacking you wham across the face. *It's only a job, isn't it?* Did I really hear her just saying that?

'Eva, not to put too fine a point on it, I'm unemployed, broke, up to my armpits in debt, out of my mind with worry, not to mention staked out by the press and now, on top of everything else, I haven't heard a single word from my boyfriend all night or all morning, although apparently he's well able to ring Nathaniel!'

'Shh, shh, honey, take a deep breath. In for two and out for four, like they tell us in power yoga class. You need to de-stress. I'm sure Sam's just busy. You know what he's like when it comes to work, Jessie.'

'Are you kidding me? My whole life has gone into freefall and you're telling me that Sam is too busy to talk to me?' I'm trying my best to keep the rising hysteria out of my voice, but not really succeeding.

'You know, Jessie, listening to you, all I can think is, when was the last time this girl had acupuncture? Hey, here's a thought, my masseuse is calling over later, why don't you drop by and have a Swedish massage? Sounds like you might need one. Badly. Oooh, and then later on, I'm going to the Design Centre to see their new spring collection. You should come with.'

Dear Jaysus. I'm inclined to forget. To Eva, the recession is just something that's happening to other people. Somehow, I restrain myself from snapping at her, but firmly tell her I need to get off the phone to call Sam's office. Like, now.

'Oh, OK,' she yawns. 'I'm going back to sleep anyway.' I know, for a mother of twin boys, this sounds extravagantly luxurious, but bear in mind that Eva has *a lot* of home help. 'Just try to calm down, Jessie. And remember, at least we've got the trip to Marbella coming up really soon. Now isn't that something lovely for you to look forward to?'

I hang up, wondering if she even heard a single word I said.

So I ring Sam's office and am put straight through to his assistant, Margaret. Two things about Margaret: firstly, she's incredibly protective of Sam, almost obsessing over him the way an Irish mammy would with a cherished only son. Secondly, to put it mildly, she's not exactly a huge fan of mine. Can never quite figure out why. I've only met her a handful of times, but she always treats me like some telly-tottie blow-in who only distracts Sam from going out and making even more money than he already has.

'He's specifically asked not to be disturbed this morning, Miss Woods.'

That's another thing about her, she always calls me Miss Woods. I think it's an intimidation tactic. Waste of time trying to intimidate me though; I may live in a fancy gated house in Dalkey, but scratch below the surface and you'll find a true blue, working-class Dublin Northsider.

'However, I'm very happy to pass on your message.'

I know right well that she knows what happened to me over the weekend; bar she's just come out of a coma, how could she not? But I don't give her the satisfaction of hearing me sniffle down the phone – just thank her politely and hang up.

Right then. So Sam is alive and well and going about his day's work and not lying comatose in a hospital bed. Which is something, I suppose. Then a surge of optimism; of course he's going to call me back later. Come on, this is Sam I'm talking about, Mr Perfect Boyfriend. Yes, it's a bit odd he never came back here last night, but I'm sure there's some perfectly plausible explanation. So when we eventually do get to talk and when he inevitably asks me what I've been up to since yesterday, what will I tell him then? That I lay in bed all day whinging like a crazy lady? Or that I took his advice, picked myself up like a winner who's just taken one of life's knocks, and is now bravely dealing with it head on? Right, that's it. Decision made. Let Operation Damage Limitation begin.

An hour later and I'm up, dressed in jeans and a sweater with my hair tied back under a baseball cap, along with the biggest pair of sunglasses I can find for maximum face covering. Just so no one gets to see my face which frankly is looking like a bag of chisels from all the crying and sleep deprivation. For better or for worse, I'm ready to face the world. Plus I've been busy lining up appointments in town for the week ahead with my agent, publicist and, the one I'm actually dreading most of all, my accountant.

First hurdle though, is getting out the front gate without the hounds of hell stationed there having a pop at me. Added to this particular dilemma is the fact that a) I've no car and b) if I get the bus into town, there's every chance the bastards will follow me and God alone knows the craic they'd have doing that. Right, nothing for it but to get a taxi to come through the security gates and right to the front door of the house, so I can hop into it and slip past the photographers at maximum speed. Slight problem though: I've no cash in the house to pay for said cab. Not a brass farthing.

I can't believe I'm doing this, but next thing, I'm rooting through coat pockets and old handbags foraging for loose change. Dear Jaysus; not one week ago, I spent around €180 on a La Prairie face cream and now I'm scrambling around looking for a few spare coins which I might have forgotten about. But I'm in luck; right at the bottom of a ridiculously expensive, impulse-buy Gucci bag, there's a €20 note and about €4.50 in coins. Well whaddya know. I'm rich.

Week from hell: day one
I meet with my agent, one Roger Davenport, in his offices in town. Roger, I should tell you, is a sixty-something bachelor whose ideal client would probably be Audrey Hepburn. Always dresses a bit like a magician in velvet suits and bow ties, usually accessorised with a brolly; a bit like Steed in *The New Avengers*. He's also a thorough gentleman of the old school and never loses his temper with the kids who always follow him, as he strolls from his converted Georgian townhouse to his equally elegant Georgian office. I've often seen him sauntering through town, like it's permanent Bloomsday, chased by kids all chanting, 'Here mister, where's your boyfriend?' Water off a duck's back though; Roger is famous for his unflappable cool and permanent good humour. Until I go in to see him, that is.

He's sitting at his antique desk when I arrive at his office, surrounded by this morning's papers. 'Dear Lord, Jessie, what precisely were you thinking?' is his opener, peering up from over Churchill-esque half-moon glasses. I fill him in, with particular red-eyed snivelling saved for the part where I stress that I didn't know I'd done anything wrong. It's fast becoming my new catchphrase.

'Well, my dear,' he frowns, looking like a consultant about to give me bad news, 'naturally I shall do my best to source alternative employment for you. However, be warned. This will be no easy task.'

Then I meet with Roger's publicist Paul, a prematurely grey chain smoker with so much manic energy that after ten minutes in his company I'm so exhausted, all I want to do is lie down in a darkened room and take sedatives. Together with Roger, we draft a press release, which I think just about hits the right, apologetic note between deep contrition and remorse for what I did, yet gently touching on the fact that had I suspected for a second that what I was doing was wrong, I'd have been a distant speck on the horizon.

On his way out the door to have a cigarette, statement tucked under his oxter, Paul turns to me. 'Oh, by the way, I do have one bit of good news for you, Jessie.'

I look at him stunned, but then, optimism is an unfamiliar sensation for me right now.

Then he tells me that some topless glamour model who I never heard of has just left her boy band drummer husband who I also never heard of, for a Premiership footballer whose name I couldn't even attempt to pronounce.

'Sorry Paul, excuse my addled brain, but how exactly is this good news?'

'Means you're relegated to page four.'

I see what he means. By the time I get back to the house, the photographers and press who were there yesterday and this morning have completely dispersed. So now I know exactly what they mean by 'yesterday's news'.

By nine that night, I've broken the magical half-century barrier with the amount of messages I've left for Sam, which in stalking terms is probably the equivalent of running the four-minute mile. And not one single call answered. I'm too exhausted even to cry, so I just collapse into bed and sleep the sleep of the damned.

Week from hell: day two

My policy of call bombardment to Sam continues. Except now that I've actually had a night's sleep and am thinking a bit more clearly, I'm *furious* with him. Madder than a meat-axe. I mean, for feck's sake what exactly is going on here? Me going through career meltdown and him ignoring me? Cowardly bloody bastard. With woman's intuition, the only possible reason I can come up with for his bizarre carry on is that Sam, media lover, with a book about to be published in a few months' time and an ongoing campaign to become a panellist on that entrepreneur's TV show, can't hack being around the PR disaster that I've become. So if it comes to a choice between his precious career and me, his girlfriend, then guess who gets the boot? Which leaves me with exactly two courses of action to choose from: Plan A, I barge into his office to have it out with him there. Except then I'd only have to face snotty Margaret acting like a sentinel, who'd probably force me to wait in reception for the rest of the day out of pure badness. And to be perfectly honest, I wouldn't give the old bitch the satisfaction. Plan B is just to go round to his house and stake him out there, but he lives in deepest County Kildare, about fifteen miles from any bus route and let's face it, there's no way I could ever afford the taxi fare. Probably just as well for him that neither plan is a runner, because the mood

I'm in right now, if I did get to see him, I'd bloody kill him, then feed his rotting carcass to starving alsatians.

I leave about six messages for Nathaniel too, but, surprise, surprise, he doesn't get back to me either. I've always liked Nathaniel, but in my yo-yoing emotional state, now I'm furious with him too. I always thought he was a bit weak, a bit too easily dominated by Sam and his Type A personality. Now here's the proof. I ring Eva too, the only one of our foursome who's still actually speaking to me, but it turns out she has another yummy mummy friend over with her kids for a play date, so she can't talk. She swears she'll call me later on though. Which of course, she doesn't.

Roger calls to say that, as he suspected, no one is hiring right now. He'd put out a few feelers on my behalf, but nothing doing. 'Best lie low for a bit, Jessie dear,' is his sage advice. 'When this unpleasantness all dies down, I'll try again. Perhaps not a primetime show, but maybe something on one of the digital channels.' This is about as close as polite, gentlemanly Roger would ever come to saying, 'Your stock is so low in this town, you'll be bloody lucky to get a job in community radio reading out the funeral notices on the 5 a.m. graveyard slot.'

Then Paul the publicist rings with an update; our press release has done the trick and seems to have killed the story for the moment at least. I'm now further relegated to page eight, which is marginally better than being publicly stoned.

'Any actual . . . em . . . *good* news?' I ask hopefully.

'Are you kidding me? You don't pay me for good news; you pay me to make bad news go away. You're now on page eight beside the horoscopes and the weather report; as far as you're concerned, that's a miracle up there along with the second coming of Christ.'

Funny, my entire career, which I worked so hard for, is lying in ashes around me and yet all I can eat drink or focus on is Sam and this disappearing trick he's pulling. I don't even sleep that night. Every time I hear a car on the road outside, I keep thinking that it's him and that he'll knock on my door and that there'll be some completely rational explanation for this crucifying silence and then he'll hold me in his arms and everything will be just fine.

Week from hell: day three

There *is* a completely rational explanation! I ring snotty Margaret at the office who tells me that Sam is in London on business and will be back tomorrow! A wash of near-euphoria comes over me. Of course, Sam wasn't ignoring me, he's out of the country, that's all and when he gets home everything will be back to normal. Well apart from my being broke and unemployed that is. But like I say, once he's back in my life, everything else will seem bearable again. I conveniently brush aside the fact that every other time he's away, he never fails to call day and night. He was probably just stressed up to the ceiling about all his meetings in London, that's all. I actually have a spring in my step for the first time in days, which lasts all the way up until 11 a.m., when the phone rings. It's the letting agency who found this house for me. 'Bad news,' says the property management guy, who sounds about fifteen. 'You're now almost four months behind in rent which means you're in breach of the lease agreement. The owners have instructed me to request that you vacate the premises and return the keys ASAP. Otherwise, they'll be left with no choice but to instigate legal proceedings.'

For a second, I think I'm going to black out as I slump against the stairs, with my back to the wall. It's official; I'm on the express train to hell.

'Listen to me, Jessie,' says Teen Boy kindly. 'This could be an awful lot worse. I know these people and trust me; all they want is you out of the house by the end of the week. Fair's fair, you do owe them well in excess of €12,000 in back rent.'

'€12,000?' is all I can think, fresh beads of panicky sweat forming in the small of my back. How in the name of Jaysus did I let that happen?

'Go quickly and quietly,' he says, 'and I'm pretty certain that they'll leave it at that. Going to court will cost time and money and the owners already have interest from people who want to come over and view the place.'

By now I'm actually drenched in sweat. Just when I thought things couldn't get worse, I'm made homeless. I thank the poor guy as politely as I'm able to; after all, none of this is his fault and like he says, go quietly and I won't get sued. But go where?

Now the tone of all my messages to Sam has completely changed from angry to pleading. I urgently need to talk to you, I almost beg. Something calamitous has happened. Ring me and I'll explain. Then, a brainwave; he always stays at the Mandarin Oriental Hotel when he's in London; vintage Sam, only the best will do. So I call them and ask to be put through to his room. The over-polite receptionist asks me for my name first, checks the room, then comes back to me and says Mr Hughes isn't there. Trying my best not to sound like some kind of psycho stalker, I explain that I'm his girlfriend and would she pretty please with knobs on have any idea when he'll be back?

The blind panic in my voice seems to do the trick.

'Well, I normally wouldn't dream of giving out personal information, but seeing as you are his girlfriend . . . OK then. He should be back in the room in about an hour or so. He's down in the spa at the moment having a sports massage.'

So he's not up to his eyes in meetings, too busy to return my calls. He's lying naked, wrapped in a hot towel having aromatherapy oil rubbed into him. I spend the rest of the day trying to pack, then collapsing into floods of heaving tears. Ask not for whom the bell tolls. It's the ambulance coming to take me away.

Week from hell: day four

Funny thing is, when the final blow falls, it happens fast. I'm lying in bed with all the life and energy of a used teabag. My phone rings and it's him. It's Sam. I almost drop it with nervous anxiety and before he's even said a word, my heart's already twisting in my ribcage.

'So . . . you got my messages then?' is my opener. Shit, I didn't mean to sound sarky, it just slipped out.

'Yes.'

'That's all you're going to say? "Yes"? A monosyllable?'

There's an awkward pause, so I do what any TV presenter does when faced with a hiatus, fill it up with gabble and shite. The nightmare the last few miserable days have been, the agonising worry over why he was blanking me out—

'Woodsie,' he interrupts and I jibber over him. But then nervous tension tends to have that effect on me.

'I need somewhere to stay,' I stammer. 'So – and I know

it's an awful lot to ask – is it OK if . . . Look, what I'm trying to say is . . . and of course, it would just be until I get back on my feet again . . . but the thing is . . . can I move in with you?'

There's silence. I didn't expect silence. I have to say 'Sam?' a few times just to check that he's still on the line.

'I'm here,' he says dully and I swear to God, now I can actually feel the beads of sweat starting to roll down my face. 'To be honest, Woodsie, I think right now, that would be a bad idea. A really bad idea.'

For a second I can't speak. Then more gibberish comes tumbling out, Tourettes-like. 'Look, I know it's a big ask, and an even bigger imposition, but Sam, it's just temporary, just until I find another job, that's all . . .'

'I've got my parents coming to stay, so I'm afraid it's not going to work.'

'But your house has seven bedrooms! It's not like we'll all be on top of each other!'

'Look, there's no easy way to say this, but I really feel that . . .'

The breath catches in the back of my throat. 'You really feel that . . . *what*?'

'That you and I should take a bit of a break. I need to be honest with you; I'm finding all of this negative media attention very difficult to live with.'

There it is, the one cold, bald sentence that I've been dreading this whole, horrendous week. Funny, now that it's out in the open, a dead calm comes over me. 'Just so you're clear on a few things, Sam,' I say icily, almost spitting, staccato style. 'The negative media attention as you call it, is dying down. We put out a press release and that's pretty much killed the story—'

'Woodsie,' he interrupts, 'you know where I'm coming from here.'

I'm cooler now so I let him talk. And out it all comes, all my worst fears, verbalised. He's worked so hard to get to this level of his career and bad press is the last thing he needs right now, he feels his position is utterly compromised because he and I are so publicly linked together . . . blah-di-blah-di-blah.

It's like he's reading from an instruction manual on how to break up with someone and leave them with absolutely no hope of reconciliation. And all I feel is numbness, like I'm anaesthetised from pain that's going to hit me like a sledgehammer any minute now.

'What you're trying to tell me, Sam, is that you don't want to be tarred by association with me. Like my fall from grace is something contagious.'

'Woodsie, look—'

Then I throw in an old classic. What the fuck, I've nothing to lose. 'I thought you loved me. But here you are, at the first real hurdle we've ever had to face, bailing out, running for the hills. You're the single most important person in my life and I mess up once and suddenly you decide that I'm flawed and therefore dispensable. Have you any idea how that makes me feel?' My voice is shaking so much, I'm amazed I even managed to get that much out coherently.

'Woodsie, you're taking this the wrong way . . .'

'What other way is there to take it? You're dumping me over the phone? After two years?'

'Can we drop the dramatics? No one is dumping anyone. I'm just suggesting we take a break, that's all.'

It's an odd thing when the man you love asks you for 'a

bit of time out'. Makes you feel like the first quarter in a basketball game.

'Woodsie? Are you still there? Because there's something else I need to say to you.'

I catch my breath, waiting on some crumb of comfort he might throw my way.

'I'm having my PR people put out a press release to say we're not together any more. I think it's best for both of us to put a full stop to this. Don't you?'

Week from hell: day five

Somehow I manage to get out of bed and haul myself to the one meeting I've been postponing all week but have now run out of excuses for. My accountant. You should see me; I'm like a dead woman walking. Literally. Dead on the inside and dead on the outside. The whole way there, all I can think is, *If I were to get run over by that bus . . . it wouldn't necessarily be the worst thing that could happen.* Given the rate at which my entire life is unravelling, I'd be surprised if Satan wasn't waiting at the gates of hell for me with a fruit basket and a complimentary robe.

My accountant is called Judy: she's a widow with four sons all of whom she's single-handedly putting through schools and colleges, and I'd say she's never been in debt once in her whole life. I think she realises that there's rock bottom, followed by another 500 feet of crap before you finally arrive at where I'm at right now. So, for once, she's going easy on me.

She sympathises over my being turfed out of the house and even manages not to invoke the one phrase that really would send me over the edge, 'I told you so.' Then, for a full hour, Judy goes through every sickening, nauseating entry on my credit card statements, household bills, the works, trying to figure what we can write off against my tax bill versus debt that just has to be saddled onto all of my other loans and toxic debts. I've even come clean with her about the secret Visa card I'd been hiding all along. At this stage, on the brink of bankruptcy, what's another few thousand? But, try as I might, even in my numb, deadened state I still can't tune her out entirely and snippets of past extravagances keep filtering through, stabbing me right in the solar plexus.

Shopocalypse Now. Story of my life to date. Veni, Vidi, Visa.

'The fifteenth of last month, crystalware from Louise Kennedy, €485.'

I remember. Six beautiful long-stemmed champagne flutes. An anniversary gift for Nathaniel and Eva. Who by the way, I rang this morning to ask/beg/plead for a temporary roof over my head. Eva didn't even have the good grace to sound concerned about me; just said that they'd now decided to stay down in Marbella with the kids for longer than they'd thought, so it just wasn't a runner. Anyway, she'd spoken to Sam and knew about our break-up. Knew about it before I did, I'll warrant. And her final word on the subject? 'Yeah . . . you know, we're really sorry but I suppose these things happen. Shame you won't be coming away with us this Easter. You're always such fun to be away with.'

Like I'm some kind of court jester. But however vague and dismissive she sounds, the subtext is clear as the crystal I bankrupted myself to buy for her; Sam was their friend long before I came along, so, foursome or no foursome, if anyone is going to get jettisoned, it's me. Of course it is. I'm utterly dispensable. In Eva's eyes, I'm broke = I'm out.

In fact, the only real friend that's come out of all this for me is Emma. Before I'd even had a chance to ask, she said that I'd be more than welcome to stay at her flat in town. The only person I know who actually *offered* to put me up. There was a catch though; she's on a few months' paid leave from Channel Six and is going down to stay with her parents in Wexford for a few weeks, so she'd already sublet the flat before she'd heard about my, ahem, domestic difficulty. Nice of her to offer though. More than some people. A lot more.

'So to recap,' Judy the accountant is still droning on, 'I'll have to get on to credit control at Visa and explain the situation. Needless to say, your card will be cancelled forthwith. But, with luck, maybe we can stall them from referring this to their legal team.' She smiles at me. God love her, she must think this'll cheer me up. 'Obviously with a commitment from you to come to a long-term payment arrangement with them,' she adds.

'A payment arrangement?' I say, temporarily stunned out of my deadened stupor. 'Emm . . . sorry to state the obvious, Judy, but payment from what exactly? I have nothing.'

'Come on, you must have valuable items you could possibly sell? When you were earning, did you invest in paintings? Jewellery? Anything?'

I'm too embarrassed to tell her that the only investments I ever made were in handbags/shoes/designer clobber etc, so instead I just focus on dividing the snotty Kleenex that's lying on my lap into half, then quarters, then eighths and not bursting into tears. Yet again.

'Jessie,' she says, softly, 'you have to understand that I'm trying to help you as much as I can. And I want you to let me know if there's anything else that I can do for you.'

'You could lend me the bus fare home.'

'Please, be serious.'

'I was being serious.'

'What I meant by that was, do you have any assets at all which I could liquidise for you? Something that would give you a cash injection to get you through this?'

Me? Assets? For a second I want to laugh. I'm a live now, pay later kind of gal.

'Jessie, I hate bringing up a distasteful subject but needs must I'm afraid. When your father passed away, didn't he leave you anything at all?'

'No,' I mutter dully. 'Poor Dad had nothing to leave. Well, apart from the house that is.'

Her eyes light up.

'He left you a house? Explain, please?'

'Nothing to explain. Dad left our family home equally to my stepmother and me. That's all.'

'So this would be the house that you grew up in?'

'Yup.'

'And he left it to be divided fifty-fifty between both of you?'

'Ehhhh . . . yeah.'

'So, all this time, you've been part-owner of a house and you never told me?'

Swear to God, the woman's eyes look like they're about to pop across the room like champagne corks. 'And was it sold? Is it rented out?'

'No, my stepfamily still live there. The three of them. But I have absolutely nothing to do with those people and they've nothing to do with me. Trust me; it's an arrangement that suits all of us.'

'But you're the legal owner of half of this property.'

'Judy, I'm not with you. What do you suggest I do here?

Turf them all out and sell the place from under them? They'd get a hit man after me. You have no idea what these people are like; they'd have me knee-capped. This is their home.'

'You needed somewhere to stay, didn't you? Well here's the answer staring you in the face.'

For a second I look at her, my mouth I'm sure forming the same perfect 'O' that the kids do in the Bisto commercial.

'Jessie, welcome to the wonderful world of "Got no choice".'

Chapter Six

It's like a mantra with me the whole of the next day: I have no choice, I have no choice. I. Have. No. Choice. And in fact, if I don't get a move on, chances are I'll come home to find all my stuff in cardboard boxes outside the security gates, the locks changed and new people already living there. All of which fits in beautifully with the recurring theme of my life right now; when you've got everything, you've got everything to lose.

It's late Saturday afternoon and I'm still in bed, paralysed. Praying that at this exact moment Sam is doing the same thing. That he's dead on the inside too. Despondent. Missing me. Willing himself to swallow his pride, pick up the phone and beg me to get back with him.

I've been practically a 'Rules Girl' since our last, harrowing conversation and by that I mean I've only texted him approximately a dozen times and left around eight voice messages on his mobile. Per day, that is.

TV is my only friend, but as I'm avoiding the news for obvious reasons, I stick to the History Channel where there's bound to be nothing on that'll only upset me more. An ad comes on where they quote Buddha saying that all suffering stems from failed expectations. Yup, sounds about right to me. Next thing, out of nowhere, there's a massive, urgent walloping on my hall door downstairs, which my first instinct is to ignore, but then it flashes through my mind, *Suppose it's Sam?* Standing there with a huge bouquet of flowers and a speech all prepared about what a complete moron he's been? I dive out of bed like I've just had an adrenaline shot to the heart and race downstairs, still in my pyjamas. Course, it's not Sam at all though. It's the estate agent, with a middle-aged-looking couple standing on either side of him like twin bodyguards, wanting to view the house. The estate agent is super-polite and says he's mortified for disturbing me, but his implication is clear; just disappear for the afternoon and let people who can actually afford to live here get a once-over of the place in peace.

Which is how, about an hour later, I end up back in our humble little corporation estate in Whitehall, on Dublin's Northside. My first time back to the house since I was eighteen, all of eleven years ago. I'm absolutely dreading what lies ahead and at the same time, so punch drunk by all the body blows I've taken in the last week, that the part of me that's numb just takes over everything; all bodily functions like walking down streets and holding conversations without crying. Anyway, like I said, where I come from is not posh. Nor, from what I can see so far, has much of it changed since I used to live here. It's basically 1950s corpo-land that's so close to the airport, you can actually see the wheels going up and down on the bellies of all overhead flights. It also gets so deafeningly noisy at times that you feel like you could be living on the near end of a runway. But it just so happens that deafening noise suits me right now. As does anything that drowns out the loop that's on eternal long play inside my head: *dumpedhomelessjoblessdumpedhomelessjoblessdumpedhomelessjobless* . . . etc., etc., etc., repeat ad nauseam.

The house is right at the very end of a cul-de-sac, which means that when I get off the bus, I have to do the walk of shame down the whole length of the street, alone, unprotected and totally exposed. Which, I know, makes it sound like I come from Fallujah Square and it's not that I'm worried about broken bottles or other random missiles being flung at me; no, it's the kids on this street you've got to watch out for. They're complete savages and their cruelty knows no bounds. Plus, as it's a warm, balmy evening, they're all out swarming round the place like midges. Sure enough, right across the street, there's a gang of them led by a boy of about ten, a dead ringer for the kid in *The Omen*, all harassing someone I can only presume is a Jehovah's Witness making door to door calls.

'You says there's no Our Lady, you says there's no Our Lady!' they're chanting at the poor gobshite, hot on his heels. I pull the baseball cap I'm wearing down even lower over my forehead and pick up my pace a bit, head down at all times. But just then an elderly neighbour out doing her hedges spots me.

'Jessie Woods? Mother of God, it *is* you!'

Shit. Caught. And by a neighbour who's known me ever since I was a baby, worse luck. 'Oh, hello, Mrs Foley.'

Right then, stand by for the sideshow. And sure enough, Mrs Foley yells excitedly over at another pensioner who's busy doing the brasses on her front door. 'Mrs Brady? Would you look who it is! Jessie Woods herself, as I live and breathe! She's come home!'

'Suffering Jesus, I don't believe it,' says Mrs Brady,

clutching her chest, then abandoning the hall door and waddling over to Mrs Foley's front gate.

Nononononono, you see, this is exactly what I wanted to avoid. The thing about our street is that it's considered rude to walk past a neighbour without having at least a ten-minute chat about the most intimate details of your private life. God, the difference between life here and life in Dalkey, where my house – sorry, my ex-house – is. Over on that side of town, I couldn't even tell you who my neighbours are. Everyone lives behind high security gates and apart from seeing the odd four-wheel-drive zipping in and out, you wouldn't have a clue who's living next door to you. There were always rumours flying around that Bono and Enya lived locally, but you'd never, ever get a glimpse of them out buying cartons of milk, Lotto tickets or similar. There was a Southside snobbery at play too; even if you met people locally, say in Tesco's, they were all far too cultured and sophisticated and up themselves to even admit that they recognised me from TV.

But Toto, I'm not in Kansas any more.

'Terrible about what happened to you last week, Jessie love,' says Mrs Foley kindly. 'Big fuss over nothing if you ask me. And they really fired you just for doing that? For taking the offer of a free car?'

'Yes, they really did.'

'But sure I watched the whole thing myself. They made it very hard for you to say no. Nearly forced it on you, they did.'

'Yeah, you're right, they did,' I agree, touched and grateful to her.

'Well, if you ask me, you should have had more sense, Jessie Woods,' snaps Mrs Brady, treating me exactly like I'm still the kid she used to give out to for sitting on her front wall and damaging her geraniums. 'You big roaring eejit. No such thing as a free lunch, sure the dogs on the street could tell you that. You should have told them where to go with their flashy car and then you'd be on the telly tonight, wouldn't you? Instead of walking the streets, looking like a refugee.'

I'd forgotten that about Mrs Brady. She has a very nasty side to her.

'So what'll you do now, love?' says Mrs Foley gently. 'The papers all said no one would come near you for work, you poor pet.'

'Emm ... well, I'm actually hoping to take a bit of time out and just, emm ... you know, reassess my options,' I manage to say, weakly.

The pair of them look completely unconvinced, so I try changing the subject instead.

'So how's Psycho, Mrs Brady?' Psycho is her son. He's my age, we were in junior school together and from what I heard, he went on to spend most of his teenage years in juvenile prison. Everyone calls him Psycho, ever since he was about three. Even his mother.

'Ah, he's grand, love. Thanks for asking,' she smiles proudly, instantly brightening. 'He's getting out on TR tomorrow, so we're having a bit of a knees-up for him. You should drop in if you're still around. He was always very fond of you. And I happen to know that he's single at the moment.'

'Ehh, sorry ... TR?'

'Temporary Release. Please Jesus, with a bit of good behaviour, he could be out before the summer. Only a short stretch this time, thank God.'

I ooh and aah about how brilliant that is and am just about to make my excuses when the gang of kids, led by *Omen*-boy, spots me.

Shit.

Next thing, there about eight kids all clustered around me, demanding to know whether or not I'm your one off the telly?

'Go on,' says one. 'Take off the baseball hat and sunglasses till we can get a decent look at your face!' says another one, while a third, who can't be more than about eight, whips out a camera phone, shoves it right under my nose and starts taking photos.

''Cos if you really are Jessie Woods,' he says cheekily, 'then I'm emailing this to the *Daily Star*. Might make a few quid.'

Which serves me right of course. I should have remembered that round here the only safe, harassment-free time to walk down this street is in pitch darkness, preferably between the hours of 2 a.m. and 5 a.m., when it's a kid-free zone. They really should have a sign up, warning people.

'Leave the poor girl alone, you ignorant shower of pups!' says Mrs Foley, shooing them away with her apron. 'How would you like it if you got the sack and then your fella dumped you, all in the one week?' Then she realises that I'm still standing right beside her and claps her hand over her mouth, mortified. 'Oh, Jessie love, I'm sorry. I hope I didn't embarrass you, pet. It's just that it's been all over the news ever since yesterday. About you not going out with that good-looking businessman any more, what's-his-name.'

'Imagine getting dumped and the first thing your ex does is go running off to the papers,' sneers a third neighbour who's just joined us. She's leaning on a yard brush and has a perm so tight that it's almost as if someone poured a tin of baked beans over her head. I haven't the first clue who she is, but she seems to know more about my own private life than I do myself. Sam and his bloody, bollocking press release included. He warned me he was going to do it, 'Put a full stop to this,' as he'd said during our last, nightmarish phone call, so I knew it was inevitable. But it still somehow feels like someone's physically taken a shovel to my insides. Right. Officially had enough. Got to get outta here.

'Sorry, but I'm afraid I really should get going . . .' I say lamely in an attempt to make a run for it. No such luck though.

'You should have married that Sam Hughes when you had the chance, Jessie,' pontificates Mrs Brady. 'Then at least you'd have a few quid to show for yourself. Or you could have had a baby with him, then maybe he'd think twice about running to the press to tell everyone it's all off with you. Plus you'd have the child maintenance coming in every week, which would have come in very handy, now that you're jobless . . .'

'The secret to a long and happy marriage', says Baked Bean Head, leaning on her yard brush, 'is that the man has to be scared shitless of the woman. They only really respect you when they're completely terrified. You must have gone far too easy on him, Jessie . . .'

OK, it's at this point I officially can't take any more. 'I'm really sorry, ladies, but I have to get going.'

They turn to glare at me, like I'm being rude to just walk away when they're all busy throwing out their pearls of relationship advice, but at this point I'm beyond caring. I take a deep breath and turn into our tiny front yard. And almost fall over when I see the state of it. I'm not messing, there are actual statues of stone angels blowing into trumpets dotted around the tiny grassy bit, the original agony in the garden. Trying my best to keep my stomach from dry-retching at the very sight of it, I knock firmly on the front door.

And wait.

And wait again.

A kafuffle from the TV room inside, followed by a clearly audible row about who's going to get up and answer the door. Which is followed by another glacier-slow wait before the door is eventually opened. By Joan, my stepmother. Dressed, and I wish I were joking here, pretty much like Cher on the Reunion tour. It's almost scary the way everything matches; her suit is deep purple and so are the nails, lipstick and shoes. With, the final touch, tights the colour of Elastoplast. Honest to God, there are mothers of brides out there who'd blush to be seen in this get-up.

'Jessica!' she says, with a horrified, icy smile so fixed that it almost makes her look embalmed. That's another thing about her; she's the only person in the northern hemisphere who calls me Jessica. 'What in God's name are you doing here? It's not Christmas Eve, is it?'

'Emm, I did phone to say I was calling today, do you not remember, Joan? About an hour ago? You told me to be sure to call after *Britain's Got Talent* but before *American Idol*.'

Now coming from any other family, that might sound pig rude, but the thing about these people, certainly when I lived with them, was that their lives entirely revolved around the TV schedules. And clearly that hasn't changed.

'Oh, did I? I really have to start writing things down. I also have to have a drink. Right then,' she sniffs, looking down at me like I'm about as welcome as a fungus. 'Seeing as you're here, I suppose you'd better come through to the drawing room.'

By which I'm assuming she means the TV room, which is the only reception room in the house, apart from the tiny kitchen. But then that's Joan for you, everything gets talked up. In fact, I'm surprised she doesn't refer to the minuscule patch of grass in the front garden with the ludicrous gakky stone angels as the 'meditation and contemplation' area.

So in I go and am instantly struck by just how garish the place looks. So utterly different to when it was just me and Dad living here. The hallway, which is minute, dark and poky, now has a patterned cream Axminster carpet with loud polka-dot wallpaper in pink, blue and green. The overall effect of which is to make me feel like I'm trapped inside a bottle of prescription pills. No trendy, 'less is more' minimalism going on here; this has turned into the house that taste forgot. Joan catches me staring gobsmacked into the kitchen, which is straight ahead of us, and completely misinterprets my dropped jaw.

'Oh yes,' she waves airily, brightening a bit. 'You've noticed the dining area. Elegant, isn't it? I've just had the vinyl flooring redone in liquorice and marshmallow.'

This, by the way, would be Joan-speak for 'black and white'. Now while that might sound reasonably tasteful, factor in the bright peach fake festoon blinds in oceans of nylon draped over windows that you can barely see out of, the net curtains are that thick, along with peach stripy wallpaper and you'll get the picture. Dear Jaysus, it looks like a Mississippi paddleboat from Mark Twain's time washed up in a tiny little kitchen in Whitehall. Put it this way, you wouldn't want to be sitting there with a minging hangover. Gak, gak and gak again.

Anyway, to the right of us is the TV room, nerve centre of the whole house, where I wouldn't be surprised if they all eat, drink and sleep rather than, perish the thought, actually miss a TV show. Joan flings the TV room door open, says, 'Girls? Finish up your takeaways and watch your language, we've a visitor,' and I follow her. Into the portal of hell. May God help me.

'Well, well, well,' says Maggie looking at me with her stony, dead, grey eyes. 'Look who took a wrong turn on her way to the dole office.'

Pure, vintage Maggie; she always fancied herself as a bit of a one-woman Morecambe and Wise Christmas special.

'What the FUCK are you doing here?' is Sharon's stunned opener. 'And would you look at the state of you? Jeez, you look like you're on life support.'

'So it's the traditional warm, friendly welcome then,' I fire back at them, attack always being the best form of defence with my stepsisters, as I learnt a long, long time ago.

It's been eleven years since I've set foot in this room and I'm astonished at how little they've changed. You should just see the pair of them. The Borgias on a bad day. They don't even budge when I come in, but then lethargy was always pretty much the theme of this house. Maggie is sprawled out on what still appears to be her favourite armchair, which is positioned so that it faces the TV exactly head on, with a cider tin clamped to one hand and a forkful of takeaway Indian curry in the other. And if pulling the tabs off tins was a recognised Olympic sport, I would now be saying, 'Ta-da . . . Let me introduce you to the world champ.'

Now that I get a good, decent look at her, two things strike me; has this girl ever met a tracksuit she didn't like? Including the beaut she has on her today which is a shade of Hubba Bubba pink so nauseatingly sickening that no girl over the age of eight should ever go near it. The second thing is that she actually seems to be ageing in dog years. Maggie's only thirty-three, but could nearly pass for twenty years older; the wiry, woolly hair is now almost completely grey and what's more, she doesn't even seem to care. Plus, and there's no politically correct, sensitive way of saying this, but she and Sharon are both BIG girls. Legs the approximate size of tree trunks with necks roughly the same circumference as my waist. Nasty thought, but I remember as a kid looking at the pair of them and wondering who exactly their biological father had been anyway. A circus freak, perhaps?

Meanwhile, Sharon is stretched out on the sofa beside Maggie like she's sedated, with a *Cosmo* magazine balanced on her belly, opened on the quiz page, 'Is Your Guy a Stud or a Dud?' She's still in her brown serge uniform from Smiley Burger, where she works as 'food preparation and hygiene manager' (don't ask). There's also a big, roundey badge on her lapel that says, 'Hi! I'm Sharon and I care about your experience here!' Oh, that a cheap bit of plastic could contain so much blessed irony.

Anyway, unlike Maggie, Sharon always was at least aware of the directly proportional relationship between the amount of food she shovelled down her gob and the size of her arse. When I lived here, she was one of those people perpetually on a diet and yet whose weight never fluctuated by as much as a single gram, either upwards or downwards. And again, *plus ça change*. I'm guessing she's on yet another one of her crash diets right now, judging by the Low Fat Smiley Chicken Caesar Salad she's wolfing down. As opposed to Maggie, who's horsing into the remains of her Indian, eating straight out of the tinfoil container, like the fastest way to get food into her is to completely bypass all kitchenware. God Almighty, I'm astonished she's even using a fork.

With only a year between them, Sharon and Maggie are what's known as 'Irish twins' but at least Sharon manages to look in her early thirties, mainly because she hasn't let grey hair get the better of her. At least not yet, she hasn't. Trouble is, her hair is cut into a style so bizarre, it looks like it's in talks to play the Jane Fonda role in *Klute*.

Something else catches my eye; the Saturday supplement of today's paper on the coffee table, lying open on one of those 'What's hot/What's not' pages. No prizes for guessing which category I fall into. Bastards.

Anyway, this is not a social call, so nothing for it but to say what I came to say then get the hell out of here before the law of the sibling jungle kicks in and we all start killing each other. I plonk down on the far end of the sofa and switch off the TV, this being the only sure way to get everyone's full attention.

'If you value your miserable life,' Maggie snarls at me, with enough venom to wither a city, 'you'll turn the telly back on. I was watching that!'

'It was the ads,' I smile back, as politely as I can.

'Drinkie?' says Joan, trying to diffuse the tension that's ricocheting off the walls like ions before an electrical storm. 'Girls, one of you go into the fridge and get your sister a tin of Bulmers.'

'She is *not* our sister,' the two of them growl, both sitting back and lighting fags in such perfect synchronicity, you couldn't rehearse it.

'Besides,' says Sharon, all brave and feisty because she has Maggie right beside her for moral support, 'if her majesty wants a tin, she can get up off her skinny arse and get it herself.'

'I don't actually drink cider,' I say to Joan, trying to block out Pattie and Selma from *The Simpsons*. I will *not* let them get to me. Instead, I'll just do what I always do whenever I'm in their company. Lock my voice into its deepest register and remain cool. This also being the surest possible way to piss them off.

'But if you had a glass of wine please, Joan, I'd love one.'

Feck it, alcohol is about the only thing that'll get me through this. Joan disappears off to the kitchen, and the second she's out the door, Maggie and Sharon immediately start chanting, like a pair of bullies in the kids' playground, 'OH, I DON'T DRINK CIDER . . . I'M TOO FAR UP MY OWN ARSE.'

I totally forgot they could be so horrible. Dear Jesus, how did I edit this out? I must be off my head doing what I'm about to do, but then my accountant's words from yesterday come floating back to haunt me. *I. Have. No. Choice.* Besides, this was my family home long before the bloody Addams family ever moved in and took over. Dad bought this house, Mum died here, I grew up here. I legally own half of it. If I have no choice in this, then neither does anyone else.

Joan totters back in on her scaffolding heels with a bottle of Chardonnay, my least favourite wine in the whole world, but it'll just have to do. Then she pours a thimbleful for me and a full to the brim glass for herself.

'Wine with a cork?' mutters Maggie. 'What is this, Christmas Day?'

'Thanks,' I say, taking it from Joan. 'Now will you sit down please?'

'Would if I could but I can't. I'm going out tonight and this suit creases if I sit in it. Besides, I look thinner if I stand and then the Spanx don't cut off circulation.'

Right then. I take a huge gulp and launch into my semi-prepared speech. 'OK, I've something to say to you all, so I need you to listen. As I'm sure you know, seeing as how the dogs on the street seem to, this hasn't been an easy week for me.'

'I *see*,' says Maggie, slooooooowly. Scarily slowly, as she picks up the paper with my name plastered all over it and thrusts it at me. 'Would this perchance have anything to do with the reason why her majesty is gracing us with her presence today?'

I'm in mid-patter though, and determined not to let her pointed jibes get to me.

'I slipped up at work and lost my job—'

'You call what you did a "slip-up"?' sneers Sharon, sucking on her fag so deeply it's like she's inhaling all the way down to her feet. 'Should have taken the bloody car and run, you gobshite. A Merc like that would go for eighty grand on the black market, easy.'

'Hmm,' says Maggie dryly. 'Now if only there was some mechanism in your head that controlled the shite that comes out of your mouth.'

It's as if they know exactly why I'm here and are toying with me now, like starving rottweilers teasing a kitten just before going in for the kill. So I'll just give them the last sentence first. Easier and far, far quicker. 'I've lost my home and until I get another job and get back on my feet again, I'm coming to stay here. Believe me, I don't like it any more than you do, but it's happening, so suck it up.'

Stony silence.

Then, all of the sudden the tension that was hovering over the room earlier breaks like a storm and now everyone's jabbering viciously over each other.

'Sure what's that to do with us?' says Maggie. 'Go and stay with one of your celebrity friends. How do you spell celebrity if your name is Jessie Woods? Oh I know, L. O. S. E. R. Or you could stay with your boyfriend. Oh wait a minute, I forgot, you don't have one. At least, not any more you don't. Oops. Silly me.'

Bloody ouch. That comment cuts to the quick, like Maggie's comments have been cutting me most of my whole life. Meanwhile Sharon sniggers so hard at this that cider actually comes down her nose.

'Nice one,' she smirks over at Maggie, grabbing a Smiley Burger paper napkin and wiping her face with it.

'Thank you, gag copyrighted to Maggie Woods.'

Christ alive, there's so much about the pair of them I'd completely blanked out. That Maggie has by far the tougher, stronger personality for starters and where she leads, Sharon, who's that bit weaker, will invariably follow. But the trick with them is never, ever to react, so I just gulp back yet more revolting vino and eyeball them, waiting to see who'll blink first.

'Well, I'm terribly sorry to put a damper on this,' says Joan, sounding panicky, 'but it's out of the question. We have . . . emm . . . visitors coming to stay . . . emm . . . from Canada. For ehhh . . . three months.'

'Fine, then we'll just all be a bit crowded, won't we?' I say firmly. Joan always was a crap liar.

'You can't stay here! This is *our* house, not yours!' snarls Sharon.

'Technically, no it's not. It's half mine. Dad left it to Joan and me equally and my name is on the title deeds.'

'Excuse me, your majesty, but has it occurred to you that we don't actually get on? I mean, you're sitting there now, drinking our wine and looking down your nose at us like we're cave dwellers.'

'No I'm not! Besides you're looking at me like you want to have me . . . diagnosed.'

'She can't stay here and that's all there is to it. Besides, it's not a runner because there's no room for her,' says Sharon triumphantly to the other two and completely ignoring me. Like the Chardonnay has suddenly made me invisible.

'This house only has three bedrooms and I'm fucked if any of us are going to share with her.'

'So? I'll sleep on the sofa. Not a problem.' Funny, the more they protest, the more I'm digging my heels in, mainly because I know this is the surest way to annoy them even more.

'I don't see why you can't just check into a hotel until you get back on your feet again,' says Joan, nearly spitting out the words. 'Far easier and far less stressful all round.'

'Do I have to spell it out to you? Gimme a B, gimme an R, gimme an O, K, E.'

'Hang on one minute,' says Maggie, leaning forward in her armchair like a sumo queen squaring up for a fight. 'I hate to be the fingernail in the salad here, but we all pay the mortgage on this house, as we've done ever since the happy day when you first fecked off. Even Ma and she's only working part-time. All the bills are split equally between us and we pay for our own food, booze and fags.'

'So?'

'So, if you're out of a job, how are you going to pay your way here? Because if you think we're supporting you, you can feck right off.'

Shit. I never thought of that.

There's another silence while I gulp back the disgusting Chardonnay and rack my brains to come up with something.

Eventually Sharon speaks, 'Here's a thought.' We all turn to look at her and by now even my bum is starting to sweat. 'If Jessie can't contribute to bills and stuff, then . . . well, maybe she could earn her keep by doing all the housework, couldn't she? Just imagine, we could come in from work every day to all the laundry done . . .'

'And all the groceries bought . . .' says Maggie slowly, with an evil glint lighting up the stony grey eyes.

'And a home-cooked dinner served up to us . . .'

'That she has to wash up after, not us . . .'

'And all the ironing done. I bleedin' hate ironing . . .'

'And the garden looking immaculate . . .'

'Be like having an au pair, except without the hassle of kids . . .'

'And one that we'd never have to pay . . .'

'Right then, Cinderella Rockefeller,' says Maggie, with murder in her eyes and spinach in her teeth. 'If this is what you really want, then move in, soon as you like. Because you have yourself a deal.'

I get the hell out of there as soon as I can. And as I slam the hall door behind me, I'd swear I can hear the sound of cackling.

Chapter Seven

Sunday
Packing is a nightmare. I pick up something to fling into a suitcase, then remember exactly where I was when I bought it, time, date and place, the works, then dissolve into floods of tears, then try ringing Sam again, then round off by leaving a tonne of voicemails for him. What the hell, if you're going to boil the bunny, you might as well turn the heat right the whole way up. If I'm turning into Glenn Close with the bubble perm, might as well go the whole hog. And all of my desperate, pleading messages are ignored. Of course they are; at this stage, what the feck else did I expect?

So far, all I've managed to pack is three pairs of knickers and an old deodorant. I am officially a basket case.

Sunday night
Sleepless. Wondering how much longer before I'm turfed out of this house and am forced to move back into Whitehall, a.k.a. the Sandhurst of emotional emptiness. A week possibly, maybe even less? Maybe that couple from yesterday loved it and want to move in here in a few days? And find me still wandering around here, like the mad wife

in the attic from *Jane Eyre*. Then a fresh worry: suppose the estate agents sue me for not clearing out of here fast enough?

Suddenly I get a nightmarish flash of myself standing in the dock, in handcuffs and a neon orange jumpsuit, pleading for clemency, like in one of those witness for the prosecution-type courtroom thrillers. Right. Gotta pack. Gotta clear out of here. Got. No. Choice. In a blind panic, I hop out of bed, switch on the lights and start flinging stuff that's strewn on the dressing table into an abandoned suitcase on the floor. But then I come to a cherished old black and white photo of Mum and Dad taken on their wedding day and start bawling all over again. Times like this I'm almost glad neither of them is around to see what a sad disappointment I've become to them.

No, on second thoughts, packing is a bad idea. Sleeping for twelve hours = miles better.

Monday morning

After five goes, Eva eventually answers her phone to me. Yes, she did see Sam at the weekend, she reluctantly admits, but before I get a chance to launch into further in-depth questioning, on cue, one of her babies starts squealing in her ear so she just does that thing you can only get away with if you're a mum, and immediately hangs up without even saying goodbye.

Mind you, maybe she was only saying that to get me off the phone. Maybe that was a tape she had on standby to play in the background just in case I rang. Jaysus. That's another thing about being dumped and frozen out. Makes you incredibly paranoid.

Monday evening

The estate agent rings. The guy with the barely broken voice. 'Bad news,' he says. 'You only have until Thursday to clear out.'

Three bleeding days?! 'Can't be done,' I tell him. 'I've been living here for two years, you can't seriously expect me to pack up two years of my whole life in three lousy days?'

'We feel it's very generous of us even giving you until Thursday,' he says, suddenly managing to sound all manly and assertive. 'However, if you fail to meet this deadline . . .'

I don't hang around to hear the end of the sentence.

Not in the form for threats right now.

Monday night

What's killing me now is that there's no one, absolutely no one to help me with the Herculean labour of trying to pack my entire life up in three miserable, measly days. Not a sinner. Sam? Yeah, right. Eva and Nathaniel? Don't make me laugh. Emma would, I know. In fact she'd be around here right now organising all my stuff into neatly labelled cardboard boxes and making pots of tea for me, sainted angel that she is. But she's away until at least the end of the month, so that's out. There's not a day goes by that I don't hear from her though; always leaving cheery, positive messages and texts telling me that everything will work itself out and that I'll be fine. Utter shite, of course, but I do appreciate the thought.

Still, it's devastating to think that with only one exception, the very core of people who not two weeks ago I'd have counted on as my nearest and dearest, not only won't lift a finger to help me, but won't even return my calls.

Unbelievable. Like so much in my life lately, you couldn't make it up. Spend the rest of the evening wondering why they ever bothered hanging out with me in the first place. Can't figure it. The one thing Sam, Nathaniel and Eva all have in common is money; vast, bottomless pits stuffed to the overflowing brim with it. And OK, so I kind of inveigled my way into their exclusive 'members-only', club by overstretching myself to keep up with them all, losing all sense of reason in the process. That much, even in this highly distressed state, I'm fully able to grasp and accept. But here's the real killer; I think the main attraction I held for all of them, and it stabs me to include Sam in this, is that I was 'yer one off the telly'.

Fame opened doors for me, like Alice in Wonderland finding the low door in the wall that led to a magical world, except mine was full of five-star hotels, business-class flights, fabulous Michelin-starred restaurants; *la dolce vita*. Everything I'd ever wanted and never had, suddenly offered to me on a plate. But the very second the rug was pulled out from under me, that was it. As if I'd stumbled into the VIP room by mistake and it was only a matter of time before they showed me the door. I've been chasing a pot of gold that turned out to be all glitter and no substance and now have nothing to show for it apart from debts I'll probably be paying off for the rest of my natural life.

Tuesday morning
Eventually dozed off with Sky News on in the background, then couldn't believe it when I came to and it was 10.30 a.m. Ten bleeding thirty in the morning means my allocated clearing out time has now been whittled down to less than two days, so in a rare burst of energy I'm out

of bed, down to the kitchen to make some heavy duty coffee, then back upstairs to start operation Attacking the Packing.

Yes, admittedly, I've left it a bit late in the day, I think, trying my best to be positive, but it's quite do-able. I am after all, the girl who once had to do military boot camp à la Private Benjamin for the TV show and still survived to tell the tale. So if I can handle eighteen-hour days of intensive exercise in three degrees below freezing on an empty stomach, then a bit of light packing shouldn't pose any problems, now should it?

The other thing in my favour is that I rented this house fully furnished, right down to all the kitchen appliances, the works. So all I really have to worry about packing is . . . well, you know, *stuff*. Clothes, shoes, books, DVDs, CDs, all that sort of thing.

A doddle really, when you think about it.

Twenty minutes later

Ohgodohgodohgodohgodohgod! Found a book which Sam gave me two birthdays ago. A first edition of Margaret Mitchell's *Gone with the Wind*, my Desert Island favourite book of all time, ever. Inscribed with the words, 'To Woodsie. I know we'll always be together. Sx' Sam always signs his name like that. Like he doesn't actually have enough time to write all three letters of his name. Collapsed into yet more tears and this time, really thought that my heart would break.

Midday

OK, at this stage I've accepted that there's just no way to get through this without getting distraught, so now the plan is to pack and howl simultaneously, with a box of Kleenex beside me at all times. Believe me, easier said than done.

I'm flinging make-up and face creams from my dressing table into a wheelie bag and doing quick mental calculations, working out that the La Prairie moisturiser and night cream alone would have set me back the guts of €400. Not including the Crème de la Mer eye cream which I spent no less than €165 on, used once, then broke out in spots.

Think I might have to have a lie down. Except there isn't time to indulge in lambasting myself over the huge sums of cash I frittered away, is there? I'll have nothing else to do but whinge about that when I'm stuck on a sofa in Whitehall, worrying about whether Maggie and Sharon will come down in the night and stab me in my sleep.

Right then. I head for my wardrobe and realise with horror that I have no fewer than twenty pairs of jeans... twenty! What in the name of Donatella Versace was I thinking? And I wouldn't mind, but most of them look identical. Into my suitcases they go and when I run out of luggage space, I start flinging them and just about everything else into black plastic bin liners. Then I move on to all my evening dresses. Beautiful, so beautiful that all I want to do is prostrate myself on the ground before them and gape in awe at their beauteous beauty.

A thought; wonder if there's some kind of second-hand swap shop where people could buy all this gear, that might generate a few quid for me? Or maybe I could flog it anonymously on eBay? Then, a miracle, I manage to find three tops, two skirts and a brand new winter coat, still with the tags on them. Money in the bank, I reckon. Because the shops will have to take them back, won't they? So I'll just get the cash back instead. Brilliant! I grab the phone which is lying on my bed and call the customer service department in Brown Thomas. No, the assistant says very politely, sorry but, no cash refunds are ever given, just store credit instead. Which leaves me with almost €980 worth of store credit and not enough money to take a taxi to Whitehall with all my stuff.

Another panic attack. Hadn't thought of that. I haven't a bean to my name; how exactly am I supposed to deal with the sheer logistics of hauling a mountain of suitcases and bin liners like a bag lady all the way to the Hammer House of Horror? Panic, panic, panic.

Just then my mobile rings and I do a leap over the bed worthy of the Grand Slam rugby team to grab it, in case it's Sam. But, of course, it's not. Instead it's, of all people, Joan. Wondering when exactly they can expect me? And did I need to get a spare key cut? She's so helpful and nice in fact that I keep having to repeat her name just to check that this is in fact the same Joan I think it is. I tell her that I've only got until Thursday to clear out and miracle of miracles, she actually offers to come over in her car to help me shift my stuff.

Well, well, well, I think, hanging up and catching sight of the photo of Mum and Dad on my dressing table. Whaddya know? Maybe they made this minor miracle happen from beyond the grave. I continue packing with fresh vigour, in complete wonderment at just how spectacularly wrong I can be about people.

Half three

Joan arrives bit late but then, who am I to complain about the one decent human being who has actually offered to help me in my hour of need? She breezes in, groomed like a storm trooper in a bright, floral patterned dress with every single accessory matching, shoes, bag, the works. But then, why am I surprised? This is Joan. Everything always matches.

Anyway, the minute she gets here, she clicketty-clacks in on her scaffolding heels, surveying the place like a Japanese tourist in the Sistine Chapel and asking if she can have a good nose around. I say yes, of course, then offer her a coffee. She follows me into the kitchen and there's a silence as we both look at each other, but neither of us has anything to say. The funny thing is, that now she's here and it's just the two of us on our own, there's so much I want to tell her. Because maybe, after all these years, I've completely misjudged her and now I'm at the lowest ebb of my life, she's turned into some kind of guardian angel that'll get me through this horrible, horrific time.

Be ironic if, after all these years of me being busy despising her that now, at the ripe old age of twenty-nine, I did actually manage to forge some kind of working functional bond with her. Growing up, I had all the normal grievances you'd expect a kid to hold against any kind of surrogate guardian; Joan constantly taking Maggie and Sharon's side in all rows against me, with the added complication of me resenting her for trying to take the place of a mother that she couldn't possibly come near.

But if Maggie and Sharon were openly hostile to me, Joan was more . . . glacial. Frosty. I remember one time, when I was about eleven, she lost me in a huge department store and while I was terrified the whole time that I'd end up kidnapped by some pervert, the ordeal barely knocked a feather out of her. In fact, to this day I can distinctly remember the security guard finding me white-faced and frightened, wandering around the cosmetics hall, then handing me back to Joan. Poor man honestly looked as if he was weighing up whether or not to call in social services. Well, what was he supposed to think? My guardian was neither bothered that I was gone nor particularly relieved to have me back. She never as much as broke a sweat. But there you go. Some women just aren't cut out for motherhood. And in a million years, I'd never have gone whining and complaining to Dad; he'd quite enough stress on his plate as it was and the last thing I ever wanted to do was add to that.

Rebelling as a teenager with Joan around was a tall order too, mainly because if you plonked yourself down on the sofa beside her, aged fourteen and smoked one Marlboro Light after another, she wouldn't bat an eyelid. Likewise, if you staggered around the house pissed out of your head, her only concern would be whether you'd been at her stash of Chardonnay. Or if you decided you wanted to live off batter burgers and chips day in, day out; again, in Joan-land, not a problem.

With poor Dad out slaving away in the pub where he worked every hour God sent, she was the only authority figure in my life for most of the time. So therefore my teenage rebellion usually involved eating healthily and trying to actually get the odd vitamin into me. While other kids in my class envied that I could get away with never doing homework and watching telly all evening eating McDonald's if I felt like it, I'd be in the kitchen washing heads of lettuce and juicing carrots.

And here she is now after all these years sitting on a bar stool in my kitchen; OK, maybe not exactly full of friendly chat and warmth – Joan doesn't do warmth – but she's an ally and, feck it, she's here. More than some people.

I make her a coffee using the fancy cappuccino maker for probably the last time (like so much else, it came with the house) and ask her whether she'd like the grand tour. It's the first time she looks animated since she got here, so off we trot, me still in my pyjamas and dressing gown, her all eager to see the place, inquisitiveness on heels, scanning the place so thoroughly, you'd nearly think she was about to put an offer in on it. In fact, it strikes me that her real reason for coming over was to see where I live, but am I complaining? Hell, no.

So we start with the huge hallway and suddenly I get that sensation of seeing the house through someone else's eyes. In all my time living here, I don't think I ever really appreciated how beautiful it really is till now, just when I'm being flung out. Can't believe I used to give out about all the pink marble floors; looking at them now, they're just so elegant and classy. And the doric columns gracefully adorning each entrance off the main hall – breathtaking. Dear God, I actually deserve to be thrown out for not giving this fabulous mansion all the love and care it needed.

Joan pulls me out of my reverie. 'And were there ever any celebrities here?'

I remind myself that she's come all this way to help me; the woman is doing me a massive favour, so in return, the least I can do is tell her what she wants to hear. Yes, I answer. Loads of them. An actress who's a household name once snogged a well-known and very married libel lawyer on the exact spot you're standing on now. And a boy band member snorted a line of coke off the hall table, then was sick into the ivy growing on the steps outside. Then there was the time I went upstairs while a party was in full swing to find a well-known model *in flagrante* with a property developer friend of Sam's, whose wife was at home nursing their four-week-old baby boy.

It's a good thing these walls can't talk, because the last days of Sodom and Gomorrah would have nothing on some of the antics that went on here. The house would be packed to the gills with 'celeb friends' and 'well-wishers' and I'd be right in the middle of them, pouring the entire alcoholic content of my house down people's throats. I don't know who exactly I thought I was, the Great Gatsby? Living not just in any house; oh no, only the Elton John of houses would do me. *And where are all those so-called friends now?* I find myself wondering. Feck knows, but I can tell you this much: not a single one of them has as much as picked up the phone to even see how I am. Not one.

Anyway, Joan drinks it all in, gimlet-eyed, then goes back to wandering around, checking out the décor. 'Well, I suppose a place like this is all very well and good if it's the kind of thing you're into,' she says coldly, reaching into her handbag and fishing out a box of Dunhill. 'But if you ask me, it's all just a bit . . . sterile. Needs colour. And warmth. Not to mention wallpaper. The lovely polka-dot one I have in my hallway now would work very well here. Festoon blinds would be gorgeous too, give the place a bit of character. And I hope you don't mind my saying, Jessica, but what in the name of God is that awful smell?'

I explain about the downstairs loo being, let's just say, out of action, like, forever.

'And why did you not just ring Dyno-Rod?'

'Story of my life: no money.'

'Hmm,' she sniffs, disapprovingly and for some reason I

get the feeling that the story of my blocked, knackered loo is the one she'll be retelling later on. 'OK if I light up a fag to disguise the smell?'

I lead her through the dining room ('A table that seats fourteen, Jessica? And where do you all sit when there's something you want to watch on telly?') and then on out to the massive conservatory. She wanders around, freely tipping cigarette ash everywhere, passing disparaging comments about how expensive every single thing must have been, all the while comparing and contrasting with the soft furnishings in her own house.

Anyway, I hasten to remind myself, the thing to remember is that she means well. She's the one person who volunteered to give me a dig out and if it's the last thing I do, I'm determined to build bridges with her. If nothing else, on the principle of divide and conquer; if I have Joan on my side, it should make life with Laurel and Hardy that bit more bearable. Shouldn't it?

She plonks herself down on a wicker two-seater, wincing a bit at how uncomfortable it is, then asks me the one question calculated to reduce me to a blubbering wreck inside of four seconds. 'So, what none of us can understand is . . . has that Sam Hughes really just broken up with you and disappeared off the face of the earth? Where, I'd like to know, is he in all of this?'

'Dunno,' I say weakly, slumping down beside her. Desperate to talk and yet knowing that it'll only bring on yet another tsunami of tears.

My latest theory is actually way too painful for me to articulate out loud, but for the record, it's this: you see, while Sam juggles so many balls in the air when it comes to his career, in his private life, he's a pure minimalist. From

6 a.m. when he starts his day, he's like a puppet master, buying this, selling that, hiring this person, letting that one go, taking this meeting, having a high-powered business lunch with some top executive then off again in a whirlwind of activity and money making and success and all the trappings. But when it comes to his private life, he doesn't just crave, he *demands* peace, tranquillity and absolutely no hassles of any kind whatsoever. Ergo, the very second I became a problem, I was unceremoniously dumped so fast that my head is still reeling from it.

And the reason I landed on this particular theory? Because this is history repeating itself. It's all happened before. Years ago, when I was still pointing to warm pressure areas on maps in the TV weather room and Sam was dating a high-profile politician who was never out of the papers. Anyway, big scandal at the time, but basically she lost her shirt on stocks that crashed, was forced to declare insolvency and ended up having to resign from her party on account of some mad rule that bars anyone bankrupt from sitting in government. Huge deal, headline news, the papers even called it 'Stock-gate'. But I distinctly remember reading in the gossip columns not long afterwards that she and Sam had split up. Coincidence? I think not.

I say none of this to Joan, of course. In time, I'd like to think she would become a confidante, but right now, if I have to articulate these thoughts aloud, there's a good chance I'll have a full-blown breakdown. So I go for a gag instead, 'Oh, you know Sam, out helicopter shopping, probably.'

'Well, no Jessica, I don't know him, do I? Only through what I read in the papers. We were never introduced. Or even invited here before you fell on hard times. Remember?'

There's a hint of ice in her voice now, which wasn't there before.

Shit. I was kind of hoping that wouldn't come up. Right then. Nothing to do but deal with this head on. Build bridges, keep allies and at all costs, get her onside. 'Joan, I know I haven't exactly been a model stepdaughter in the past, but please know how much I appreciate you taking me in.'

'Well I can't say we're exactly looking forward to it . . .'

'I know, I know, we fight like Italians . . .'

'Oh please don't say that. It makes us sound so . . . garlicky.'

'Come on, I know we're family and everything, but let's face it, Dad's anniversary mass once a year on Christmas Eve is taxing.'

She just pulls on her cigarette and doesn't answer, but I know she agrees with me.

'But, the thing is, Joan, I want you to know that I will try. To make an effort, I mean. If it's one thing the last few awful weeks have taught me, it's that I've been completely wrong about everyone who was closest to me up until now and I'm really hoping that . . .' The actual end of that sentence is '. . . that I've been wrong about you, Sharon and Maggie and that somehow we'll all miraculously morph into the Waltons over the next few weeks, right before I get offered a fabulous TV gig that puts me back on top of my game again. And gets me out of Whitehall and back to a life of luxury, with luck. And then Sam will realise what a moronic gobshite he's been in letting me go and will come begging for me to take him back, with an engagement ring tucked under his armpit to woo me with.' Not too much to ask, now is it? But of course I can't manage to get a word of this out, so I settle for just sobbing my heart out instead. A real *cri de coeur* this time.

'Oh Jessica, for God's sake stop that right now, you're getting carried away,' snaps Joan, coughing on her fag now, but then this is a woman who hates all overt displays of emotion. Even at Dad's funeral, the only way you'd have known she was having any kind of emotional experience was by the number of fags she chain smoked. 'Do you know, driving here I saw a car with a bumper sticker that said "All men are bastards. Best you can hope for is to find a nice bastard." Quite apt for you at the moment, I'd say.'

Through choked-up tears, I thank her for her pearls of wisdom courtesy of some bumper sticker, but as anyone on the verge of a breakdown will tell you, once the crying really starts, there's just no stopping it. Next thing, Joan starts fishing around the bottom of her handbag, I'm presuming for a tissue, but no. She whips out a blister of tablets, pops out two, one for me and one for her and tells me to knock it back, that it'll shut up my whinging. And that I can keep the rest of the pack.

'Zanax,' she explains. 'Very mild sedative.'

'Ah Joan, no,' I sniffle, handing them right back to her. 'The state I'm in, I doubt a sedative would know what to make of my central nervous system.'

'Oh for God's sake, Jessica, these are no stronger than a glass of vino. That's all. Gets you through the day. It mightn't take away the pain but it'll make you not give a shite about it any more.'

The funny thing is, she's right. Because half an hour later, I'm loading all my boxes and bags into the boot of Joan's little Toyota Yaris and for the first time in ages, I'm actually feeling . . . all right. OK, so I mightn't exactly be dancing on the rooftops singing 'Oh What a Beautiful Morning' but you get the picture. I've finally stopped whinging and from where I'm coming from, that's a pretty big deal.

Joan's defrosted a lot too; she even says that if I drop her off at the hairdressers where she works part-time as a receptionist, that I can have her car for the rest of the evening to keep moving the rest of my stuff into the house. 'And don't worry about where to put everything,' she calls back to me as I drop her off at Curl Up and Die (the salon's actual name; couldn't make it up, could you?). 'Plenty of room in the garage!' Friendly as you like. Amazing.

Half eight that night
Right then. By now, the tiny garage in our little corpo house looks like Ellis Island at high tide, with the amount of suitcases and bin liners belonging to me. I've done three runs back and forth to my house and am almost finished moving. Best of all though, the Zanax haven't even begun to wear off and I feel wonderful. Blissed out and *totally* relaxed. So chilled, in fact, that I'm seriously considering joining Maggie on the couch inside, where she's fast asleep and snoring, sedated after two Chinese takeaways and four tins of Bulmers. Sharon is working late tonight at Smiley Burger, so I know that for once, there might actually be room for me on the sofa too.

Next thing, the garage door trundles open and in thunders Joan demanding to know what the hell all my things are doing here and archly ordering me to get them out of her sight *right now*. You should see the vicious state of her; honest to God, it's like she should be wearing a pointy Dracula cape with a dry ice machine behind her billowing smoke.

'But . . . Joan . . .' I stammer, momentarily taken aback at the severity of her mood swing. 'You said this was OK, remember? You said I could store everything in the garage . . .'

'Did I say *garage*?' she snaps icily. 'Silly me, I meant to say *garbage*. Now clear that crap out of here to make room for my car. If you think I'm leaving it parked out on the road at night with Psycho Brady out on the loose, then you've another thing coming, missy.'

Bugger it anyway. I completely forgot that she could be like this. Mercurial. Lovely to you one minute, then would clip the side of your face off the next. Her moods are like the moon; they come in phases and are ever bloody changing. Right now though, I don't particularly care. Because I'm on Zanax.

Chapter Eight

Having lived here in humanity's petri dish of hatred for almost three long weeks now, I feel somewhat qualified to set the following down in stone: *The Heaven of my old life versus the Hell I'm sentenced to live in now.*

It's true what they say, you really haven't a clue what you've got till it's gone. For starters, in my old life, I never slept. Hardly at all. Dunno how I managed it, but I just seemed to whiz through the day, buzzing on the sheer adrenaline high of having a job I adored, a social life that wouldn't quit and a boyfriend that even Angelina Jolie might gratefully consider trading up to. Now, I sleep all the time. Ten, sometimes eleven, hours at a stretch. And when I actually am up and about, I'm staggering around the place in a living coma, full of tears that I won't let fall. Then there's the small matter of where I'm sleeping. In my old life, I'd crash out in a four-poster bed, on two-hundred-thread Egyptian cotton sheets, wearing sexy nighties straight out of the La Perla catalogue, with my sex god of a boyfriend by my side, more often than not. Now I sleep under a duvet on a three-seater sofa with bum imprints embedded deep into it from my stepsisters. And as for nightwear, these days, I just sleep in the comfiest fleecy pair of pyjamas I can find. Sleep in them, eat in them, go round the house in them, do all my chores in them, you name it. One outfit only. No need for anything else. No one sees me and no one cares. Least of all me.

In my old life, back in those long-forgotten days when I used to have energy, I'd bounce out of bed, zip into the TV studio and then spend most of my day having high-powered pre-production meetings about that week's episode of *Jessie Would*, followed by a fabulous, expensive lunch in whatever restaurant happened to be hot at the moment. And lunch, by the way, would usually involve myself and Eva spending a minimum of two hours lingering over three courses, discussing men, clothes and beauty treatments, in that order. Taking the world apart, then putting it all back to rights again. Now, I think, *Lunch? Are you kidding me?* Between the marathon sleeps and the long To Do house-work lists I get flung at me every day, I'm doing well if I can manage to grab a Pot Noodle and a Jaffa Cake in between unclogging plugholes or, I'm not making this up, hand washing the heavy-duty, double-gusseted tights that Maggie wears to work. You should have seen the state of them, honest to God, I picked them up off the floor and wondered where the hell she even goes to buy tights in that size. Harland and Wolff? That, by the way, was item number one on Jessie's To Do list, which I think the bad bitch wrote purely on purpose to humiliate me. Yeah right, Maggie. Like I could possibly be humiliated any more?

Messing aside though, the housework list that she and Sharon handed me on my first morning here led to one of out bloodiest rows to date, and God knows that's really saying something. And, yes, I'm fully aware that I'm a person who comes with no boundaries, but what they expected me to do really was pushing things to the giddy limit. It would have taken three highly trained maids working round the clock to get through what they expected me to do in a single day. Gak jobs too, that you'd blush to ask a paid professional to get stuck into. Like clearing out all the drains on the outside of the house. Yes, *all* of them. Including one that would have involved me climbing up a ladder to the outside of the bathroom window, then trying to simultaneously pour bleach down a gulley with one hand, while clinging on for dear life with the other.

'Are you kidding me with this?' I confronted the pair of them as soon as I read the list. Or should I say, page one of the list, given that it ran to well over seven pages long. Double sided. 'Trained circus performers would demand danger money for doing that.'

'Think of it like just doing a dare on your TV show, except this time there's no cameras pointed at you,' Maggie coolly puffed back at me, in a cloud of cigarette smoke. 'Remember when you used to have a TV show? It was back around the same time you used to have a boyfriend. Oops, sorry, how tactless of me.'

'Gee, thanks so much for that, Maggie. One of your kinder and more sensitive comments, may I add,' I muttered at her as I stomped back to the kitchen, mop and bucket in hand.

The only household job I'm exempted from is cooking, which goes back to my first night here, when I tried to make a chilli con carne that ended up tasting like a cross between paint stripper and dog diarrhoea. Put it this way: with me at the cooker, Nigella Lawson's job is safe. Anyway, no one really cared, given that this is the house where evening meals invariably come courtesy of Domino's Pizza or else the local Chinese takeaway down the road. (We're far and away their best customers and even have the loyalty mugs to prove it.)

But to make up for that, they expected me to spring clean the garden shed, which still has stuff belonging to Dad inside and which I don't actually think any of them have even set foot inside since he died. Well I took one look inside the cobweb-ridden door of it and could go no further. Because there, flung in a corner on top of a broken wheelbarrow was his favourite armchair, all saggy and torn, with bits of yellow foam and stuffing hanging off it. And beside that was his bookcase; I can still vividly remember him reaching down for my favourite book of fairy stories and reading them aloud to me when I was little. And over in a far corner was yet another container load of stuff belonging to him. Mum dying so young left Dad with a lifelong fear of losing things, with the result that he became a terrible hoarder. And here it all still was; except covered in dust and cobwebs with rain leaking down on top of everything that he'd treasured.

Funny, they say that grief takes two full years to heal but it's not true. Because it never really does heal, just gets duller and more bearable, that's all. Bad enough that every corner I turn in this house holds a ghost of his memory, but believe me, all the Zanax in the world couldn't block out the searing pain of seeing all of his old things discarded into a manky, filthy shed and forgotten about. So I stand my ground and say no: the only job I'm prepared to do here is to bring all his things back inside the house again and restore them back to their rightful place. And that's it. End of story.

So now, most of the time I settle for doing the bare minimum, which by the way isn't laziness on my part; that still amounts to several hours' worth of washing, scrubbing and polishing, then having a fight with them about it when they all come in from work and make me justify what I've been up to all day.

Sharon works shifts in Smiley Burger, so you never know when she'll be around, whereas Joan seems to swan to and from her job at the salon whenever it suits her and unlike either of her daughters, actually has a social life and occasionally goes out the odd evening. Usually only as far as the Swiss Cottage pub down the road, but at least she's out of the house.

'If anyone rings looking for me, you're not to say I'm in a bar, you're to say I'm out at a wine tasting,' is her invariable warning to me as she clatters out the door, looking like a perfume ad from the 1970s. Blue eye shadow, flicked hair, the works.

Maggie, on the other hand, is always home first. She finishes work at 5 p.m. and has her bum on the sofa by 5.30. Could set your watch by her. So generally, the first big humdinger row of the day will tend to be with her. Anyway, one particular howler went something along these lines:

Maggie (plonking onto her favourite armchair and cracking open her first tin of Bulmers of the night): 'Why is my ironing only half done? What the feck have you been doing with yourself all day?'

Me (in the middle of hoovering): 'Why Maggie, how lovely to see you too. How kind of you to inquire so politely about my day. I've been out riding unicorns in Never Never Land. Can't you guess?'

Maggie (lighting a cigarette and sprawling herself out on said armchair, like an uncoordinated hippopotamus):

'Listen, you. I work for the Inland Revenue. I'm in the suspicion business. And right now, I suspect that you spend the whole day sitting on your bony arse watching my DVD box set of *Dancing on Ice*.'

Me (knowing I shouldn't rise to the bait, but not able to help myself): 'As a matter of fact, I've actually spent most of today changing your bed sheets, washing your industrial strength tights, then picking up the empty tins and pizza boxes that you left strewn all over the floor last night. Now, I'm sure that you meant that last remark to be brimming over with gratitude and deep appreciation, so I'll just assume that some of it got lost in translation.'

You'd want to see the pair of us squaring up to each other. Honest to God, we're like a full-length episode of *Jerry Springer* just waiting to be Sky-Plused. But then, as I constantly remind myself to prevent me from losing my temper and flinging a scalding hot iron into her face, my stepsister has a heart condition. She doesn't have one. I'd also like to add that, in my defence, I only did her disgusting gusset washing job once and then only because I was out of my head on the Zanax. But never again. Because, come on, even desperados like me have to draw the line somewhere.

Anyway, back in my old life, I would change outfits a minimum of three times a day. Funky designer jeans for work, something dressier for lunch and then I'd pull out all the stops for a night out with Sam. Which usually ended up being approximately six nights out of seven. Now I find it's far easier to stay in my pyjamas all day. And if it gets chilly, I just throw a sweatshirt over them. Practicality and comfort all in one. In fact, if they made giant baby-gros for adults, then I'd just stay in one of those all day. Yes, the garage is stuffed full with bin liners and boxes full of clothes that I could shoehorn myself into if I wanted, but I frankly couldn't be arsed. *Waay* too much effort involved. Besides, who sees me now anyway? So, in other words, this season the devil's wearing Primark.

In my old life, I was rarely home except to sleep, change, then run out the door again. On and on with the never-ending whirlwind. Now, I'm starting to think there's agoraphobics out there who have better social lives than me. I hate this horrible house, I hate the polka-dot wallpaper, I hate the elephant ornaments on top of the TV, I hate the patterned cream Axminster carpets everywhere, I hate the peach festoon blinds in the revolting kitchen and I reserve special hatred for the people who live in it, but the funny thing is . . . I can't bring myself to leave.

Weird, that this place I despise so much has now become my hideaway and sanctuary. So weird in fact, that I sometimes wonder if I'm suffering from depression. I even run a check list in my head just to be on the safe side. But no, I don't feel like self-harming, and I don't think that life's not worth living any more. I'm just deeply sad, irritable and so, so unaccountably tired all the time. Like having flu but with no symptoms. Anyway, going outside the front door = meeting people = exposure to comments such as 'Didn't you used to be someone?' = more misery, humiliation and heartache. No, total isolation from the outside world is a far, far better idea.

In my old life, my house was so ridiculously, ludicrously vast, that I had whole rooms dedicated just for storing all my shoes/handbags/coats etc. Now I'm reduced to having a sofa to sleep on and, get this, my own shelf in the fridge which Maggie allocated to me, telling me in no uncertain terms that I wasn't allowed to touch anything on anyone else's shelf. Like I'm a flatmate that they're all dying to get rid of. Her exact words, I recall, were, 'Ever wondered what it would feel like to live somewhere where no one wanted you? Well, now you do know!' Dear Jaysus.

Funniest of all though, is that in my old life, even though I made TV for a living, I never watched it. Ever. I'd see *Jessie Would* on tape, of course, but only a few days after a broadcast and always on a big TV monitor in the production office, along with Emma and Liz Walsh. Then the three of us would critically analyse every little detail of the show to flush out any gaps where there might be room for improvement, notebooks on our knees and constantly hitting the freeze frame button. But somehow that only ever counted as work, never entertainment. But now that I'm living in a house where the shagging TV is never off, I've become a complete addict. It fills a void. And frankly anything that stops me obsessing about Sam can only be a good thing.

By now, my days have settled in a kind of pattern, entirely revolving around the TV schedule. It usually starts at about 7.30 a.m., when Maggie comes into the living room and wakes me up by switching on breakfast TV while she eats a brekkie fit for a builder, wolfing it down in seconds. A truly astonishing sight to behold, take it from me. Then, she flings my day's instructions at me, but the minute she's out the door I drift straight back to my second sleep of the morning, thinking, *Great, only another two hours to go until Jeremy Kyle.* By mid-morning, Sharon and Joan will usually have surfaced, depending on how late Sharon's shift was the previous night and how sozzled Joan was when she staggered home from the boozer. Sorry, I mean the 'wine tasting'. Then we move on to the morning repeats of last night's soaps, which to be honest, I'm actually starting to get hooked on. So, after they've both left for work and when the bulk of my chores are done, it's on to all the afternoon shows, magazine programmes aimed at a target audience of grannies, that kind of thing. Grannies or else people on sedatives like me. Not forgetting *Oprah*, which is fast turning into the highlight of my whole day. Then as soon as Maggie gets in, we watch the evening shows like *Xpose* and repeats of *Friends* which at this stage I've seen so often, I'm starting to say the words along with Jennifer Aniston.

What passes a lot of the time too is working out all the mini-civilisations that go on within families. Take Joan for instance. From the minute she stumbles down the stairs each morning, wearing the kind of fluffy dressing gowns that Barbara Cartland used to wear on her book covers, it's a crap shoot trying to predict what her mood will be. You might as well try to predict the Euromillions lottery numbers in next Saturday night's draw. Some days, she's actually great company and will cook a big fry-up breakfast for myself and Sharon, while chatting happily away about whoever is on the cover of this week's *Heat* magazine, required reading in this house. Well, that or else her second favourite topic of conversation: the neighbours on our street and whatever gossip happens to be going on with them.

'I ran into Mrs Hayes from across the road, Jessica,' she said to me over brekkie the other day, when she was in one of her better moods, 'and she was wondering why you still haven't called in to see them all yet? Hannah's just had another baby you know. Apparently herself and the article she married have moved into a house only just a few streets away. And you know that brother of hers, Steve, has been back from the States for a few years now. I don't know where he's living these days or what he's at, but apparently he heard you're back here again and wants to come and see you.'

My heart sank. Last thing I'd be able to do, go out and face people. Particularly ones who I used to be friends with in times gone by, but then drifted away from. Far too many explanations and apologies involved. Sorry, but I can't do it. No energy. *Way* too much to ask.

It's interesting to hear that Steve is back in town though. Suddenly I get a flashback to when Hannah and I were in school together and I was permanently hanging around their house. He was older than us by about three years and when we were about fifteen or so, Hannah always swore he had a crush on me, backed up by the fact he'd go bright purple in the face and his stammer would get far worse if I as much as said hi to the poor eejit. He used to call here to do odd jobs for us too: mowing the lawn and general handy work, that sort of thing. But he stopped coming after a while, not only on account of how horrible Maggie and Sharon were to him, but because Joan rarely, if ever, remembered to pay him.

'Oh, I know what Steve Hayes is doing,' Sharon piped up, between gobbling down mouthfuls of leftover pizza, which she always microwaves the morning after the night before. 'He's playing in a band now. They're called The Amazing Few and I hear they're shite. Bono's job is safe.'

'Don't say shite, say manure,' said Joan.

'Jeez, excuse me, your highness. Manure.'

'How you do know all this about him anyway?'

'He comes into Smiley Burger for the Smiley Fries.'

'How can he be in a band with that awful stammer?'

'The stammer's gone now. Anyway, he's the guitarist. He doesn't have to sing. Oh and by the way, Ma, if he does call here, for fuck's sake don't let him in. We still owe him money.'

Anyway, those are the good days in Joan-land. Other days, it's frost over Whitehall and she'll nearly cut the snot off you for even daring to ask her something as innocuous as whether she enjoyed herself last night. Once I even made the cardinal mistake of asking her if there was a good crowd at the bingo the night before? 'I was at *bridge*, not bingo,' she hissed back at me. Even though I happen to know that not only is she a regular at the bingo, but she's always winning cash prizes too. But bear in mind that underneath the over-polished veneer this is a woman well in touch with her inner shrew. With the result that I constantly feel like I'm treading on eggshells with her. In a banana skin factory. In a hurricane.

Sometimes, on the nights when she's been out, she'll teeter home on her high heels with bags of chips fresh from the chipper for everyone, brimming over with good humour, all chat and gossip about who's making moves on who, who got the most drunk, who got barred down the local at one of her 'wine tasting' soirées. Other times, she'll thunder in, having, I can only guess, drunk enough to knock the pennies off the eyes of a dead Irishman, and clatter her handbag down so loudly on the hall table that the ornamental elephants on top of the TV all rattle. Then she'll pick a row out of thin air with whatever unfortunate happens to be sitting nearest to her on the sofa.

'Look at the bloody useless state of the three of you,' was one particular gem she spat out at us last weekend. 'It's a

Saturday night and not a fella to show between the lot of you.'

Well, it was all I could do to throw her a dead-eyed look. Because my survival mechanism in this house is to never, ever let the taunts get to me. And believe me, there are many... Anyway, her eye caught mine and she back pedalled a bit, realising what she'd just said.

'I'm leaving you out of this, Jessica, on account of you getting so spectacularly dumped only recently and on the principle that it's better to have loved and lost than never to have loved at all.'

'Where did you get that quote from, Ma?' asked Sharon, sucking on a fag. '*OK* magazine?'

'I don't know who said it and I don't care. Celine Dion or someone. But my point is, here's Jessica going around the place like the zombified dead because she can't figure out how to hang on to her fella—'

'Joan,' I interrupted, not sure how much more of this I was able for in, shall we say, my frail emotional state. 'I'd leave it there if I were you. Or else...'

'Or else what?' Maggie sniped across the room at me. 'Or else you'll trash her in your memoirs?'

'I was going to say, "Or else I might start howling over the TV, thus interrupting your enjoyment of this episode of *Little Britain*, which you've only seen about two hundred times before," but what the hell, yours is better.'

Like most bullies, Maggie is always bested when you give back as good as you get. Tell you what though, it sure as hell sharpens your wits just being in the same airspace as her. The only downside is that I'm fast becoming every bit as horrible as her.

'So what I want to know is,' Joan continued on with her

rant, turning to glower at Maggie and Sharon, 'why can't you bloody useless pair get your arses off the sofa for a change and start acting like normal young ones? Why can't one of you come home married or engaged or at least pregnant? Look at Mrs Foley across the road, with seven grandchildren already and only one of her daughters ever got married and even *she's* separated now. But at least hers are out knocking around with fellas at night instead of sitting in staring at the telly night in, night out. Plenty of other mothers would have a seizure if their daughters had boyfriends staying overnight in the house. Me? I'd gladly cook up fried breakfasts for them the next morning if I thought at least one of you was getting a decent shag every now and then. For feck's sake, when I was your age I had buried your father and was already back out dating again . . .' She was working herself up to a crescendo by then as we all stared dully at her, waiting on the grand finale. 'Why in the name of God,' she snapped, 'didn't I have girls who took after me? Or better yet, why didn't I have *sons*? Look at the pair of you; the elder disappointment and the younger disappointment.'

I couldn't help noticing that neither of her daughters reacted to this tirade; their eyes never as much as flickered away from the TV. Which made me think that this must be a regular occurrence in this house. Then the minute Joan was out of the room, Maggie, queen of the one-line put-down, piped up, 'As soon as she dies, I'm burying her in a drawer.'

'As soon as she dies? Are you kidding me?' said Sharon. 'That one will outlive Styrofoam.'

Which neatly brings me to Sharon. Right then. Now while she's every bit as silent and grunty as Maggie, stop the presses, but I did happen to make an interesting discovery about her only last week. One of the many jobs on my To Do list was to give her bedroom a good dust, polish and hoover, so up I went at a convenient gap after *Judge Judy* finished and before *Oprah* started. She now sleeps in what was my old room, so it was beyond weird seeing it as it is now, decorated in Joan's OTT taste, all Laura Ashley flowery patterns and matching bedspreads that nearly make you feel like you're on hallucinogenic drugs. Anyway, I was just about to start dusting the shelves and was trying hard not to gape at a particularly horrible photo of Sharon and Maggie taken when they were about six and seven, where they're dressed identically and look exactly like the two little girls from *The Shining*. But then something else caught my eye: Sharon's entire DVD collection is made up of romantic movies. Every single one of them. *Gone with the Wind*, *Rebecca*, *Sleepless in Seattle*, *When Harry Met Sally* all here. Plus she has a DVD of just about every film that Hugh Grant has ever made, even the really shite ones. Then, when I get to her bedside table, I find it's stuffed full of romance novels. Each one of them pretty well thumbed too, I can't help noticing. Mills & Boon books with saccharine titles like *The Duke and I*, Barbara Taylor Bradford, there's even a few Danielle Steels in there.

I'm not passing any comments, I'm just saying it's surprising, that's all. I wouldn't have had her down as someone with a happy-ever-after addiction. Anyway, as chance would have it, a few days later I had a chance to ask her about it. A proper conversation, that is, as opposed to the monosyllabic grunts that I normally get out of her. She had some kind of bug and she wasn't making it up either, I knew by her face that she was genuinely ill. The giveaway was that Sharon loves nothing more than to talk about the food she's going to eat, while already eating. But this particular day, she physically turned green at the sight of me opening the fridge and producing the leftover pizza from last night, which would be her normal breakfast.

'Do you want me to ring in sick for you?' I offered.

She look at me, surprised at my being nice to her. 'Jeez, would you mind? It's not a word of a lie either. Look at the state of me, I'm sicker than a plane to Lourdes.'

So I rang Smiley Burger for her and over-egged it, as you do on these occasions, making it sound to the sixteen-year-old junior floor manager that she was in stage four of swine flu. 'Well, if she's that unwell, she can have the day off,' he said. 'But no more. Back to work tomorrow, Saturday, no excuses.' So, all delighted, Sharon settled onto the sofa for a twenty-four-hour TV marathon.

Now it so happened that particular Friday was the very day Sam was due to travel to Marbella with Eva and Nathaniel, so I was on double doses of Zanax and moving around the house at quarter speed. I really did try my best to get through my list of jobs, thinking that hard work and manual labour was just what I needed to distract me, but no such luck. Sure, how could it? By then I was clutching at straws thinking, maybe, just maybe, he didn't go on the trip at all. Maybe he figured he'd only miss me too much. Which of course was immediately followed by the tacked-on awful, aching thought, *So if that's the case, why hasn't he just picked up the phone to call me?* OK, I decided, enough with the housework. Need a distraction. Need telly. So I plonked down on the sofa beside Sharon. But, as bad luck would have it, she was watching one of those glossy holiday magazine programmes about Spain, full of sandy beaches and sangria and fabulous tapas bars. Where I should have been headed to with my boyfriend, right there and then. Suddenly, it was just all too much for me and next thing I was howling, really wailing from the bitter depths like I hadn't allowed myself to do in weeks and with nothing to wipe my nose in, only a J Cloth that smelt of Mr Sheen.

Sharon looked over at me, puzzled and confused, not knowing what to do with me, without back-up. If Maggie was here, she'd cut me down with some one-liner and they'd both snigger at my expense and that would be that. But Maggie wasn't there. It was just her and I, alone.

'Ehh . . . Jessie, what's wrong with you? Is this about me asking you to dust my room?' she asked tentatively, clearly uncomfortable with all overt displays of emotion.

'No,' I wailed back at her. 'It's just . . .' But I was too choked to finish the sentence, so I just waved the J Cloth vaguely in the direction of the TV instead.

'Oh!' she said, misinterpreting. ''Cos if you hate travel shows that much, I can easily change the channel for you.'

'It's not the travel show,' I sobbed bitterly. 'It's . . . it's . . .' Then I looked over to where she was sprawled out under my duvet, looking a lot weaker and more defenceless than she normally would. And so in that second, I made a snap decision. What the hell, having someone to confide in and talk to was better than no one, even if she mightn't exactly be the most sympathetic of audiences. 'Sharon, can I ask you something?'

She just looked at me, puzzled.

'Have you ever had your still-beating heart ripped out and dangled in front of you by a man you loved so much that it hurt? Because if you have, then you'll know exactly how I'm feeling right now.'

There was a long pause and I swear I could physically see her weighing up whether or not she could talk to me. Really confide in me, I mean, girl to girl. Then a thought struck me. God, maybe Sharon with her romance addiction did once have a boyfriend, maybe more than one and maybe she too came off worst like I did and just maybe . . . it could be something we could bond over. Maybe. An outside shot I know but stranger things have happened.

'No,' she said, firmly.

Now I could have let this go, but some voice in my head told me not to.

'Well, if you've never had your heart broken, never once in your whole life,' I sobbed, 'then lucky you.'

Then it all came pouring out, about how right then I should have been snuggled up with Sam on a flight to Malaga, how much I miss him every day, how I just don't work without him. Simple as that. Maybe it was just the release of being able to actually talk about him out loud after so long, instead of just having endless conversations about him in my head, but pretty soon the tears started to dry up and the howling abated. I looked over to Sharon, where she was staring back at me, with a funny look on her face.

There was a long, long pause where I was silently willing her to say something. Anything. After all, I'd just spilt my guts out on the table in front of her, surely this was something that might, in theory, bring us a bit closer?

Eventually she spoke. 'Well, if you ask me . . .'

'Yeah?' I said, hopefully.

'That fella Sam Hughes is just a big knobhead. With no knob.'

'Oh right. Well thanks then.'

'And his hair is very tufty. I mean, I know I've only seen him in photos, but he always struck me as having seriously crap hair.'

OK, so it wasn't exactly the Gettysburg address, but nonetheless one small step for mankind and all that. So then I figured, the least I can do for her is ask her if there was anything she needed. Quid pro quo and all that. 'Emm, do you want me to call a doctor?' I offered tentatively.

'No, ta. I just drank a bad pint last night. There's nothing really that wrong with me.'

'Dad's last words,' I said and we both smiled.

But if I thought I'd chipped away at some of her armour and gained an ally here in the Hammer House of Hell for myself, I was sadly mistaken. Because that night as soon as Maggie got home, it was right back to the grunts and monosyllables and horribleness. So that's my relationship with Sharon for you then. A perpetual game of one step forward, two steps back.

God I miss my old life. Back then, I used to hold actual, proper conversations with people. We would discuss art, politics, music, culture, whatever was going on in the world. Well, actually, that might be a bit of an exaggeration, as a lot of what I used to talk about was a load of gossipy shite, but you get my point. I once lived a life where you conversed with other human beings and they conversed back and it was all lovely. Now the only person from those glory days who bothers contacting me is Emma. Even though she's down in Wexford with her family, she still calls regularly, telling me to keep the faith, that everything will be OK. Sending a bright blast of positive energy through my day. Course, that rosy glow only ever lasts for about three seconds or so after I hang up, but you see what I mean. It's cheering to think that at least someone remembers me and is actually prepared to talk to me. Because the golden rule in this house is that you're never, ever in any circumstances allowed to talk while the TV is on, which is pretty much most of the time, and basically if my stepsisters aren't watching TV then they're talking about it. And nothing else. You want to hear some of the conversations.

For instance, last night, myself, Maggie and Sharon were tucked in front of the TV watching an old black and white movie on TCM, *Brief Encounter*. Or rather, they were watching it and I was supposed to be dusting in the background, but then exhaustion got the better of me, so I just collapsed down on the end of the sofa beside them and no one said anything. Wonderful, poignant, romantic tearjerker of a movie and all Maggie could say was, 'Could you imagine how much easier life would have been if they'd just all had mobile phones back then? No pissing around waiting on some bloke in a railway station in the back arse of nowhere, for starters.' Then we watched *Pride and Prejudice,* one of my all-time favourite books and movies and as the credits rolled, Sharon's one and only comment was, 'Jaysus. Imagine living in a world with no gay men.' So then they switched over to a TV documentary called *Three Sisters Make a Baby*, about one sister who surrogates for another, so the third can adopt the baby.

In the mirror above the fireplace, I caught a glimpse of the reflection of the three of us. Three sisters can make a baby together and look at the state of us. We couldn't make a cheese toastie together without the riot police being called in.

Come nine o'clock, we went over to RTE One to get the news headlines and Maggie's comment was, 'Why do they let ugly people read the news? I don't pay a TV licence to watch complete mingers.'

I had to bite my tongue as I looked over at her. God made her in his image, I reminded myself, and I'm sure he doesn't regret it that much.

Then later that evening, at about 10 p.m., Joan breezed in with Bacardi breath and a whole stack of magazines from the hair salon which she filches from time to time on the grounds that here is the only place she gets to read them properly. I knew she was in one of her better humours; it's getting so I can usually guess by how loudly she clatters her handbag down on the hall table.

'Nothing but bloody bad news in the papers,' she said kicking off her shoes and lighting up a fag as she flung herself down onto the spare armchair. 'Recession. Global warming. Plane crashes. The Britney miming scandal. So I brought these home for us to have a laugh at. Look Jessica, I found a wonderful article in *Cosmo* that's right up your alley. It'll give you great hope. And there's some wonderful advice for the newly unemployed too.'

'What's that?' I asked, half relieved not to be talking about TV for bloody once.

She flicked through the index until she found the right page, then read it aloud, 'Losing your job is like being given a gift.'

'Joan, that better make sense soon, because otherwise there's a good chance I might start self-harming,' I said, wondering if she was even aware of the sheer number of calls I'd made to my agent begging and pleading for work. Something, anything. At this stage, I'd gladly welcome a 5 a.m. radio gig broadcasting to a North Sea oil rig. Complete waste of time, of course. Every time I call the office, his secretary says he's 'out at a meeting'. To the point where I was starting to get a mental picture of Roger holding up a placard whenever I rang saying, 'If that's Jessie Woods, tell her I'm NOT IN. And that I've left the country with no immediate plans to return.'

'Let me finish, will you? It says here, "Starting at rock bottom is a precious bequest". So don't knock it, will you? Eh . . . oh yes, here's the bit I wanted you to read. Says here that a crisis is a terrible thing to waste. Then it talks about Simon Cowell.'

'What about Simon Cowell?'

'Bit here about how he was a millionaire in the 1980s, then he lost it all and ended up moving back into his mother's house. And look at him now, for God's sake, richer than the Queen.'

'I don't understand, Joan. What exactly are you saying? That I should go on *X Factor*?'

'If you pair want to talk shite, can you go into the kitchen?' Maggie snarled at us, looking like she was about to have an embolism. 'Some of us are trying to watch telly here.'

'The point I'm trying to make, if I could be allowed to finish my sentence please, is that there are some great pointers here about hauling yourself back up from the depths again. All you have to do is follow a few simple steps. Listen to this: "With a positive mental attitude, you could be back in the game in no time."'

I grabbed the magazine from Joan to see for myself what this wonderful advice for the newly unemployed was, but all I could see was a *Cosmo* quiz where question one says, 'Describe your life in a single word.'

Hmm. Is 'shit-hole' one word? I wonder.

'Not the quiz, you eejit,' said Joan, getting up to go to

the drinks cabinet and pouring herself out another Bacardi chaser. 'Read down to the bottom of the page. The bit where it tells you the first things that you should do in the short term.'

'Joan! What?'

'Well sign on the dole, of course.'

Hours later, long after the others had dragged themselves up to their comfortable beds, I lay on the sofa, still wide awake. Dole. Brilliant. Genius. Never thought of that. My mind raced. I mean, I paid taxes all my working life, surely I must be entitled to get something back from the system? Then I'd have cash. Actual cold, hard cash. Then I could pay some money towards the housekeeping here. Then I wouldn't have to wash industrial-size knickers day in day out any more. Then I could ... My thoughts were interrupted by the light streaming through from the kitchen behind me. Maggie probably, getting one of her late-night snacks. Because sometimes the wait between supper and breakfast just gets too much for her. It wasn't Maggie though, it was Sharon. She came into the TV room and plonked down on the armchair beside me.

'You awake?'

'Uh-huh.' Jeez, all the grunting in this house must be contagious.

'It's just that ... well ... if you were going to sign on the dole then ... well, I can help you.'

'What did you just say?' I sat up, stunned.

'I've signed on loads of times. I can tell you where to go, what to bring with you, which welfare officers are nice and which ones are the bastards. If Ma gives us a lend of the car, I'll even drive you.'

It took a beat for all this to sink in. 'Sharon, that's really nice of you to offer, but why are you doing this for me? I don't get it.'

'Because I need a favour in return. And if I help you, then you can help me.'

'Help with what exactly?'

There was a long pause before she eventually spoke.

'I'd like you to help me get a boyfriend.'

'You would?'

'Yeah. Remember the other day when you asked me if I'd ever had my heart smashed and I said no? Well, I've been thinking, maybe it's . . . you know . . . time that . . . I did. I don't want to spend the next twenty years sitting at home getting pissed on cider and watching TV, night in, night out. Sure I've my twilight years for all that, haven't I?'

After she'd gone, I was left staring in disbelief into the dying embers of the fire.

Well whaddya know? *Breakthrough*.

Chapter Nine

If anyone I know sees me here, I will die.

Mind you, that equally applies if anyone recognises me, but I think I'm fairly well camouflaged, with my trusty baseball cap pulled so low down over my eyes that I keep inadvertently bumping into Sharon. Add to that a pair of shades so huge they disguise most of my face, along with my hair scraped back into a tight ponytail and, for God's sake, *I* barely recognise me. Besides, as Sharon keeps on saying, there's no shame in signing on the dole these days, not with almost twelve per cent of the country out of work. OK, so maybe most of them were made redundant through no fault of their own and didn't necessarily make holy shows of themselves live to the nation like I did, but the fact is we're all in the same boat now. Plus, Sharon, who turns out to be something of a welfare expert, tells me that I can qualify for €204.37 every single week for a full twelve months. A king's ransom where I'm coming from. Then I get a lightning-quick stab to the heart when I think back to the money I used to make in Channel Six, and how €200 would barely have lasted me a morning, forget about a full week. But the guilt quickly passes. That was then and this is now. If there's one thing I've learned about my life in the last few miserable weeks, it's this: when fate teaches me a lesson, it really goes the whole hog.

Anyway, true to her word, Sharon got me up and out the door early this morning and even paid my bus fare all the way here to the gates of hell. Sorry, I mean the dole office. Unbelievable. It's not even 9 a.m. and already the queue is snaking half-way down the street. And that's not the queue to sign on by the way, that's just the queue to get in the door. It's like humanity's giant melting pot here. I'm not messing, there are be-suited and bewildered-looking business people, all pale and stressed, looking like they don't belong here, shell shocked as to how this could have come to pass. It's a mystery all right. One minute, our economy is the envy of Europe, next thing it's like a flashback to Depression-era America. It would break your heart to see these people. A lot of them look like they should be on their way to senior management meetings in boardrooms, not standing on the pavement in one of the roughest parts of town, on a chilly Monday morning, utterly dependent on welfare to get them through the week.

God, just standing here in this queue is the most monumental reality check you'll ever get. Dole queues really are the great leveller. By the look of these people, I'm guessing some of them have mortgages to pay and young families to look after. Some of them might even have bought houses at ridiculously over-inflated prices at the height of the property boom and now find themselves in dreaded negative equity situations with absolutely no hope of ever getting out of it. Loads of young people are queuing up as well, looking like they just left school. In fact, there's more boob tubes and hoop earrings here than you'd normally see in late-night bars in town any night of the week. A few enterprising barrow women from nearby Moore Street have come round too and are now working their way down the queue selling everything from pineapples to kids' toys.

'Six mandarin oranges for the price of five, only one Euro, Dolebusters' Special' one of them is yelling. But they're not doing much in the way of trade. The business types just bury their heads in their newspapers, desperately trying to blend into the background and look invisible. Just like me, hoping and praying that no one sees them.

Tell you something else: I'm bloody glad to have Sharon with me. Turns out she was on the dole, or 'the scratch' as she calls it, for almost two years. Then they threatened to stop it on her, unless she did a CERT back-to-work course.

'But can they do that?' I ask her innocently.

'Course they can, you eejit,' she says, lighting up her third fag since we got here. 'The whole point of being on the scratch is that the government want to get you off it as quick as they can. They made me go on a personal development course with a load of women who were out of their heads on methadone half the time. A few of them had even been in prison. Then I got the job at Smiley Burger which paid me more than I ever got on the scratch anyway, so that was the end of that. Best day of my life, the day I was able to tell the aul' bitch of a welfare officer where to shove her personal development course.'

To Sharon's credit, she's really keeping up her side of our little Faustian pact and has been amazing about all this whole signing-on lark. I hate to put a hex on it but I think we're actually starting to get on reasonably well. But then, I figure, if Robbie Williams and Take That can put their differences aside, why can't we?

Anyway, according to her, the doors don't even properly open until 9.30, so to pass the time in the queue, I start to ask her loose, broad questions about her dating history/ideal man/perfect relationship. Fair's fair and I've gotta keep up my end of the bargain. Least I can do after she's sacrificed her lie-in and more importantly, all her early morning TV shows.

'Right then. The way I look on the whole dating game,' is my opener, 'is that it's a bit like buying a house. You've got to work out a list of what you absolutely refuse to compromise on, versus things that may drive you mad in the short term, but that you're ultimately prepared to put up with.'

'Is that what you did with Sam?'

Sam. Although he's never out of my mind, just hearing someone else say his name still is like a kick right in the solar plexus. Funny, how a heart can be broken and yet still beat. 'No, no it was never like that with Sam,' I eventually force myself to answer her. 'He was . . . well . . . pretty much perfect.'

Well, OK, so maybe not perfect, I mean, come on, what bloke is? Yes, he was a bit work obsessive and yes, all his talk about winners versus losers and mental discipline could drive me scatty at times, but then . . . but then in the end, he wasn't the problem, was he? I was. And now the best I can hope for is that he'll get bolter's regret and come crawling back to me. It's been weeks now and yet every single time my mobile rings, I keep silently hoping that it's him to say that he's made a terrible mistake and that he wants nothing more than for us to get back together again. Whereupon I'll finally get a chance to vent my anger and chew the face off him for ignoring me/airbrushing me out of his life running to the papers etc. Whereupon he'll grovel and crawl and declare undying love . . . whereupon we'll both live happily ever after and treat this whole miserable episode as an amusing anecdote to tell our grandkids. I've the entire fantasy conversation all worked out in my head. But then that would be asking for miracles wouldn't it? And miracles don't happen in dole queues.

Anyway, something in my expression must give Sharon the hint that this is one of those deeply painful, out of bounds topics because next thing she's looking at me, almost with kindness in her eyes. 'Do you want a Crunchie?' she offers, fishing one out from the pocket of her tracksuit. Like a baby gorilla in a zoo thrusting out a spare banana at a teary child.

'No, thanks.'

'I don't care what you say,' she says firmly. 'Sam can't have been that bleeding perfect. There must have been some things about him that annoyed you. You know, the kind of things women are always bitching about in problem pages. Are you telling me that he never once, ever . . . like left the toilet seat up, or something?'

She means well, so I haven't the heart to tell her that his house has approximately seven bathrooms at the last count, so toilet seats were never really that much of an issue. I'll say this much though, I'm getting to like this more humane side of Sharon. The side you never get to see when Maggie's around.

'It'll get easier, you know,' she eventually says, stubbing out her fag on the pavement.

'It is easier. Look at me, I'm dressed. And out of the house.'

Anyway, right now a subject change would be really good,

so I get back to asking Sharon what's on her boyfriend 'cosmic ordering' shopping list.

'OK then. I'm assuming you're going after the big three?' I ask her, trying to sound efficient and business-like. 'Looks, manners and money.'

'Jessie, I'm a realist. I live at home with my mother and sister and I flip burgers for a living. What the feck do you think I'm doing with my life anyway, living the dream? And you might have been too dazzled by personality to notice, but I'm not exactly Scarlett Johansson in the looks department either. Now if women's magazines have taught me anything it's that you have to punch your weight in relationships. So all I really want is . . . just . . . just someone who doesn't make me miserable.'

'Come on, you're setting the bar way too low! You can do far better than that. What you want to find is a soulmate.'

'Anyway,' she says, but she's gone off on a bit of a tangent. 'I'm back on my diet. I lost three whole pounds when I was sick, you know. And I was doing really well yesterday too. I'd a Smiley Salad in work for lunch and then the low-fat Smiley Chicken Soup for dinner. You saw me, didn't you?'

'Yes . . . yes . . . I did. You were, emm . . . a model of discipline and self-control.' We're getting on well here so it's probably not the best time to remind her about the fish supper she had right before she went to bed. Washed down with three tins of Bulmers.

'And I might join Weight Watchers too. They have meetings in the Whitehall Parish Centre and that's only five minutes away from us. 'Cos, be honest with me now, Jessie. Do you think I've a better chance of meeting a fella if I can get a stone off me?'

'Emm...'

'Tell me the truth, now.'

'Well... you see...' There's just no right answer to that question.

'Then on the other hand, I look at you and think, sure you're skin and bone. You go around the place looking like all you weigh is your keys and clothes and you've no fella to show for yourself either, do you?' A vintage Sharon comment, but to be fair to her, she's being honest, not cruel.

'Do you want a Polo mint?' I ask her, rooting around in my bag, all this talk about dieting making me suddenly aware that I'd no breakfast.

'Yeah. Givvus two to make up for the hole.'

Half nine on the dot and the queue slowly begins to shuffle forward as the doors are opened. More waiting, then as soon as we get inside, Sharon tells me I need to queue up again at hatch fifteen. New claims. So yet more queuing as we slowly inch our way forwards. At the very top of the queue there's a woman stridently saying at the top of her voice, 'But you can't do that to me! I know my entitlements!' Then, at the hatch right beside her, there's a little kid of about four scribbling on the walls in crayon while his dad signs on.

'Could you kindly ask your child to refrain from drawing on my office wall?' asks the welfare officer, a youngish guy with roundey glasses that kind of give him a look of Harry Potter.

'What do you mean, *your* office wall?' he retorts. 'This is government property and the government work for me, so when you think about it, this is really *my* office, isn't it?'

Sniggers from everyone in the queue behind. And still

more sniggers from Sharon when I naively ask whether or not I'll get any actual cash today.

'No, eejit. All you're here for now is to make an appointment to come back to see the welfare officer. Then you come back in a few weeks and they'll means test you.'

'You mean we've queued for this long just to get an appointment? Couldn't I have just . . . I dunno . . . rung up instead?'

'Where exactly do you think you are, Cinderella Rockefeller? The hairdressers? The beauty salon?' she almost guffaws into my face.

'So when do I get to see any money is what I really want to know.'

'Depends. Your claim will be backdated to today but if they feel sorry for you, then they might give you an emergency payout.'

'So . . . is there any chance they might give me some of that emergency cash today?'

'Are you joking?' she nearly guffaws into my face. 'You have to go to the local health centre to apply for it from the HSE. Oh yeah, and you have to be sure to tell them you're actively seeking employment or else you won't get a bean. And you have to say it like you mean it. You've no idea what a shower of suspicious bastards they can be.'

'But how am I supposed to actively seek employment when no TV show for miles will touch me with a bargepole? Even my agent says there's nothing for me at all until . . . well . . . until what happened blows over. Can't I just explain to them that I'm like . . . a unique case?'

'Well excuse me, your majesty. For feck's sake, Jessie, just look around you. Everyone here is a "unique case". Now build a bridge and get over yourself. And would you ever take off the sunglasses? Only Goodfellas wear sunglasses indoors.'

'The point I'm trying to make,' I argue back at her, reluctantly taking off the glasses and shoving them into my bag, 'is I'm an un-hireable TV presenter. Which has to make me a special case.'

'Listen to you, Little Miss Oh Don't You Know Who I Am. Everyone here is in the exact same boat as you, except none of them got fired for being greedy and grabbing free cars in front of half the country. Now shut up and sign on.'

It's at this point that I'm about to give up, run outside and open a vein, but lo and behold, miracle of miracles, my turn finally comes. The dole woman is brisk and business-like as she hands me out a UB90 form to fill out, completely uninterested in who I am or what my 'special' circumstances are. When she sees the name on my passport, it's the first time she actually makes eye contact with me, with a tiny flicker of interest in her eyes.

'You're Jessie Woods? Oh yes, well, under question fourteen of the Jobseeker's Benefit Form, where it asks why your previous employment ended, just put that your employment was suddenly terminated.'

Living in total isolation from the world at large as I am now, I'm inclined to forget that the dogs on the streets know all my business. Anyway, expertly groomed by Sharon, I must have answered all her questions right because after less than five minutes she's going, 'Next!'

And that's when it happens.

I turn around and head over to where Sharon's grabbed a free seat for herself, delighted to be done and dusted, and with a 'can we go now?' expression etched onto my face. But there's two women standing right beside her, one with a buggy and one with a stroller, with about three kids each hanging out of them.

'It *is* her!' one of them says, staring at me like I'm some kind of exhibit in a wax museum. She has tattoos of all her kids' names on her forearm written so large that even from a few paces away, I can still read them clearly: Kylie, Britney and Rihanna.

'No, it's not,' says her pal, who looks like she's dipped her head in waaaay too much peroxide.

'It *definitely* is! Sure she got fired from her TV show, didn't she? Makes sense that she'd be here to sign on.'

'Jessie Woods is miles better looking than her,' says Peroxide Head. 'That one looks like death warmed up.'

Next thing, one of the kids is over to me. 'Givvus your autograph, will you?'

'Emmm . . .' I stammer. 'Well, actually, if you don't mind, you see, I'm in a bit of a rush . . .'

'If she takes off the baseball cap, then we'd be able to get a decent look at her. Tell her to take it off!' says Tattoo Woman bossily.

'Ehh, excuse me? Take off that baseball cap there for us, will you love? We can't see your face.'

Just get us out of here, I semaphore furiously over to Sharon, who seems to take the hint and slowly peels her bum off the seat to leave. But now it's like a ripple has spread through the entire welfare office and all I can hear is, 'Jessie Woods? From the TV show? For real?'

Next thing there's people whipping out mobile phones and taking photos. One guy is even videoing me on his iPhone.

'Maybe she's doing this for one of her dares!' some bright spark at the back of the packed room calls out, as I battle my way through the crowd to the door. I've lost Sharon and now I can't even see her.

'Feck, does that mean there's hidden TV cameras here?' another guy with white emulsion paint streaks in his hair mutters to his pal as I inch my way past them. 'I don't want to end up as an extra on the telly. I'm not even supposed to be here. I'm working.'

'She can't be doing it for her TV show!' yells a woman's voice from the very back of the queue. 'She got fired and the show was taken off the air. And now there's nothing to watch on a Saturday evening except for bleeding Ant and Dec. I *hate* that pair of gobshites.'

Christ alive, it's a nightmare. By now I'm a public spectacle and what's worse is I'm still a good ten feet from the bloody door. There's people grabbing at me and in the mêlée I lose my baseball cap but I just keep battling my way through the throng thinking *getmeoutofheregetmeoutofheregetmeoutofhere.*

I'm not joking; at one point a tall girl who looks a bit like a model actually thrusts a CV into my hand. 'I always wanted to work in TV,' she almost shrieks at me, 'so if you wouldn't mind passing that on to your agent or, you know, any producers you might still be on speaking terms with . . .'

Then some joker sitting with the paper on his knee pipes up at the top of his voice, 'What's the difference between Jessie Woods and a pigeon? At least a pigeon can still make a deposit on a Mercedes, waa-haaa!' He cracks up at his own gag and so do half the dole office and I swear I'm *this* close to bawling when out of nowhere, a rough hand grabs me, grips me tight and strongarms me towards the door, almost lifting me as we barge our way out. I look up gratefully to this knight in shining armour . . . and it's none other than Sharon.

'Will you all relax for feck's sake?' she yells at the crowd at the top of her voice. 'She's only a look-a-like! Used to make a fortune on the side doing twenty-firsts and thirtieths, but now God love her, she can't get a gig to save her life on account of what happened to the real Jessie Woods!'

I don't know how she even does it, but somehow she manages to shove me safely outside with the speed of a presidential bodyguard and all I can do is gratefully whisper a barely audible 'Thank you' as I try to catch my breath.

'No worries,' she says, cool as you like, fishing out a fag from the depths of her tracksuit pocket. 'Now all you have to do is find me a boyfriend and we'll call it quits.'

Later that evening, as soon as she's home from Smiley Burger and after all her soaps are finished, I go for it. Because let's face it, after today, I owe her big time and I'm determined not to renege on my end of the deal.

'Sharon? Can we go upstairs? I need to talk to you. We might also need to use your computer, if that's OK?'

'Oh, right. Eh . . . would this be about . . . emm, you know what, by any chance?' she asks, hauling herself up and bringing a tin of Bulmers with her. 'Yeah, sure, OK then.'

Maggie's antennae immediately shoot up. 'What are you two at?'

For a second Sharon and I lock eyes.

'Nothing,' Sharon mutters.

'Nothing?'

'Well, something all right, but not really . . . emm . . . anything.'

'Oh, if I begged you, would you share?' says Maggie, thick with sarcasm and, I swear to God, Sharon actually looks mortified.

I'm looking at the pair of them, thinking how bizarre and ridiculous this is. I mean, Sharon looks like a rabbit caught in the headlamps. Like she's actually embarrassed to tell Maggie what we're up to. And OK, so maybe she did sneak down in the middle of the night to ask me about this but for God's sake, it's not like what we're doing is something we have to keep as classified information, now is it?

'As a matter of fact, Sharon has asked me to help her find a boyfriend,' I say firmly, 'and I need to talk to her about it privately, that's all. The only reason we're going up to her room is so we don't disturb you watching *What Not to Wear*.'

'A boyfriend?' says Maggie, so shocked you'd swear I'd said, 'Oh, Sharon's anxious to join a local Al-Qaeda cell and I might just have a few underworld contacts who might help her out.'

'Emm . . . well, you see . . .' mutters Sharon weakly.

'You want a boyfriend?'

First time in my life I think I've ever heard Maggie being cutting to Sharon.

'Come on, let's get going,' I say, leaving the room first.

But Sharon stays behind me and when I'm half-way up the stairs I can't help overhearing Maggie growl at her, 'And you're taking dating advice from Cinderella Rockefeller? The most publicly dumped woman in the country? Isn't that a bit like taking PR advice from Princess Anne?'

'Just back off and leave me alone, will you?' says Sharon, slamming the door behind her.

Tell you one thing. That is one helluva dysfunctional relationship.

As soon as we're safely up in the privacy of her room, she plonks down on the bed and launches into me. 'What did you have to go and tell Maggie for? Now I'll never hear the end of this.'

'Well, excuse me, I hadn't realised it was a state secret.'

'You don't know what she's like. She'll slag me about this for weeks.'

'That's daft, why would she do that?'

'I dunno. I suppose she just wants, well, someone who'll always be here to watch TV with her in the evenings. She doesn't want me out and about, meeting fellas and dating.'

'But what about when you were out with other boyfriends you had before?'

She looks at me sheepishly. 'That's the thing, you see. I've never really . . . well . . . you know.'

I don't believe this. 'Sharon! Are you telling me that you've never gone out with anyone? Ever?'

'No! I've had loads of snogs and flings,' she says defensively, 'but never really anything . . . sort of . . . long term. Like you had with that Sam fella. Oh, sorry, I keep forgetting not to bring him up.'

'It's OK.'

'But I think Maggie's afraid that if I do meet someone, then I'll be out gallivanting with him every night of the week. And then she'll be stuck here on her own. Or worse, on her own with Ma.'

'Not necessarily on her own. She'll have me, won't she? Come on, it's not like I can afford to go out anywhere.'

We both crack up laughing at the thought of me and

Maggie cosied up together in front of the TV, without managing to gouge each other's eyeballs out.

'Seriously though,' I say, 'I don't get it. Why neither of you ever want to get out of the house now and then, is what I mean. It's ... well ... it's ...' I have to stop myself from saying, '... it's beyond weird,' so I just trail off into silence instead.

'Well ... Maggie says she's only anti-social when she goes out, then finds there's no one there that she actually wants to talk to. And we're close so it's just comfortable and easy to stay in. Tell me the truth, do you think we're a bit odd?'

'No, you're not odd, you're ... emm ... special. I mean, maybe it's ... you know, a bit unusual to see sisters quite as tight knit as you both are, but it's ... nice.' *Nice* being the only euphemism I can come up with on the spot for 'freaky'.

'And then you see, the other thing is I'm always so knackered when I get in from work, I can't face getting dressed up and going out anywhere. Not when I can just get a takeaway, a few tins and relax here.'

'Well, then my next question is, how exactly do you ever expect to meet someone? Eligible guys tend not to go around knocking on doors wondering if there're any hot, single chicks home. You've gotta get out of your comfort zone and put yourself in the line of fire. Which is why I'm suggesting that we go online and start you internet dating. Right now. Tonight. I'm throwing the baby into the paddling pool and not taking no for an answer.'

'Internet dating? Ah Jessie, no,' she almost splutters on her cider. 'I want to meet normal fellas not perverts.'

'It's not like that any more,' I reassure her. 'When I was at Channel Six, half the women on the production team were at it. From the office, when they were meant to be working, more often than not. There's no stigma about meeting people online any more you know, it's just a way for busy people like you who work long hours to meet people from the comfort and safety of home.' I threw in the 'comfort and safety of home' bit on purpose to try and lure her in.

'Hmm,' she says suspiciously. 'But don't some of these fellas have websites that say things like "Retired farmer seeks nubile young lass for fun times. Must have own chicken."'

'If they do, then we just ignore them. Simple as that.'

'But supposing I do meet someone and I go on a date with him and he turns out to be a total weirdo?'

'Ahh, then that's what the emergency escape call is for.'

'The *what*?'

'It just means that about fifteen minutes into your date, your mobile rings and your dating wing woman, in this case, me, gives you an out. Just in case you need it. But if all's well and the guy doesn't turn out to be some pervey farmer, then you just tell him it was only work ringing and he's none the wiser.'

'God,' she says, looking at me, impressed. 'You must have done this loads of times.'

'Actually, yeah. You know, before I met . . . himself . . . I was out there too. At the dating coalface. Plus we once did a whole *Jessie Would* programme about dating, a few years ago. I had to speed date, read date, internet date and even go eye-gazing dating.'

'What's that?'

'Same as speed dating except you're not allowed to talk. The idea is to see whether there's any non-verbal chemistry between you.'

'And what's read dating?'

'A fancy word for multiple blind dating except it happens in Waterstone's. You're supposed to get chatting to blokes about their taste in books, then figure out if you're compatible from there. You know, like if a guy is reading Jane Austen, chances are he's gay. Or if he's reading Jeremy Clarkson, chances are . . .'

'. . . he's a tosser. And did you ever meet a proper boyfriend at any of these dos?'

I blush a bit, remembering. Probably best not to tell her that the only boyfriend I did actually get out of my foray into speed dating was my cheating boyfriend pre-Sam. I don't mention this to Sharon of course, who's looking at me with such hope in her eyes, it would break your heart. So instead I tell her what she wants to hear, which is basically a load of lies about love. Yes, you will kiss frogs, I tell her, but dating is just a numbers game and you've got to crunch your way through those numbers until you find your perfect match. Who is out there waiting for you, no question. And you're going to be so happy with him and life will be wonderful and you'll never look back again. All complete shite of course, but she seems to buy it and half an hour later, she's even offered me one of her tins of Bulmers while we sit companionably side-by-side at her computer, scrolling our way down through all the online dating agencies.

You'd howl at some of the website names. There's even one called ForgetDinner.com, you can only presume for would-be couples who want to cut straight to the chase and bypass the whole first date preamble. Then there's the online user profiles. We actually find one guy who calls himself Mr Ever Done It In The Back Of An Audi?

'Well, I'll give him this much,' Sharon sniggers, 'at least he's upfront about what he's after. Look at this fella here. "Married man seeks fun times with like-minded young lady. Available daytimes but not evenings or weekends." The gobshite's even posted up his wedding photo with the wife cut out of it. Tosspot extraordinaire.'

We both cackle at this and for a moment it flashes through my mind that I can't remember the last time I laughed. In fact, I haven't even smiled in so long, I can barely remember what my teeth look like. Course it could just be the Bulmers.

Then we stumble across a site called NeverTooLate ToMate.com.

'Look at their tagline,' I giggle, pointing at the screen. 'It says "We delete members unfit to date." Guerrilla dating clearly is their *modus operandi*.'

'That's what I want,' says Sharon, taking a swig from her can. 'A site that filters out all the messers and eejits for you. Go on, click on some of their members so we can have a good laugh at them.'

But some of the guys on this site actually seem relatively normal. Even Sharon is a bit taken aback at the lack of swingers, perverts or openly married men.

'Ignore all the ones who didn't bother posting a photo,' I tell her, scrolling through profile after profile.

'Why?'

'Because it's cowardly. Like going into a pub on a Friday night with a paper bag over your head. And by the way, just a tip. When a guy describes himself as "fun" that means "annoying". Just like "cuddly" means "morbidly obese and has to be hauled around on a mini-crane".'

'Really?' She's looking at me like I've suddenly transformed into this wise, sage dating oracle.

'Yeah, sure. Common knowledge. And by the way, "Enjoys pubbing and clubbing" can be loosely translated as "Would suck the alcohol out of a deodorant bottle"."

'Oooh, here's a live one,' says Sharon, clicking on another profile. 'Listen to this. "I may not have gone to college, but I have qualified from the University of Life."'

We both make gagging gestures and stick our fingers down our throats together, then crease up laughing.

'Here's one,' I say, taking another glug of the Bulmers, which shock, horror, is actually starting to grow on me. 'An actor, if you don't mind. Look, he's done a rep season at the Old Vic and two years at the RSC.'

'Feck that. I don't want anyone with a prison record.'

Eventually, Sharon narrows it down to about six guys she'd like to message, or 'wink' at as you can do on this site. Right then. Next thing is I have to sign up for her and write a profile. So I hit the 'Join now' option on the computer and get the ball rolling.

'OK,' I say, 'now you're going to need a fun-sounding user name. Something that'll catch a fella's eye. And we need to post a photo of you too.'

'Hang on, I've one on my bookcase that was taken five years ago when I had the blonde streaks and was half a stone lighter.'

'We've got to write your profile too, so that means we've got to list all of your interests and hobbies too. Except the trick is not to give too much away either; no harm to cultivate a bit of mystery.'

'Well,' she says, lighting up a fag and looking a bit lost. 'My interests are . . .'

'Yup, fire away,' I say, tapping away at the keyboard.

'Well . . . watching the telly.'

'Sharon, I can't write that, it makes you sound like a couch potato. What else?'

A long, long pause.

'I like . . . ehh . . .'

'Theatre? Sports? Music?'

'Yeeee-ah. I sometimes watch MTV, so I suppose it's OK to put down music.'

'Anything else?'

'Well . . .'

'Sharon! You must have interests and hobbies apart from watching MTV!'

'I like . . . ' she racks her brains to think. 'Well . . . food.'

Then I look over at the shelves which are groaning with her chick-flick DVD collection and her Danielle Steels and an idea comes. Half an hour and two tins of Bulmers later, we've posted the following profile, under the user name MOVIELOVER: 'Home bird, loves cosy evenings in, reading, fine dining and all kinds of music, WLTM like-minded guy for friendship and maybe more.'

Not great, I know, but I had a right job getting her to delete the line, 'Seeks Hugh Grant look-alike for fun times.' Fun times, I patiently explained, being a well-known dating euphemism for hot, anonymous sex. What's really great is that Sharon and I are getting on so well and this is the happiest I've seen her without a remote control in her hand. Come 11.30, we say our goodnights and I head back downstairs to make up my sofa bed. But, just outside the TV room door I hear Joan in mid-conversation with Maggie. Joan sounds in one of her snappy, irritable moods which is never, ever good news.

'Sheila Nugent showed this to me at the cheese and wine reception tonight and I don't want Jessica seeing it, so shove it somewhere that she won't. That one has taken about a month's supply of sedatives off me already. If she gets a hold of this, she'll be streeling around here like some self-medicated zombie for the next fortnight.'

As soon as I can hear the lights and TV being switched off, I know the coast is clear. In I go and start searching around . . . but there's nothing there, just leftover tins and an empty pizza box. Nothing out of the ordinary. Next thing, I spot a pile of newspapers beside the fire, waiting to be burned. I scramble down on my hands and knees and go through them, but there's nothing at all. Then, in the gossip pages of today's *Evening Star*, I spot my name, and instantly shove it into the 'To be burnt' pile. I've resisted all temptation to read anything about myself in the last few weeks; why start now? But then I spot a different name in the same article. Sam's. I grab at the article, nearly ripping it in a blind panic. I know this column well; it's written anonymously, fabulously and bitchily by someone who just calls themselves Ulysses. No one has a clue who the mysterious Ulysses actually is, or even if it's a man or a woman. But given how poisonous the column is, I know plenty of celebs who'd gladly get a hit man after him or her.

> *Having just returned from a delightful spring sojourn in Marbella, who did Ulysses happen to bump into while strolling in the sunshine? Only a source close to Sam Hughes. For those of you just coming round from a coma, Sam has recently broken up with former TV presenter, Jessie Woods. (Did Ulysses dare invoke the phrase 'has-been'?) My mole tells me that while Sam had enjoyed a delightful holiday, sadly he cut it short for 'personal reasons'.*

Which set Ulysses to wondering why. Another lady love on the scene already, whom he was anxious to rush home to? Surely a catch like Sam need only pick and choose from a bevy of beauties available to him? But my source hinted to me that the real reason is far more romantic; Sam simply missed his ex-girlfriend and was unable to enjoy a holiday so far from her sparkling company. So, who knows, maybe Ms Woods is a little luckier in love than she is with work. Could news of possible reconciliation be in the air? One thing is for certain, wherever Ms Woods has been shielding herself away from the public gaze lately, she may very well find herself on the receiving end of a phone call from a contrite and lonely ex any time now. My Deepthroat assures me that a reunion appears to be little short of imminent. Just remember, you read it here first.

Chapter Ten

The really critical thing here is for me to stay utterly calm. Zen-like, if you will. Because this is a clear-cut, A or B situation. Either Sam cut his holiday short to rush back and beg me for a reconciliation, or . . . in fact, no, there is no B. Because Sam already seeing someone else, so soon after we broke up is just completely unthinkable. In fact, maybe in a weird way, we actually needed this time apart so we could both realise just how much we mean to each other. Or rather, maybe Sam needed this time out to cop onto himself, because while he might well be on his way to becoming the next Richard Branson, like most men, he's a complete gobshite when it comes to matters of the heart. And if all the daytime TV I've been watching recently has taught me anything, it's this: there is only one impossibility in life and that's trying to keep two soulmates apart (thank you, *Oprah*). So basically, all I have to do is sit tight and wait for the phone to ring.

Which it will. Course it will. I mean, it said so in the paper. 'A reunion is little short of imminent.' That's what it said. I'm guessing that the 'mole' referred to was either Nathaniel or Eva because come on, I mean who else could it be? I called them, got no response, left a few messages for each of them, then gave that up as a bad job. Because, let's face it, I have FAR bigger things to focus on, don't I? The main thing is for me not to be the one to blink first. At least, not now that the tide's finally turning in my favour. I shudder a bit, remembering that as far as Sam is concerned, I've been acting like someone out on day release since we broke up, but that was then, this is now and I make myself one solemn vow. This time, it'll be different. Now that he's clearly on his way back to me, it's not too late to try and regain some degree of self-respect.

The best thing, I decide, is to get on with my usual morning's work and not even think about going near my phone, because everyone knows the watched phone never rings. So, like the model of patience and restraint that I've newly become, I deliberately leave the mobile at the very bottom of my handbag in the hall, and head into the kitchen to start my day's work. Trouble is, I keep dropping things every time I think I hear a noise that just might be the phone. By 10.30, I've smashed two of Joan's revolting peach side plates (with ivy leaves growing round the edges, gak, gak, gak) when I could have sworn I heard a text coming through, but it turned out to be a Mr Whippy van on the street outside. Easy enough mistake to make; my ring tone and the ice cream van are virtually identical and both equally annoying. Then, I let a china shepherdess I was dusting smash to smithereens on the floor when the front doorbell rang. (Which was no harm, actually; there's so many of them dotted around the place, it looks like there was a mini Laura Ashley explosion in here.) Well, it has to be Sam, it just has to, I figure, nearly impaling myself on the hall table as I ran to open it. Who else could it be? Reasonable assumption, given that it would take a very brave neighbour to call here to Wuthering Depths, The House That Manners Forgot. No, he's probably figured that there's just no way of saying what he wants to over the phone, i.e., grovelling apologies and profuse expressions of undying love, you know yourself. Miles better just to call here and sweep me off my feet with flowers, champagne, the whole works.

But when I fling open the door, with my most 'surprised' smile hardwired onto my face, it isn't Sam at all. Turns out just to be some guy trying to sell raffle tickets to raise money for the local hospice. I'm a bit deflated but quickly brush it aside. It's only mid-morning. I have to be realistic; he only got back to Ireland yesterday, I need to chill out here and give the guy some time. He probably went straight into his office this morning to catch up with everything, but no doubt is saving the big romantic reconciliation scene with me later.

Just hope Maggie is back home from work in time to see it, hee hee.

Anyway, the point is that this time tomorrow, I'll probably have moved into Sam's house, with all my boxes, bin liners and all, and life will be rosy again. Course I still won't have a job, but with him beside me, somehow that won't matter quite so much. I certainly won't miss sleeping on a lumpy sofa, I won't miss Maggie and her never ending put-downs or Joan and her mood swings, but in a funny way, I will miss Sharon, who's turning out to be far more sisterly than I could ever have imagined.

OK, you know what? Housework = crap idea. I'm way too jittery to get anything done, so to pass the time I knock on Sharon's bedroom door and find her glued to her computer screen, tapping away on the NeverTooLate

ToMate website. She's on her day off and her plans for the day appear to be sit on arse in front of computer and find cute guys to wink at.

Perfect. Couldn't ask for a better distraction. Plus there's that smug feeling of gently guiding someone else towards love and romance, while knowing deep down that this time tonight, I'll be the one with the boyfriend.

'You won't believe this!' she screeches excitedly at me before I even have a chance to sit down.

'I've news for you too, but you go first.'

'I got up about five times during the night to see if any cute guys had messaged me and guess what? *Seventeen* messages so far!!! *Seventeen!* Can you believe it? And the best bit is I never even had to go outside the front door to meet them! Didn't even need to shoehorn myself into a pair of Spanx or put on make-up or anything. You're a bloody genius, Jessie Woods. Why didn't I sign up for this internet dating lark years ago?'

She's still in her pyjamas and, I can't help noticing, is so animated she's forgotten to even come downstairs for her normal breakfast of leftover pizza.

'That's fab!' I say, pulling out a chair and plonking myself down beside her. 'OK, so let's scroll through all your messages and then start eliminating all the eejits from the eligibles.'

'Good plan. Hey, get a load of your man here; I think I might end up deleting him.'

'Why?'

'Because how could I ever bring him back to this house with Maggie sitting here? You know what she's like; her favourite hobby is slagging off visitors.'

'I'm not with you.'

'For feck's sake, look at his photo, will you? If a fella is covered in bruises and has most of his front teeth missing, then the chances are he's a bit sensitive to criticism. Maggie would start having a go at him and he'd end up annihilating her.'

'Well, I know we shouldn't reject anyone based on their photo at this point, but his profile doesn't exactly scream "hopeless romantic" either, now does it?'

We both read it together, then crack up giggling.

'STOCKY, 30, SHAVED HEAD, INTO HEAVY METAL SEEKS SIMILAR FOR RAW, HOT FUN.'

'Can I delete this one here?'

'What's wrong with him?'

'For feck's sake, Jessie, he looks like a younger version of Santa and his user name is Desperado.'

'Show me his profile.'

'He's a sixty-four-year-old divorcee with four kids. He's a non-smoker and his tag line says "Get me out of this rut." Gakkety gak gak. Can you imagine me as a stepmother? With Ma as a shining example to guide me?'

I won't argue with her on that one, so I let her delete. Anyway, we manage to kill a whole half hour like this before it even crosses my mind to go downstairs and check my mobile for messages.

By 11 a.m. though, I'm starting to get just the teeniest bit antsy, so I run down to my handbag, whip out the phone and keep it close by me. No harm in that. I also show Sharon last night's paper and fill her in on this latest twist in my love life, mainly because I do really sincerely hope she'll keep in contact with me after I move out of here.

It's really sweet actually, she kind of looks disappointed when I break it to her that my days here are numbered.

'So, like . . . are you getting back with him, or what then?'

'Well, not exactly, but I'm confident it's just a matter of time. He'll call today, maybe any minute now. But in the meantime, I'm just sitting tight and doing absolutely nothing and you're going to do the same with me.'

'What?'

'Oh Sharon, you have so much to learn from me,' I smile, a bit patronisingly. 'You see the thing about guys is that they only really appreciate you if you're like a prize to them. And prizes have to be won. So I'm advising you to do exactly as I'm doing. Leave it a good twenty-four hours before you message back any of the guys you like. Don't let them know you're interested. Just play it cool. Look at me, and learn from the master. I mean, do you see me picking up the phone to Sam?'

'You did loads of times when you first moved in here. Me and Maggie used to think you were talking to yourself the whole time, until Maggie copped on you were leaving about two hundred voice messages for him. Jeez, you were like Sky News, every hour on the hour.'

OK, I was kind of hoping that mightn't come up.

'Yes, well, that was then and this is now,' I snap back defensively. 'The point is, there are times when you have to let a fella chase you and this is most definitely one of those times. For both of us. And if a guy chooses not to pursue you, then you're gracious and dignified, but you move on. Plenty more fish and all that.'

'Can I not just message back this guy here? His profile sounds really funny. Look, he says, "Please don't ask my age; in dog years, I'm already dead." And he's online now.'

'Sharon!'

Anyway I do amazingly well and manage to hold out

until well after 11.30 without going near the phone, but then I think, you know, this could actually be very hard for Sam. After all, he's not a guy who finds it easy to admit that he was ever in the wrong, so . . . in that case, why don't I drop him a little text message? Just to let him know I'm thinking about him, that's all. Except I don't want Sharon seeing what I'm at, so I slip in the bathroom and text him from there. Nothing furtive about it, I just need a bit of privacy for this.

By lunchtime, there's no reply. So, same drill, I slip back to the loo and send a second text.

Still no answer.

So a few minutes later, I head back to the bathroom again and text again. Then I slip back to Sharon's room and give her a great lecture about how when a fella is interested, you don't need to do a single thing. They'll make all the running and what's more they'll enjoy it. She's totally engrossed in the computer screen and I've the phone in my dressing gown pocket, which I keep surreptitiously checking, oh, about every two minutes or so.

'Is there something wrong with you?' she asks after a while, worriedly.

'No, why?'

'Because you keep staring down into your nether regions. Anything you want to tell me?'

'No, I just . . . emm . . . might need the loo again. Something I ate last night is . . . ehh . . . disagreeing with me. That's all.'

Feck it, might as well leave a proper voice message for him. To hell with all this texting lark. In for a penny, in for a pound. He doesn't answer, so I wait for the beep on his message minder to come on. I'm in the tiny bathroom, balancing on the edge of the bath, in the middle of a message for Sam so long the beeps cut me off, when the door suddenly bursts open.

'I *knew* it! You were in here ringing that Sam Hughes fella all the time, weren't you?' Sharon yells, grabbing the phone off me and checking the number on it. 'And here's me, like a gobshite, taking dating advice from you?' She's so infuriated, you'd swear she'd caught me in here mainlining heroin.

'Now there's absolutely no need for you to overreact . . .'

'And why is that, exactly?'

'Because . . . it's different for me. Remember, I've been with him for two years you know, so the same set of rules don't apply.'

'Bugger that, Little Miss Do As I Say, Don't Do As I Do. You're completely deluded. Jeez, you could give lessons in self-delusion to Heather Mills.'

By 2 p.m., all pride is abandoned and I've rung eight times, not including all the text messages. I didn't count, but Sharon did. And still no reply. I even tried calling Eva, who's still in Spain with Nathaniel, but, surprise, surprise, she didn't answer either.

By 2.10 p.m., I've convinced myself that Sam will just do the obvious thing and call here after work. Then another alarm bell. As I'm frantically pacing up and down the tiny hallway, I suddenly catch sight of myself in one of the half dozen mirrors Joan has hanging here. Christ alive, look at the state of me. In all the time I've been here, I don't think I've even bothered once to actually take one long, hard look at my appearance. I look grey, washed out and so scrawny you'd think I weighed approximately the same as your average carton of milk. The circles under my eyes are pitch black, like a two-year-old attacked me with a Crayola, and I'm also wearing the same manky dressing gown and pyjamas I've been living, eating, drinking and sleeping in for weeks now. Don't get me wrong, I have flung them in the washing machine the odd time, but basically now they're so minging, they could do with having a stake put through them. Then there's the small matter of my hair. The mousey brown roots on show are so glaringly bad, I'm staring at them in horror. It's so long since I've seen my natural colour, I'd actually forgotten what it was.

In a blind panic, I leg it upstairs, race to the bathroom, fling off the PJs, switch on the shower and hop in. Then, a far better idea hits me. Two seconds later, I'm hammering on Sharon's door, wrapped in a towel and still dripping wet.

'Come in.' There she is, still so engrossed in NeverTooLateToMate.com that she doesn't even bother looking up at me.

'Sharon, dire catastrophe. Will you lend me some money?'

'Piss off. I've already lent you money to pay off your mobile phone.'

'I told you, I'll pay you back as soon as my emergency dole money comes through. But the thing is, now I need more.'

'What for?'

'To get my roots done. Now. Today. Look at the state of me, would you? For God's sake, Myra Hindley had better hair. Can't believe you never pointed out to me how utterly crap I look. So if you think about it, in a way . . . this is all your fault. So you have to lend me the cash.'

No response.

'Come on, Sharon, don't make me beg.'

She glances up to where I'm standing in her doorway, half naked and leaving a pool of water on Joan's Laura Ashley country floral carpet.

'Is this because in your deranged state, you think Sam Hughes is on his way over here now to whisk you back to his country residence?'

'I don't just think it, I know it.'

'Even though he's ignored every one of your two dozen phone calls and hasn't even bothered his arse getting back to you? You read one stupid article in one of Ma's trashy papers and now you're acting like a complete and utter headcase.'

Right then. This calls for, shall we say, a more subtle form of negotiation. 'If I could have a further moment of your time,' I say, sashaying towards her computer and standing with my dripping wet arm on top of it. 'One of these days, you're going to be going out on a date, with a straight, single guy. Correct?'

'Straight and single means he passes the Sharon test, yeah.'

'So, let's just take a moment to think this through, will we? You'll want to look your best for said date. You might even want to be styled for it.'

'If you think I'm taking style advice from someone who spends all day every day in their pyjamas, you've another think coming.'

'What I was getting at, dearest, is that I have a garage full of designer clobber downstairs. There's Gucci handbags down there. And Hermès scarves.'

She looks up sharply.

'And you might just care to see this season's Louis Vuitton

black clutch bag, which is lying downstairs in a Tesco's bin liner as we speak.'

Now there's a spark of interest in her eyes.

'Not to mention a whole suitcase full of La Prairie face creams. And Laura Mercier foundations. And a mountain of Mac make-up.'

'The stuff J-Lo uses?'

'The very one. And it can all be yours . . .' I'm starting to sound like a panto villain now, '. . . just for the lend of a few measly Euro.'

She sighs so deeply, it almost comes from her feet.

'Right then. How much do you need?'

I try to hide my triumph. 'OK, let's see, cut and colour, plus a blow dry . . . two fifty should do it. Better make it an even three, to allow for tips.'

'Three Euro? You could have got that much out of the loose change jar in the kitchen, you moron.'

'Ehh . . . that would be three *hundred* Euro.'

For a second I think the girl is about to have an aneurism.

'Three hundred bleeding Euro to get your hair done? For feck's sake, Jessie, Cheryl Cole wouldn't fork out that kind of money and she gets extensions!'

'But you don't understand, I've been going to Chez Pierre for years now, he's like an artist, he understands my hair . . .'

'Does that three hundred Euro include flights to France where I can only presume this gobshite Pierre is based?'

'Ehh . . . no he's on . . . emm . . . Dawson Street,' I say in a little voice.

'And you have the cheek to wonder how you got yourself into a financial mess?'

In the end, she grudgingly hands me over €15 so I can

run to Tesco's and pick up a Nice and Easy home colour kit in Champagne Blonde. And at that I had to promise her an entire La Prairie starter kit which sells for around €200, so not exactly the best trade in the world. Anyway, by 4.30 p.m., I'm washed, exfoliated, all made-up, back in my DVB jeans with a little top Sam always used to admire and all I have to do is rinse the colour out of my hair.

'A child of five could handle Nice and Easy,' Sharon assures me, standing in the bathroom beside me, playing with all the La Prairie she's just looted from the garage. Like a kid on Christmas morning that's focused on their toys and nothing else. 'Jeez, tell you something else,' she says, with her face pressed right up against the bathroom mirror, 'this concealer stuff is seriously good shite. You can hardly see my acne scarring. OK, you can rinse your hair off now, Jessie, the time's well up. You'll be gorgeous and you'll have saved yourself a fortune.'

She's absolutely right, I think, shoving my head under the shower hose. Just think of the dosh I could have saved myself over the years just by doing home treatments! And they're so easy too. Sharon told me what to do and I just followed her instructions to the letter. Doddle. All delighted with myself, I towel off my hair and stand in front of the bathroom mirror, prepared to be dazzled.

OK, my hair is now orange. Bright orange. Like a puppet in a kids' show. Not red, not ginger . . . orange. Think of the worst ginger going and right now I'm trumping them. I'm even more carroty than Mick Hucknall. Or Prince Harry.

I'm rooted to the spot, staring horrified into the mirror, my mouth in a perfect 'O'.

'It's ehh . . . a nice change, isn't it?' Sharon says hopefully.

'Sharon. I'm about to have a longed-for reunion with my boyfriend. And I look like Beaker from the frigging MUPPET SHOW. And it's YOUR EFFING FAULT!'

'You must have left it on for too long,' she says, reading the side of the box.

'Oh, NOW you read the instructions?'

It costs me a brand new jar of Crème de la Mer to bribe her to go back to Tesco's and get another colour that'll tone this one down. Either that, or a pair of garden shears to cut my hair off with. In fact, the amount of expensive stuff I've given her would have got me about three sessions in Chez Pierre so this whole cost cutting lark is turning out to be a bit of a false economy.

Two hours and another home colour later, the orange is now a few tones lighter, still red-ish, but at least now I'd be able to walk down the street without people thinking that I've a traffic cone stuck on my head.

'Very Nicole Kidman,' nods Sharon approvingly, as she blow dries it for me out of guilt. 'Strawberry blonde suits you. Plus there's another advantage.'

I just glare in the mirror by way of an answer, still hopping mad at her for not reading the shagging instruction box.

'At least no one will recognise you now. Which can only be a good thing, can't it?'

Anyway, by 5.30 and with the hair crisis averted, I try calling Sam's office and manage to get a hold of his snotty assistant, Margaret. 'No,' she tells me crisply, 'Mr Hughes is in meetings all afternoon and can't be disturbed.' Her standard 'kindly get off the phone, please' clause. So I leave yet another message and I'd nearly swear I can hear a note of triumph in the bitch's voice when she says, that yes of course she's happy to pass it on. But her subtext is loud and clear; don't hold your breath waiting for him to get back to you, baby. Well feck her anyway. She obviously didn't read last night's paper and hasn't a clue about the latest development. Tell you something else, the minute I'm back with Sam, she'll be out on her ear and with a bit of luck, propelled to the back of the same dole queue I had to suffer my way through.

5.45 and by now my nerves are ricocheting. I keep checking the phone every few seconds, but nothing. By now, both Maggie and Joan are home from work; Maggie's in the kitchen and I can hear Joan clattering her handbag on the hall table downstairs, rattling all her china ornaments. Clearly in one of her bad humours, then. Then from the very depths of my mounting hysteria, suddenly . . . a brainwave! I don't need to put myself through all the misery and torture of waiting, do I? Not when I could just borrow Joan's car, drive to Sam's house and wait for him there. Perfect! I am such a moron. Because no matter where he is, he's got to go home sometime, doesn't he?

But my cunning master plan totally hinges on Joan lending me her car a) because Sam's house is in Kildare, miles away. Even if you got the bus to Kildare village, you'd still have an approximate fifteen-mile hike ahead of you. And b) a taxi would end up costing about €200, which, quelle surprise, I don't have.

'Well hello there, Joan, how are you? Wow, can I just say that you look absolutely amazing today. Nice . . . emmm . . . pant suit. Very . . . ehh . . . Jackie O,' I smile as I pad downstairs, trying the softly, softly, kill-her-with-niceness approach.

'Christ Almighty, Jessica, what on earth did you do to your hair? You look like Bianca from *EastEnders*.'

'Oh, well, you see I'd a bit of an accident with a home colour kit...'

'Oh I *see*,' she says, throwing me a look that could freeze mercury. 'So in other words, you've been messing around with your hair all day instead of doing the list of housework I left for you? The breakfast china in the kitchen hasn't even been washed since this morning yet. And one of my Lladro figurines has mysteriously gone missing. You're not pulling your weight around here, Jessica, and I simply won't stand for it.'

Jesus, Joan and her shagging ornaments. I wouldn't put it past her to have diagrams drawn of where they all go.

'I can explain about the figurine, honest, but the thing is right now I need a lend of your car... It's sort of an emergency.'

'A lend of my car? Well Madam Woods, I've a few home truths for you. You're constantly borrowing it to go to the supermarket so you can avoid meeting neighbours on the street and you've never once put a single drop of petrol into it.'

'I know and I'm sorry and I will, as soon as—'

'I know, I know, as soon as your emergency dole money comes through. You're like a broken record. You'd think you were about to collect on the Euromillions lottery, the way you keep going on about it. May I remind you that at the end of the day, it's only dole.'

'Please Joan, it's just for tonight, I'll make it up to you.'

'Out of the question. Besides, tonight I'm going to my musical society meeting.'

'For "musical society" read "sing-song down at the Swiss Cottage",' snorts Sharon, thudding down the staircase and barging past us on her way into the kitchen. 'The landlord got a piano put in the back room and the last time Ma got up and sang, he barred himself. Boom, boom.'

'We're rehearsing for a production of *The Mikado*, if you must know,' Joan fires back at her. 'And look at the holy state of you, still in your night attire at this hour of the day. You're a holy disgrace, so you are.'

'Give me a rest, it's my day off.'

'Don't suppose . . . you're in any way . . . emm . . . flexible on this?' I plead to Joan in a last-ditch effort to get around her.

'Do I sound flexible? Now not another word out of you; the matter is closed,' she snaps on her way upstairs. 'And that kitchen better be tidied by the time I get back down.' She glares at me furiously and then, to really ram her point home, snatches her car keys off the hall table and takes them upstairs with her.

Bugger it anyway. I half feel like shouting up after her that she could always use her broomstick to go out tonight. What's really annoying is that she was in wonderful humour only this morning. In fact, if I'd told her what I was at then, she might even have offered to drive me, purely so she could get a good look at the inside of Sam's house. Then, out of the corner of my eye, under a stack of unpaid bills, something glittering catches my eye. The keys to Maggie's little Fiat Uno.

Well whaddya know, my luck's turning. Two seconds later, I'm in the kitchen where she's snacking on the microwaved remains of last night's chicken tikka masala, while Sharon peruses the collection of takeaway menus, deciding what the pair of them will order in for dinner later. Brilliant timing. Perfect. Couldn't have planned it better, in fact. Maggie is always at her most agreeable directly after food. A bit like a hippo.

'Maggie, could I talk to you for a second?'

She looks at me a bit puzzled, then, being Maggie, reaches for a wisecrack. 'If you want to communicate with me, Cinderella Rockefeller, then I suggest you leave a Post-it note on the fridge. And by the way, is your hair on purpose?'

'Ha, ha, HA!' I force a laugh to try and win her round. 'You are so dry and witty, ever thought of going into stand-up?'

'Not a bad idea actually, Mags,' Sharon chips in, with her mouth full of grub. 'You're always saying it would be the ultimate doss job and you'd be amazing at it. Jeez, you'd be like another Jo Brand.'

'I insult you,' says Maggie, folding her arms and slowly turning to glare at me, 'and then you compliment me? Hmm ... can the request for a favour be far behind?'

'I need a lend of your car. Please. Just for a few hours. And in return, I'll emm ...' I was going to say '... do all your laundry and clean out your room for the next month,' but I do all that anyway. 'Well, I'll find some way to pay you back, Maggie. And that's a promise.'

She sits back, flinty-eyed, and, for a split second, I get a flash of how terrifying it must be to be stuck in the Inland Revenue office with her, having a tax audit.

'There are thousands of reasons for me to say no,' she eventually says. 'Would you like me to enumerate them all, so you can pick your favourite?'

'You know what the best bit is?' sniggers Sharon, a bit disloyally. 'She only wants your car so she can stake out Sam Hughes's house. Isn't that the most mental thing you ever heard? I'd nearly go with you myself for the laugh, Jessie, only *Coronation Street*'s on tonight and I've been dying to see it all day.'

Next thing, there's a ring at the doorbell and we all stare at each other in shock. No one calls here. *No one.* Only total strangers who don't know us.

'You get it,' the two of them say to me together.

'And if it's anyone looking for either of us,' adds Sharon, 'we're not in. I mean, what kind of a gobshite calls to your house on a Wednesday night, when everyone knows *Corrie* is on?'

I race down the hallway, muttering *PleasebeSampleasebe SampleasebeSam*. But when I fling the door open, it's not him at all. It's a ridiculously tall guy in white linen shirt and black leather jacket, in his early thirties or so; light, fair-ish hair and thin as a reed, carrying a neat little bouquet of chrysanthemums and carnations, all wrapped up in cellophane. Something familiar about him too. I'm slowly taking him in, like he's a foreigner whose accent I can't quite place and he's staring back at me hopefully, expectantly. As though I should know who he is, but I don't.

'Em . . . I'm really sorry, but I think you might have the wrong house,' I say as politely as I can, given that I'm in the middle of an emotional meltdown. Perfectly reasonable assumption; I mean, come on, who'd be calling here with flowers?

'Jessie? Don't you remember me?'

I squint up at him and while, yeah, there is something vaguely familiar about the light blue eyes, otherwise I haven't a clue.

'I'm Steve,' he says, a sounding a tiny bit disappointed. 'Didn't Joan tell you I was going to call?'

Steve, Steve, Steve . . .?

Oh for feck's sake, I do not believe it. 'You're Steve *Hayes*?'

'The one and only,' he smiles down at me, all delighted.

Oh my God, Hannah's big brother. I've a vague memory of Joan mentioning something about bumping into him recently and him promising to call, but what with everything else that's been going on, I must have just blanked it out.

'Hannah's just living a few streets away from here now, you know,' he beams just as another trait about him comes floating back to me from all those years ago. I'd forgotten that he's one of those always happy/good-natured/glass-half-full, /even-tempered people. God, no wonder Maggie and Sharon used to make his life hell. 'She's just had another baby, number two. Mad, isn't it?' he grins cheekily. 'I often feel like we're still just kids ourselves.'

'Yeah! Yeah, completely mad. Well . . . you've . . . ehh . . . changed so much, Steve, I'd hardly have known you!' The truth too. Last time I saw him I was barely twenty-one, right before I got my first job in Channel Six. His hair was far blonder back then, and he used to wear roundey jam-jar glasses which kind of gave him a look of the Milky Bar Kid from certain angles. Funny how the intervening years have changed him; he's grown, not so much in height as in stature. The guy I used to know was slightly gawky and unsure of himself, but the Steve standing in front of me now is a man. And a very cool-looking one at that too.

'Oh, these are for you, by the way,' he smiles, thrusting the flowers clumsily at me. 'Just to say welcome back to the estate and that I'm sorry about what happened to you with your job. Like the hair, by the way. Big change to the way you used to look on TV. Very . . . let me pick my words carefully . . . yes, got it: very Nicole Kidman.'

I laugh nervously, at the back of my mind wondering

how the hell I'm going to get rid of him. Sorry, no rudeness intended, but cosy reunions with ghosts from the past are NOT on tonight's agenda.

'I'm glad it was you who answered the door, by the way,' he adds, his ridiculously tall physique taking up most of the frame. 'Not Maggie or Sharon, is what I mean. If they saw me arriving here with flowers, I'd never hear the end of it. Unless they've both changed drastically since the days when I used to live here, that is,' he adds, winking at me.

I'm only half listening, my mind's too busy racing, but suddenly the words Maggie and Sharon catch my ear. I look up at him, suddenly all interested as an idea forms in the back of my head. Perfect. A diversion. Couldn't have asked for better.

'Yes . . . you know, they're both here . . . and, you know what? They'd be so annoyed if you called over without saying hi. Come on in!'

Before the poor guy knows what's hit him, I've grabbed his arm, swung him into the hall and shoved him in the direction of the kitchen.

'Jessie,' he hisses, panic beginning to rise in his voice, 'you don't understand, I came here to see you.'

I'm not even focused on him though. I just want to create a distraction and get out of here. Not very nice of me, I know, but it's all in aid of the greater good. Besides, plenty of time to apologise later.

'Go on through to the kitchen,' I call back at him gaily, 'and will you tell them all that I'll see them later!'

Thirty seconds later, I've grabbed Maggie's car keys and am sitting in the driver's seat, reversing out of the garage. I'm almost there . . . almost home and dry . . . when suddenly, like two imploding missiles, Maggie and Sharon hurl themselves against the bonnet, Maggie's mouth frozen in a silent movie expression of horror. I'm forced to brake or else run them over, so I brake; but just as I'm about to zoom off down the road, I lose two crucial seconds trying to figure out the gear stick on Maggie's manual car.

But it's two seconds too much.

Next thing, the two of them are in the car beside me, breathing fire and stale Indian food at me.

'Fecking insane BITCH!' roars Maggie from the back seat, grabbing a fistful of my hair. 'Pull the car over or else I swear, you are so DEAD!'

'Let go of my hair, or I'll crash your precious car.'

She does what I tell her without further argument.

'And I'm not pulling over. We're going on a road trip.'

And there's nothing they can do about it either. I'm the one in the driver's seat.

So, here I am, on my way for a romantic reunion with my ex-boyfriend at his palatial mansion house in the country. Just never thought I'd be bringing Laurel and Hardy along with me for the ride.

Chapter Eleven

'Will you cool the head, for feck's sake, Maggie?' says Sharon, fishing around in the glove compartment for a box of Marlboro Lights, then passing the entire box back to her in an effort to calm her down. 'Can I remind you that it was either this or else stay at home making small talk for the whole night with Stuttering Steve.'

'That's not fair. The stutter's well and truly gone,' I say.

'Ah, but sadly the moniker lives forever.'

I actually think that as soon as she realises just what this evening's alternative was, Maggie does start to calm down a bit. Mind you, this takes about ten miles and fifteen cigarettes. However, I figure that I'm on slightly safer ground with her as soon as she starts having a go at poor, harmless old Steve. But then that's Maggie for you. A tree hasn't fallen in the forest until she's slagged it off.

'Christ alive, Steve fecking Hayes,' she says, sucking on a fag. 'The very thought of having to entertain that big long string of piss . . .'

'He's in a band now, you know,' says Sharon. 'With some eejitty name. The Amazing Few, I think they're called. Hey, we should go to one of his gigs some night, so we could have a proper laugh.'

'Well, it'll cost you. Because you'll have to pay for the wild horses it'll take to drag me there.'

Sam's house is miles, and I really do mean miles, away from Whitehall, well past Kildare town, down a twisty, narrow, secondary road where the houses gradually get bigger and bigger, growing more and more spaced apart, until after a while, you only see a gateway about every five miles or so. Anyway, as soon as we're through the worst of the rush hour traffic, I drive like a brain-damaged test monkey, not even entertaining Maggie's demand that she drive instead. Would take way too long with me having to shout navigation instructions at her.

Too rushed. No time. Just got to get there.

Plus if I did give her the wheel, she'd only turn the car round and head straight for home. I'm like a woman consumed; all reason has completely gone out the window and I honestly think that if I hit one more red light, I'll end up hyperventilating into a paper bag. As it is, my breath is coming nervously in quick, sharp stabs, my head is starting to swim and my heart's palpitating so much that I think there's a fair chance I might throw up. Just at the thought of how Sam will react when he sees me. Of what he might say. Or worse, what he might not say.

Then I make a Herculean effort to cop myself on. Because I'm being ridiculous. Of course Sam will be over the moon that I've made all this effort to prove how much he still means to me. It's just a simple case of one of us having to swallow their pride and take the first step, and in this case the fates decreed that it should be me. I just happened to have more time on my hands than him to make the first move and bloody lucky that I did. In a few hours' time, we'll be snuggled up in bed together, drinking champagne most likely, toasting our reunion and having a good old giggle about this. The words in that newspaper article, which I've memorised and am now silently repeating like a mantra, are keeping me sane and focused, 'A reunion is imminent.'

Between heavy traffic and seeming to get every bloody set of traffic lights red, the drive takes the guts of an hour. And as if that wasn't bad enough, I have to put up with Maggie whinging about how hungry she is while Sharon lists out all the TV programmes she's missing, with particular moaning reserved for the fact that now she won't get to see *Coronation Street*.

'All that was happening on *Corrie* tonight,' I snap at her, unable to take much more, 'is that Kevin was being stalked by his ex-girlfriend who breaks into his house to have it out with him.'

'Very interesting plot synopsis,' quips Maggie from where she's sulking away in the back seat, now in a haze of smoke. 'Can I eat it?'

'Well I was looking forward to it all day,' moans Sharon, who I'm on the verge of slapping any minute now, if she keeps this up for much longer. As soon as I'm safely back with Sam, my solemn vow is to buy the girl a subscription to Sky Plus as a thank you for helping me out with the dole, and maybe then that'll shut her up.

'In fact, it was the highlight of my whole TV week and what's more, you *knew* that, Jessie Woods.'

'Well instead of watching someone getting stalked on *Corrie*, now you get to see the live floor show instead,' says Maggie and just for a split second I catch a glimpse of her lizard eyes staring at me from the rearview mirror, unblinking. 'And speaking of which, Cinderella Rockefeller,' she goes on, 'suppose he takes one look at you waiting for him like a complete basket case and decides to call the police? Did that ever once filter through your addled brain, before you turned to car theft?'

'I'm calling in to see my boyfriend, that's all. What's wrong with that?'

'*Ex*-boyfriend.'

'What I'm doing is entirely within the boundaries of the law.'

'You know, I didn't *like* you before this, but at least I *respected* you. Now I just think you're a nut job. It's not the dole you should be applying for, it's day care.'

'Why thank you for that, Maggie. Can't tell you how much your support means to me. For your information though, I happen to be doing the right thing.'

'Just what the Germans said before they invaded Poland.'

'Oh I just thought of something else,' Sharon chips in. 'If you do get back with him, you'll be able to tell your grandchildren, "If I hadn't stalked your granddad and acted like a complete mentaller, then none of you would have ever been born."'

'Can you both please stop using the word stalking? I'm not sure how comfortable I am with it.'

'Well what else would you call it?' says Maggie. 'I assume your crackpot master plan is to camp out at the front gate until he shows up?'

'Or maybe you could scale a ten-foot-high wall to get in?' Sharon asks hopefully. 'You know, dodging past hordes of salivating rottweilers and alsatians. Then you could break in through a window and try to dodge the alarm's laser beams. It'd be cool, wouldn't it? Like Tom Cruise in *Mission Impossible*.'

Actually, what I'm slightly too shamefaced to admit is

that right up until late this afternoon, that was my plan. Like a good cat burglar, I even had it all worked out, right down to which was the best point of entry into the house. Through the French doors round the back, because half the time Sam forgets to lock them . . . sure I'd be through them in two minutes.

Then it dawned on me. I still have a set of keys.

Ten minutes later and I'm pulling up to the huge iron security gates outside Sam's house. Sorry, make that Sam's palatial mansion. I hit the zapper button on the remote and seconds later the gates glide elegantly open. Sharon's awed into silence, but Maggie's not.

'So, if you lived here, how far away would your nearest neighbour be?'

'About five miles.'

'Feck off! So what happens if you have to run next door for a cup of sugar or a jug of milk? Does one just send one's butler in one's helicopter?'

The driveway is so long that the house isn't even visible for a while; all you can see are vast, rolling, immaculately kept, well-manicured lawns on either side of us.

'Don't know if Ma would be much into this,' says Sharon, head out the window like an over-eager puppy. 'It's all a bit too under-decorated. Not a pretendy Grecian urn or a statue of a naked angel in sight.'

Then I turn a bend and there it is, glinting in the evening sunshine: Casa Sam. For a second, I see it through Maggie's and Sharon's eyes, thinking back to how wowed I was the first time I came here too. It's the approximate size of a country house hotel, but an uber-posh, five-star one with plenty of room for a golf course in the front garden. In fact, it's so huge that I remember when Sam first took me here, I debated whether I should leave a trail of breadcrumbs after me so I wouldn't get lost.

I'm not messing, it looks like a mini-Versailles, right down to the fifteen-pane, full-length sash windows on each of its double-fronted, mock-Georgian sides. There's even an elegant water feature in front of the main door, which isn't switched on, but still looks so mightily impressive that Sharon actually starts taking photos on her camera phone.

'Ma will get great mileage out of these,' she says to me, by way of explanation. 'You know how much she loves laughing at other people's crappy taste.'

There are two cars in the driveway, a Porsche and a BMW Z4, but I still know just by looking that Sam's not home.

'So who do those cars belong to?' says Maggie, hauling herself out of the back seat. 'The staff?'

'No, they're both Sam's. On weekdays, he always takes the Bentley into work with him.'

'For feck's sake. What is he anyway, a rapper?'

'He's an entrepreneur,' I say proudly.

What's weird is that, even though I wouldn't necessarily have chosen to bring Tweedle Dum and Tweedle Dee along with me for the ride, I'm kind of glad that they can see for themselves first hand the life I actually do lead. OK, so at the moment, I may spend most of my day scrubbing floors and picking up empty pizza boxes, but as a matter of fact, here's my natural habitat. Sleeping on sofas and washing their dirty knickers isn't my normal thing, this is. To the manor born. Funny, but Sam tends to role play a bit when he's down here too, effortlessly slipping into the part of the country squire, right down to the Burberry checked jackets and wellies that have never seen as much as a drop of mud. He doesn't like too many people knowing this; far preferring the world to think he was born and reared in this mock-Georgian mansion, but the truth is he only bought it about four years ago, when he'd made his first €5 million.

The house isn't even period either; it was only built about ten years back by a property developer, who spared no expense in getting the best interior designers to fully kit the place out. So although everything is made to look like it's about 200 years old, it actually comes with all mod cons like underfloor heating and a highly anachronistic indoor swimming pool. And if Maggie and Sharon think this is a sight to behold, wait until they get a load of the place inside. The stone hallway so massive that you could almost have a party in it, the basement wine cellar, the entertainment room, with its own private cinema, Sam even has a bar that serves Guinness on tap. As it is, the pair of them are sauntering around the front forecourt, with Sharon snapping away on her camera phone as Maggie does her best to look nonchalant and not a bit intimidated at all. While standing on a helicopter landing pad.

'You know what? I could *really* get used to this lifestyle,' Sharon laughs over to me, from where she's wandering around behind the fountain. 'I mean, I know Sam dumped you and everything, but I still don't blame you for trying to get him back. I'd do the same myself, even if he was a three-foot-high dwarf with breath like owl droppings.'

She means well, I remind myself, so I force a weak half smile.

'You OK?' she asks, suddenly concerned and picking up on the nervous tension that's practically hopping off me.

'No,' I say back to her in a tiny voice. 'I'm about as far from OK as you can get.'

Thing is, I'm frightened and don't even know why. Which is ridiculous. I mean, this is *Sam*, for God's sake. My perfect boyfriend. Who, granted, may be acting a bit weirdly right now, but who will no doubt return to standard Prince Charming behaviour when this little blip we're going through is sorted out.

Anyway, another deep, nerve-calming breath and I trip up the steep, stone steps to let the three of us in through the huge, heavy oak door, mentally reminding myself of his alarm code. It's an easy one to remember because it's the month and year of his birthday; 081975. Leo, wouldn't you know it? High achieving, driven, successful and doesn't know his arse from his elbow when it comes to women.

I push the door open and the three of us clamber into the hallway, so vast it could easily double up as a cathedral. As the warning alarm beeps, I head for the security box, which is just to the right of the cloakroom as you go in the door, knowing that I've about ninety seconds to punch in the code and deactivate it.

Meanwhile, Maggie and Sharon are strolling around the hall, gazing upwards like tourists in the Louvre museum.

'Get a load of the ceiling,' says Maggie, looking weirdly out of place amid all this neo-Georgian splendour in her favourite Hubba Bubba neon pink tracksuit. 'What did Sam do anyway, have it imported directly from Saddam Hussein's palace in Baghdad?'

If they think that's impressive, I smile smugly to myself as I punch in the alarm code, wait until they get a load of the kitchen, which is so huge, you could have a sit down dinner party for twenty people in it with plenty of room over for dancing on tables later.

I wait for the beep beep warning noise to stop. But it doesn't. Which is a bit odd. I try again. Same code, except this time I do it slower in case I made a mistake the first time. I'm positive I did it properly, but for some reason now a computerised red message is flashing up on the alarm box, saying 'Incorrect code, please retry.' I know you only get three goes at getting it right, so I take a deep breath and really concentrate this time.

One by one, I stab in the numbers, then wait with my heart walloping. No joy. I'm just about to break into a sweat when next thing, disaster. The alarm goes off in all its ear-piercing, glass-window-shattering glory. It's beyond deafening, so much so that I have to stick my two fingers in my ears and mime to Sharon and Maggie to get back outside. The three of us run out to the front garden hands clapped over our ears and mouths agape like three exact replicas of that Edvard Munch painting, *The Scream*.

'WHAT THE FECK DID YOU DO?' I think Sharon's screaming at me, but over the alarm racket I just have to lip read her.

'HE MUST HAVE CHANGED THE ALARM CODE!' I mime back, whipping out my mobile phone to ring him. He doesn't answer and it's ridiculous me leaving a message for him because I can't even hear myself over the unmerciful racket.

Then more panic sets in. His alarm is monitored, so right now, the alarm company are probably ringing both him and the police to let them know that it's gone off. In the panic and the pandemonium, we're all screaming at each other, so completely deafened that I think we'll end up having hearing difficulties for life . . . and that's exactly when a neat little squad car comes trundling up the driveway, blue lights flashing.

In all the sleepless nights I've had since moving back home, and believe me there have been many, I'd sometimes lie awake, staring at Joan's stupid-looking eight-arm chandelier in the TV room, fantasising wildly about possible reconciliation scenarios between me and Sam. Him arriving in his flashy Bentley to Whitehall, walloping on the front door and shoving his way past Maggie and Sharon, sweeping me up into his arms and back to my old life . . . always a particular favourite. Him have a screeching go at Maggie for being such a minging cow to me this last while, resulting in Joan's revolting plates being hurled around the room by the two of them like flowery peach-ringed missiles, also made it into my top five. But never, in my greatest, wildest flights of imagination did I imagine this. That I'd be sitting in Kildare Police Station, with Sharon and Maggie on either side of me, facing some highly embarrassing questioning from one Superintendent McHugh. Who's a perfectly nice man, kindly in a patrician, fatherly sort of way, but clearly has me written off as some kind of lunatic/stalker/amateur burglar who's crying out to be admitted to the nearest day care unit.

'And these are your two sisters, you say, Miss Woods?'

'*Step*sisters,' Maggie snaps back. 'Which means we're not actually related at all really. Just in case you were thinking that insanity runs in families.'

'What's of concern to us, Miss Woods, is why a valid key holder wouldn't be aware of a change in the alarm code.'

'But as I've explained to you time and again,' I insist

firmly, ready to leap up and start thumping on the table like they do in all those miscarriage of justice movies, 'the owner of the house, Sam Hughes, has been out of the country for a while and . . . you see, the thing is that he must have changed the code before he left.'

'Without mentioning it to the key holder? Seems a bit odd, wouldn't you think?'

'I promise you, Superintendent; this is all just a silly misunderstanding . . .'

'Jessie just broke up with Sam, you see,' Sharon chips in and I'm sure she means to be helpful but I actually could strangle her.

'Oh, so then you were in a relationship with the home owner?'

'Emm . . . yes.'

'And you didn't think to mention this before? Now why was that?'

'Because . . . I just didn't. I mean . . . that is to say, I didn't think it was relevant.'

'So what was your reason for calling to his home when he wasn't there?'

'Well . . .' *Think, think, think!* 'I didn't know that he wouldn't be there you see.'

'Ah for feck's sake, just come clean, Jessie, will you?' says Sharon, prodding me under the table. 'Then we can all get out of here. You see, Superintendent, basically she was trying to get back with him. That was the plan. I know, I thought it was a mental idea all along too.'

'Can I just point out that I've never, ever done anything like this before?' I plead.

'Well your first time was a roaring success,' says Maggie from out of the corner of her mouth. 'Look, why don't you just plead insanity and then we can all get out of here? And by the way, Guard, can I step outside for a cigarette now? I'd nothing to do with any of this and I haven't even had dinner yet.'

Then another Guard comes in, a woman this time about Joan's vintage, who briskly plonks a polystyrene cup full of milky tea in front of the Superintendent and is about to turn on her heel to leave when . . . disaster . . . she recognises me.

'Excuse me, it's Jessie Woods, isn't it?'

I nod and manage a watery half smile, thinking *Shit, shit, shit.*

Last thing I need is this leaking to the papers.

'I thought it was you. Almost didn't know you with the red hair. Sorry about what happened to your show and everything.'

'Ehh . . . thanks.'

'Don't suppose I could get an autograph, could I?'

'Yes, of course.'

'Thanks.'

'You're welcome.'

'It's not for me, of course. I never watch lowest common denominator television. It's for my daughter.'

'Oh. Right then.'

'And just to let you know, Superintendent, Mr Sam Hughes has just arrived and is ready to identify Miss Woods now.'

No, no, no, no, please for the love of God, noooooo. I do NOT believe this.

But before I have time to gather my thoughts, Sam is being ushered into the tiny questioning room, all good humour and bonhomie and radiating his usual bullet-proof self-confidence. He doesn't make eye contact with me, just instantly identifies the Superintendent as the main man in all of this, and torpedoes straight in on maximum, high-alert charm offensive. It's Sam at his most gulp-inducingly handsome, dazzling best. A terrible misunderstanding, he beams winningly, flashing a smile that practically pings. Perfectly easy to explain away though. Quite simply, Miss Woods wanted to collect some of her belongings from the house and hadn't realised that the alarm code had been changed. So awful to have involved the police in all this . . . such a storm in a tea cup and profuse apologies all round.

'Ah, sure, not at all,' says Superintendent McHugh good-humouredly, already like putty in Sam's hands. 'We just can't be too careful now can we? And of course when we found Miss Woods at the property with no positive identification on her, we'd no choice but to bring her in for questioning. Standard procedure, we'd do the same for anyone, ha, ha, HA.'

During all of this, I'm completely agog, having forgotten the sheer force of nature that Sam can be. And now that we're sharing the same airspace again, I'm also silently willing the oxygen to stop my body from shaking. It's tough though, because as he's chatting away, a whole kaleidoscope of memories keep flooding back to me, including one particular gem; the first time Sam ever said he loved me.

We were on a mini-break in Venice, I remember. He was there on business and I flew out to join him for the weekend. We had two blissfully romantic days of pure luxury in the Cipriani Hotel . . . well, that is to say, it was blissfully romantic in between all of his business meetings. But then, I knew he was going to be busy, Sam's always busy. Anyway, on our last night, at my insistence, we went on a gondola ride through the city. I had it all planned, I'd even smuggled along two snipes of pink champagne for us to sip while gliding under moonlit bridges through the twisting canals. I'll never forget it, maybe I was a bit tipsy, but I snuggled up into him and whispered that I loved him so much, that he was the single best thing that had ever happened to me. Then, in the half-second delay before he answered, his iPhone rang and he answered it, telling me it was important and that he had to take it.

If he doesn't say it back to me, I remember thinking while he took the call, *I will jump into this canal right here and right now*. He didn't. At least not in so many words. But what he did say later on was, 'I heart you.' The L-word, he explained, doesn't come easily to him, which I understood perfectly. I mean, aren't all Alpha males a bit emotionally retarded when it comes to expressing how they feel? So, 'I heart you' became our little private in-joke, which we'd say to each other last thing at night and at the tail end of phone calls if we were apart. And that's what I'm thinking as I look at him now, all tall and commanding, explaining everything away. *I heart you, Sam. So, so much.*

Somehow, it all comes to an end and we do actually get out of there, but the next few, awful minutes are a nightmarish blur. Us being ushered out of the cop shop and blinkingly pouring out onto the street outside. Me, Maggie, Sharon . . . and Sam.

'Emm, by the way, these are my sisters, Maggie and Sharon,' I say to him, to break the silence more than anything else, as the tension between us is starting to crackle like an electric current.

'*Step*sisters,' says Maggie, scowling at him and lighting up a fag.

Sharon, meanwhile, is gazing up at him fascinated, like he's some kind of alien from another planet. But then there's not too many blokes with Rolex watches, Prada loafers and Bentleys hanging around Smiley Burger in Whitehall. I throw her a quick flash of a warning look, mainly because knowing Sharon, there's a fair chance she'd ask him straight out if he's any single friends he could match her up with.

Next thing, Sam politely excuses us, then grabs my arm and firmly steers me away from the others and towards where his car is parked, a few feet away. I look up at him, determined to let him speak first. But when he does, it's not what I expected at all.

'I could have pressed charges back there, you know,' he says coolly. 'Trespassing on private property? Letting yourself into my home without my permission? How would you like it if I pulled a stunt like that on you?'

No, no, no, no, no, no, no. This is not how this conversation is supposed go. There are coherent sentences ready formed in my brain. Trouble is, not one them will come out.

'What exactly were you thinking?'

I manage to stammer out something about the article in the paper about him coming home early from Spain and how rumours were flying around that this meant he wanted to get back with me, but he immediately cuts me off. This is all because of one crappy piece in a gossip column? At my advanced stage of working in the media, don't I realise that journalists make stuff up? Besides, the only reason he cut his holiday to Spain short was because he was asked to deliver a keynote speech tonight at the K Club on start-up businesses. Which is where he's meant to be right now.

On and on he goes, working himself up to a crescendo of quiet, understated fury. Detail always coming before emotion. He'll get his people onto this straight away, he says and with great luck, maybe, just maybe, it can be kept from being leaked to the papers. And I can hand him back his house keys right here and now so there'll be no repeat performance of this horrible, horrible evening.

Sam never raises his voice, ever, and somehow when you're on the receiving end of a tongue lashing from him, it makes it all the more intimidating.

But there's no calling me Woodsie, like he always does. No 'I heart you.' I'm rooted to the spot, staring at him like an imbecile with nothing to say for myself. And still he goes on. Why was I pestering him with phone call after phone call? And harassing Margaret in the office too when she'd quite enough to be getting on with? Wasn't it obvious that he didn't want to speak to me? Didn't I understand what was meant by 'taking a break'? Then the real killer. The one that makes my heart physically twist in my chest. Maybe, he said, maybe there was a time a few weeks ago after the split when he might have considered a reunion, but now it's out of the question. Not after this. The subtext being: because who wants to be with some kind of obsessive, house-breaking bunny boiler?

I don't even bother defending myself. I just stand there taking it. Like an abused wife who somehow feels it's all her fault in the first place. Because he's right. I have behaved like a woman demented. I deserve my carpeting from Axminster. I'm not quite sure how much longer I can stand it without my eyes beginning to seep and I'm determined not to let him see me crying. But as usual, my body lets me down. I hear sobs and realise they're coming from me.

Then, sure enough, the tears start to fall. Big ugly tears too that signal to Sam he should run as far away as possible but under absolutely no circumstances get involved. A second later it's all over. And I really do mean, all over.

'Gotta go,' he says brusquely. 'I was just about to start my speech at the K Club when the call came for me to drive here to troubleshoot this. Little did I guess I'd end up having to deal with all this crapology.'

He's leaving. Really leaving this time. Getting into his car to go. Out of my life forever. I'm on the pavement beside him, numbly willing him to say something else to me. Crapology can't be the last word he ever says to me. It just can't.

Next thing, the window of his car glides down and he sticks his head out. His sunglasses are on now, so I can't make out his expression. Irritation? Annoyance? Or, worst of all, pity?

'Oh and by the way?' he calls back to me, revving up the car to pull out.

'Yes?'

'The red hair is bloody awful.'

Half an hour later, I'm sitting in a pub across the road with Maggie and Sharon. They're both stuffing their faces with sausage and chips swimming in a disgusting, gloopy-looking oniony gravy while I nurse a brandy, shaking and shivering, looking and feeling exactly like a car crash victim. I don't even remember much about how we ended up here. All I know is that after Sam whooshed off, I felt exactly as if someone had just stuck their fingers down my throat and squeezed right down into my bowels.

Then I remember Sharon and Maggie's voices beside me,

bickering amongst themselves. Maggie threatening that if she didn't eat a proper dinner within the next five minutes, that she'd torch down the whole town of Kildare, which with her wouldn't necessarily be an idle threat. So they linked me, one arm each and dragged me into this pub.

Anyway, now that the pair of them have eaten and are happily rubbing their tummies waiting for dessert to arrive, they're both in miles better form and are actually making touching little efforts to drag me out of the deep mire I've sunk into. Without even realising it, they're fully obeying all ex-boyfriend break-up rules. Rule one: they're both bitching about Sam as much as is possible. Rule two: they even order a second brandy for me. Which, considering I can't afford to pay for it, is more than kind. It takes ages to come, so long that Sharon snaps at the lounge boy, 'How exactly is that brandy getting here anyway? By Saint Bernard?' Also, the pair of them are missing all their soaps just to sit here. Which is the equivalent of diehard soccer supporters missing the FAI cup final, just to put it into context. Even Maggie, who loves nothing more than kicking me when I'm down, is keeping her claws well and truly reined in. Which, just for tonight at least, I appreciate.

'Tell you something,' says Sharon, 'I've seen Sam Hughes's photo in the paper loads of times, but up close, he's not even all that good looking. He has very tufty hair for starters. Even worse than Simon Cowell's.'

'And the head is nearly a perfect square,' Maggie throws in. 'He's built like a rugby player, but with a really stupid-looking unibrow.'

'And here's another thing,' says Sharon, 'he was really angry. Vicious. White hot anger. Never seen anything like it.'

'How exactly is that supposed to cheer me up?'

'Well if the movies of Sandra Bullock have taught me anything, it's that the opposite of love is indifference. Now you can say what you like, but he was definitely not indifferent to you back there. So from now on, the best thing you can do is to deflect indifference with more indifference. Then you'll be grand.'

You're quite wrong, I think, looking dully at her. *The opposite of love isn't indifference. It's disembowelment.*

'Or else, if you fancied a laugh,' says Maggie, hauling herself up to go outside for a fag, 'I could get him audited for you? If there's anything he hasn't declared to the Inland Revenue in the last few years, even as much as a pair of jocks, we could make life very uncomfortable for him.'

I just sniffle by way of a response. Sorry, but it's all I'm able for.

'Ah for fuck's sake, Jessie, you're going to have to snap out of this. I don't think I can put up with you trailing around the house out of your brains on whatever pills Ma's been slipping you for the past few weeks. The guy's a prick and the sooner you draw a line under this the better. Simple as.'

'Yeah and I mean, it's not like he ever asked you to marry him or anything, now did he?'

'No. No, you're right. He never did.'

MAY

JUNE

Chapter Twelve

OK, good news and bad news to report. First, the good: I'm no longer sleeping on the sofa at home any more. I know, miracle. Sharon, in a flush of generosity which I'll forever be grateful for, took pity on me and said that from now on it would be OK if I crashed out on a makeshift fold-up bed in her room. A vast improvement to sleeping on the bum-imprinted sofa downstairs, let me tell you.

We've become close, Sharon and I. She's been helping me and I've been helping her. Every spare minute we have, we're online vetting out suitable men for her and weeding, as she puts it, the WLTMs (the Would Like To Meets) from the RAMFs (the Run A Mile Froms). Then, at night, we lie awake giggling and messing and talking about boys and about some of the more eejitty email replies she's got, usually until Joan wallops on the bedroom door and tells us both to shut up, that we're keeping her awake.

So it's kind of like being a teenager again, minus homework/spots/hopeless crushes on band members/older, unattainable boys in school. I swear to God, this is doing me good on several levels. Renews my faith that love and romance do exist in the cyber world, if nowhere else, for starters. And any topic of conversation that takes my mind off that other matter can only be a good thing, can't it? We've reached an unspoken agreement in the house to draw an iron veil over that bowel-withering event back in April and the general embarrassment of my carry-on, which is probably just as well. Even Maggie, queen of the quip, has left me alone and hasn't had a go at me. At least not on the subject of He Whose Name Shall Forever Remain Unspoken, that is. On just about everything else, though, she's the same as she ever was, a wise-arse that looks like she's about ready to throttle me if I as much as look sideways at her.

After said event, Sharon told me in no uncertain terms that I'd made the big romantic gesture, it blew up in my face, so therefore it only proved the theory she'd espoused all along. Namely that Sam was never anything more than a big knobhead with no knob. Furthermore, she reckoned that his behaviour towards me that horrible night was exactly the electric shock treatment to the heart which I needed to jolt me back to reality. From then on though, she started to monitor my behaviour and began by stealing my mobile from my handbag and deleting Sam's number, as well as removing the photo of him and me together on a Caribbean holiday, which I had kept as my little screensaver. Her heart was in the right place, I had to keep telling myself, even though it was a complete waste of time, I've had that number memorised pretty much since the day he first gave it to me.

Then, as we lie in our beds at night, she often tries to get a laugh out of me by imagining all sorts of wild and wacky 'serves him bloody right' scenarios. Since we've broken up, he's turned to drugs and has now mortgaged his life away to support his two grand a day habit, is a particular favourite.

'Or, hang one, I've a good one,' Sharon said to me hopefully one night while she stared at the ceiling smoking a fag and I tried to get into one of her Danielle Steel novels. 'Did you ever think that he might be gay and is only realising it now? I've seen it happen before, you know. Toxic bachelors who flit from girlfriend to girlfriend but never settle down; next thing, before you can say Gianni Versace, they've gone and shacked up with some skinny-arse David Furnish type.'

'Where exactly have you seen this before?'

Someone on the street maybe, I'm thinking? Some local hot gossip I don't know about?

'On *EastEnders*. Sorry, when I said I'd seen it before, I didn't mean in real life. By the way, do you think I'd sound more glamorous to fellas if I changed my name?'

'Changed it to what?'

'Shazwanda.'

'Ehhh . . . no. Definitely not. Now, goodnight . . . Shazwanda.'

Heartache, I've decided, is a bit like measles; the later it comes to you in life, the worse it is. But now that the healing has begun, in my quieter, calmer moments, and with the benefit of hindsight, I've come to accept the following: if Sam is able to deadhead me out of his life so easily, then our entire relationship was a bit like Communism; good in theory but lousy in practice. Yes, he knew every incarnation of me, from humble runner in Channel Six to weather girl to fully fledged TV presenter. But the one incarnation of me that he couldn't handle was unemployed loser. Which, when you think about it, says far more about him than it does about me. And my contacting him all the time was, to borrow Sharon's metaphor, a bit like her relationship with Pot Noodles. Irresistible in the short term, deeply satisfying and nigh on impossible to say no to, but afterwards you're guaranteed to feel like complete shite and end up hating yourself even more for not having any self-control. Sharon's very fond of any metaphor that involves food.

So, anyway, I've stopped. No phone calls, no incessant texting; I don't even read the papers just in case there might be a bit of gossip about him. Like a recovering alcoholic, I'm taking it one day at a time. But right now I'm almost seventy days without contacting him and as far as I'm concerned, that's one of my proudest achievements.

Anyway, only middling news about Sharon's love life to report. After intensive site-trawling, and much gentle guidance on my part, she did eventually whittle all the guys she'd been in regular contact with down to one special someone. A guy called Dave who worked in IT: thirty-five, separated, no kids. Looked cute in his photo, even if it was hard to tell, given just how far he was standing away from the camera. The only tiny point in his disfavour was that, during a late-night email to Sharon, he made the cardinal error of letting it slip that she appeared to watch a lot of TV, whereas he was someone who found real life far more stimulating. It took me several hours to convince her that this was actually a perfectly normal stance and that he wouldn't necessarily be alone in thinking so. Anyway, they got to a point where they were messaging every day, sometimes several times a day and when the time finally came for them to meet up, she was up to high doh with excitement. Her cunning plan was to meet for dinner somewhere posh in town; a proper, grown-up date, right down to beard rash and love bites to show for it at the end of the night, with any luck.

Bad idea, I argued, hating that I had to play devil's advocate, but knowing I'd no choice. You can get to know so much about a person online, but the one thing you can't ever gauge from a computer screen are the mysteries of human chemistry. Supposing you meet and within five minutes you realise you don't fancy him. Then what? You end up bored stupid and yet still having to get through a two-hour meal that could end up costing you a week's wages, that's what. Or worse, and really I hated saying this, but someone had to; suppose he stands you up and you're left in a swishy restaurant on your own with a glass of tap water in front of you? No, far, far better to meet in a coffee shop for the first date. That way, it's only half an hour and if you do get on, then it's a doddle to arrange to see each other again. But if you don't, then you've only wasted thirty minutes and the price of an Americano.

'Then there's the other huge advantage of a coffee date,' I added smugly.

'Namely?'

'You can tell a lot about a guy from the way he drinks. Example: if he blows on a coffee, chances are he's ultra-cautious in bed. And if he slurps, then you can bet he's a sloppy kisser.'

'Jeez, you should do this for a living.'

So before we knew it, Sharon was going to loads of bother getting ready for her big date. I took full charge of her makeover, something I'd been itching to do for a long, long time, and even bullied her into making an appointment at Joan's salon to get something done with the awful hair. As if that wasn't enough, I also plucked every single excess hair from her eyebrows and amazingly, managed to talk her into tackling her moustache, which, after much whinging about how painful it would be, she eventually did. She even treated herself to a brand new pair of jeans and I found a cute little vintage Whistles twinset lurking at the back of Joan's wardrobe which fitted her perfectly. Then we jointly raided all my stuff in the garage and rummaged out one of my Birkin bags, as well as some costume jewellery earrings and a necklace for her.

Overall effect? Complete transformation.

Maggie's comment? 'I think you need more accessories. Like a pimp and a lamp post, for instance.' Then, when Sharon was out of the room, Maggie turned on me, snarling, actually *snarling* that if anything happened to hurt Sharon, she'd hold me personally responsible. I got defensive, muttering something about how it's better to have loved and lost than never to have loved at all (it's all the Danielle Steel I've been reading), and Maggie's response was, 'Oh please. Just look at the state you have her going out the door in. Why don't you just drop her down the docks in a pair of hotpants?'

I said nothing to Sharon about this exchange, just silently reminded myself that people always want you to reflect their status in life so they can feel good about themselves. Which has to be the only reason why Maggie's so threatened by all this. She's single and therefore wants the whole house to keep her company.

Joan, on the other hand, was completely fantastic about the whole thing. I actually think the thought of one of her daughters out dating might even have propelled her into one of her good moods. The only slight problem being that a lot of her well-intentioned dating advice clashed violently with mine. Example: me gently guiding Sharon to be funny and warm but still to keep something in reserve, on the grounds that it's never any harm to cultivate a bit of mystery around guys. Whereas Joan told her, 'Put on your available face and remember you've just had about a twelve-year dry spell, so best to grab whatever you can get your hands on.'

Then, I was coaching Sharon to keep a close eye on the time, and after about forty minutes, to let on she had to leave. To say she'd a pressing engagement elsewhere, on the showbiz principle that it's always best to leave 'em wanting more. Whereas Joan told her she was more than welcome to bring him home, so she could get a decent look at him for herself and furthermore, if he fancied staying overnight, she'd even cook him a big fry-up for brekkie the following morning.

'Jeez, could you imagine that?' Sharon muttered to me on our way out the door. 'Me bringing the poor eejit back here for the first time and Ma waiting here for us? And you know what she's like; the nicer she'd be to him, the more she'd frighten him off. Like some kind of giant dating scarecrow.'

Anyway, I borrowed Joan's car and dropped Sharon off at Starbucks in Dame Street, right in the middle of town; her nervous as a kitten and me fully immersed in my role as relationship guru, calmly assuring her that I'd dropped a lot of babies in the bathwater in my time and that they'd all been absolutely fine.

I was so full of high hopes that it all might go somewhere but . . . disaster. I hadn't even made it back to Whitehall when my mobile rang. Sharon, in tears, wanting to be collected. Now if she'd been stood up it mightn't have been quite so bad, but what happened was far, far worse.

Your man arrived in, took one look at Sharon, then said he'd forgotten to feed the meter back where his car was parked. And never came back again, the bastard.

'I've never felt so humiliated in my whole life,' she sniffed in between fags on the way home. 'And I flip fecking burgers for a living. It was like his lips said no and his eyes said read my lips. Useless gobshite.'

So, basically, it's one-nil to Maggie.

I'll never forget the row that night. Mainly because, for once and most unusually, it didn't happen to involve me. In fact, I was innocently loading the dishwasher in the kitchen when, from the TV room, I heard the highly unusual sound of Maggie having a go at Sharon. 'You see? This is what happens when you turn a gobshite like Cinderella Rockefeller into your new best friend. Bet she's having a right laugh for herself over this. Getting you done up like a dog's dinner and all for some fella who took one look at you and then ran.'

'Leave Jessie out of it, will you? This wasn't her fault. How could it have been? Just back off and give the girl a break, will you?'

'And, unsurprisingly, you're sticking up for her. My my, we're very matey these days, aren't we? Sharing the same room, all gossip and chats and trawling the computer together looking for complete tossers you'd run a mile from if you met them down the local. She's playing you like a violin and you can't even see it. She's wormed her way into your life purely so she can get what she wants. And she's succeeding too; she's got you to share your room with her and now she has you and me at each other's throats.'

'You know something, Maggie?' says Sharon, sounding stronger than I think I've ever heard her before. 'When

Jessie first moved in here, we gave her all of our shittiest jobs to do, totally on purpose. And she did them and she never moaned or complained. Not once.'

'Oh please, Jessie Woods and manual labour lead mutually exclusive lives.'

'Would you listen to yourself? Why don't you just stop being so down on her all the time? And while you're at it, you can bloody well stop being so down on me too. Because I'm fed up being on my own—'

'You're not on your own . . .'

'I'm fed up doing nothing but watching TV night after night and most of all, I'm fed up of being single. I'm only thirty-two for feck's sake and I'm sick of Ma having a better social life than either of us. I don't want you and me to end up being two weird old ladies who the kids on the street all call names at and play knick-knock on our door then run away.'

'What is going *on* with the pair of you?' I can hear Joan yelling down from the top of the stairs.

'NOTHING,' they both yell back up in perfect unison.

'Well can't you keep it down then?' Joan shouts back. 'And if there's blood spilt on a carpeted area, you'll have me to answer to.'

A slam of the bathroom door and the row continues, but in lower voices this time.

'It's like this,' says Sharon, a bit more calmly. 'I want a fella and I'm going to do my best to get one and maybe it won't work out, but at least I'll have tried. At least I'll have got my arse up off the sofa and actually tried to get something that I wanted out of life, for a change.'

'I do *not* just sit here with my arse on the sofa night after night . . .'

'Maggie, take a look at yourself, will you? There's so much more you could do with your life. Jeez, you're the funniest, sharpest person I know and you're always saying that being a stand-up comedienne would be your dream job, aren't you? You'd be amazing at it and what's more you know you'd love it and you could do it in your sleep. But no, you're content to just crash here on the sofa night after night watching repeats of the same programmes time and again. Well I've have enough. I want more.'

'Hang on here a minute . . .'

'Because if it's one thing I have learned from having Jessie around, it's this. These are the golden years when we prove our mother wrong. And that's what I intend doing.'

Door slam. Exit. Just like in a soap opera.

I was standing in the kitchen, tea towel in one hand, the other hand over my mouth, hanging on to every word. But I could only think one thing. *Bravo Sharon.*

More news. About two weeks ago, Emma called over bright and early one morning. She rang first to see if I was free (Me? *Not* free? Now there's a laugh) so I gave her directions and an hour later, she was sitting at our kitchen table drinking coffee out of one of Joan's gakky peach mugs. It was so lovely to see her, I almost had to fight back the tears. We've been in touch on the phone, of course, but it was just so sweet of her to take the time and trouble to look me up all the way out here in Whitehall.

She looked as gorgeous as ever, in one of her neat little newsreader suits with her usual pristine grooming. Tanned and golden too; she and her boyfriend Simon had just come back from a week in Portugal, where they're planning to spend this Christmas. She invited me to join them, which was more than kind, but short of my winning the lottery between now and then, I'd say there's zero chance of my being able to go. Bless her, she even admired my new redhead look. But as she chatted on about everyone and everything back at Channel Six, it was beyond weird being reminded of my old life. Of what might have been.

Anyway, she had a meeting recently with Liz Walsh, the Head of Television, and it's looking likely that she'll be given her own talk show to spearhead the late summer/early autumn schedule. Something primetime too, and no one deserves it more. Emma didn't even condescend or patronise me by commenting on shall we say, my reduced circumstances, just kept telling me that somehow everything would work itself out and in the meantime, she was only on the other end of a phone if I ever needed her.

Ever the lady, she even chatted away to Joan, after she'd eventually hauled herself out of bed and come downstairs to discover a bona fide TV star sitting at our kitchen table. Needless to say, Joan instantly snapped into one of her better moods at the very sight of Emma and made a point of getting a few shots of her on her camera phone, 'So I can show all the girls later on in work, don't you know.'

Then, between the two of them, they came up with an idea for me to raise a few extra quid; finally selling the bag loads of stuff belonging to me in the garage. One of those gak jobs I'd intended doing ages ago but just never got around to. I think mainly because it would mean really saying goodbye to my old life, like cutting the very last tie. But on the other hand, I desperately needed the cash and when Emma said she knew of a second-hand clothes shop in town which only took designer goods, handbags and shoes etc., then gave you a percentage of the profits, it seemed as good a time as any to get cracking.

'What a wonderful idea,' Joan chirruped, looking fondly at Emma. She reckoned that if I was going to do a massive clear-out, then it would be the perfect opportunity for her to throw out a pile of Sharon and Maggie's crappy old clothes too, which she could then leave down at the local Oxfam; a job best done when the pair of them were safely out of the house at work.

'No time like the present,' Emma said gamely, volunteering to give us a hand as she had the rest of the morning free and even offering to drive me to the second-hand store, seeing as how her car had a massive boot that held loads. So for the next hour, she and I ploughed our way through all my bin liners in the garage, ruthlessly purging anything that I had a reasonable chance of making a few quid out of. Prada dresses, Vuitton luggage, Jimmy Choos, the works.

Having Emma beside me was amazing; I really did my best to mirror her positive, can-do attitude and didn't allow myself to wallow about the happy days when I actually used to wear all this gear, just kept focusing on the fact that I might end up with extra cash and not a minute too soon. The only things I held back on were a few jeans and tops which I definitely would need, a suit in case a miracle happened and I got a job, plus a few accessories like scarves and bits of costume jewellery which I thought Sharon might get some wear out of. In her own words, she was 'reworking her look', so anything I thought would look good on her, I kept. But nothing more.

I needed money far, far more than I needed memories.

Meanwhile, upstairs, Joan worked her way through Sharon and Maggie's wardrobes and filled no fewer than four black bin liners with the more offensive and gakkier of their tracksuits, sweatshirts and jumbo-sized underwear. So by lunchtime, the three of us were all set to go; Emma and I to town in her car and Joan to the Oxfam shop down the road in hers. We loaded up both cars with the black sacks and went our separate ways; Joan practically making poor, patient Emma swear on the Bible to call back and visit us sometime very soon.

Now, you might think that was all very straightforward and simple, but like so much in my life, it quickly turned to disaster. By way of farce. Emma and I arrived in town at a store called Second Avenue and the sales assistant told me to empty all the clothes out on the counter so she could have a look. Which I did.

I stuck my hand into the bin liner nearest to me and out came ... not one of my Prada dresses or a beautifully elegant Jimmy Choo sandal, but Maggie's most revolting tracksuit, the one in bright Hubba Bubba pink. Panicking, I spilled out the rest of the bags all over the shop floor; same thing. Maggie's horrible gusset tights, nighties belonging to Sharon with holes in them, knackered bras with hooks missing and knickers, long gone grey from years of washing. None of my designer stuff, not a single thing.

Which meant that somehow the bags got mixed up and right about then, every stitch belonging to me was sitting in Oxfam. Where I'd never get as much as a bean for it. I'll never forget the horrified look on the shop assistant's face when she politely but curtly told me that she was terribly sorry, but really this wasn't the type of thing they were looking for at all. And later on, as we drove past the charity shop, sure enough, I saw a model in the window wearing my Marni evening dress and a pair of my good Manolo

Blahniks. Emma even tried to make me see the positive side: Oxfam would now make a killing on my stuff and it would help all the poor starving babies in Africa, etc., etc. She was right of course, but I was still ready to sob my heart out with mortification and silent fury. The dress in the window had never even been worn. I could still see the tag on it.

Anyway, she drove me to my front door and, as I stepped out of the car, a few of the kids on the street recognised her and were over like bullets demanding autographs and photos on their phones. Then of course, our street being what it is, the neighbours had to check up on the commotion outside, so they all joined in, scrambling over each other to shake Emma's hand, like she was visiting royalty. But she greeted everyone warmly, signed every single autograph and took on board every comment like, 'Ah love, could you not put in a good word to get Jessie back on the telly again? She's like a recluse here. Never even comes out for a chat, just runs to and from the car with a baseball cap and sunglasses on her.'

Which, I know, gave me more than a touch of the Norma Desmonds from *Sunset Boulevard*, but then that's my neighbours for you. Well intentioned but cutting. Hence my long-term survival policy of avoid, avoid, avoid. Emma of course just laughed and smiled and took it all in her stride. And when she finally had to leave, she hugged me tightly before slipping into her car, zooming out of my new life and back into my old one.

And now . . . Ta-da! . . . the actual good news. I have a job. Don't get too excited though. It's nothing like what I used to do. At all. Not by the longest of long shots.

How it came about was thus: my emergency dole money finally came through, but honest to God, by the time I paid Sharon back what I owed her, not to mention the good people at Visa who've set up a 'long-term debt repayment schedule' for the rest of my natural life, there was nothing left over. Nada. And I hated borrowing more, particularly from Joan who's one of those people who hold a bad debt over your head like a whip.

That aside, having feck all to do day in and day out was certainly contributing to the low-level depression I'd been going through these past few months. And, in a funny way, seeing Emma again brought it all back to me. In times past, I was just like her; always on the go, busy and active from the minute I hopped out of bed to whatever God-awful hour I crawled back into it again. And, OK, a lot of that time was spent getting myself into toxic debt, but you get the picture. Being busy = good for me. Earning cash = even better.

I rang my poor agent Roger so many times in the past few weeks that I almost formed a mental picture of him waving his monogrammed hanky at his assistant and mouthing at her, 'If that's bloody Jessie Woods yet AGAIN, tell her I'm not in and no, there are NO JOBS.' And it's not just in the entertainment industry either. No one's hiring anywhere. NO one. Not the huckster shop down the street, not in the takeaways, not even in our local Maxol garage. Believe you me, I've tried them all. This is the first summer in living memory when even students can't get part-time jobs and anyone lucky enough to have a Saturday job is politely but firmly being let go.

Plus, there's the slightly bigger concern. I'm not exactly trained to do all that much, am I? I mean, yes, I did a certificate course in media training years ago, but since then my work experience to date has all involved doing wild and wacky dares, bits and pieces of freelance reporting, pointing at areas of low pressure on chromo-key maps and acting as general dogsbody to a lunatic. And I'm up against college graduates with BAs and MBAs and MAs hanging out of their earlobes. You know, useful qualifications.

Then there's the other, slightly more delicate problem. Who wants to hire someone who made such a spectacular show of themselves live to the nation? When there's a queue forming behind me of, let's just say normal, reliable, more trustworthy candidates? The problem was driving me nuts and I was on the verge of throwing in the towel, when, not for the first time, Sharon came to my rescue.

About a week ago, she bounced home from work so delighted with herself that I thought some handsome, TV-addicted, fast-food-loving stranger had walked up to her and asked her on a date. But it turned out to be even better.

'News for you,' she beamed. 'You'll never guess, so don't even try to. Smiley Burger are looking for a new crew member and guess who has an interview tomorrow morning? You do! I had to put in a good word for you though, but don't let on we're sisters or else they'll all think it's nepotism.'

Useless my protesting that I know as much about the fine art of burger-making as I do about flying the space shuttle, Sharon was having none of it. Think of it like one of your dares on telly, she said. A child of five could do it and in fact, if it was up to Larry the boss (who they all call Larry the Louse) he'd have the kitchen entirely staffed with underage kids like in a Chinese sweatshop, just so he wouldn't have to bother paying them minimum wage.

Then there was the small question of wages. €9.31 an hour. Which works out at a bit more than €446 per week, if I can manage to work a six-day week. Exactly *double* my dole money. It would mean I could finally start paying my way at home and therefore be exempted from doing all the housework. And just the very thought of never, ever having to stand in that God-awful, long, snaking queue at the dole office is enough to have me grabbing Sharon's uniform, name badge and hat and running down to Smiley Burger to start chopping gherkins right now.

Sharon even spent hours coaching me through the type of questions I was likely to be asked at the interview. Interview, I thought? Surely I just turn up, fill out an application form and get kitted out with a uniform straight away? You'd think that, but no. Apparently, I'm expected to wax lyrical about all their products and as Sharon put it, show that I actually do eat the shite.

So she gave me a crash course on every single thing they make, Smiley Burgers, Smiley Fries, Smiley Shakes; they even do a whole range of low-fat Smiley Calorie-Counter meals, all of which taste like cardboard and by the time you add on the Smiley Salad Dressing, end up with exactly the same fat content as a big, greasy burger and chips. But there again, I'm quoting Sharon.

Then, on the morning of the interview, when she spotted me getting into my usual jeans and a casual top, she almost had a coronary. 'Jeez, smarten up a bit, will you? Larry the Louse will be interviewing candidates kitted out like they're going to appear in court. People with actual degrees. So cop the feck on.'

I did what she said, albeit a bit sulkily, thinking, Yeah right, degrees in what exactly? How to deep fry chips?

Anyway, I did manage to find a solitary Peter O'Brien crisp, tailored suit among the few clothes I'd held on to for just such an emergency, so I shoehorned myself into it and off I went. And bloody glad I was too that I wore something demure, mainly because Larry the Louse spent pretty much the entire interview staring at my chest. Honestly. He's well named too, he actually does have a lousey look about him, with eyes that bit too close together and teeth that bit too pointy and sharp. And when he wasn't looking at my chest he was looking at my legs, one or the other. The git never even asked me a single thing about all the crap I'd memorised; how many calories were in a Smiley Chicken Salad, was the beef in the burgers one hundred per cent locally sourced and organic? No, all he wanted to know was did I regret leaving Channel Six and whether or not Emma Sheridan was single. Dear Jaysus help me.

I must have done something right though, because the last thing he said to me was, 'So, when can you start?' And as I stood up to shake his hand on my way out the door, he leaned in and gave me a highly inappropriate peck on the cheek. Now there was a layer of skin I'd be exfoliating later.

So now I'm one full week in the job, it's Saturday lunchtime and today I'm being trained on the till. At all times remembering the two Smiley catchphrases, which have been drummed into me: 'Did you want fries with that?' and my personal favourite, 'You have a Smiley day now!'

Till duty is actually considered something of a promotion here, mainly because on hygiene duty, you're expected to mop floors and clean toilets which most of the staff hate and despise. I'm not so bothered though, as let's face it, up until a few days ago, I was doing all that stuff at home anyway, for free. But interacting directly with customers has caught me a tiny bit off guard, mainly because, new-look red hair or not, I'm quietly terrified that someone will come in and recognise me as 'your one who got fired off the telly'.

It's also very busy. Packed. Now this is a hectic branch at the best of times, given that it's near the Omni Park shopping centre and also fairly close to the airport, but it's one o'clock now, peak lunchtime and the queues are long. Six of us are working flat out on the tills, including Larry the Louse who's supervising on this shift and who's right beside me, taking let's just say more than a keen interest in everything I'm doing.

Anyway, my head is down and I'm slaving away, taking orders, accepting cash, handing out food the second it's come from the sweatshop of a kitchen that's steaming away at full throttle behind us. I glance up, checking to see how many customers are left in my queue . . . and that's when I spot them. Eva and Nathaniel standing in my queue, while their two little twin boys run riot around the place.

No, no, no, no, no, no, no, no. This can't be happening, this can't be happening.

'Josh? Luke? Come back here this instant or else there'll be no TV when you get back home!' I can hear Eva shrieking.

It is happening. OK, the main thing is to stay cool and calm. They haven't seen me. I can still get out of here. There's still time. Think, think, think . . .

'Emm, Larry? Can I go on my break now?'

An irritated, rodent-y glare from him. 'What are you talking about? You've just had your break.'

Shit. Eva and Nathaniel are getting closer now, as the queue moves on, so close that now I can hear them rowing.

'Nathaniel?' she's griping at him. 'I don't see why we couldn't have gone to the Four Seasons to feed the kids. You know I hate them eating this rubbish. It's utter junk, full of nothing but wheat and E numbers.'

'For the thousandth time,' I can clearly hear Nathaniel replying, 'because I am NOT driving all the way home with the kids wailing at me that they're starving. You're the one who wanted them to sleep on the flight instead of letting them eat the airline food. I'm tired, I'm jet-lagged, I'm stressed and as far as I'm concerned, they can eat whatever crap they like if it'll just shut them up so I can drive home in peace.'

I chance a lightning-quick upwards glance at them and notice that they're all suntanned, wearing 'just stepped off a long haul flight'-type gear. Eva's in chinos and a T-shirt, with a very new-looking set of highlights glimmering through her long, swishy hair.

'Well, the boys will just have to eat in the car,' she moans, sulkily. 'Because if you think I'm sitting down in this kip, you've another think coming. Someone might see us.'

'Small chance of anyone we know being in a dump like this.'

'Well you needn't bother ordering anything for me. I wouldn't eat the food here, not if you dragged it through a pool of disinfectant.'

'Larry,' I say, getting panicky now, as they're only two places in the queue away from me. 'Emm . . . I need to . . . use the bathroom. Now. Dire emergency.'

'Well you should have gone when you were on your break, shouldn't you?'

Bugger him anyway. If Sharon was supervising today, I'd have no problem, but, as bad luck would have it, it's her day off today.

'*Please* Larry,' I beg, the hysteria in my voice rising up another notch. 'It's—' Then I have the brainwave of seeing whether embarrassment will get me further with him than pleading. 'The thing is, you see, I have, well it's . . . women's problems. Time of the month, you know . . .'

He sighs deeply, like it's not the first time this one's been pulled on him. 'Right then. When you finish dealing with these customers, you can take five minutes and no more.'

A glimmer of hope. I might, just might, get out of this and live to tell the tale. I serve the customer in front of me as fast as I can and am just about to make a run for the sanctuary of the staff loos downstairs . . . when hope dissolves like a Smiley Muffin in the rain.

'Two Smiley Meals with Smiley Juices and a Smiley Latte,' Nathaniel says, with his head in his wallet, counting cash and not looking at me.

'Ehh . . . sorry sir, this till is closed,' I mumble, head down. Then I think, disguise my voice. *Now*. 'If you wouldn't mind using the till just here,' I add, in a crappy attempt to pull off a Cork accent.

'Don't be ridiculous. How can you be closed when you just served the family in front of me? Now get me two Smiley Meals . . .'

Shit. He's looking directly at me now, really staring.

'Dear God, I don't believe it! Jessie? Jessie Woods? Can that really be you?'

I blush like a forest fire as clammy, cold flop sweat breaks out all over me. Down my spine, everywhere.

'Jesus Christ, it *is* you! What's with the funny accent?'

'Emmm . . . sore throat,' I cough weakly.

'Eva? Come here, wait till you see who it is!'

No, no, no, no, no, please let there be an earthquake or some global catastrophe right now, just so I can get out of here . . . But Eva, who'd disappeared down to the back of the queue to chase after one of the kids, is straight back up to us.

'Jessie? I don't believe it! What are *you* doing here?'

'Emm . . . well, long story, you know . . .'

'And you're a redhead!'

'Ehh . . .'

'Are you doing this, like, for charity or something?'

The loudest scream is slowly starting to build up inside me, gathering strength like a tidal wave. 'No you fecking dopehead, I am not standing here, in a revolting brown stripy uniform with a matching, equally vomit-inducing hat, waiting on you for *charity*. I'm doing it because I need the money. I got fired from my job, remember? Now piss off and let me get back to work.'

I don't say that aloud of course. Mainly because Larry the Louse is right beside me and if I do, I'll be flung straight back on the dole for insulting customers faster than you could say P45. Now the thing is, if Eva had looked me in the eye and been straight with me; if she'd said something along the lines of, 'I'm so sorry, this is awful, this is rubbish, that your once fabulous life has come to this . . .' I might just have been able to handle it. Because honesty goes a long way with me. But she didn't. Instead she went down the Marie Antoinette route of patronising me so much, that only the threat of losing a job I was lucky to get in the first place prevented me from flinging a scalding hot Smiley Tea into her immaculately spray-tanned face. She actually pats my hand and says, 'Well, it's *so* wonderful to see you back working again! This is terrific for you and . . . hey! Congratulations! Right then . . . we'd better get going now. Must dash! Lovely seeing you!'

They don't even wait for their order, just bolt out the door, the whole family and I swear to God, as soon as she's safely outside, I see her through the glass doors whip out her diamante-encrusted mobile to call, oooh, probably everyone she's ever met in her entire life to tell them. Including, it goes without saying, He Whose Name Shall Forever Remain Unspoken.

No time to brood though. Or get angry. Or even call Sharon to tell her that I've pretty much had a shovel just taken to my insides. Because Larry the Louse, who's famous for inflicting petty torments if you dare annoy him (he's not unlike a prison warder that way) takes me off till duty and puts me onto mopping the floors. Fine. In the mood I'm in. Because frankly, I feel like a Viking village right after being pillaged. Five minutes later and I'm furiously bashing the mop off table legs and chairs, white hot with rage and full of smart-alec indigestion of all the things I should have said to Eva and Nathaniel when next thing, someone grabs my arm. A man's hand. Connected to ridiculously long legs that are in my way.

'So do you charge extra for wiping my shoes or what?'

'Sorry sir,' I mutter, not meaning it. Actually thinking, move your fecking feet, moron, can't you see I'm trying to clean up?

'Jessie, it's me.'

For the first time I look up and . . . it's Steve. Hannah's big brother. Oh shit. Oh bugger. Steve Hayes that I abandoned to Joan that horrible night, when he called to the house with flowers and . . . OK, gotta get out of here.

'Oh, hi Steve. Look, emm . . . sorry about, you know . . . everything, but I really better get back to the kitchen . . .'

'Jessie, sit down.'

I don't know why I do as he says. I rarely do what anyone tells me. But now I'm sitting opposite him, in a Smiley booth, looking straight into the big blue eyes and there's no getting out of this.

'OK. Here goes,' I sigh deeply. 'I know that what I did that night was unforgivable . . .'

He waves this away and instead leans forward, pushing a Smiley tray out of the way and focusing on me directly. 'Jessie, are you OK?' he asks, concerned.

'Emm . . .'

'I don't mean to be nosy, but I was standing in the queue just now and I saw those people you were talking to. Tell me to mind my own business if you like, but whatever they said seemed to upset you.'

'Long story,' I say wryly.

'People from your past life? Gave you grief about working here?'

'How'd you know?'

'Wild guess. Tell you what you should have told them though.'

'What's that?'

'That you're on the witness protection programme. That would have shut them up pretty pronto.'

I smile in spite of myself. Then I remember. I still owe him an apology. 'Steve, that night when you called to the house, I have to explain what happened. I feel awful about it. You see, well . . . I had to be somewhere, it was important, so important that I wasn't even thinking straight . . .'

'You don't need to explain,' he smiles.

A nice smile. Friendly and warm.

'No, I really do . . .'

'No, you really don't. Sharon told Joan who told my mother who told my sister who told me. About, where you rushed off to that night and . . . well, about what happened when you got there.'

Shit. I'm always inclined to forget that life on our street is lived under a microscope. Even if you're a semi-recluse like me. Everyone knows everything. It's like if one neighbour hears you sneeze at 9 a.m., by 9.30, someone will have knocked on the door to say they heard you were laid up with a terrible dose of pneumonia.

'I'm sorry you broke up with your ex. But if you don't mind my saying, what an arsehole.'

It's the first time all day I've cracked a smile.

'I'm also glad you didn't end up with a prison record for breaking and entering.'

'So am I.'

'So you're one of the Smiley crew now.'

Absolutely no judgement in that statement.

'Yeah, and I was lucky to get any kind of job at all. Anyway, speaking of which, I'd better get back to work, or . . .' I glance over to the tills to see Larry the Louse glaring at me and pointing at his watch.

'And do you enjoy working here?' he asks innocuously. Faux-casual.

'Come on Steve, what do you think?'

'It's just that, if you didn't, I might be in a position to offer you something else. Something let's just say a bit more suited to your talents.'

An utterly unfamiliar sensation washes over me: hope.

Chapter Thirteen

I think Sharon's met someone. Can't be too sure until I worm the whole story out of her, but when I get home from my shift later that night, she meets me in the hall wearing a smart new jacket, fully made-up with her hair all washed and glossy. Then she stuns me by saying that we're going out for a drink. Which is so completely unheard of in this house for anyone other than Joan, that I have to ask her to repeat herself.

'OUT out? Outside of the house? Like as in . . . away from the TV?'

'What's wrong with that? It's a Saturday night and we're going out. Like people do.' Then, dropping her voice, she adds, 'I've something to tell you, and we may as well get out of here so we can chat properly.'

She gives me exactly two minutes to whip off my minging Smiley uniform and change into jeans and a T-shirt and next thing, we're out the door and on our way down to the Swiss Cottage, leaving Maggie in the TV room all on her own for her usual Saturday night telly-fest of *American Idol* and *X Factor*.

Fifteen minutes later, we're tucked into a fairly quiet corner of the pub, with two glasses of Bulmers in front of us. Funny, but I'm actually developing quite a taste for cider these days.

'I've news for you,' she says, taking a big gulp out of her drink.

'I've news for you too, but you go first.'

'Oh Jess, I've met someone. OK, pause for reaction.'

I ooh and ahh accordingly, prodding her for more info.

'Well, you won't believe it, but he's actually nice and normal. At least I hope to Jaysus he turns out to be nice and normal and not, like, emailing me from a prison library or something.'

'Tell me everything,' I say firmly, taking a sip of the cool, sweet cider. 'And omit no detail, however trivial.'

A quick, grateful smile from her. 'He's called Matt and he's an actuary, whatever the feck that is.'

'Oh, something to do with working out probabilities, I think. Like when you go for insurance, they calculate whatever the likelihood is of your having an accident might be. Pretty much the same with the online dating, if you think about it. Didn't I tell you that it was a numbers game and that if you just stuck with it for long enough, then in all probability you were bound to meet someone?' I grin, delighted to be proved right. For once.

'An actuary,' she says, slowly. 'Jeez, I hope he doesn't turn out to be some kind of anorak, train-spotter type. You know, the sort of eejit who goes out to the airport on Sundays just to look at the planes. A gobshite, in other words.'

'Well, you won't know until you meet him, will you?'

'Well when I do meet him, you've got to get me ready for the date and drop me off too. As far as I'm concerned, you're part rabbit, Jessie.'

'What?'

'You know, a bit like a rabbit's foot. I need to rub you for luck.'

I let that hang, thinking that I didn't exactly bring her much luck last time around. Then something else strikes me. 'Of course I'll drive you to your date, hon. But this time I've a tip for you. Maybe best to say nothing at home, for the moment at least. If things don't work out, it's hard enough to cope with your own disappointment, as well as having to cope with everyone else's as well. If you're with me.'

'Yeah, but I'm still wary, Jess. I mean, you would be too if you hadn't been with a fella since the Clinton administration. And that other gobshite who took one look at me in Starbucks and ran away did nothing for my confidence, I can tell you. Maggie still slags me about it.'

'He was your Defibrillator Guy, nothing more,' I say firmly.

'My what?'

'Defibrillator Guy. The one who brings you back to life after you've been off the dating scene for a while. Or possibly, you could call him your Sight of Land Man.'

'Explain?'

'You know how, centuries ago when explorers went in search of continents to discover? They'd always see a sight of land first. Like a small island or something. It wasn't what they were searching for, but it was a sign that you were almost home and dry.'

'Oh, right yeah, I get it,' she nods. 'I'm nervous though, Jess. I mean, this guy Matt sounds lovely. He keeps messaging me all the time saying he's dying to meet up, but suppose he turns out to be just another eejit?'

'Then we write him off as Knock Off Guy and move on.'

She looks at me, so I explain, 'Knock Off Guy? You know, one that initially seems to be the real thing, but when you get to know him better, he's just like one of those Prada handbag knock-offs. Looks the biz short-term, but ultimately you know it'll only fall apart in a few weeks.'

'You are really good at this.'

'Well, I used to be out there, you know, at the dating coalface. Before I met, well . . . you know. Before.' Not an avenue of misery I particularly want to reopen, so instead of going down that route, we keep on messing and inventing dating code words and silly nicknames for guys. As the cider kicks in, we've pretty much devised the Jessie and Sharon Woods Definitive Dating Guide.

The Punxsutawney Phil of dating is one. Someone who takes one peep at what's on offer out there, then shrivels back into their nice, warm, cosy lair and stays there until winter's safely over. Runway Guy is another. In other words, a fella who may as well have runway lights leading from his hall door to his empty double bed, wanting sex from you but very little else. And needless to say, the minute you sleep with him, you'll never hear from him again. Guaranteed. Then there's Pamplona Guy. One of those fellas that, when you're with him, it's the greatest adrenaline rush ever, but ultimately you know you're going to end up getting gored alive.

'Or Air Bag Guy,' I suggest to Sharon, who's guffawing so hard I'm worried she might bring up an organ.

'What's that?'

'When two guys approach you in a bar and only one is interested. But he's too nervous to get chatting to you on his own, so he brings a pal with him, on the understanding that if you give him the brush-off, then the friend is his air bag.'

'Canary Guy is what I'd christen him,' says Sharon. 'You know, like when they used to send canaries down coalmines years ago, to see if there was anything doing?'

We both fall around laughing and I get up to order another round, delighted to actually be able to pay for it with money that I actually worked hard for and earned myself. Funny, the little things that can fill you with pride.

Anyway, the pub is filling up in earnest now and as I'm standing at the bar waiting to be served, more than a few people come up and say, 'Howaya Jessie?' like they've known me for years. I just nod and smile back, a bit annoyed with myself for being terrified about getting out and socialising locally, among neighbours. In fact, when I look back now, I'm completely mortified at how ridiculously agoraphobic I used to be. What exactly did I think would happen anyway? The worst thing anyone could possibly do is laugh in my face and I'm feeling so strong in myself now, that if that happened, I'd just tell them where to go. Or else set Sharon on them.

No, everyone's being lovely, really concerned about me in fact. A few people have even asked me if I'm OK tonight, which is more than kind of them. Then, on my way back to Sharon with the drinks, I see Mrs Foley and Mrs Brady from our street sitting companionably at a table together side-by-side, nursing small whiskeys.

'Jessie?' Mrs Foley calls me over. 'I just want to say it's great seeing you out and about this evening. You're dead right, love. Feck them all anyway!'

'Absolutely,' Mrs Brady nods in agreement. 'Best thing you can do is to be seen in public with your head held high. Fair play to you, Jessie. Don't let the bastards get you down, I always say!'

I smile and thank them, then head back to Sharon. 'Ehh . . . why is everyone being so nice to me?'

'Because we're nice people, dopey. Why do you ask anyway?'

'Because, well, there's being nice and then there's being a bit too nice.'

The mystery deepens two minutes later when Joan breezes in, dressed in scarily matching colours as usual (canary yellow tonight, and where she managed to find a handbag that exact colour is beyond me), and is greeted by a huge round of applause. Suddenly it seems like everyone in the pub is clapping her and she obliges by doing a little twirl and a bow, then spots us in the corner and totters over on the heels. In great form tonight, as it happens.

'Well there you both are, girls!' she smiles. 'I was wondering where you pair were hiding. Maggie's at home spewing fire at being left on her own, you know.'

Sharon and I look guiltily at each other. But then, that's one particular bridge we'll just have to cross later on, isn't it? And preferably the more canned up we are for that, the better. I don't know, maybe it's because Sharon and I have grown closer, or maybe it's seeing Sharon actively looking for love online, but honest to God, these days Maggie is acting like the poster girl for anger. And why she can't express it by coming out and getting drunk like the rest of us, is beyond me.

'What was all the clapping for?' I ask Joan, deliberately changing the subject. For a second innocently wondering if it was because of her outfit.

'Oh, you mean you didn't know? Because this evening . . .'

'What she means to say is that, this evening, she has

rehearsals for the *musical* you're putting on, don't you Ma?' Sharon interrupts, warningly.

'Oh, ehh, yes, we've a musical soirée in the back room here later on. Doing *The Mikado*, you know,' she adds uselessly, but it's already too late. My suspicions are well and truly aroused. The game is up a second later when a chunky, florid-looking middle-aged man slips his arm around Joan's waist and tells her that she's a fine-looking woman and that she should appear on TV more often. Then, as he escorts her to the bar to buy her a Chardonnay, I turn on Sharon.

'OK, nice cover-up, but would you please mind telling me what Joan was doing on TV tonight?'

But no sooner have I asked the question than the answer begins to dawn on me. Oh dear Jesus. I am such an idiot to have even forgotten in the first place. In the end, Sharon and I say it together. 'The documentary.'

I slump against the wall of the bar and rub the cool glass over my forehead, like a cold compress. Of course. The *A Day in the Life* programme which was shot over the most monumentally awful twelve-hour period of my entire professional career. And of course, Maggie, Joan and Sharon would all have featured in supporting roles, given that they were interviewed for it way back when. I can't believe I'd edited it out of my mind.

'Let me get you another drink,' says Sharon, concerned.

'No. Just answer me one thing. How bad was it?'

'Well, I didn't see the whole thing, because you literally came in the door just before it was over, but what I did see ... really wasn't that bad at all,' she lies.

'That's why you were anxious to get me out of the house tonight.'

'Sorry about that. I didn't want you to get upset. We all said some things in it that, well, that weren't very fair. Me and Maggie particularly. And I'm sorry, Jess, I really am. It's just I didn't know you then like I know you now. But if that same crowd came to our front door tomorrow, I'd say very different things. I'd tell them how cool and fantastic you are. I'd tell them that . . . that . . .'

'You don't have to finish that sentence,' I interrupt, afraid I might just start getting teary and emotional. 'But, still, thanks for starting it.'

'But I really want you to know something, Jessie. You're my best friend.'

Now I'm touched. Really touched. 'Thanks, Sharon. You're my best friend too. I wouldn't have got through the past few months without you.'

'And I'm sorry for calling you a loser.'

'You didn't call me a loser.'

'I did in my head.'

'Come on,' I say, all decisive. Determined not to get sentimental and to put the whole shagging documentary thing clean out of my head. That was my old life and this is the new. Simple as that. 'Let's get another round in. Let's stagger home tonight as stewed as newts.'

'Now that's the kind of nagging I can live with,' grins Sharon. 'Sure, we have to toast the end of your first successful week working in Smiley Burger anyway, don't we?'

Shit. Can't believe I still haven't told her.

'Erm . . . Sharon? There's something I need to say to you too. Are you drunk enough that you won't be annoyed with me?'

'Hang on a sec,' she says, knocking back the rest of her Bulmers in a single gulp. 'OK, shoot. And if it's something

I'll be furious at, then you're buying me a kebab on the way home.'

'I've handed in my notice.'

It's well after 2 a.m. when we finally stagger home with the intention of crashing out drunkenly on the sofa, so Sharon can have her kebab and I can doze off all the cider. But as it turns out, Joan's beaten us to it and is still up, still in full make-up, wearing a matching nightie and dressing gown and watching herself on TV. Glued to it, in fact.

'Oh girls, there you are, I was just playing back the tape of the documentary. Jessica, come here and tell me what you think of my interview because you know, in the pub tonight, several people were kind enough to tell me I'm a born natural on TV.'

'Tell you what,' I slur, hauling myself up, 'you watch the bloody thing. I'm off to bed.'

'Language, Jessica. Don't you want to see it? It'll be the talk of the street, you know.'

'I'll pass, thanks very much,' I say, half-way out the door.

'You sure?' Sharon says, patting the sofa beside her encouragingly. 'I mean, at least you'd know what people were talking about in the pub earlier. Plus I've lost four full pounds since I was interviewed, wouldn't you like to see that for yourself?'

I stop in my tracks. Yeah, I suppose it's no harm to have a little look, is it? I mean, everyone else will have watched it and by everyone else, I really mean Sam. So why not have a peek with my hands over my face at this car crash piece of telly so I can see for myself how bad it is? After all, I am just drunk enough to be able to take whatever's coming my way.

'Come on, Jess,' says Sharon. 'At least you're seeing it in the comfort and privacy of home. And if it gets too awful, sure you can just leave the room, can't you?'

Right then. I sit gingerly on the edge of the sofa, ready to run out of the room in case anything really horrible is said, and Joan helpfully rewinds the documentary back to the start. It opens with a sort of people on the street-style vox pop.

'Jessie Woods?' says a young girl of about sixteen or so, interviewed outside McDonald's on Grafton Street. 'Oh my God. I, like, never miss her show! She's *so* amazing. And funny and fabulous and cool. I just love, love, love her. If you ask me, I think they should put her face on money.'

'Now what was so bad about that, Jessica?' says Joan delightedly and suddenly I'm able to breathe again. Then they stop a woman in her mid-thirties wheeling a buggy down the street. 'Hang on, you mean the one who presents that crappy dare show on TV?' she snaps at Katie, the interviewer. 'What, are you deranged? I've stopped buying the gossip magazines because I am so sick of reading about her and her fella out partying like it's the last days of Rome. "Super Couple" my arse. Will someone please tell that girl that she's not so much a social climber as a social mountaineer. And that for some of us, there's actually a recession going on.'

'OK, that's it, I'm off to bed,' I say getting up. Had enough. Already.

'No, *wait*!' the other two yell in unison and Sharon forces me back down onto the sofa.

Just in time to see Margaret, Sam's snotty PA, talking straight to camera. 'Mr Hughes is in an important business conference at the moment and can't be disturbed. Though I must point out that he never comments on his relationship with Ms Woods. He did, however, ask me to confirm that he's been approached about taking part in a forthcoming series of *Dragons' Den* and will make an announcement of his own to the press in due course.'

I barely have time to react when next thing Sam's handsome, chiselled face is filling up the screen, gluing me to the seat. It's not an interview though, it's just his photo, while his voice is played over it in the background, sounding like a crackly message left on an answering machine. 'Oh and don't forget to mention that my new paperback, *If Business is the New Rock & Roll, then I'm Elvis Presley*, will be coming out in paperback soon. Available from all good bookstores.' Then a line flashes up on screen: Sam Hughes, entrepreneur, and at the time of recording this program, Jessie's long-term partner. This is an excerpt from a voice message he left to the makers of this documentary, approximately five minutes after we spoke to his assistant.

Joan and Sharon both giggle at this and for once, even I can see the gag. I've never really said it before, but Sam really does come across as someone who'd sell his mother for a scrap of publicity.

Then Maggie's on screen. Interviewed here, in this very TV room, on this very sofa. Puffing cigarette smoke right down the camera lens. 'If you ask me, Jessie should have stuck to being a weather girl. Perfect vehicle for her end-of-pier talents; standing in a mini-skirt and pointing at cloud formations on maps. That sad excuse of a TV show she's on now is barely worth the electricity it takes to broadcast it. I'd tell her myself only we only see her about once a year, at Christmas. For, like, ten minutes. Mind you, I'll give her this much; that last magazine she was on the cover of did come in very handy. To prop up a wonky table leg, that is.'

Sheepish looks from the other two in my direction. And then all the Bulmers I drank earlier just takes over. 'Would one of you please explain to me,' I say, or rather garble, 'why exactly she hates me so much? I mean, what did I ever do to her? It's like her whole chain of rage begins and ends with me. She's permanently down on me and even on the rare occasions when I try to be civil to her, she still ends up having a go at me. Why? That's all I want to know. Why?'

'Oh, come on,' says Sharon between mouthfuls of the kebab. 'You've got to see where she's coming from. When we were kids you were always the pretty one who never got spots and who had boyfriends running after her. And you were good in school, *and* you were popular and skinny. For feck's sake, you never even needed braces. I'm not defending Maggie, I'm just saying, life was very different growing up for her, that's all.'

'You were the apple of your father's eye too,' says Joan, a bit sadly.

'Then when you left home,' Sharon continues, 'every single thing you said you'd do, you just did. It all came so easy to you. Like you led this charmed life. While Maggie was stuck doing the most boring job known to man, day in, day out. I'm not making excuses for her, I'm just saying, she had it far harder than you, that's all.'

I'm temporarily silenced, wondering if we'd ever have had the moral courage to say these things to each other, sober.

Next thing, Emma's beautiful face is on screen. Shot outside Channel Six, very late at night, I'm guessing by how dark it is. 'And how did you feel after Jessie's contract was so suddenly terminated this evening?' I can hear Katie the interviewer's voice probing her. Shit. Which means this bit was taped the night I got canned. Immediately afterwards, I'm guessing. 'Utterly shocked, naturally,' replies Emma. 'However, rules are rules and I'm afraid accepting freebies is just not something any presenter is permitted to do. But of course, I'm hugely upset at this sudden turn of events . . .'

'Very sweet girl,' says Joan over the TV, 'but is she a bit dim, do you think?'

'What do you mean?' I look at her.

'Well, remember the day she was helping us clear out all the clothes from here and the bags got mixed up?'

'Do I remember? Will I ever forget?'

'The funny thing is,' muses Joan, 'that when you were in the garage, I told Emma that all black bags with a red tag on them were mine, so they wouldn't get mixed up. Distinctly told her. Most puzzling that she just . . . forgot.'

Just then my mobile beeps loudly. It went off a few times in the pub earlier tonight, but I was having far too much of a badly needed laugh to pay the slightest bit of attention.

'Switch that thing off, will you?' says Sharon. 'You're distracting me.'

So I haul myself up off the sofa and go off into the kitchen to listen properly. Actually glad of the excuse to get out of here.

'And hurry up, will you?' she yells after me. 'My bit is coming up in a minute.'

Two voice messages and a couple of texts. Both from Amy Blake, one of the runners on *Jessie Would*. A lovely girl, kind of reminds me of myself at her age. Up for it and would do anything you asked without question, just for the privilege of working in the hallowed halls of a TV studio. Both of her messages say the exact same thing. She saw the documentary tonight, felt awful watching it and hoped I was OK. That she'd really enjoyed working with me, was very grateful for the iPod I bought her last Christmas and would love if we could work together again some day (some hope there, Amy love). Then in her second message, she added that she had a whole boxful of stuff from the *Jessie Would* production office which she'd been storing for me, and wondered if I'd ring her so she could arrange to drop it off?

Thank you, universe, I think, clicking off the phone and going back in to watch TV. Yet another reminder of my old life and how it's finally gone forever. Funny though, I'm not nearly as upset as I thought I'd be.

Chapter Fourteen

Right then. Time for new beginnings. The following Monday morning and I can't believe I'm starting my second new job in as many weeks. Steve called and offered to collect me, said he'd give me a lift on the back of his motorbike. I was perfectly happy to take the bus, but he insisted.

'You offer me a decent job and you even take me there on my very first day?' I say to him, smiling. 'What are you, ... the nicest guy in the world?'

'Yup, that'd be me all right,' he grins at me from under his helmet as I strap mine on. 'Atta girl,' he says approvingly. 'Now just hop on. Boy, will this give all the neighbours something to talk about.'

I jump on behind him and grab on to his waist, raring to go.

'Got to warn you, this thing goes fast.'

'It's OK. Speed's not much of a problem for me,' I shout back from under my helmet.

'Well fair play to you, Miss Woods; you're the first girl I've ever taken on this yoke who wasn't petrified with nerves.'

I grin to myself. If only he knew.

Funny, but when he first told me back in Smiley Burger that he might have a job for me, my first thought was, as what exactly? Backing singer in the band he's in? Because, believe me, when I sing, it sounds a bit like nails being dragged down a blackboard.

No, Steve laughed when I shared my worry with him. Not a singing job at all.

Which is how I find myself hopping off the motorbike outside what looks like a perfectly ordinary office block in the centre of town, about twenty minutes later. We're now on Digges Lane, a small cobble-stoned street in the heart of the city, right in the midst of all Dublin's busiest and most bustling bars and coffee shops, and I'm looking at a discreet plaque on the wall which reads, 'Radio Dublin, Marconi House.'

Because this will be my new job. And no, I'm not here to clean the place.

Meet the new presenter of *The Midnight Hour* show. (I know, I can't believe it either.)

Steve parks the bike and leads us both inside, through revolving doors and into the foyer. He signs us both in, then guides me towards the lift and on up to the fifth floor. We step out into a huge, open plan office, with floor to ceiling glass walls full of light and air and with stunning views over the city centre below. As Steve steers me past row after row of desks, it seems like every second person looks up to give him a warm smile and a big, cheery, 'Hi Steve!'

Mostly, it has to be said, women. All young ones, pert and pretty and probably wondering who the redhead trailing behind him is. For a split second, I find myself wondering if he has a girlfriend. Only because, if he were single, there's certainly no shortage of admiring female looks headed in his direction here. It's a tough one to call.

He certainly hasn't mentioned a girlfriend, but then I've so little information about him, how would I know anyway? All I do know for certain is that he lives in an apartment in Santry on his own and, according to Sharon, eats in Smiley Burger a minimum of three times a week. Which now that I come to think about it, kind of does sound a bit like single behaviour.

Anyway, he's teasing bordering on mysterious about his connection to Radio Dublin and how he managed to get me a gig here in the first place. Not to mention the fact that everyone here is warmly greeting him by name, like he's great buddies with them all.

'Oh, just friends in high places, you know yourself,' he grins infuriatingly at me when I ask him for about the twentieth time. 'Come on, let's get you a coffee.'

Next thing, we're side by side in a tiny office kitchenette and he's pouring us out two mugs of fresh brew. Him towering above me, somehow looking even taller in all the biker gear.

Steve's older than me by about three years, which makes him early thirties, but somehow he permanently has a look of someone on a grown-up gap year. An adultescent, if they've even invented such a term yet. Utterly impossible to have a serious conversation with him; everything, absolutely everything gets turned into a joke.

Out of nowhere, a memory from years ago comes back. I remember him, aged about eighteen, out mowing our front lawn and Maggie first nicknaming him the Milky Bar Kid, on account of his fair hair and the roundey John Lennon glasses he used to wear back then. I did nothing whatsoever to stick up for him and now he's like the saviour who rescued me from Larry the Louse and eight-hour shifts of shovelling fries into Smiley cartons. I blush a bit, utterly mortified, then make a silent vow to be super-duper nice to him from here on in. So sweet, it'll nearly give him diabetes. I have a lot of making up to do. Years of horribleness from all the Woods family to atone for.

'So, Steve,' I say, smiling brightly up at him. 'You're in a band, aren't you? Is that how you're so in with the radio crowd?'

'Don't you ever listen to neighbourhood gossip?' he grins, handing me over the mug of coffee. 'Yes, I'm in a band, but only as a hobby. Just for the laugh more than anything else. If you ever heard us play, you'd understand.'

I smile and sip the coffee.

'Actually, we've a gig in Vicar Street at the end of the month,' he says. 'Why not come along?'

Oh shit. Did that just sound like he was asking me out? Because saviour or not, I'm sorry but I do draw the line there. Not only am I not in a place where I could ever look twice at another fella, but . . . I'm just not interested in Steve. Sorry, but I'm not. At least, not in that way. Thing is, I'm the single most monogamous person you're ever likely to meet. Even when I'm grieving the death of a relationship, I still can't bring myself to look at anyone else. No Morphine Man for me (you know, one who's there to dull the pain and nothing else). And now a fresh worry washes over me. Is that why Steve's being so good to me? Because, if so, then I'll just have to nip this in the bud, here and now.

'There's a huge gang from here coming, so you'd be more than welcome. Sure the more the merrier.'

Phew. Not a date then. Hallelujah be praised. All embarrassment avoided. 'Fantastic, sounds lovely.'

'Tell you someone else who'd really love to see you again. Hannah.'

Shit.

I keep forgetting about Hannah. Worse, I'm constantly saying that I'll definitely call over to see her definitely sometime very soon, then not doing anything. I am a horrible person and a very bad friend. Or ex-friend, rather.

'In fact,' Steve grins down at me, 'she's having her little baby daughter christened this weekend, why not come along to the party afterwards? You could bring your family along too.'

'Great!' I say, delighted that yet again, this couldn't sound further from a cosy à deux tête-à-tête.

Next thing, a pale, skinny guy so young he looks like he should still be ID-d in bars comes in and introduces himself as Ian. He's wearing a U2 T-shirt from their 360 tour with jeans and trainers and looks like he survives on about two hours' sleep a night.

'I'm going to be looking after you,' he says, shaking my hand. 'I produce *The Midnight Hour*, but don't worry, there's nothing to fronting the show. Bit like spinning plates in the air and never letting then fall. Piss easy once you're used to it.'

'OK,' I say a bit nervously. 'But here's the bit where I have to tell you both that I've never done anything like this before. Presenting on TV, yeah, but that was different.'

'If you can handle TV,' says Steve kindly, 'as far as I'm concerned, you can handle anything. Ian here will spend the next few days showing you the ropes. Besides,' he adds, playfully punching Ian on the arm, 'nothing this eejit does can be *that* complicated.'

'I'll pick my moment, but I will get you back for that,'

Ian grins back at him, messing, as though they go on like this all the time. 'OK, Jessie, ready when you are. Bring the coffee into the studio with you, it's cool. The station manager here lets us get away with murder.' Then, smirking, he adds, 'He's a terrible gobshite, really. Mind you, I think he's only here on some kind of temporary secondment from St John of Gods. Kind of like a work experience programme for loonies.'

I turn to Steve, 'So, emm, well, thanks for bringing me this far and everything, but . . . what will you do now? I mean will you head off, or . . .?'

'Ehh, Jessie?' says Ian, looking like he can't contain the laughter any more. 'Steve *is* the station manager.'

Without exaggeration, this has been the best week I've had in months. I LOVE my new job so much, I almost wonder why I never got into radio instead of TV in the first place. I haven't started broadcasting yet, this week has all been about training or 'learning the decks' as they say here, but according to Steve and Ian, I should be ready to hit the airwaves as early as next week! I still can't believe it. But from midnight until 2 a.m., the airwaves at Radio Dublin will be mine, all mine.

Everyone at the station is lovely, just gorgeous, full of enthusiasm and energy and if anyone does remember me from my days on *Jessie Would*, they're all far too tactful to say it. So much so that, almost on an hourly basis, I can feel my own buzz slowly beginning to come back to me. The longer I'm here, the more I remember why it was that I fell in love with broadcasting in the first place. Now, the money isn't great, in fact it's not all that much more than I was making at Smiley Burger. Put it this way, I won't be moving off the spare bed in Sharon's room any time soon. But at least I'm able to pay my way at home a bit more now. Properly I mean, instead of borrowing all the time.

My accountant is thrilled too, because she negotiated a deal with the good people at Visa so exhaustive you'd need about five days and a minimum of six barristers to comb through the paperwork alone. Anyway, she came up with a repayment plan whereby I can at least start giving them back some of the dosh I owe, on a weekly basis. It's so little that I think I'll be paying off my debts till I'm about eighty-seven, but, hey, at least I'm solvent again. Oh, and not going to debtor's prison either. Always a bonus.

In fact, the only person who counselled me against taking the job here was, ironically, the one person who I thought would be happiest for me. Emma. 'Oh, sweetie, are you sure this is a good move for you?' she said anxiously when I called to tell her the news.

'Why would it not be a good move?' I asked, puzzled.

'Come on, Jessie, to go from a primetime TV show to a late-night radio gig on a small local station? It's a backward step for you career-wise and frankly I'd be worried about the press getting hold of this and having another go at you. Last thing you'd need. Isn't it best for you just to lie low?'

She was only trying to protect me, I know, but from where I was coming from, anything that got me out of Smiley Burger was a minor miracle to be grabbed at with both hands. I was just a bit surprised by her reaction, that was all. Surprised and if I'm being honest, a bit disappointed.

Meanwhile, Sharon has her first date with Matt the actuary, with a second date lined up before they've even met, as he's insisting on taking her dog racing later in the week and she's already agreed. Said they're getting on so well online that he wouldn't take no for an answer. All against my better judgement, it had to be said, as I'm always a bit wary of things moving too fast, but then, given my unspectacular relationship history, who am I to lay down the dating law?

So, early in the week, as my training finishes at about 6 p.m. and, as Sharon's on a day off, she and I arrange to meet in town at 7 p.m. and I walk her right to the door of the Insomnia café on Dawson Street, punctual to the dot for her very first meeting with him. I even offer to linger around the shops to wait for her, but she waves me away, claiming she already feels like a five-year-old being walked to school.

Gotta hand it to the girl, she's looking well, the make-up (all mine) is flawless, the dark bobbed hair is sitting perfectly and she's wearing yet another new outfit that the two of us went shopping for last weekend, a summery floral dress this time. She didn't want to, but I strong-armed her to buy it, because she looks good in dresses. Very casual and feminine yet kind of sexy too. All part of the image overhaul and I couldn't be more proud of her.

'Want me to come in with you?' I offer as she has a last fag on the street outside before heading in.

'No. But thanks. I'm nervous and I'd only end up biting the face off you. Besides, suppose we both meet him and I like him but you don't?'

'Sharon, I am without doubt the worst judge of character in human history as I think I've already proved. Why would my opinion even matter?' Nice though, that she thinks it does.

'Suppose he has breath like an autopsy?' she asks, fiddling with her hair and starting to sound a bit edgy.

'Then, when I ring you in exactly half an hour with the emergency get-out call, you get out. Simple as that.'

'Suppose he takes one look at me, then runs faster than . . . than a ladder in my tights?'

'In that case you sit there, calm as you like; you sip your coffee, flick through a magazine and then you leave, head held high. It's only half an hour. Thirty minutes, you can do, hon. Now do you need anything before I go? Fags? Money? Pepper spray?'

She just looks at me blankly.

'That was a gag.'

'Oh, ha, ha. Very droll. Look, are you sure I don't look like I'm wearing one of Ma's shower curtains? You'd tell me if I looked crap, wouldn't you? Last time I wore an actual dress was to my First Holy Communion.'

'Come on, Sharon, you look stunning. Now go in there and knock him dead. And remember, it's just a coffee date. That's all. Now what's the worst that could possibly happen?'

'Yeah, you're right,' she nods, perking up a bit and sounding a bit less jumpy now. 'And I mean, as Ma said to me on my way out this evening; it's not like I've a cold sore on my lip and a couple of kids at home, now is it?'

I give her a big bear hug and watch my girl go inside. At this stage it's just after 7 p.m. and, as promised, precisely half an hour later I phone her with the standard 'air bag get-out' emergency call. But she doesn't answer, which I take to be a good sign, so I hop on the bus and head for home.

By 9 p.m. there's still no word from her. So now I've turned into the world's most over-protective mother hen, constantly texting her to check if she's OK, pacing up and down the hallway, worried out of my mind that Matt the actuary turned out to be some serial killer who lured her to the boot of his car and then on to her doom.

Anyway, all my worry was for nothing, because Sharon eventually staggers home at about midnight, stewed off her head, but saying she had a great night. Apparently they hit it off immediately, neither one wanted the coffee date to end, so he suggested going to a movie, then a few drinks afterwards.

'He definitely isn't a core shaker,' she says drunkenly getting into bed while I glare furiously at her, arms folded. 'In fact he looks a bit like . . . well . . . like you'd expect an actuary to look. Short guy too, only five foot five, but says he likes big women. Jeez, wait until he gets a load of Maggie.'

'And would it have killed you to have rung and let me know you were OK?' I demand, with my face like thunder, effectively doing Joan's job for her. 'I've been pacing up and down here, worried sick about you . . .'

'Jeez, come on, Jessie. Can't you just feel what I want you to feel?'

'Which is what?'

'Jealous.'

Two nights later, Matt takes her dog racing. Even offered to pick her up at the house, which I actively discouraged. Waaaaaay too early to meet the Munster family yet.

With Sharon out and about and Joan hardly ever home anyway, it's just been Maggie and me on our own together a lot lately and it's not been pleasant. What's worse is that, ever since my chat with Sharon the night we watched the documentary, I've been trying, really trying to make an effort with her. Complete waste of time though; if I as much as initiate a conversation, all I'll get is a grunt in return. If I'm lucky and she doesn't just ignore me, that is. So most of the time we don't speak at all.

Until the night Sharon's out on her second date, that is. Maggie and I are watching a re-run of *Frasier* when out of nowhere, she turns to me with poison in her eyes and Bulmers on her breath.

'Not happy until you've waved a wand and changed all of our lives, are you?' she almost growls at me from her armchair, holding the fag in her hand like it's a dagger.

I just look at her, determined not to rise to the bait. Trouble is, I've had two tins of Bulmers as well, so if she wants to pick a row with me, I'm just sozzled enough to make a stand against all her bullying and low-level passive aggression. No, on second thoughts, make that her full-blown naked aggression.

'These days, your nickname should be Pollyanna Rockefeller, not Cinderella,' she says, glaring at me with the flinty eyes. 'Personally, I preferred it when you were acting like Cinderella though. You were mildly less irritating.'

OK, I know I shouldn't rise to the bait, but I do. Can't help myself. Sorry, but I've had enough of her sniping at me and it's time to draw the line. What can I say? There comes a time when you get tired of being treated like the antichrist.

'Maggie, when are you going to stop being so angry all the time?'

'On the day that I get married,' she sneers back at me. 'That's the answer you want to hear, isn't it? The only answer a dolly bird like you would understand. So you can give me a makeover too, send me out of here looking like a dog's dinner and force me on dates with complete strangers too. Because in your eyes you're not validated unless you're in a couple. For feck's sake, I think that to a vacuous bimbo like you, the feminist movement was just something that happened to other people.'

I slump back into the sofa, take another gulp of cider and abandon the fight before it even begins. Poor Matt the actuary though, I think, feeling sorry for him before we've even met.

Imagine being introduced into this?

Next day, when I come home from Radio Dublin, there's about half a dozen cardboard storage boxes lying in the hallway waiting for me. Joan's there too, in thunderous form.

'I almost lost the heel off one of my good shoes tripping over this mountain of rubbish,' is her greeting to me, as I let myself in. 'I'm warning you, Jessica, this pile of crap better be cleared out of my sight by the time I get home.'

'This is all mine?'

'No, Pope Benedict's. Who do you *think* it belongs to? Some girl called Amy dropped them off when you were at work. I mean it, I want it all gone by the time I'm back from my soirée tonight.'

Shit, I've had so much else on that I completely forgot. She means Amy Blake, the runner on *Jessie Would*. So sweet of her. Anyway, before I start shifting all the boxes to the safely of the garage, I stop to give Amy a quick call and to apologise for not being here when she called. She answers immediately.

'Hey, it's so good to hear from you!' she laughs cheerily and for a moment it's just like old times. She chats away, telling me she'll be working on Emma's new talk show soon, so she's all buzzed up about that. 'Won't be the same without you though, Jessie. We all miss you so much. You've no idea. The place is dead without you. No one treats the runners like you used to.'

'Aw, thanks Amy. And look, I owe you one for going out of your way to deliver all those boxes. I really do.'

'Not a problem. I'm sure most of it is for the bin anyway, but I thought I should at least let you decide. I found Emma shredding everything in the entire production office right after the show was canned, so I salvaged as many of your things as I could. You never know, there might be something in there that's of use to you.'

I thank her again and as I hang up, we promise to meet for coffee soon. Bit odd, I think as I start shifting boxes. Emma shredding documents in the production office, that is. I mean, apart from anything else, why would she be bothered?

Come the following Saturday and things are on such a sure footing with Sharon and Matt, that not only does she want to invite him to the christening at Hannah's later today, but says he's even insisting on collecting her at our house, so he can give us both a lift there.

Steve made sure I knew that all the family were invited, but Joan is, surprise, surprise, heading off to the Swiss Cottage, this time she claims for a 'business meeting'. She even whispers the word 'business' as if it's all top secret and Donald Trump is waiting in the pub's upstairs room to invest in whatever this mysterious project is. I just smile at her, presuming this is another euphemism for 'wine tasting' but no, she says, it really is business and that she'll tell us all about it 'once the business plan is finalised'. Honestly, there are times when I wonder why she bothers talking everything up with me. I washed her knickers, for God's sake; we have NO secrets.

Anyway, I arrange to meet Steve at Hannah's house that evening, as it's family only at the church bit; the neighbours are only invited to the knees-up afterwards. I'm actually a bit nervous about seeing Hannah after all these years of not being in contact. And I'm even more eager to finally get a look at Matt the actuary.

Under strict orders from Sharon, he arrives to our house punctual to the dot of 6 p.m. and, as Sharon herself is still upstairs drying her hair, I'm charged with letting the poor guy in and entertaining him until she's good and ready to come down. This, by the way, is all on account of some self-help book she read which advises that if a guy calls to your door to collect you, then you should keep him waiting as long as possible, at all costs. Ho hum. Just wouldn't have thought that daft rule would apply in this particular house, but there you go.

Anyway, I trip downstairs and open the door to say hi. Sharon's right, Matt isn't tall, but round and bald with black-rimmed glasses and dressed in an immaculately pressed suit. Hard to tell his age, but I'm guessing that he's looking down the barrel at about forty.

'Good evening. You must be the lovely Jessie, I presume?' he says, holding out his hand.

Formal manners, I think, smiling and shaking hands. Old fashioned. Which is nice, cute and kind of endearing. I make him as welcome as I can, and am about to usher him into the kitchen, when Sharon shouts from the top of the stairs to bring him into the TV room. Where Maggie is watching *Deal or No Deal*, or some similar Saturday evening crap, all while indulging in her favourite hobby: planning out the rest of her night's viewing with the TV guide plonked on her lap. Feeling mortally sorry for the poor fella, I lead him in and introduce Maggie, who's sitting like a sumo wrestler in her armchair, glaring at him with the stony grey eyes. Warming up for the fight.

'And this is my sister, Maggie.'

'*Step*sister.'

Then I offer him a drink. Anything to make the poor fella feel comfortable.

'Coca Cola please, I'm teetotal,' he replies and I swear to God, Maggie's frozen non-reaction speaks volumes.

Then I realise this entails me leaving the room and going to the fridge to get the drink for him, thereby exposing him to Maggie at her foulest, i.e., when her TV's just been interrupted. So I race to the kitchen as quick as I can, but just as I'm coming back into the TV room, I'm in time to catch her saying, 'So, Matt. Are you sure you're not going to try to get me to join a cult? No offence, but you have that look about you.'

I hand him the drink and of course, overcompensate for her horribleness by patting the sofa beside me and asking him to join me. Like some maiden aunt in a black and white film; all I'm short of is a hairnet, a lace mantilla and a pair of knitting needles.

'So, you're an actuary?' I smile.

'Yes, but it's not nearly as exciting as it sounds, you know.'

'That a fact?' snipes Maggie from under a thick cloud of smoke, waves of hostility practically rolling off her.

I think that this is probably the first heterosexual man under the age of forty to have set foot in the TV room since my dad's funeral, hence her reacting as if she's about to wave garlic and a crucifix into the poor guy's face at any minute. But Matt doesn't seem to even notice. Got a thick skin, obviously. Which augurs well.

'It's wonderful to finally meet you, Jessie,' he says to me at one point. 'It's not often someone in my line of work gets to meet a genuine household name.'

'Well, well, well. You must be an actuary *and* a comedian,' Maggie smiles like a cobra. 'Because, let me tell you, Jessie is barely a household name in her own house.'

I don't want to let the entire Woods family down in front of him, so, like the majority of Maggie's jibes, I let it slide. More long pauses, then purely from the point of view of filling up dead air (a radio phrase I just learnt), I pass some inane comment about how lucky we are the weather is so fab, considering the forecast for today was complete rubbish.

'In actual fact, it's nothing to do with luck at all,' Matt explains. 'It's a mathematical certainty that weather forecasters are inaccurate forty-five per cent of the time, so it's perfectly probable that good weather was likely after all.'

A quick glance at Maggie tells me that the probability of Matt being about ten seconds away from one of her nastier, more cutting comments is a dead certainty, but mercifully, Sharon bounces in just then, looking absolutely gorgeous in yet another new outfit that she bought without me. In fact, with the amount of new gear she's been bringing home this week, I'm thinking she must have spent her entire wage packet in the boutiques of the Omni Park shopping centre. Dear God, I have created a shopping addict in my own image.

As we all get up to leave, I make a point of letting Maggie know that she was invited to the christening too and is absolutely more than welcome to join us. On the principle that it's one thing less for her to bitch about later on.

'I'm not much of a kid-lover,' is her reply, puffing smoke at me.

'Are you sure?' I ask, really making an effort here. 'It'll be fun.'

'Oh please, fun? At a christening party? If you ask me, I've always thought the witch in Hansel and Gretel is a deeply misunderstood woman. She builds her dream home and two brats come along and eat it? Deserved what they got really.'

Knew it was a complete waste of time asking her. Dunno why I even bothered. Then Matt's phone rings and as he goes out to the hallway to take the call, Sharon turns to us both.

'Well? Thumbs up or thumbs down? You can tell the truth, 'cos I'm just using him for practice really. My Defibrillator Guy,' she adds, with a knowing look in my direction.

'Well Sharon, I think he's absolutely lovely,' I say, really meaning it. 'Mad about you too. Couldn't take his eyes off you when you came into the room!'

'Jeez, do you really think so?'

'Honestly. He was looking at you adoringly. Like . . . like . . .' I scramble around for a metaphor. 'Like a cute little . . . seal pup.'

'Yeah,' says Maggie. 'That you want to clobber.'

As the three of us head for Matt's car, I turn to Sharon. 'Something has to be done about her. She's been in a bad mood for about twenty years now and I'm not sure how much more of it that I can take. The nicer I try to be to her, the worse she gets.'

'I know,' Sharon nods, as Matt goes to link her arm and she shoves him off. 'But what the hell do we do?'

* * *

Anyway, we drive to Hannah's house, which by car is only about five minutes from our street. Although neither Sharon nor I have ever been here before, you'd know we had the right house from about a mile off. Dozens of helium balloons are hanging off the gateposts, and the tiny driveway is completely stuffed with cars. It's still early but already the party is looking wild and raucous. As we park and make our way to the front door, we can already see the front garden heaving with kids, all playing screaming fighting with each other.

For a split second my thoughts go back to my old life; I remember a children's do Eva and Nathaniel had for their twins where they'd hired an actual string quartet to play and the kids just looked bored off their heads while the adults stood around sipping Bellinis and talking about money. It was so sedate compared to this; a real, old-fashioned knees-up where even this early in the evening, you can see most of the grown-ups slowly starting to get arseholed drunk. I know where I'd far rather be too, I think, gratefully giving Sharon's arm an encouraging squeeze. Among real friends, thanks very much.

Hannah's mum, Mrs Hayes, answers the door and it takes a second for her to recognise us.

'Oh my God, Jessie? Is that you under all the red hair? Sure I'd hardly know you! Hannah will be absolutely thrilled you came by. She's upstairs changing the baby, but the minute she's down I'll let her know you're here. And Sharon, I barely recognise you, you're looking so well and so SLIM! Come in, come in and welcome!'

We introduce Matt and she's so warm and lovely to him as well that it instantly takes me back to when I was a teenager, permanently lounging around her house. Never once did this generous, kind-hearted lady ever make me feel like I was just another kitten sharing the litter tray. At a time when money was tight for everyone, I think she must have guessed that things were rough at home for me and just automatically included me in all her own family meals and activities with no questions asked, bless her.

'Mrs Hayes, I'm so sorry I haven't been round to see you before this,' I make a point of saying, feeling the apology is necessary.

'Don't be daft, Jessie. We're old friends, aren't we? And old friends don't stand on ceremony. Steve tells me you're doing a great job down at the radio station; but you'll have to play a request for me, won't you? Promise?'

'Faithfully promise,' I smile at her, thinking how lucky he and Hannah were growing up with a mum like this.

'"Yesterday" by the Beatles will do me grand, love. I'm sixty-five years young next Monday, so if you could play it for me then, it would really make my day.'

'Consider it done.'

Other guests arrive hot on our heels and Mrs Hayes turns to greet them, so Sharon, Matt and I work our way across the packed living room then on through to the kitchen. There's at least three generations of families here, all having a blast. I walk past a teenager who looks barely old enough to drink saying to his mum, 'I swear I'm *not* pissed! I only had nine!' Then I see a woman about my age breastfeeding a kid who looks old enough to eat Smiley Burgers. Funny being at a christening when you're single and childless; it's like the life you never had flashes in front of your eyes.

'OK, there's the bar, straight ahead, twelve o'clock,' Sharon says, picking her steps across a train set that a gang of kids are fighting over on the floor. Just then, Matt reaches out to take her hand. Which again, she shakes off. I'm not making any comment. Just noticing, that's all.

When we get to the kitchen, it's even more jammers, this time with people battling over the food laid out on the kitchen counter. I'm just about to suggest we go out to the back garden when a hand grabs me by the shoulder.

Steve.

'Hey, you made it, didn't think you were coming!' he says bending down from his ridiculous height to warmly peck me on the cheek. There's a very tall, pretty brunette at his side with poker straight hair down to her bum which she keeps swishing over her shoulders, and trendy square glasses that make her look like an architect. He introduces her as Elaine but she doesn't shake hands, just hovers proprietorially at his shoulder, clutching a glass of white wine. So I introduce Matt to Steve, then point out Sharon. It's hysterical, his eyes nearly bulge out of their sockets when he cops a load of her.

'Wow, Sharon? Is that you? I mean . . . you're looking . . . I mean, you must have lost . . . and the hair . . .' Then he just laughs at himself in that permanently good-humoured way that he has. 'What I'm actually trying to say is that it's good seeing you again and nice to meet you too, Matt. Now what'll you all have to drink? In case you hadn't noticed, Hannah has me doing barman for the night. All tips gratefully received.'

After taking our orders, he tells us to go on out to the back garden where it's a bit less crowded and that he'll bring our drinks to us there. So out we troop and bump straight into Mrs Foley and Mrs Brady, sitting like twin sentinels on two plastic garden chairs. The pair of them give Matt a very obvious once over, then demand to know who he is. Sharon stays to introduce Matt and is clearly having a great time seeing the looks on their faces when they clock that she's on an actual date. With a normal enough looking fella, to boot.

I let her have her moment and move on, trying to find somewhere for us all to sit. Eventually I spot two free kitchen stools at the very bottom of the garden, so I leave them empty for the others and plonk down on a kid's swing seat, glad of a bit of peace and quiet after the mayhem of the house. Steve's out a few minutes later balancing a trayful of drinks which he hands out to Sharon and Matt, then spotting me, ambles down the garden in that long-legged way he has, sitting on the spare swing seat beside me. We chat a bit about work and he asks me how I'm feeling about going live on air next week. Can't wait, I tell him, enjoying the drink, the late summer evening sun and the conversation.

'We're all very proud of you down at the station, you know,' he smiles.

'Why's that?'

'Oh, you know. Coming from the height you were at professionally, to a late-night/early-morning slot on a small local radio station. Plenty of celebs would have had a complete diva fit, but not you. You just bounced in, knuckled under and got on with the gig. No airs and graces at all. I really like that. We all do.'

'Are you kidding me? Steve, you're the guy who rescued me from flipping Smiley Burgers, chopping gherkins and asking bratty kids if they'd like fries with that. As far as I'm concerned, if you'd offered me a job washing the windows at Radio Dublin, I'd have considered it a step up in the world.'

'You seem so fine about what happened. I'm not sure I'd be as cool about the whole thing as you are.'

'Well, I wasn't. Not for a long, long time. But I am now. At least, I'm getting there. And getting this job has been a big part of that, let me tell you.'

Suddenly he gets serious. 'You know, Jessie, I saw that documentary about you. That *A Day in the Life* thing. It was horrendous and I'm not the only person who thought so. Did you ever consider the possibility that you might have been set up?'

I shake my head and smile. 'Listen to you, you've been watching waaay too many conspiracy movies.'

'Maybe,' he grins. 'But think about it and ask yourself, was there anyone who stood to gain by getting you out of the way?'

'Oliver Stone himself couldn't have come up with a better concoction.'

'Sorry,' he says, shaking his head. 'It's just, watching that programme, there was something not quite right about the whole thing.'

'Steve, the only person who set me up was myself. Believe me, I've been over and over it a thousand times in my mind and the only conclusion I can come to is that, just like in the fable, I flew too close to the sun on borrowed wings and paid the ultimate price. I learnt a huge lesson though. The hard way, the way I seem to learn all my lessons in life, but there you go.'

'Jessie Woods, you're without doubt the spunkiest, bravest girl I know.' He's looking at me a bit more intently now.

'Not a bit of it,' I laugh off the compliment. 'Just getting on with things.'

'I can't imagine what it must have been like for you

though. There were so many shots of you in that incredible mansion you used to live in. To go from that to living back at home . . .'

'Sleeping on the sofa, by the way . . .'

'With Maggie and Sharon . . . although I have to say, Sharon's changed so much since you came back into her life. It's like she's a different person. Not just her appearance, she's . . . I dunno . . . softer somehow. If that makes any sense.'

'She's been terrific. Throughout all of this. She even apologised for the things she said about me in the documentary.'

'Good,' he nods, looking into the middle distance now, where some kids are having a water fight with the garden hose. 'Because some of what was said . . . well, no matter now. All I'm clumsily trying to say is that you've had quite a journey in the last few months and I think you're incredible to have come out fighting.' A sideways glance at me, then he qualifies it. 'That is . . . what I mean to say is, I think you're handling it incredibly well.'

'Well there you go. That's my life story,' I grin back. 'I'm the original Celtic Tiger cub who fell to earth.'

'But who lived to tell the tale.'

In the distance, just coming out of the house is Elaine, the swishy-haired girl, head swivelling around looking for Steve. She spots him and strides down to where we're sitting, not saying much, just glaring at me through the architect glasses as if to say 'Push off, babe, your time's up.' Unsure of what the story is between them, I leave them alone, with the excuse I'm going inside to look for Hannah.

I eventually find her in the TV room and just seeing her

again after all these years brings so many memories flooding back. She's the same old Hannah though. Tall and lean like Steve, with blonde hair (natural, natural, natural, used to make me sick with jealousy years ago) and not a single gram of baby weight on her.

'If somebody doesn't turn off that fecking Beyoncé Knowles song, I'll throw the CD player out the window!' she yells at her husband Paul.

'Ah, come on, it's catchy!' says Paul.

'Yeah? So is thrush.'

Definitely the same old Hannah. And if I'd thought it would be awkward meeting her for the first time after so many years, I couldn't have been more wrong. Thank God.

'Sorry,' she says distractedly. 'I hate that song. Gets into your head and stays there for three days. This is the first chance I've had in twenty-four hours to sit down and relax with a glass of wine, and that crap song isn't going to ruin it for me.'

'It's good to see you, Hannah,' I say, clinking glasses with her. 'And congratulations again. Your daughter is a little beauty. Just like her mum.'

'Tell that to her father. I had a fight with Paul on the way to the church because he said the baby looked like Khrushchev. Then he tried to qualify it by saying that ALL babies look like Russian premiers. There was nearly a riot in the car.'

I snort laughing, visualising the scene only too well.

'Well, it's lovely to see Paul too. You must be thrilled to have him home safe.'

Paul's a cadet in the army and only just back from a tour of duty in Chad. Hasn't changed a bit since I last saw him though; still wiry and muscley, with absolutely no neck at all. Just a head, then shoulders.

'Good to see you too, Jess,' she smiles, collapsing exhaustedly onto the sofa beside me. 'I wasn't even sure whether you'd come or not. I know you've been lying low lately. And I don't blame you either.'

'I'm sorry, Hannah, I really am. I should have called months ago, but half the time I could barely haul myself out of bed.'

'Can't have been easy. Especially for someone like you.'

I just look at her, wondering what she means, someone like me?

'You were always so driven, I mean,' she says, by way of explanation. 'As long as I've known you, which is a long, long time, babe. Right the way through primary school, right up till we finished secondary school, even back in the days when we first started sharing that poxy flat in Beggar's Bush together. You were just consumed with ambition. You wanted a TV career so badly. Remember when you first got the job as a runner? It was like you'd been given the golden ticket to paradise. You were like a greyhound, out of the traps and gone.'

I'd forgotten that Hannah was such a straight talker. A tell-it-like-it-is kind of gal.

'Oh God, was I really that bad? How did you not murder me? I must have been a nightmare to live with!'

'No, you weren't at all,' she grins. 'But then, I knew where you were coming from. I knew how tough things were for you at home and how much you wanted to get out and get away. I don't even blame you for airbrushing your past, so you could reinvent yourself as this hot, tellie-tottie babe. You worked hard and made a huge success of yourself and no one could have been more proud of you than me.'

And that's when her tone completely changes. Now there's hurt in her voice, that wasn't there before. I brace myself for what's coming.

'But, Jessie, all I'm asking is . . . did you have to airbrush me out of your life too? After everything we'd been through together? When I got married and had my first baby and then moved back here, be honest, Jess, and admit it. You just stopped calling me. The odd Christmas card, but that was pretty much it.'

The guilt feels like heartburn. 'Hannah, I'm so sorry . . .'

'Don't get me wrong, I do understand to an extent. I mean, you had your life and I had mine. And I know once you've had a baby, it's very hard for your single friends to understand how different life is. Would have been nice to hear from you once in a while though, that's all I'm saying. But you were all pally with that Emma Sheridan by then; you had new mates to play with, new places to go.'

'I still am friends with Emma. In fact, she's about the only person from my TV days who still bothers to pick up the phone to me.'

'Hmm,' says Hannah, unimpressed.

Another memory from years back resurfaces. Hannah never liked Emma. I'd completely forgotten. When they first met, all those years ago, they just didn't get on. 'Too sweet to be wholesome,' Hannah always used to say about her. One of the few things she turned out to be wrong about. Although she's right about pretty much everything else. I did airbrush Hannah out of my life and it was a horrible thing to do. I just figured our lives had drifted apart and that we'd nothing in common any more. And, to my shame,

I assumed Hannah felt the same way too. Tell you something; if there's one big life lesson the past few months have taught me, it's this: in a single word . . . humility.

'Well,' says Hannah, topping up our glasses of wine, 'if Madam Emma has stood by you, then I suppose that's to her credit. But you know, even when she's on TV, I could never take to her. Too much of a cold fish for me. She's one of those women that never puts a foot wrong and I can totally see why they had to pair you up with her. You livened things up and weren't afraid to fall flat on your arse, then laugh it off. Unlike Miss Ice Queen, goody-two-shoes.'

'I can't believe you used to watch the show . . .'

'Are you kidding me? Of course I did! I've followed your whole career, Jessie. Kind of made me feel like I was keeping in touch with you. I'd see you on TV and read all about you in the papers, going to this party and that glamorous do. And I'd think to myself, well she certainly got what she wanted.'

'It certainly didn't last though,' I say, knocking back a mouthful of wine. 'The minute things started to unravel for me, every single one of those people vanished into thin air.'

'I know and that must have been tough for you. Especially with what happened with Sam Hughes.'

I've no answer for that one. Besides, I think you're only allowed a certain number of tears per guy and I've already used mine up.

'Sorry, Jessie,' she says, a bit more gently now. 'I know how much he meant to you. Remember how, just after you first met him in Channel Six, we used to scroll through all the papers together to see if we could find any mention of him? Then years later, when I read that you were actually with him, I couldn't believe it. You just went after your goal and somehow you made it happen. I thought wow, Cinderella finally got her Prince Charming.'

'For all the good it did me,' I smile at her wryly. 'I suppose I'm a walking cautionary tale. You know, one of those people that you point at and say, be careful what you wish for. But I'm a very different person now.'

'No,' she says shaking her head firmly, with the killer insight only someone you've grown up with can possess. 'You were a different person then. You used to be so hungry for it all. So driven and obsessed with shaking off your past and getting on in the world. But you know something? You've changed. You're calmer now, more grounded, more realistic about life. In fact, I prefer you like this.'

'You know something? I prefer me like this too.'

Chapter Fifteen

'And a huge big hi to all our listeners out there, hope you're having a great night wherever you are and whatever you're doing. This is Jessie Woods, at *The Midnight Hour,* saying welcome to the show and stay tuned. The lines are open if you fancy ringing in for a chat but before we get started, I'd like to play a very special request for a very special lady. Mrs Mary Hayes of Whitehall is celebrating her birthday today, so now that it's exactly one minute past midnight, we at Radio Dublin want to be the very first to wish you a fantastic day. And so, especially for you, here's the Beatles singing your favourite song, "Yesterday".'

'That was a stunning gig . . . Jessie Woods, you're a born natural at this game!' Steve grins jubilantly at me two full hours later, the minute I'm off air after my first ever live radio show. Now given that it's past 2 a.m., I'm kind of impressed that he's hung around to hear the whole thing, but then I figure, he's the boss, wouldn't he have to? I step out of the boiling hot little DJ booth to a big thumbs up from Ian the producer and an even bigger bear hug from Steve.

Feels hilarious hugging him, as I barely come up to his shoulder, he's that tall and gangly.

'I can't believe you're still here, at this ungodly hour!' I laugh back at him.

'What can I say?' Steve smiles, still in his perpetual good humour, even at this hour. 'Gotta look after the talent, don't we, Ian? Especially when you're playing requests for my mum. She stayed up late to listen in to your first show, by the way, and even texted me to threaten that if I didn't thank you, I'd be disinherited.'

I punch him playfully and then thank Ian warmly too. If it hadn't been for the intensive crash course he gave me in the past week, I'd never in a million years have been able to pull this one off.

'Now, come on you,' Steve says to me, 'grab your bag, I'm taking you out for a late bite before you go home for your beauty sleep. It's the least Radio Dublin can do after such a terrific debut.'

A yawning Ian understandably declines to join us, but I'm so buzzed up and pumping full of adrenaline, that there's just no way on earth I'd ever be able to go home and sleep, so I do what I'm told. Half an hour later, Steve and I are sitting in the Eddie Rockets diner on South Anne Street, in a booth facing each other. He's tucking into a hamburger while I'm having a hotdog with chilli fries on the side. What can I say? After a show, I need the carb-hit. It was ever thus, even after doing an episode of *Jessie Would*. And, yes, I know that boring through these tiny wormholes back to the past is akin to scratching at a scab then wondering why it's not healing, so I'll just make this one, small little comparison.

Back then, in a different life, after-show relaxation would usually involve duck liver pâté and foie gras washed down with enough bottles of Cristal to take a bath in. Plus all of my post-work conversations seemed to be about one of three things: Sam, Sam's career or how much money Sam was raking in. Whereas now with Steve, it's actually hard to get him to chat seriously about anything; somehow the conversation always seems to descend into messing and giggles. Always playful, always lightweight, never, ever serious or professional.

'Anyone ever tell you that you eat far too much junk food?' I ask him, pretending to smack his hand after he robs a fistful of my chilli fries. 'And what I can't get over is that you're still so thin! Whenever you give me a lift on the back of your bike, I can actually feel your ribs sticking out. It's not fair. If I ate the amount of junk you do, I'd be the size of . . .' I was about to say the size of Maggie, but don't because it's a bit too mean.

'Hey, you're speaking to a loyalty-card-carrying member of the Smiley Burger rewards club, I'll have you know,' he teases, wolfing back the chips two at a time. 'What can I say? Apart from a big mammy Sunday dinner at my mum's house, crap food is pretty much my staple diet. But if it's my health you're wondering about though, don't worry. I draw the line at deep-fried Mars Bars.'

Now there's a single guy statement if I ever heard one, but I say nothing, just smile and let it pass. Who knows what the story is with him and that swishy-haired one at Hannah's party the other night?

Anyway, we chat some more, with me trying to get him to open up about himself and how he came to manage a radio station in the first place, but as ever with him, even serious chats somehow revert back to joking and messing. So then we talk about *The Midnight Hour*, where I can go with it and what more I can do. Funny, but now I've one show safely under my belt and my confidence is slowly starting to come back, I feel like a racehorse whose gate has finally opened.

Steve's full of apologies about the lateness of the slot, saying the audience is largely made up of late-night truckers and people staggering in from bars, but does make the point that if there's any particular item I'd like to do or try out, that I'm more than welcome to. 'As long as it's not nude juggling on the radio that is,' he grins, shoving a plate away from him and lazily stretching out, like he could stay here all night.

'What?' I nearly choke on one of my chilli fries.

'Your predecessor chanced that one time. Course being a complete eejit, I hadn't realised the date. April the first. I was a laughing stock in the office for weeks afterwards, I can tell you.'

'I promise, *The Midnight Hour* will be a nude-juggling-free zone,' I smile back. But my mind starts to race. Because I really want to bring something else to the show, to put my own stamp on it. Who knows? Maybe after the holy show I made of myself back at Channel Six, it's my small way of proving to the world that I'm not a completely useless gobshite after all.

It takes a while, but my body clock is slowly beginning to adjust to the new working hours too. Most of the time I can't get to sleep until well after 4 a.m., then stay in bed until midday, kind of like being a teenager all over again. Right down to Joan hammering on the bedroom door and screeching at me to get my lazy arse out of bed. I'm not officially meant to be at Radio Dublin until 9 p.m., but lately I've been heading into work hours earlier, mainly because Sharon's been out with Matt more often than not and I've no intentions of spending my evenings stuck beside Maggie on the sofa, thanks very much.

At this stage, Matt's called to the house a fair few times to collect Sharon, so I've had a proper chance to observe the two of them up close and personal, without the distraction of a christening party and a lot of drunken rowdiness going on in the background. From what I can see of the relationship dynamic, it's like this: the more offhand and dismissive she is of him, the more he seems to like it. The highest form of affection she shows for him could best be described as a sort of irritated fondness. Whereas, he seems to be getting in deeper and deeper with her on a daily basis. She's actually being a complete and utter Rules Girl without even realising it; doing all the things you're supposed to do to keep a fella on his toes. You know, like never calling him, rarely returning his calls and treating him with a combination of mild annoyance and as a sort of emotional punch bag if she has something to give out about. And he seems to be loving every minute of it. It's as if every time she tells him to feck off, he gets turned on. Weird. To think that I started out as Sharon's dating guru and now it looks like I'm the one who should be taking tips from her.

Anyway, it's about 7 p.m. on a warm, sunny evening about a week later, when I skip into the Radio Dublin offices. My head's buzzing with ideas for tonight's show and I'm still not sure which one to go with. By the time I get upstairs to the main office, it's surprisingly busy with the drivetime show still on air and being broadcast live. I make my way to the tiny kitchen to grab a quick coffee before mapping out tonight's play list then filling in the blanks between.

I'm absentmindedly pouring out the coffee with my mind in fifth gear when, out of nowhere, something catches my eye. I drift over to the noticeboard just beside the fridge and take a closer look. No. I wasn't seeing things. There it is, in black and white. The possible answer to all our prayers.

I read it again, just to be certain. It's a flyer, buried at the back of about a dozen other flyers with ads for things like second-hand Fiat Puntos for sale and holiday cottages in Ballynahinch to let at recessionary rates. Without thinking twice, I do a lightning quick over-the-shoulder check to make sure there's no one hovering behind me, then rip it off the wall and stuff it into my jeans pocket.

Because this one calls for extreme diplomacy and tact. In other words, this is something Sharon and only Sharon can handle.

It's coming up to 10 p.m., getting close to show time and the office is by now almost deserted. I've been at my desk all this while, surrounded by scraps of paper with my ideas jotted out on them, utterly absorbed. Next thing, Ian drifts past my desk, looking tired and a bit hung over. But then he's one of those guys with the permanently ghostly pallor of the night dweller. Like he's allergic to daylight.

'Hey Jessie, another great show last night, well done you,' he says in a husky just-got-out-of-bed voice. 'By the way, the boss wants to see you.'

I head into Steve's office, which is a complete shambles with mountains of newspapers on the desk in front of him and an electric guitar propped up against the doorframe. I can't help smiling as I look at him; you just couldn't meet anyone less boss-like. He's sitting on the desk, long legs stretched out, wearing faded jeans and a black T-shirt that

I'm guessing has never been introduced to an iron in its entire existence.

'There's our rising star!' he beams, jumping up to peck me on the cheek as I come in. 'Get a load of this,' he says, shoving a copy of the *Daily Herald* at me. 'Then you'll appreciate why I'm sitting here basking in reflected glory.'

I turn to the page he's pointing at to see what he's on about. Not a news item at all, just the smallest little column buried in a corner of page eight, tucked up in between the weather report and today's horoscopes. There's a passport-sized photo of me taken when my hair was still blonde, with the caption: *COMEBACK KID.*

Fair play to Radio Dublin who've taken a chance on the previously unhireable Jessie Woods and have now allocated her their Midnight Hour show. We'll be listening with great interest to see how she fares in this particular presenting medium, but in the meantime, we'd like to wish her every success and a warm welcome back to doing what she does best. Jessie, it's been too long.

I can't talk for a second, just look at Steve, gobsmacked. I've been on a self-imposed media blackout for ages now, petrified I'd only read something that would take a shovel to my self-confidence, so to see something kind appearing about me in the print media is . . . well, it's lovely actually.

'You deserve it,' he grins, shoving the floppy hair out of his eyes. 'And hey, I'm going down in history as the guy who got you back on the air again . . .'

'It's OK, you can finish that sentence. When no one else

would,' I laugh, sitting down on the empty seat opposite him.

He laughs, then stabs a biro at the pile beside him. 'Quick idea for tonight's show. These are all first editions of tomorrow morning's papers; how would you feel about doing a short piece about what's in them during your show? Nothing too heavy, just the lighter, more showbizzy stuff. And all distilled into your trademark style, of course.'

'Terrific idea. Do you mind if I have a quick scan through all these?' I ask, grabbing a newspaper and flicking through it.

'Not at all, that's what they're here for. Here, I'll even give you a hand.'

Pretty soon, the two of us are poring over the huge mound of papers on Steve's desk, me with a highlighter pen in my hand, ready to mark anything that might just work. I stumble on a feature about Emma, an At Home piece, with a gorgeous photo taken in her state of the art kitchen, where she looks as groomed and flawlessly perfect as ever. All to plug her new TV chat show, which goes to air later this month. She's been up to her tonsils with work lately, as have I, so it's been a while since we've had a decent natter, but still, I make a mental note to call her and wish her all the luck in the world.

Then something else catches my eye. 'When you said lighter stuff, does this count?' I ask Steve, pointing to page fourteen of the *Star*.

'Gimme the gist of it,' he says without looking up from the *News of the World*.

'OK, how's this for a crap first date? A woman met a guy for dinner, but while she was in the bathroom, he filched the keys from out of her handbag and stole her car.'

'You are *so* making that up.'

'Cross my heart, it's right here. There you go, real life trumps any fiction you could come up with yet again.'

'Cool. Maybe chat a bit about rubbishy first dates and then you could segue into—' He breaks off abruptly, tossing away the paper he was reading. I'm so engrossed in the stolen car story that I mightn't even have noticed, only he made the fatal error of tagging on, 'Ehh . . . no, no nothing at all in that paper, just ignore it.'

I look up at him.

'But that's the *News of the World*. Usually that's the best for this kind of thing.'

'Don't worry about it, just leave it.'

Of course now my antennae are well and truly up, so I stroll faux casually over to where he flung the paper, then snatch it up to see whatever it is that he doesn't want me to. Nosy bitch that I am.

'Jessie, don't, really, there's no need . . .'

'Ha, ha, too late,' I laugh at him, scanning through it at speed.

Oh holy fuck.

I do not believe this. There it is, on the inside, page three. Sam. On the way to the launch of his new book, *If Business is the New Rock & Roll, then I'm Elvis Presley*. Held in the Mansion House this evening. And probably only getting into full swing right about now. Considering it's only a book launch, they've printed a massive two-page colour spread; I'm only surprised they didn't print a special pull-out-and-keep supplement to go with it, like they did with the moon landings.

Vintage Sam, his PR people had the press all lined up and ready to snap him and his celeb pals on their way in, nicely in time to make the early edition of all tomorrow morning's papers. I know I shouldn't read on but I can't help myself. *La douleur exquise* and all that. Reading through the guest list is like a roll call of every single person who wouldn't return my calls in the last few months. All present and correct, may it piss rain on the whole shower of them. Sam included. I mean, why can't he just recoil from the public like a normal billionaire anyway?

Next thing I feel a warm, comforting arm around my shoulder. 'Jessie, I'm so sorry,' says Steve. 'I didn't mean for you to see this. I had no idea it was in the paper. I never would have suggested you read through them if I'd known . . .'

'It's fine. Really.' I shrug his arm away. Because that's how absolutely OK I am with this.

'It's completely understandable that you're still cut up about it. These things take time. Sure you're all right?'

'Yes. Honestly. Stop worrying. I'm a big girl.' Who's starting to speak in jagged sentences, I'm suddenly aware.

'You know what we say in showbiz,' he says gently. 'Today's papers are nothing more than tomorrow's glorified cat box liners.'

I smile, appreciating that he went for a gag.

'Tell you something though, Jessie, when I saw that Sam Hughes on the documentary they made about you, I just felt like punching the git right in his smug, self-satisfied over-privileged gob.'

I look up at him and suddenly the biggest surge of deep gratitude comes over me. Now why weren't you around when I was going through the break up? You're the perfect combination of brotherliness and violence.

* * *

Show time and if I say so myself, I'm on fire. Got a lot to prove. Plus every time I think of Sam and his posh launch party in the Mansion House with his even posher friends and all their rarefied, over-moneyed lives, a huge wave of 'I'll show you' energy surges up through me like a volcano.

'So here's one for all you listeners out there; why not phone me at *The Midnight Hour* with tips about . . . break-up behaviour? What is it that you like to indulge yourself in to help get you over someone? The phone lines are open, on 1850 . . .'

It's incredible. I could never have seen this coming. The phone never stops once for the entire duration of the two-hour show. In fact, I could stay on air until 4 a.m. and still not get through everyone. Men and women all calling in to describe how they cope or don't cope in that nightmarish situation when you're the dumpee in a relationship which you never wanted to end in the first place.

'My top tip,' one female caller rings in, 'is to destroy all photos of you as a couple, where he looks hot and you look happy. It could set the whole recovery process back months if you happen to stumble on it at a weak moment. And of course, certain parts of the city are just out of bounds. Places you went together, bars where you know he hangs out . . .'

I barely have time to answer her when another line lights up. Joe from Irishtown rings in to say that the crucial element in recovering from a break-up is to constantly play on a loop in your head everything you hated about your ex. Over and over again, he insists, until you're actually delighted NOT to be still dating them.

'Get out more,' says Gemma from Sandymount. 'A lot more. Worst thing you can do is hole up in your house, like Anne Frank.' Lizzy from Clontarf rings in to agree, with the added caveat that you must never, under any circumstances ever leave the house un-beautiful, on the grounds that the day you do saunter out in a manky tracksuit with three-day-old hair and no make-up, is the very day you're guaranteed to bump into him.

Then Tara from Temple Bar calls to say it helps to make out an iTunes list of the best break-up songs of all time. 'Any suggestions?' I ask tentatively. 'I'm Not in Love' by 10CC is her personal favourite, which by a miracle, Ian in the production box manages to root out of the library and we play it to take us out, as the show wraps.

Never in my whole life have two hours gone by in such a blink.

Steve is still there when I get out and offers me a ride home on the back of his motorbike, which I gladly accept.

'I don't know how you did it, Jessie,' he says as we leave the deserted building together. 'But it's like you've tapped into something big here. Sure, I knew there were a lot of lonely hearts out there, listening in at this hour of the night, but what's amazing is that they're all fully prepared to ring in and talk about the most intimate, personal details of their break-ups.'

'I know, I thought I'd never get that last caller to shut up about her ex. If she'd had a guitar, she'd have written a ballad about him.'

He snorts laughing.

'Please tell me I'm not that bad,' I say suddenly.

'Jessie, *no one* is that bad.'

We speed through the near empty streets and he drops me right to my front door. I hop off the bike, hand back the helmet and hug him warmly.

'Now I know we work you hard at Radio Dublin, so into

bed and get your beauty sleep,' he smiles. 'And I'll see you tomorrow.'

'Are you sure you wouldn't like to come in for a coffee?' I ask, feeling I should but kind of half hoping he'll say no.

'Another time. But tell Sharon I said hi, won't you? And that she and that fella of hers are invited to my gig this Sunday night. You're coming too, but then you don't have a choice, even if it is your one and only night off. All Radio Dublin employees are required to attend the boss's band sessions. It's compulsory.'

A lovely feeling of deep warmth comes over me. 'You're a good friend, Steve, you do know that, don't you?'

He nods from under his helmet, waits until I'm inside, then zooms off into the night.

Given that Sharon and I have been working in what feels like totally different time zones this week, I'm actually glad when I come to the next morning and she's still in our room, straightening her hair. Mind you, I think it could be the smell of burning that wakes me.

Delighted that I caught her, I nip out of bed and pull the flyer I robbed from the Radio Dublin kitchen out of my jeans pocket. And just like me, she reads it, stunned.

'Jeez, this is . . . I mean . . . this could be . . .'

'I know,' I say, nodding.

'But do you think she might . . .'

'Not if it comes from me she won't. But maybe if you were to broach it with her . . .'

'Leave it with me. With a subtle mixture of bullying and reverse psychology, I'd be surprised if I don't have an answer for you by tonight.'

* * *

Joan has news for me too. Now I'm the first to admit that I laughed when she talked about going to her wine tastings, I sniggered when she yakked on about doing re-enactments from *The Mikado* and yet again, I nearly choked on my Bran Flakes when she'd swan off for 'business meetings' down in the Swiss Cottage night after night.

But I'm not laughing now.

Next morning, after Sharon's left for work, it's just Joan and me for a mid-morning brekkie. I pad my way softly into the kitchen, all set for our usual morning game of tip-toe round the mood swings. But as luck would have it, she's in top form today, happily bouncing around the place. She even offers to cook me one of her big fries, which I gratefully accept. I'm still in my pyjamas, even though it's well past eleven, but she's dressed to kill in a neat little black suit with matching everything.

'Looking good,' I wolf whistle at her, messing. 'Very Joan Collins circa the *Dynasty*/Nolan Miller years.' I'm running a risk saying that much; in one of her foul moods she'd have cut the face off me for less. But for some reason today it's like she's the Prozac version of her usual self.

She does an obliging twirl then sits down beside me.

'Exciting news, Jessica. Huge news, in fact. And I want you to be the first to know, because I may need you to give us a little plug on your radio show. Oh and I need another small favour too. And in return, I have a little surprise for you.'

'Sure, what's up?'

Then she says that, seeing as how Sharon and I have been sharing a bedroom for so long now, she's thinking of redecorating it, which completely stuns me. Bear in mind that this is as close as Joan could ever possibly get to expressing affection for another human being. In this house, all outward displays of emotion are done via the Laura Ashley catalogue. I thank her, really touched, then ask what the other big news is.

'I'm going into business,' she announces, glowingly. 'You are looking at a director of a newly formed company. I'm getting business cards printed up and everything. No expense spared.'

'That's fantastic, but . . . . what exactly is the business?'

'Oh, very cutting edge. Not my actual idea, credit for that goes to Jimmy Watson in the Swiss Cottage, who I really think is something of a business genius . . .'

'And . . .?'

'. . . but I am a principal investor and employee in the company . . .'

'Joan! Gimme the last sentence first, will you?'

'As a matter of fact, we're a web-based company. On the internet, you know.'

Joan pronounces 'internet' like it's a brand new thing that only got invented yesterday. I also refrain from reminding her of how she used to have a go at myself and Sharon for spending so much time online. Her exact comment, I recall, was that the World Wide Web existed purely so that nerds could find out what other nerds thought about *Star Trek*.

'Now Jessica, you're not to laugh . . .'

'Course I won't.'

'It's called IPrayForYou.com.'

'Excuse me?'

'Like all great ideas, it's actually very simple,' she smiles smugly, as if she's reading a voice over for a new kind of bank account. 'You see, we've already bought the web space and as soon as it's properly designed, Jimmy and I are going to launch it together online.'

'IPrayForYou.com?'

'Well, the idea is that people can go online, give us all their credit card details and in return, we'll pray for them. Our rates are very reasonable I'll have you know. Fifty cents to light a candle, one Euro for a Hail Mary or an Our Father, five Euro for a decade of the rosary and a tenner for a full rosary. Of course the real beauty of it is that I can do the actual praying anywhere. In the car, in work, even while I'm watching the telly.'

'But you're not even religious!'

'Did I say I was? This is *business*, Jessica. Try to keep up.'

I just look at her, dumbfounded. 'And do you think people might actually go for this?' I manage to splurt out in between mouthfuls of fried egg.

'Oh listen to you, so cynical. You know some people look at things as they are and ask why. I dream of things that never were and ask why not.'

'Well, what can I say? Best of luck with it, Joan.'

'You're most kind. Oh and I need a favour from you too. That stuff you've been storing in the garage will have to be cleared out as soon as you possibly can. Those boxes are all just going to have to go upstairs to your room.'

'Sure . . . but why?'

'Because our garage is going to be the official IPrayForYou.com headquarters, of course.'

Unbelievable. The woman is unbelievable.

And there's yet another surprise later on that evening. I'm in Radio Dublin at my desk and just going through some notes I made for this evening's show when Sharon calls me.

'You'd better be sitting down for this!' she squeals excitedly.

'What's up?' I ask, wondering if it's something to do with Matt. Then again, she never gets that animated over anything to do with poor old Matt. In fact, every time I ask her how things are going between them, she just shrugs and lights up a fag.

'I did exactly what you told me to. Followed your instructions to the letter. Handed her the flyer you took from the radio station wall and everything . . .'

'And?' Now I'm all excited.

'Now, I don't want either of us to get our hopes up on this one. I mean, you of all people know what she's like, but . . .'

'But . . .?'

'. . . I think she's going to go for it.'

Well, bravo Sharon.

In the meantime the show continues to whiz by and some nights I stagger out of the booth at 2 a.m. and it feels like I've barely been in there five minutes. All week, the phone lines haven't stopped hopping. Like *The Midnight Hour* has suddenly become Dating Horror Stories Central. It's a complete phenomenon and Steve even gives me the loveliest compliment of saying that by the time the audience ratings come in, this could be the first time in the station's history that a late-night show eclipses a primetime one. That confidence boost alone made me feel like I was walking on water.

Some positive pieces have started appearing in the media about *The Midnight Hour* too. In fact it got a mention in *The Times* under their 'If you do one thing this week . . .' listings, which was mega cool. Even Roger Davenport, my agent, who I haven't heard from in months, called to say that he'd heard a download of this show that everyone was suddenly talking about and he wanted to congratulate me. I'm not entirely sure what surprised me more. That someone as old-fashioned as Roger knew what a download was or that he actually picked up the phone to me after all this time. Anyhow.

You wouldn't believe some of the calls we're getting into the show either. Maybe it's something to do with the anonymity of radio, but there's a freedom here that you just don't get on TV.

For instance, the other night the topic was cheating and a married woman calling herself Caroline rang in to tell us that she'd got married ridiculously young, to a guy she referred to as 'Mr Ah Sure He'll Do'. 'I panic dated,' she told me in a wobbly voice and then, just because everyone else was at it, she panic married. And started cheating on her husband about two years ago with a guy she works with. The affair has been over for months now but she insisted she was going to confess all to her husband and come clean. He may not be the love of my life, she said sadly, but he's still a good man who deserves the truth.

Cue about half a dozen calls and texts in to say, 'But you got away with it!' Which then led on to a heated discussion about cheating in the broadest sense, is it like a tree falling in the forest? Is it only really classified as cheating if you get caught out?

'But I don't get it, why would you risk your whole marriage over something that's finished?' one caller rang in to ask Caroline.

The sheer, bald honesty of Caroline's reply startled me.

'Because it's the getting away with it part that I can't live with.'

Then a guy calling himself Brad (I know, I know, they make half the names up) rang in to say that he'd dated someone who he thought was his absolute dream woman. He got engaged and then married her in a whirlwind courtship during which he couldn't believe they'd never had as much as a single cross word. He honestly thought that he was the luckiest guy alive not only to have met, but then to have married her. However, that all changed the second she got the ring on her finger. It was like a Dr Jekyll/Mr Hyde situation; gone was his sweet-tempered, adorable girlfriend and left in her place was this toxic harpy who seemed hell bent on making his life a misery and spending every penny he'd ever made. So now he's met someone else, someone kind and understanding, a shoulder to cry on. Nothing's actually happened between them, so technically he hasn't actually cheated per se, but his argument is that he was duped by the woman he married and now feels entitled to run after a chance at real, lasting happiness. 'When we were dating,' he said, 'my wife played a great game. A fantastic game. But she was doing nothing more than acting a part the whole time. And once she landed me, her real personality emerged.'

The switchboard in front of me instantly lit up, some with irate callers to remind 'Brad' that he had taken a vow for better or for worse and now had to live through the for worse bit whether he liked it or not. Others were more sympathetic, telling him that if he'd met someone else, then he shouldn't let the new potential girlfriend out of his sight.

We sign off for the night with one single woman's wry comment. 'You know something, Jessie? Listening to all of this talk about cheating just reaffirms what it is that I'm looking for in a partner. I want the Ronseal Man. A fella who does exactly what he says on the tin. Loves me and only me and that's it.'

What can I say? I *love* this gig. Everyone here at the station has been tremendously supportive, as if sensing that I've a lot to prove and a long way to crawl back. And then there's Steve, sweet, adorable Steve who's fast turning into my best-friend-next-to-Sharon. There was only one night in all of last week when he wasn't around after the show, so the two of us could either stuff our faces with late-night fast food or else zoom home on his motorbike. He texted me though, to say that he was at a rehearsal for his band and apologised for not being there for me.

The funny thing is that I missed him.

By the time Sunday comes around, I'm wall-falling with tiredness, but it's Steve's gig with his band tonight and not only did he almost make me sign an agreement in blood that I'd be there, but I've asked Sharon and Matt to come along too. The long-suffering, gentlemanly Matt even offered to drive the two of us there, saying he'd come and collect us at Whitehall first.

I'm running behind getting ready so by the time I get downstairs, poor old Matt has already been introduced to Joan. She's on the highest of high alerts for this, fussing and fawning over him like he's minor royalty. In fact, if I know my stepmother and unfortunately I do, chances are she has a copy of some mother-of-the-bride magazine upstairs on her bedside table with all her favourite outfits already marked in highlighter pen.

The thing about Joan is that when she's pulling out all the stops to impress you, it can often be worse, far worse than when she's in one of her foul humours, so it's hard to know what's going through Matt's mind at this moment. We all just sit around awkwardly with the TV on low and me trying to make inane small talk. Eventually, Joan leaves the TV room to get him a Tropicana juice from the fridge, which I happen to know she bought specially for him when she found out it was his favourite. And which no doubt she'll serve in the good crystal glasses which only ever come out at Christmas.

So now it's just him, with myself, Maggie and Sharon.

'You have that slightly glazed, shell-shocked look that everyone seems to get when they first meet my mother,' says Maggie, sucking on a fag and staring at him, unblinking.

'Had to happen sooner or later,' he shrugs, completely unfazed by the whole ordeal. 'Sharon and I are now past our tenth date, you know, so the probability of our relationship proceeding further is now at well over sixty per cent.'

The gig is in the centre of town and I'm doubly delighted to see that a huge gang from Radio Dublin have turned out in force to support Steve. Including a lot of the pretty young things, Steve's office fan club, in other words, all looking as pert and young and gorgeous as ever. Anyway, Sharon, Matt and I grab a table and I rush to the bar to get a round of drinks in. Ian is there, in yet another one of his astonishing T-shirts. Tonight's is no exception, it says, 'My mother is a travel agent for guilt trips.'

'Steve will be pleased you came,' he smiles. 'I think someone has a crush on you.'

'Come on, Ian, that's ridiculous. We're friends, going back years. Nothing more!' A good, forceful nip-this-in-the-bud-right-now statement. Just wish I wasn't flushing to my roots as I said it.

'Oh yeah? So you think it's normal for him to hang around the station most nights till past 2 a.m. so he can escort you home?'

I put this out of my head and get on with enjoying the band. The gig is absolutely brilliant too. Turns out The Amazing Few write all their own songs and they're surprisingly good. Steve is terrific onstage, not a nerve in his body, as he plays lead guitar, looking like he's approximately a foot taller than the rest of the band.

Sharon and Matt seem to enjoy it too; although it has to be said that Matt spends most of the night either a) staring adoringly at Sharon or b) laughing at Sharon when she puts him down with that weird mixture of distain and fondness she treats him with. He disappears off to the loo at one point and Sharon immediately starts neck-swivelling around to check out any other single fellas that might be loitering around and on the loose.

'May I remind you that you're here with someone?' I say sternly, after I catch her ogling some guy sitting opposite us who's covered with tattoos.

'Listen to you, the dating police. I'm only checking out what else is on offer. You know, on the principle that when you have a fella on your arm, suddenly other guys start paying you a bit more attention. Its like they look at you in a whole new light. Admit it, Jess, in your heart you know I'm right.'

I shake my head and go back to watching the band. Sometimes I wonder if I've created a dating monster.

Anyway, when it's all over, at about 11 p.m., Steve saunters past all the girlie girls from the station who are catcalling him to join them and instead ambles over to our table. I jump up to give him a bear hug and tell him how fabulous he was. Only the truth.

It's one of those wonderful, fun nights; Steve messing and joking like he always does, everyone in good form and relaxed. Sharon and Matt decide to leave early-ish as Matt has a meeting first thing in the morning and Sharon's on the Smiley breakfast shift too. They offer me a lift home but Steve insists on my staying, saying he'll give me a lift on his bike later.

'If I'm sober enough, that is,' he laughs, heading off to the bar to get another round in.

'The more I see of Steve Hayes,' says Sharon as I hug her goodbye, 'the more I'm getting to like him. He's . . . Fertiliser Man.'

'By that, I'm hoping that you don't mean full of shite?'

'No, you eejit. I mean he grows on you. Just slowly and over time, that's all.'

After they've left, he's full of lovely things to say about Sharon too.

'I can't get over how different she is,' he keeps telling me. 'She's looking fantastic but it's like her personality has changed too. I used to be terrified of her and Maggie and now I think Sharon's completely cool. One of us.'

'I'll be sure to pass that on.'

'Congratulations, Jessie, you've done a complete Pygmalion on her. Except that you're Henry Higgins and she's Eliza Doolittle.'

For the first time in I don't know how long, I can honestly say this.

I'm happy.

Chapter Sixteen

This lasts right all the way up until the end of the following week and then the blow falls. What makes it worse is that, up till then, everyone's in top form. And I really do mean everyone, including most astonishingly of all, Maggie.

Remember the flyer I whipped off the kitchen wall at Radio Dublin? It was an ad for an open mike contest, to be held at the Comedy Cellar in town in just two weeks' time and called, appropriately enough, So You Think You're Funny? A one-off night to give first-time stand-up comedians a chance at performing in front of a live audience. With a prize of €1,000 *and* the chance to be seen by one of the top comedy agents in town. The only stipulation is that all entrants must be novices. Complete unknowns, so it's a level playing field.

Now, knowing full well that if I mentioned this to Maggie, she'd do the exact opposite of what I was suggesting purely just to spite me, I got Sharon to pitch it to her instead. With one hundred per cent success. She took one bite of the cherry and said what the hell, nothing to lose, she'd give it a go.

But that's only part one of the miracle I have to report. The big news is that, finally, after all this time, there's been, let's call it a 'cessation of hostilities' between Maggie and me. Hard to believe, I know, but it all dates back to a few nights ago, when it was just she and I alone in the house in, *quelle surprise*, the TV room.

For starters, there was a very different atmosphere. Maggie was all twitchy and what's more I could sense it. She was sitting in her usual armchair, but instead of giving the telly her usual laser-like focus, she had a notepad on her lap and kept either staring into space or else scribbling down into it. Every now and then, she'd throw a furtive glance in my direction, as though she was about to ask me something, then would think better of it and look away just as quick. At first I thought I was imagining it, so I did a little experiment.

'Mind if I change channels?' I asked her innocently.

'Hmm? Yeah, go ahead.'

Immediate alarm bell. Because we were watching *EastEnders*, Maggie's favourite soap that she never misses and would knife you if you even talked over, never mind changed the channel. So, figuring it would be a long, long time before I got a golden opportunity like this again, I went for it.

'Maggie, I hope you don't mind me asking, but is everything OK?'

Silence. I could practically feel her wondering whether she should open up to me, the arch enemy, or not. And then the miracle happened. She did.

'Well, as a matter of fact . . .' she began, sounding more unsure of herself than I think I've ever heard her.

'Yeah?'

'The thing is . . . there's this open mike night at the Comedy Cellar coming up that Sharon told me about and . . . well . . . I've decided to enter.'

'Hey, that's great news!' I said, mentally reminding myself to act all surprised. 'You'll be wonderful. I've no doubt.'

'Yeah, but . . .' she went on, 'you see . . . I need to test out my material. I mean, I have loads of ideas and that, but I won't know if they'll work until I actually try them out. So I was wondering . . . only just because you happen to know a bit about performing in front of an audience . . .'

'Maggie, if you want to test your material out on me, I'd be absolutely delighted to lend an ear. Just get us two tins of Bulmers out of the fridge and let's do it right now.'

She smiled, actually *smiled* at me and we spent the next two hours going through her gags. With the TV . . . drumroll for dramatic effect . . . switched *off*.

It was amazing. She paced up and down the TV room, notebook in hand, rehearsing her material as I listened attentively, making helpful comments and remembering at all times to keep her confidence up. Some of her stuff was great, but very Maggie, if you know what I mean. For instance, she had this whole riff about being a civil servant in the Inland Revenue and the pitfalls to avoid if you want to have a long career there. From there, she segued into a whole sequence about how she's going to turn thirty-four soon, referring to it as the 'Is this all there is?' age. 'It's the age when you finally accept that you're not going to win *X Factor* or the National Lottery on a Saturday night. Or that you're not going to enchant George Clooney over a muffin in Starbucks on your way into work.' And off she went spinning into this whole existential routine about how mid-life can do funny things to the most normal and conservative of people, even ones that work in the tax office. How, in her own case, the shock of reaching her mid-thirties now has her doing something she's never thought possible before:

attempting to be funny in front of a drunken cellar full of hecklers, all expecting to see the next Jo Brand.

As soon as she was finished, I leapt to my feet, gave her a standing ovation and told her I thought if there was any justice she'd win the shagging thing hands down. And that I was there for her if she ever wanted to rehearse in front of someone again.

'Look, thanks for doing this,' she said, over yet another tin of Bulmers. 'It was . . . emm . . . nice of you.'

'Maggie, give me a chance. I *am* nice. In spite of what you think, I am not the antichrist.'

'I know, I know. It's just . . . not been easy.'

'Yeah, well. Me being back here can't exactly have been a barrel for laughs for you. I do understand, you know. Particularly with myself and Sharon getting so pally.'

'No. It's not that,' she said, surprising me. 'Or at least, it's not just that.'

I looked at her, puzzled. Puzzled and half pissed, if I'm being honest. Boy is this is one road I don't think she and I could ever have attempted to go down sober.

'I know you must have thought that I had it in for you all this time,' she said, lighting up a fag, 'but it was tough for me having you living back here, you know. Brought back so many memories of us all being teenagers under the one roof all those years ago. Remember?'

'Do I remember? I'm still having therapy.'

She snorted at my gag a bit and went on.

'It's just, you were always Daddy's Little Princess, weren't you? The apple of his eye. You walked on water as far as he was concerned. But Jessie, the thing is . . . he was my dad too. He may not have been my real father, but he was my father figure and I . . . really loved him. He encouraged me in a way that Ma never did, praised me when I did well I school and was delighted for me when I got into the Inland Revenue. Meant I was set up for life, he said. Then he died and it was like you had the monopoly on grieving for him. But you weren't the only one who loved him and who misses him. For feck's sake, who do you think organises the anniversary mass for him every year? Only me.'

I couldn't speak. Just sat on the sofa, actually dumbfounded and feeling about an inch tall.

To my shame, I just never thought of Maggie as someone with sensitivity and the same raw emotions as the rest of us.

'Remember the stink you kicked up when you discovered all his things lying out in the garden shed?' she went on, stubbing out a fag. 'Well it was me who wanted to hang on to all his stuff in the first place. If Ma had her way, she'd have fecked the lot into a skip years ago. You know how unsentimental she is. Not to mention what she's like for doing clearouts.'

'I do remember,' I said, in a very small voice. 'And Maggie, for what it's worth, I'm sorry. I just hadn't realised that you missed him too. I mean . . . I never knew.'

And ever since that night, honest to God, it's been like the iron curtain coming down between us. Maggie and I actually converse now. For real. What can I say? If Dad was looking down on us, he'd be proud of how well we're getting on. I'm certain of it.

Night after night, she rehearses her material pacing up and down the TV room, surrounded by scraps of paper with ideas scribbled across them, testing out material on me. Then I chip in my two cents' worth and off she goes, rewrites, and does the whole thing all over again for me the following night, without fail.

You want to see her, she's like a completely different person these days. The old Maggie is gone and in her place is the new, improved, more energised version of her. It's a wondrous sight to behold; the girl has a raw, basic talent that's slowly beginning to flower as her confidence grows and boy is she getting there. Day by day, step by step. And what's even more astonishing is that the TV guide remains lying on the sofa, unopened and un-looked at. Meantime, Sharon continues to date the long-suffering Matt, although I did challenge her on this and told her in no uncertain terms that if she's not interested, then she really should let the poor, besotted guy down . . . but gently.

'I'm not ready to,' is her resolute answer. 'At least, not till I've someone else lined up. Besides, going out on all these dates is good practice for me. And I don't want to tell him to his face that he drives me up the walls sometimes; it's way too early in the relationship to show him my true colours.'

In actual fact, she doesn't want to let him go, is my conclusion. She's having far too good a time having a single man chasing around after her and making all the running. So I say nothing more. For now.

Meanwhile, Joan's week involved buzzing around the place in one little 'dressed for business' outfit after another, and spending most of her time down in the Swiss Cottage with Jimmy Watson, her 'investment partner'. So much so that I'm seriously starting to wonder if she has shares in the place. Funny, but whether her whole IPrayForYou.com business actually works out or not is kind of beside the point. Because one good thing has already come out of it;

her mood has been a bit like good weather can be sometimes; lasting for day after unbelievable day.

This wondrous humour lasts right up until Saturday afternoon, when she catches me crashed out on the sofa listening to a new riff in Maggie's material. We both hear her thundering into the hall then clattering down her handbag and keys, instantly alerting us to a one hundred and eighty degree reversal in her mood. As bad luck would have it, I'm the first person she lights on when she bursts in, therefore I'm first in line for a tongue-lashing.

'Why aren't you at work?' she snaps at me the minute she flings open the TV room door.

'I don't have to be there until nine,' I stammer back.

'Jessica Woods, have I or have I not spent the whole of last week asking you to move that mountain of stuff belonging to you out of the garage? Honestly, how many times do I have to nag and nag at you before you'll get up off your lazy rear end?'

'I'm doing it already!' I groan, hauling myself up from the sofa.

'Oh, by the way, Jessie?' says Maggie as I'm on my way out the door. 'Thanks for listening to my routine. I owe you one.'

And I'd swear I catch a half-wink from her. Bloody hell. Not so long ago, that was the kind of civility you'd nearly have to strangle out of her.

Anyway, as soon as I open the garage door, I realise I'd forgotten just how much there actually is here, all with my name on it. Tons of cardboard storage boxes, all full of stuff from the *Jessie Would* production office. Course I never went through them, I just did what I always do with unpleasant reminders of my past: dumped it in the garage and airbrushed it out of my life. Put in a pile and mentally labelled 'To be dealt with at a later date when am a bit more able to handle sheer, unquantifiable misery.'

Right then. It's pointless cluttering up mine and Sharon's bedroom with a load of storage boxes from Channel Six, miles better to dump the whole lot into the green wheelie bin and let the rubbish men deal with it. I'm about to do just that, when some sixth sense stops me in my tracks.

Hang on one second. I spent the best part of three years working on *Jessie Would* and apart from the ignominious end it all came to, it was far and away the happiest time in my life. Do I really want to consign all that to the dustbin of history? Isn't there some little memento or keepsake that could be in one of these boxes that I could hang on to, as a reminder of past glories? A mug maybe, with the show's logo on it. Or maybe one of the *Jessie Would* T-shirts that we used to hand out to all the kids in the studio audience? So I sit myself down and start at the very beginning.

Pretty boring, actually, most of it. There's dozens and dozens of memos that would have flown around the office and camera scripts from long-forgotten shows, but not much else. No joy in finding the mug or T-shirt I'm looking for, so I move on to another box. And that's when I first see it. A neat file, with the date of my very last show written across it. Just seeing that date in bold print makes me catch my breath. Because I remember it like a heart attack.

I'm about to shove the file back into its box and dump the whole lot in the bin when suddenly, a piece of paper flutters out and lands right at my feet. It's the heading at the top of it that catches my eye. Because it's from Mercedes Ireland. I recognise the logo immediately. It's a printout of an email addressed to Emma, care of the production office, and is from some guy called Joe de Courcey.

Dear Emma, it reads. *Further to our phone call yesterday I just wanted to confirm in writing that everything is now set firmly in place for tomorrow night's show.*

Tomorrow night's show ... Then I look at the date at the top of the printout. It was sent the Friday before what turned out to be the last ever *Jessie Would* broadcast.

OK, something is beginning to sound very, very wrong about all this. Because why would Emma have been in touch with Mercedes in the first place? So on I read.

After tomorrow evening's stunt at Mondello Park involving your colleague Jessie Woods, we're now pleased to confirm that, at your suggestion, the company are now in a position to invite her to be brand ambassador for Mercedes for a period of one year.

Suddenly I can't breathe. At Emma's suggestion? I read on, with disbelief mounting.

Of course, we understand that the element of surprise is a huge factor in getting her to agree, but as you state below, given that her own sports car was repossessed so recently, we feel that an inordinately generous offer like ours is one that surely can't be refused. Naturally, we are terribly sorry at your declining our offer, but fully understand that you're not in need of a new car, having just purchased one so recently. But we're most grateful to you for selflessly putting forward your colleague in your place. I'm happy to say that we're all in agreement with you here, Miss Woods would make an ideal candidate for a Mercedes brand ambassadorship.

We trust this will be the beginning of a long and fruitful relationship between us.

Sincerely,
Joe de Courcey

It gets worse. Far worse.

Emma's original email to him is on the printout below his reply, there in black and white for me to see. Even though I can barely believe what it is that I'm actually reading.

Dear Joe,
Firstly, apologies again for my not being able to take you up on your kind offer, but thanks so much again for being so understanding about it. Believe me, had I not changed my own car so recently, I'd have jumped at your generous suggestion!

About my other idea, I forgot to mention that Jessie's car was repossessed only a few weeks back and I've no doubt that, if faced with a brand, spanking new Mercedes SLK in showroom condition, will be only too delighted to accept. Who wouldn't be? The main thing to remember is not to take no for an answer. She's proud and will really need this forced on her! I'm thinking, maybe personalised number plates might be an idea? However, I'll leave the details in your more than capable hands.

Many thanks again for all your kindness and

generosity in this matter, I couldn't be more grateful and I'm certain that Jessie will feel the same.
　Best wishes,
　Emma

Now I think I might be sick. My hands are trembling, my heart is palpitating and my breathing is short and jagged, like I'm having a full-blown panic attack. I read and re-read it over and over again, but there's no mistake.

Emma set me up for a fall.

Emma, my trusted friend.

I have to keep saying it out loud because it just sounds so completely ridiculous, I mean this is Emma I'm talking about here! Apart from anything else, why would she do something like that to me? I was her co-presenter, for God's sake, her team-mate!

Then like a thunderbolt, it hits me. Because until I came along, *she* was Channel Six's rising star, not me. I started out with just a little five-minute dare segment on what was then her show and it all mushroomed from there.

Could she really have wanted me out of the way that desperately?

The more I think about it the more mental it sounds, but then I keep coming back to the email and reading it over and over again.

There's no mistake. Emma was the only person alive who I'd confided in about my own car being repossessed, so she knew my weak spot and went in for the kill. There's no other way of looking at it. Plus, according to this email, she was initially offered the car herself and turned it down, knowing it was a sackable offence, but put me up for it instead. It's at this stage that I honestly think I might need to start breathing into a paper bag. I don't, but I do desperately need to confide in someone and NOW. Sharon's out with Matt, Maggie's pacing around the TV room downstairs, immersed in her routine, Joan's in a fouler, so instead of turning to any of them, I call the one person who I know will talk me off the ledge I'm perched on. In other words, Steve.

I've barely said hello when he instantly asks if everything's OK. But there's just no way that I can possibly begin to tell him over the phone. So I just tell him that I urgently need to talk to him, somewhere private.

'Where are you now?' he asks firmly.

'Home.' Honest to God, my voice sounds so tiny, you'd think it was coming from another room.

'Stay right where you are. I'm on my way.'

Half an hour later, he's sitting on Sharon's bed, with his long legs stretched out in front of him, reading the email printout for about the tenth time. I'm on my own bed opposite him, white-faced and physically shivering from the shock of it all.

'Jessie, are you sure you're all right?'

'Yes. I mean no. I mean, I don't know. I just . . . this can't be happening. Just can't be.'

'It's a lot to take in all right.' Then a wry grin at me. 'And you said I watched too many conspiracy movies.'

I look guiltily at him. 'Sorry about that.'

'You know when I saw that documentary about you, it did strike me that the whole thing stank to high heaven. There was something not quite right about it. I remember thinking that it really looked like you'd been set up for a fall. And I'm not the only one who thought so either.'

'But this is Emma we're talking about here. Emma!' I

repeat for about the hundredth time, slumping back against the pillows in frustration. 'We've been friends for . . .'

'For how long now?'

'Since I first started doing freelance bits of reporting for Channel Six. Then I got a tiny little feature-ette on what used to be her talk show . . .'

'Oldest motivation in the book. She was jealous of your popularity and in one fell swoop this got rid of you in such a way that it would almost be impossible for you ever to come back.'

'It has to be a mistake. I just can't believe it of her . . .'

'Like in all conspiracy theories, the first question you have to ask yourself is, who stood to benefit? Answer: Emma Sheridan. Look at what she's gained; not only has she got you out of her hair, she's even got her own talk show.'

'But why would she do something so daft as to leave an incriminating email lying around the office? Suppose someone had found it?'

'She slipped up. Look at the date on the email; the day before your very last show. Sounds to me like she saw her opportunity and grabbed it, but was up against the clock. Which didn't exactly leave her much time to cover all of her tracks, did it? Maybe she meant to delete the email but printed it off accidentally because she was in such a blind panic. Maybe, I dunno, maybe someone in the office interrupted her, so she shoved it somewhere, fully intending to shred it later on when she had more privacy. But the point is, no one did find the email, did they? Even you only stumbled on it by chance.'

'Oh my God, I just thought of something else!' I interrupt him, suddenly sitting bolt upright.

'The runner who dropped all my stuff from the office

around here? Her name is Amy and I called her to say thank you. But now I remember . . . She said something that struck me as really odd . . .'

'Namely?'

'That right after that awful last show . . .' My voice is actually breaking now.

'Come on, Jessie, deep breaths.'

I do what he tells me. In for two and out for four. In for two and out for four . . . 'After I was fired and everything,' I go on, a bit calmer now, 'Amy said she went to the production office and found Emma already there, shredding stuff. Which I thought was beyond weird. Why shred documents? It didn't make sense.'

'Well it does now. It's classic,' says Steve, shaking his head. 'I'm sorry to have to say this, but it seems to me that all along, Emma was nothing more than a smiling assassin.'

'A smiling assassin,' I repeat dully. Knowing deep down in my heart that he's right. Other things start coming back to me too. The day she helped me clear out all my good clothes and I ended up bringing the wrong bags to the second-hand store. Joan said she'd distinctly told her that the labelled bags were hers, destined for Oxfam, but there was still a mix-up. I thought nothing of it when Joan told me this, figuring it was just one of those unfortunate things that was no one's fault. And I know it's nothing I can ever prove, but now I'm thinking, could it have been deliberate? Pure malice? To keep me down and out and broke and in my place?

Then something else hits me. 'She didn't want me to take the radio gig either.'

'Now why does that not surprise me? Of course she didn't. Last thing she'd want is you back in the public eye again. Hard to hear, Jessie, I know, but it's true.'

There's a silence while I try to digest this. But I can't get away from the facts that are staring me in the face. And now there's something else bothering me.

'The guy from Mercedes Ireland, this Joe de Courcey fella,' I say, thinking aloud. 'Here's what I don't get. Given the momentous coverage my sacking got in all the papers, wouldn't he have come forward to tell the truth about what happened? That he offered Emma the car first, but she turned him down and suggested me to him instead? Why would he stay as silent as the grave and watch me hang?'

'I'm sorry to have to say this,' says Steve gently, 'but welcome to the world of big business, Jessie. The question is, why would he even need to come forward? What did he want out of all this anyway?'

'Well . . . publicity.'

'Yeah, now work from there. Not only did he get about two hundred times more press than Mercedes could ever have hoped for, but it didn't even cost him the price of a new car either. That de Courcey guy is in a win-win situation and don't you forget it. It's in his interests to keep his mouth shut.'

I slump back on the bed, utterly stunned.

'Are you OK?' Steve asks, warm and concerned.

'It's just an awful lot to take in. I mean, look at me. I've just found out that I was betrayed by the one person from my old life who I actually thought was a decent, honourable human being.'

'Caesar liked Brutus and look where that got him.'

Suddenly I'm up on my feet. Because I can't just hang around here any more, I have to do something.

'Steve, I need a favour.'

'Name it.'

'Will you give me a lift on your bike? There's somewhere I need to be. And it can't wait.'

'Sure, but where do you want to go?'

'Channel Six. Right now.'

Chapter Seventeen

The conversation between myself and Steve on his bike goes a bit like this:

Him: 'Jessie, are you absolutely sure that this is a good idea?'

Me: 'Doesn't this fecking yoke go any faster?'

'Seriously,' he says, turning to me when we're stopped at traffic lights. 'Why not just call Emma?'

'Because . . . because I want to show her the email printout, don't I? I want her to know that these aren't just false accusations, I have proof of what she did to me.'

'You do have the printout safely on you, don't you?'

'Yup, shoved down my bra for extra protection.'

Then a fresh worry. 'Steve, just tell me that there's no room for misinterpretation here. We didn't read it wrongly, did we? I mean, it's not going to be something she can explain her way out of, is it?'

'Hard one for her to wriggle her way out of. The facts are there, in black and white. All I'm asking you is, are you quite sure this is the right time and place to do this?'

'Never been more certain of anything in my entire life. I want to wave the email in front of her, then watch her face turn funny colours. I want to hear what she has to say for herself.'

Although the truth is a bit more complex. As we zoom on, I'm rehearsing loads of great sentences to hurl at her in my head, but what I really want more than anything is to look Emma in the whites of her eyes and confront her directly, face to face. Where she can't dodge me or try to brush me off. I want to point my finger at her and say 'J'accuse.' I want to say that, for months now I've had this one thought pressing on me: that I was the architect of my own downfall, when all along I was nothing more than a puppet on a string. Most of all though, I want this shagging motorbike to go faster.

'Why do you want us to go to Channel Six anyway?' Steve yells back at me, shouting to be heard over the wind. 'What I mean is, how do you even know she'll be there?'

'She'll be there, trust me!' I shout back. Because I know the way the station works like the back of my hand. Emma's new show is scheduled to go out live next week, so the Saturday night before the show gets aired is always what they call 'dry run night'. Kind of like a dress rehearsal. With a studio audience, a full camera crew, the whole works. And that's where I'll nab her. Privately in her dressing room before she goes on, with any luck.

I'm going over and over the whole thing in my mind and the part that really stabs like a knife to the heart is that I honestly thought that Emma was my friend. That she was on my side. The one person who stood by me in the dark days. But Steve's on the money; the only reason she even bothered doing that was to make herself feel better. To ease her own survivor guilt and nothing more.

After what feels like a bloody age we eventually whiz

through the gates of the industrial estate where Channel Six is. Funny, but up until today, I would have been all maudlin and nostalgic coming back here, seeing the same building where I worked for so many happy years, seeing my old parking space, now most likely reallocated to Emma.

But not now. I'm not even trembling. There's not a nerve in my body; I'm like ice. Nor will there be any emotional bungee jumping on my part this evening. No regrets, no wondering if I called this wrong and above all no letting Emma wangle her way out of it. I've been picking lumps of humiliation out of my teeth for far too long and now it's payback time. Bring on the fight.

'Do you want me to come in there with you?' Steve asks when we pull up at the main reception door.

'No need.'

'I'm coming anyway.'

'OK. Thanks.'

He squeezes my hand, we whip off our helmets and in we go.

First hurdle: getting past security. As we burst through the main reception doors, I'm silently praying that it's some nice security guard who recognises me and who'll let us through without a fuss. Trouble is that you need either a security tag or a visitor's pass to get through and we have neither. There's a TV monitor on the wall behind the security desk with a live feed coming directly from the studio floor, but the dry run hasn't begun yet; all you can see are technicians fiddling with lights and the set decoration people busy doing their thing. So in other words, this couldn't be a more perfect time for me to strike.

But I'm out of luck. The security guard on duty is a guy I've never set eyes on before, wiry, small and so thorough in his questioning that in the Cold War, he'd have done brilliantly working for the Stasi. 'And you're here to see who exactly?' He glares at me.

'Well, we're actually here on kind of . . . emm . . . personal business, you see . . .'

Stasi guy folds his arms and I'm just waiting on him to tell us he'll escort us off the premises if we don't leave, when next thing I feel Steve's arm slip around my waist.

'What she's trying to say is that we're here for the show tonight, aren't we, love?' he grins cheekily. 'We won two audience tickets and I can tell you this is the highlight of our week. Neither of us have ever been in a TV studio before, have we, honey?'

Now why didn't I think of that?

'May I see the tickets please, sir?'

'Yeeeeeeah, that's the problem,' says Steve, cool as you like. 'You see, I thought all along that my girlfriend here had them, and she thought that I had them, but the thing is that neither of us do. In fact, they're probably sitting on the kitchen table at home right now, aren't they, sweetheart? Which is kind of funny, when you think about it.'

But Stasi guy looks unconvinced. So I pull out all the stops and join in the improv.

'Please, you've no idea how much this means to us,' I beg him. 'We had a terrible fight on the way here about whose fault it was leaving the tickets at home and we've just come all the way from . . .'

'Kerry,' Steve finishes my sentence for me. 'And it's our anniversary. And being here for the show tonight is just so exciting for us. You've no idea.'

There's a long, scary pause while Stasi guy looks at us, weighing up whether we're two whack jobs on the loose or an actual, genuine case. But outright lying seems to do the trick because next thing he's flourishing a biro at us and shoving the visitor's book under our noses.

'Sign here, please.'

We do as we're told, both of us trying to conceal our triumph. Then we're both issued with visitor's passes and waved in the direction of the main door.

So far, so good.

'It's worse than bloody Fort Knox in here,' Steve whispers to me as we pass through the door, then find ourselves in the long, narrow corridor that leads directly to the studio.

'This way,' I say, steering him down yet another tiny corridor which then leads on to the make-up and dressing rooms.

'Good line-up for tonight,' says Steve, noticing a few names on the dressing room doors. I take a quick glance too and it is pretty impressive, for a late summer talk show when a lot of A-listers would be on holiday. The Deputy Prime Minister for one, a boy band member who's just announced his engagement is another; there's even a bona fide Irish movie star, who's been based in LA for years but must be in town to promote a new film. It has all the makings of a terrific programme. Shame about the presenter, is all I can think as we race down to the end of the corridor.

Next thing, a familiar face steps out of one of the dressing rooms and instantly spots me.

'Jessie? Jessie Woods? Is that you under all that red hair? My God, it *is* you! Come here and give me a hug!'

I can't believe my luck. It's Amy, the lovely runner.

'Oh my God, you've no idea how good it is to see you!' I say, hugging her so tight I might break her.

'Right back at you, babe. You've been sorely missed, I can tell you. I never remember there being any diva fits when you were working here.' She shoots a significant look at the dressing room she's just come out of and it's then I notice the nameplate on the door. Ms Emma Sheridan. 'Hey, introduce me to your friend, will you?' Amy says, spotting Steve and immediately going to shake hands with him.

'Oh, Amy, this is my good friend Steve. Steve, Amy.'

'So what brings the pair of you here? Have you come to wish Emma luck for the dry run?'

I look at her for a split second, weighing up whether or not to confess all. But time is of the essence here, best to leave all explanations until later, I figure. On the other hand though, feigning that we've come all this way to wish Emma luck would at least guarantee that we get in to see her . . . But Steve steps in for me.

'Yes, that's right,' he grins winningly. 'I'm a huge fan of Emma's and have wanted to meet her for so long.' God, he's good. I almost believe him myself. 'But then Jessie here suggested we pop in to see her before the show, just to let her know we're all rooting for her. If it's OK with you, that is?'

Between all his fair-haired, blue-eyed sincerity and the innocent lack of guile that Steve's able to project, I can practically see Amy being completely won over.

'Ordinarily I'd have said no problem,' she says, dropping her voice a bit, 'but the mood madam's in tonight! You've no idea, she's been on my case all afternoon with the stupidest demands you ever heard . . .'

With that, the dressing room door opens and out comes the woman herself. Emma. Dressed in a very expensive-looking cocktail dress and fully made up, with the most stunning jewellery I've ever seen. Looking like she always does: groomed, glossy and it chokes me to say it, but gorgeous.

'Amy, I asked you for sparkling water five minutes ago and I'm still waiting for it—' She breaks off, suddenly spotting me.

For a nano second, I detect a sliver of dread in her. Which she instantly covers. Covers so beautifully that I almost doubt myself and wonder if I was just imagining things.

'Jessie! Oh sweetheart, it's so lovely to see you! How are you?'

My God, what an actress is all I can think as she lunges into air kissing me. Sincere as you like, warm and friendly. As if she's genuinely over the moon to see me.

I introduce Steve and she's equally charming to him too.

'So what brings you here, babe?' she beams brightly at me.

'Actually Emma,' I say as firmly as I can, 'I need a private word with you, if that's OK?'

'Can it wait? As you've probably noticed, I'm kind of in the middle of a show here.'

'I'll only take two minutes of your time, Emma, but I'm afraid that no, it can't wait. This is important.'

'Hey, so's my new show, Jessie! You know how it is on a dry run night, all go. Tell you what, why don't you and I meet up for a coffee really soon and we can have a chat then? But in the meantime, it's lovely as always to see you. You take care now!'

I do not believe this.

She walks off, calmly as you like, as if I'm some minor annoyance that can be swept under the carpet and dealt with at a later date. Well, I'm sorry, I think, as a massive surge of rage bubbles up from my toes. Emma wouldn't have a fecking show to do tonight had she not shafted me in the first place.

So I follow her. 'Emma, I said NO. This is not something that can be brushed aside. I said I need to talk to you right now. And believe me, what I have to say will be far less embarrassing for you to hear in private.'

OK, now she's ignoring me. Actually blanking me, as if I'm not even here. It's bizarre, we're all trailing in her wake down the narrow corridor which leads to studio one, but the only person she's addressing is Amy, making some ludicrous, bossy demand about the preferred kind of mineral water she wants beside her during the show. She's striding faster and faster and I'm almost running just to keep pace with her. Then, just as we're at the door of the studio, I nab her. This is one problem that she's not going to turn her back on.

'Emma, if you'd rather I spoke to you in public, then that's your call,' I say right to the back of her head. She turns round to me, all smiles and lip gloss.

'You know, Jessie, if you'd like studio audience seats, I'm sure Amy here can organise them for you and your friend. But I'm afraid that this is where I say goodbye.'

Christ alive, she's treating us like fans, like we're her obsessive admirers.

She's right inside the studio door now, just behind all the steps where the audience are already seated and having a good laugh at the warm-up act. Then a make-up girl who I know well comes over to touch her up, before she goes on camera.

'No powder, Cheryl,' Emma orders her curtly. 'You know how powder ages me.'

'Oh, not this again,' says Cheryl in exasperation. 'Come

on, you know perfectly well that you can't go on camera without powder . . .' And that's when she spots me. Lurking in the background like the ghost of TV shows past. Just waiting to pick my moment. 'Oh my GOD, Jessie Woods . . . it *is* you! I hardly recognised you! Oh it's such a treat to see you.' She instinctively comes over to hug me but Emma stops her in her tracks.

'Cheryl, there's plenty of time for small talk later. Can I remind you that I've a show to do? Jessie, I'm sure, understands. Jessie, in fact, shouldn't by rights even be here.'

The next few moments all seem to blur into one. I'm shaking, actually trembling with rage now, at her daring to be so dismissive when she's the one who . . .

Next thing I know, I've stormed up to her, trying my best to keep my voice down, but not really succeeding. 'Emma Sheridan, it's time you listened to me. You can act the diva around here all you like and you can swan off to do your new TV show and the best of luck to you. But there's something you should know: I found out the truth. You didn't mean for me to, but guess what? I did.'

'What are you talking about?' Emma is looking at me now, utterly nonplussed.

'THIS,' I almost snarl, shoving my hand down my jumper and praying to Jaysus that I didn't manage to lose the email on my way here.

Mercifully I didn't, so I grab it and shove it in her face. '*This* is what I'm talking about, Emma. Read it and weep. Because this is your worst nightmare. The night I got fired? I was set up for a fall. By you. My friend. My best friend, who I trusted.' My voice breaks a bit now. Can't help it. Extreme emotion does that to me. But at least now, I have Emma's full attention.

'That's the most ridiculous thing I've ever heard,' she laughs. Actually laughs. 'Me? Set you up for a fall?' she snorts incredulously. 'You know, maybe it's time you and your friend thought about leaving the building. I'm happy to get security down here although I'm sure you'd rather avoid the embarrassment of being escorted off the premises . . .'

'I suggest you have a look at this!' I'm half yelling now, as I clutch on to the email with shaky hands and start reading the most damning bits, line by line.

'"Dear Joe . . .

About my other idea, I forgot to mention that Jessie's car was repossessed only a few weeks back and I've no doubt that, if faced with a brand, spanking new Mercedes SLK in showroom condition, will be only too delighted to accept. Who wouldn't be? The main thing to remember is not to take no for an answer."'

'OK, you know what, Jessie? I think we've all heard enough,' says Emma, astonishingly, still smiling.

'Did I say I was finished?' I snap back at her. Then I go back to reading.

Except what I haven't realised is that by now, I've got a bit of an audience. Puzzled by all the bickering from the side of the set, some of the studio audience have turned to look downwards from the seating rig to see for themselves what the cat fight brewing at the side of the stage is all about.

Maybe even wondering whether it's part of the gig.

'"She's proud,"' I read on, louder now, my voice growing in confidence, '"and will really need this forced on her! I'm thinking, maybe personalised number plates might be an idea? However, I'll leave the details in your more than capable hands. Many thanks again for all your kindness and generosity in this matter, I couldn't be more grateful and I'm certain that Jessie will feel the same. Best wishes, Emma."'

I break off and look Emma right in the whites of her eyes. Just waiting for a reaction. She's staring at me now and I honestly think in all the years I've known her that it's the first time I've seen her break a sweat.

'This is so absurd,' she eventually says, though her voice is icy. 'I can assure you that I had absolutely nothing whatsoever to do with your being fired. As you yourself admitted, it was entirely your own fault.'

'You were the only person who knew that my own car had been repossessed . . .'

'Another lie. My God, Jessie, don't you know when to stop?'

'. . . so you arranged everything to make sure that I was for the chop . . .'

'YOU took the free car, dearest. Not me. End of story.'

'I'm not even beginning to deny that. And God knows, I've paid the highest possible price for it. But look me in the eye and tell me that you didn't set the whole thing up, knowing full well I hadn't a clue that what I did was a sackable offence . . .'

'And frankly, to come here and start flinging around wild accusations when I'm just about to do a dry run is really beyond the beyond. Can we get security in here, please?'

She's striding away from me now, heading towards the warmth of the lights, so not quite knowing what I'm at, not even pausing to think, I follow her.

There's a round of applause as we appear together at the side of the set, then a ripple effect.

'Can that be Jessie Woods?'

'No, sure that one has red hair . . .'

'Sounds like her . . .'

'Having a cat fight with Emma Sheridan? Doubt it . . .'

Is all I'm dimly aware of in the background, but I blank it out. Plenty of time for mortification later.

'Emma, BIG mistake to turn your back on me, I'm not finished!' I say to her, calmer now.

'I'm afraid finished is exactly what you are,' Emma smiles. 'And if you think you can stride in here waving some email which I never even wrote and ruin my show, I'm afraid you're quite mistaken.'

'That's the best defence you can come up with? So you claim you never wrote this in the first place?' I take a deep breath before playing my trump card.

'Then would you mind telling me how come it's got your personal email address on the top of it? The ultra private one?'

She ignores me.

Big mistake.

'Can you please deal with this?' she appeals to the floor manager, who strides over to separate us.

'Jessie, come on, leave her alone, will you?' he says firmly, steering me back the way I came. Next thing I'm aware of, Stasi security guy is at my shoulder, telling me in no uncertain terms that it's time for me to leave and that he'll be happy to escort me off the premises. There's a rough tug at my arms and a half second later, he's propelled me right back to the studio door.

Then, something weird. Someone, I'm in such a state I couldn't even tell you who, whips the email out of my hands. My only piece of evidence.

But I just keep on yelling back at Emma, who's now in

situ on set at her desk, for once without her standard ladylike composure. 'You knew my weak spot and you took full advantage of it!' I shout back at her, halfway out the door now.

I'm making a holy show of myself and I don't even care.

'Ladies and gentlemen,' says Emma, addressing the audience and trying to reassert control. 'I'm so sorry that you all had to witness that . . .'

No one's listening to her though; they're all too busy focusing on the yelling from offstage. 'You wanted me out, you wanted me fired, you wanted to ruin me and you did!'

Knowing she's virtually lost her entire audience now, Emma redoubles her efforts to win them back. 'LADIES AND GENTLEMEN! Please let me assure you that this is just a temporary blip in what will be a fantastic night's entertainment . . .'

'. . . then, worst of all, you were hypocritical enough to pretend to be my friend! Phoning me all the time, acting like you were devastated for me. You even called over to my house just to check up on me!'

'. . . and so without further ado . . . if I can just have your attention, ladies and gentlemen, I'd like to introduce my first guest . . .'

'. . . and Amy here even said she caught you shredding documents in the production office right after I got fired. So now we all know why!'

'I'll vouch for you there, Jessie!' Amy shouts out loyally, bless her.

As I'm finally hustled out the studio door, Steve is waiting, leading another round of applause and beaming proudly at me from ear to ear.

'You DID it!' he yells, grabbing me into a bear hug and

squeezing me tight. 'You got her good! I could not be prouder of you, you were AMAZING!'

'Get me out of here,' is all I can gibber back at him. 'Now.'

Next thing, we're hand-in-hand, racing towards the main reception door, like the pair of us have just held up a bank at gunpoint or something. We make it outside, just as someone behind us screeches out my name.

'JESSIE! Jessie, wait up will you?'

It's lovely Cheryl from make-up. With the famous email in her hand.

'Here love,' she says breathlessly, thrusting it back at me. 'Sorry, that was me who snatched it from you back there.'

I just look at her, still panting and not able to talk. Or even think straight.

'You really played a blinder you know,' she wheezes.

'So why did you need this . . .?' I gasp back, clutching the email.

'To photocopy it, of course. Then I ran down to Liz Walsh's office and left a copy of it there, so she can see it for herself.'

'Liz who?' says Steve.

'The Head of Television. Just figured that this is something she should know about. Don't you?'

I hug her goodbye and thank her profusely and next thing, it's just Steve and me on our own together in the late evening sunshine. Then for some mad reason, out of nowhere we both crack up laughing, as giddy as two children.

'So, where to now?' he laughs happily, arm around my waist now, steering me towards the bike.

I'm still giddy and hysterical and still trying to get my breath back, but somehow I manage to say, 'To work, of course. Hey, Emma Sheridan isn't the only one with a show to do tonight.'

And I'm not even sure how it happens, but the next thing is, we're kissing.

Chapter Eighteen

Meanwhile, Maggie's big night is this Sunday in the Comedy Cellar and, I swear to God, the rest of us at home are practically mouthing her routine along with her at this stage. She's been working her arse off too. Night after night you'll find her pacing up and down the TV room trying some of her riffs this way, then that, constantly scribbling down notes, changes, additions, whatever. In her defence, she did hone down her act considerably as some of the gags were just a bit too ahem, let's just say personal.

'My stepsister recently got dumped by her boyfriend,' went one of her jokes, ha ha ha, 'and you should have seen the state of her; she was in absolute bits. In fact, if it wasn't for the Valium, she'd be on drugs.'

She looked at me hopefully but all I could do was shake my head.

'Cut?' she asked.

'Definitely cut.'

Nor was Sharon exempt either.

'My sister,' went another gag, 'works at Smiley Burger and was recently made Employee of the Month. Which just goes to show you that it's possible to be both a winner and a loser at the same time.'

'Cut immediately, you cheeky skanger!!' Sharon screeched, flinging a handful of popcorn across the room at her, and in fairness, Maggie obediently did as she was told.

So now, with only a few days to go to the big night, the routine is looking far sharper and wittier, with Maggie's uniquely droll take on the world practically imprinted on every line. 'I'm a toxic single female,' goes one particular riff. 'And the thing is, I get a lot of grief for not having a boyfriend. Anyway, I got fed up with all the old aunties and uncles saying to me at weddings, "Oh, you'll be next." So I started saying it to them at funerals.'

The highest compliment I give her, which I mean so sincerely, is that even though I've heard her rehearse that joke over and over again, I still laugh. The hallmark of a true comic. So I tell her this and she glows.

'You're not just saying that?'

'I'm not just saying that.'

'And you promise me you'll sit in the front row on Sunday night, not let on you know me and laugh uproariously at all my gags?'

'Wouldn't miss it for the world. It's the highlight of my week.'

'Thanks Jessie. I mean . . . for everything.'

It's the happiest I think I've ever seen her. These days she's even being nice to Matt, for God's sake.

Anyway, Steve has asked me out. At least I sort of think he did. The thing is that after the snogging incident last Saturday night, things have been kind of weird between us. In the way that these things always end up getting weird. Which I hate, because apart from anything else, he's my friend and I wouldn't want to lose that for the world.

But, after *The Midnight Hour* on Saturday night, he gave me a lift home and there was no repeat performance of us leaping on each other like we did outside Channel Six. In fact, as he dropped me off at Whitehall, it was kind of ... strange. Like something had shifted between us. I felt shy and mortified around him and I'm never shy or mortified around Steve, ever. We said a hurried goodnight, then I lay awake for the rest of the night playing the whole evening over in my head like a loop. The euphoria of the moment must be my excuse. After making such a spectacle of myself in Channel Six, having done exactly what I set out to do in letting Emma have it, it was just a huge release of emotions, nothing more. Because how could I ever even think about letting someone else into my heart? Not possible. Not while I'm still grieving the loss of ... well, you know who.

Steve calls me the next day, which is Sunday, my day off. Yet more weirdness and awkwardness. Funny to think that he and I are capable of having two-hour-long chats when we're face to face about the most inane crap you ever heard and yet now, our conversation is stilted and ikky. The pair of us are both tongue-tied, actually speaking to each other in broken sentences.

'Sorry to bother you on your day off, Jessie, but I just really called to say—'

'It's fine. I'm actually helping Joan with her website.'

'Well, that's great. I mean, isn't it? For Joan, is what I—'

'Yeah.'

'So, anyway, the thing is ... I've got band practice tonight. We've got a gig at a festival down the country next Friday and Saturday.'

'Oh, that's good.'

'Because otherwise, what I mean is . . . I mean if I didn't . . .'

'No, no, you go to band practice and enjoy.'

'Well, what I mean is, if I was free then I'd be asking you . . . except that . . . well . . . you're not free are you?'

'No . . . I'm helping Joan . . .'

'Yeah, yeah. Sorry, you already said. So maybe on your next night off, like next Sunday, maybe you and I could . . .'

'Oh, that's the night of Maggie's stand-up, she made me swear in blood that I'd be there for her. We all have to be.'

'Well then, why don't I come too?'

'Oh . . . yeah, of course! That would be . . . lovely.'

'I was going to say it to some of the guys at work too. Because it'll be a fun night.'

'Oh. OK. Good idea. Well then, in that case . . .'

'Then I could invite Hannah and Paul too . . .'

'Brilliant. It'd be lovely to see her out and about.'

'Well, then, I'll . . . see you tomorrow, I suppose.'

And he's gone. Leaving me shaking my head and puzzled. Did he just try to ask me out or didn't he? I can't figure it. Because I'd have asked him to come along and support Maggie on her big night anyway, along with a whole load of people from Radio Dublin. Which makes it sound like a groupie-groupie, non-date-type night, doesn't it? And then he was the one who suggested bringing Hannah and her husband along too. Did he say that thinking there'd be safety in numbers? So, weighing up all the probabilities, to quote Matt, the likelihood staring me in the face is that this is most definitely NOT a date. Just a gang of mates going out for a laugh. That's all.

Funny thing is I can't decide whether I'm relieved or disappointed.

But on the plus side, we've a whole week of working together ahead of us before next Sunday, so he and I should be back on an even keel by then.

Trouble is, by the time Sunday night comes around, my life has changed so irrevocably that this turns out to be the last thing on my mind.

It begins on Monday morning. Well, mid-morning would be more accurate, as Sharon's on late shifts and she and I are practically living vampire hours these days; up till all hours at night then sleeping in until almost the crack of lunchtime the next day.

My mobile wakes me, so I tip-toe out to the landing, so as not to disturb the slumbering Sharon. 'Hello?' I answer groggily.

'Jessie? This is Liz Walsh calling from Channel Six. I wondered if you had a window in your schedule at any time today? I'd like to meet with you, if that were possible. I think it's not an understatement to say that you and I have urgent business to discuss.'

I almost drop the phone.

She misinterprets my silence and says, 'That's if you're amenable to meeting me, Jessie. I understand the last time we spoke was very hurtful for you and I deeply regret that.'

OK, now I think I might just have to breathe into a paper bag. Did Liz Walsh just sort-of apologise to me? Unheard of! Liz is famous for never, ever, on pain of death apologising to anyone. One time she had the Minister for Finance complaining after a right grilling he got on Channel Six's flagship current affairs show. It was the stuff of legend; even under pressure from a high-ranking government office, Liz stood firm and told them all where to go.

So you can understand why at this very moment, I'm

slumped down against the top stair, checking the number of the incoming call to make sure it's not some eejit playing a cruel practical joke on me. Definitely Channel Six calling. No mistake.

'So where would suit you to meet?' she asks politely.

Again, gobsmacking in itself. On the rare occasions when Liz wants to see anyone, they're told to be at her office at X time and woe betide you if you've a problem with that.

I manage to stammer, 'Emm . . . well, you see, I'm over on the Northside now and I don't have a car, so it would take me at least an hour to get over to you . . .'

'Oh no, Jessie, not here. I'm taking you out to lunch. How about we meet half-way? The city centre, perhaps. I suggest Marco Pierre White's restaurant. Do you know it?'

'Umm . . . yeah.'

Everyone knows it. Mainly because it's probably the swishest, priciest restaurant in town.

'Great. Well, I'll book a table and see you there for 1 p.m. Until then, Jessie.'

It takes me ages to get ready because I'm just not used to going anywhere posh. Bizarre, getting all glammed up for lunch, when these days all I live in is jeans. Like a flashback to the old days. Plus I keep having to slump down on the bed beside Sharon and say over and over again, 'Why? Why does she want to see me?'

'Because you're a mad bitch and she feels sorry for you?' says Sharon helpfully. 'Or maybe she wants to recommend a good psychiatrist for you? You know, after you had to be hauled out of there by security men the other night.'

'She already fired me. She's done her worst. The only reason she could possibly want to see me is to read me the riot act about the scene I caused with Emma, but thing is,

I don't work for her any more. So why bother reopening old wounds?'

'Haven't a clue,' says Sharon, sitting up in bed and reaching out to light her first fag of the morning. 'But I'll tell you one thing. After everything the old witch put you through, the bleeding least she can do is treat you to a posh nosh-up.'

'She'll have to. You think I can afford Marco Pierre White's on what Radio Dublin pay me?'

I'm waiting so long for the bus that I arrive a bit late. But feeling strong and confident, I have to say, wearing my one and only Peter O'Brien suit which screams, 'You may have canned me, but this phoenix has risen from the ashes and I have another job now . . . HA!' I arrive at the restaurant, probably the only person lunching here this afternoon who used public transport to get here. I step inside and the maître d' immediately guides me to a quiet window table where Liz is already waiting. She waves away my apologies for being delayed, which again is unheard of. Liz is famously punctual herself and therefore unbelievably intolerant of it in others.

Mercifully, she comes straight to the point. 'I'm fully aware of everything that happened the other night,' she says, clipped and articulate as ever.

'Liz, I know I was out of line, but you've no idea how furious I was with Emma.'

'Perfectly understandable,' she nods, waving the waiter away so we can have some privacy.

'I knew it was the dry run of her show,' I continue, determined to get at least this much out of the way, 'and that I couldn't have engineered a worse time to have it out with her, but believe me, I'd no choice. She kept walking away from me and over my dead body was I letting her get away with what she'd done.'

'Quite right too.'

I'm gabbling on a bit, so there's a two-second time delay before it hits me; Liz is *agreeing* with me.

'Thing is, Jessie,' she says briskly, 'I've read the email. And what's more, I checked up on the facts.'

'What do you mean?'

'Well, I tracked down the infamous Joe de Courcey, Head of Mercedes Ireland.'

Now my heart stops. 'And?'

'And once I assured him that this would be a private conversation which would go no further, he verified everything for me. But he was at pains to stress that he genuinely had no idea this constituted a breach of ethics until he read about it in the papers.'

'After I'd already been fired. When it was too late.'

'Unfortunately, yes. Trouble was, Mercedes by then had been name checked in every national paper, so he felt it best for the company's corporate image not to pour more oil on the fire, as it were. He was most apologetic about not coming forward of course, but it would have meant a hugely negative press story for Mercedes. Naturally, the last thing they wanted.'

'Exactly what Steve said,' I say, thinking aloud.

'Who?'

'Oh, sorry. A friend. A good friend.'

'But that's not the main reason I asked you here, Jessie. There's something else that you should know.'

'Yes?'

'As of this morning, Emma Sheridan is no longer an employee of Channel Six.'

My jaw falls to the table. 'You fired her?'

It's at this point I have to remind myself to breathe.

'I called her into my office and demanded a full explanation from her. Firstly about the contact she'd had with Mercedes Ireland and secondly, about her sly manipulation of a fellow work colleague. Astonishing really, she behaved almost like a politician. Even in the face of incontrovertible evidence, she denied, denied, denied.'

OK, now I don't know what to feel. Half of me is vindicated that Emma finally got her come-uppance but at the same time, it's awful that another human being has to go through what I went through. Although, mind you, she had no difficulty standing by and watching me crash and burn.

But still.

'Liz, I never meant for Emma to lose her job over this, all I intended . . . I mean, all I wanted was to look her in the eye and tell her I knew what she'd done to me. That she hadn't got away with it, as she'd thought.'

'You're completely missing the point, Jessie. You were fired for breaking an ethical code. And Emma was fired for breaking a moral code. I like to delude myself that we're a team at Channel Six and she most definitely did NOT behave like a team player. You were constantly outpolling her in the audience popularity stakes and it seems this was her attempt to get you out of the way. Atrocious behaviour and I for one felt that I could never work with her again after that. Because how could I possibly work with someone I can't even trust?'

I slump back against the chair and take a gulp of water. Never in my wildest flights of fancy did I think that Emma, the model of professionalism, would do anything to endanger her precious career. In fact, I almost want to take a look out the window, just to check that the world hasn't, in fact, come to an end.

'However, my prime concern,' Liz continues, fanning herself with the wine list, 'is that this be kept out of the media. It's highly damaging to us in the long run. I'm meeting with our PR people later this afternoon and we're putting out a joint statement saying Emma Sheridan felt this was the right time for her to leave the station. For personal reasons. She's reluctantly agreed to this, but then she has little other choice. From her point of view, it means she doesn't have to leave in disgrace and at least it allows me to get rid of her quickly and quietly.'

'Some chance of it not leaking out though, Liz. Even when I worked there, Channel Six was always more like a colander than a TV station. Stuff gets leaked all the time. And remember, a whole studio audience saw the sideshow for themselves. All it takes is for one person for go on Twitter and that's the end of all containment.'

'I agree. Which is why I'm asking you not to give any interviews to the press. Who I'm sure will be in contact with you in the days to come. Let's at least try to limit this.'

I'm about to do as she asks, mainly out of shock than anything else and then it hits me . . . hang on a second.

My reputation is at stake here too. I was vilified in the papers and now I'm exonerated, so if the press ring me wanting the story clarified, why would I say no? It's not like I'm an employee of Channel Six any more anyway, so shouldn't I just be delighted at any chance to clear my good name? Plus, after everything Emma's done, she's getting to leave with her reputation intact, so why shouldn't I grab at the chance to restore my own?

'And now, the carrot,' Liz continues. 'In return for your

full co-operation, I'd like to offer you your old job back. Subject to your agreement, *Jessie Would* can be back on the air, with a new co-presenter, within a matter of weeks. What do you say? Jessie?'

Chapter Nineteen

As soon as Liz sweeps off in a taxi, I find myself wandering aimlessly up Dawson Street and into the relative calm of St Stephen's Green. Need air. Need headspace. Need to digest what's just happened to me.

I find a quiet park bench and sit down, taking deep, soothing yoga breaths. In for two and out for four. In for two and out for four. The offer on the table is thus (and frankly, it's a miracle I was even able to concentrate on what Liz was saying, my head was swirling that much): I have my old job back. With a ten per cent pay rise. I'll have a brand new contract in a few days' time. As soon as that's signed, I'll be back on full salary. *Jessie Would* could be back on the air in as little as two months' time.

Through the cloud of shock that's come over me, I have to keep reminding myself that this is very, very, very good news. This is the answer to my prayers. So why am I not dancing down the streets singing 'Hallelujah'? And then it hits me. It's not numbness or astonishment at all, is it? No, it's guilt, pure and simple. Because now I have to tell Steve that I'm leaving Radio Dublin.

Amazingly, considering *The Midnight Hour* is such a late-night, low-budget gig, Liz was fully aware that I was presenting it and even went as far as congratulating me on its success. But there's just no way that I'd be able to combine working those late hours with the full-on pressure of hosting *Jessie Would*, so it was unspoken but glaringly obvious between us that I'd have to quit Radio Dublin. When I'd barely even started. And when Steve was so good to take a chance on me in the first place. But some little voice in my head told me to stand firm with Liz, even though she's famously tough in negotiations.

So I did. I told her in no uncertain terms that the manager of Radio Dublin was a close, personal friend who'd helped me out at a time when friends were thin on the ground for me. And that the very least I could do was to stay on and work for him, until a replacement could be found.

'But Radio Dublin is only a small local station! This is national television I'm talking about here,' was her dumb-founded reply.

'And I'm more than happy to go back to work for you. But I'm not leaving them high and dry at Radio Dublin. It's not fair. It wouldn't be right.'

Liz smiled wryly, I think a bit unused to loyalty. So the deal we made was this: a contract gets sent to my agent ASAP, and on signature, I'm straight back on the Channel Six payroll, like nothing ever happened. Meanwhile I put in a few hours pre-production each afternoon on *Jessie Would*, which is just about all I'd be able to manage, given my night-time radio commitments. Then, as soon as I'm replaced on *The Midnight Hour*, I go back to full-time work at Channel Six.

It's a dream gig and she's handing it to me on a plate. Liz is even offering to put out a press release later in the month, when any fuss about Emma's leaving will have died down, to say that 'After careful consideration and in light of new information, it's been decided that the termination of Jessie Woods's contract was deeply regrettable.' She actually drafted the bones of the press release on a paper napkin right in front of me, wafting it under my nose for approval.

And in return for everything I'm being offered, my instructions are clear. Under no circumstances am I to discuss this with the press and if asked, all I'm authorised to say is, 'After weighing up all my options, I'm now absolutely delighted to be back on air with a new series of *Jessie Would*.'

You get it. Plug the show at all costs and brush all unpleasantness under the carpet.

So now all I have to do is tell Steve.

I call his mobile from my park bench in the Green and he says he's just about to go into a meeting, but that he'll call me right back. Then, sensitive as ever, he asks if everything's OK and I tell him I need to talk. Urgently. Outside of work though, if he has time for a quick coffee.

So we agree to meet in an hour's time in Bewley's café on Grafton Street. I think the wait is the longest hour of my life.

He bounces in, all tall and blond and scraggy and, it's sweet, his face actually lights up a bit when he spots me in a quiet corner table, pale and still rattled by all that's happened. Funny, but now that I'm about to hand in my notice, all the awkwardness that was between us has now evaporated.

I fill him in on everything that's happened with Liz Walsh and he's utterly amazing about the whole thing. So much so, that it actually magnifies the guilt I'm riddled with.

'Look,' he smiles gently, 'to be honest, it was a coup for

us to get someone with your experience to do a graveyard slot for us in the first, so hey, you're the one who's done me the favour. And it's decent of you, offering to stay on until I find someone to replace you. You don't have to do that. Not many people would have.'

'Hey, you rescued me from a lifetime of burger flipping, remember? You gave me a break when no one else would and the very least I can do is help you out until you find a new presenter.'

'So,' he says looking intently at me. 'You must be on top of the world right now. Everything you ever wanted, handed right back to you? I'd be cracking open the champagne in your shoes.'

I can't answer, so I just bang a spoon off my coffee mug instead.

'Jessie, is everything OK?'

And that's when the truth hits me, sharper than a chilli finger poked into my eye. What they call in TV the ta-daa moment. This doesn't feel right, it just doesn't. Yes, I'm thrilled to go back to Channel Six, of course I am, but the thing is . . . the gig at Radio Dublin saved my life. Do I really want to walk away from it just like that? I loved chatting to the listeners and really felt like, even in a small way, I'd made some kind of difference after each show. Then another back-up thought: Channel Six were so terrifyingly quick to dump me once before, who's to say they won't do it again if I messed up for a second time?

'Steve . . .' I say, sitting forward and meeting his blue gaze, 'I've something to ask, something big and I'm going to fumble it, so you have to listen. Call me a greedy cow who wants to have her cake and eat it but the thing is . . . Liz Walsh wants me to leave Radio Dublin . . . and I don't.

I love working there. I love working with you. And I know it's impossible for me to do *The Midnight Hour* and work for Channel Six.'

Suddenly he's sitting forward, all animated. 'It doesn't necessarily have to be a problem,' he says, thinking on his feet. 'Of course it's out of the question your doing *The Midnight Hour* six nights a week any more, but how's this for a suggestion? You still work for us, except now we call the programme *Woods at the Weekend*,' he says, buzzing with excitement now, running his fingers through his hair. 'And it goes out one night a week, on a Sunday, when you're not shooting for Channel Six. It would be the same basic show, maybe slightly longer, but still with the original format: listeners call in with dating horror stories and you interact with them. What do you say?'

'It's . . . I mean . . . that would be . . . It's completely perfect.'

So perfect that for a second, all I want to do is hug him. But I don't, I just look at him, smiling and teary at the same time. Not trusting myself to believe just how well things have worked out. We both get up to leave as he's another meeting later on and needs to go.

Then he stops for a second and gently takes my arm, suddenly looking . . . I don't know, confused? Conflicted? God, if there's another woman out there worse at reading men than me, I'd really like to meet her.

'Look, Jessie,' he says, tenderly. 'About the other night—'

'No, no, no need to say a thing, it was all my fault—'

'No, what I wanted to say was that, well . . . I know that you're still getting over a bad break-up and I know how hard that can be.'

'Well, yes, but . . .'

'Just in case you wondered why I'd stepped back a bit . . .'

'No, not at all . . .'

Great, now we're back to the fragmented sentences again.

'So I'll see you at the Comedy Cellar for Maggie's gig this Sunday then?'

'Yeah,' I smile. 'Definitely.'

For a split second, I think he's about to lean down and kiss me – and half of me wouldn't mind it if he did – then next thing, my mobile rings. Roger Davenport, my agent. 'Oh shit, I have to take this,' I stammer, nearly dropping the phone.

He just nods, tweaks my chin and winks down at me. And then he's gone.

By that evening, Roger has a contract from Channel Six, pay rise included, signed, sealed and delivered. Just like that. With a night off on Sunday, so I can continue to work at Radio Dublin too. It's the best of all worlds, and it's mine for the taking. But what's completely weird is that I still don't feel euphoric or even remotely like celebrating.

Because there's still someone else I have to talk to and I'm looking forward to it as much as root canal.

Sharon.

By the time I get home, she's on her own in the kitchen, reading *Hot Stars* magazine and eating a pizza, while Maggie practises her routine in the TV room. Perfect time to get her, right after food. I fill her in on all the developments then, drawing a deep breath up from the floor, go for the one sentence I've dreaded having to tell her.

'The thing is, Sharon . . .'

'Yeah?'

'Well, I mean, now that I've got my old job back and

everything, well . . . it's probably time I thought about . . . you know . . .'

'I think I know what you're going to say, Jess.'

In the end, it's actually easier for me just to come straight out with it. 'I'm moving out.'

It's heart-breaking really; for a second I think the two of us are going to cry.

'Come on, Sharon,' I say, gently taking her hand. 'I couldn't keep on sharing your room forever. Apart from everything else, won't you be glad to have the space back?'

'No,' she blurts. 'No, I'm not glad. Sod the sodding space. I don't want you to go. Anyway, you *can't* go. Ma is redecorating that room especially for us.'

For a second, I smile, touched that a Laura Ashley makeover would be a motivation for me to hang around. 'Jess, I don't want it to go back to only seeing you at Dad's anniversary mass once a year for ten minutes. I'd miss you too much.'

'I swear, it's not goodbye. I'll still visit all the time, and not just at Christmas either. Hey, we're friends now and that's what really matters.'

'It's going to be so boring around here without you. You've no idea.'

'Come on, you've got Matt now. Sure you're practically out five nights a week with him.'

She does what she always does whenever Matt's name comes up. Shrugs, lights up a fag and changes the subject.

'So where will you move to?'

'I don't know. I'll rent somewhere close to Channel Six. A small, one-bedroomed apartment maybe. But absolutely nowhere over my budget and nowhere that's too ridiculously big for me. I've been down that road and learned that lesson, I can tell you. Small and affordable will be just fine. My days of over borrowing and over spending to keep up with the Joneses are well and truly over. No more acting like a gap-year trustafarian and no more flashy cars either; I'll get myself a bike and that'll have to do me.'

'Joan and Maggie will miss you too.'

'And I'll miss them. But Joan has her IPrayForYou.com business on the go and Maggie's going to do brilliantly at the Comedy Cellar on Sunday, you wait and see. But the person I'm going to miss the most is you.'

'Me too.'

I lean over to give her a big hug and that's when the pair of us start to well up a bit.

'We've come a long way, haven't we?' she says, sniffling. 'Since you first moved in. I mean, who'd have thought?'

'Such a long way.'

'Won't miss you nicking all my cans of cider though. Jeez, for a skinny bitch, you're sure as hell able to put away the Bulmers.'

'Oh, and you think I'm going to miss you robbing all my make-up, you thieving cow?'

Now we're both giggling a bit.

'Just remember, you're my sister and I'll always be there for you.'

'I'll always be there for you too.'

Chapter Twenty

I don't know how it happened. And what's more I'm fully prepared to swear on my parents' grave that it had nothing whatsoever to do with me. But by the following Wednesday, the papers are full and I really do mean *full* of the story.

It seems that some bright spark in the studio audience for the showdown between myself and Emma, had the brainwave of videoing it on their iPhone. And by Monday it had found its merry way onto YouTube, including a clear shot of me kicking, screaming and being escorted off the premises by security.

I can't actually bring myself to watch it, but Sharon tells me it looks very well. In a Jerry Springer sort of way, that is. Anyway, that led on to a feature piece in the *Evening Herald*. Which, come Tuesday, had mushroomed onto page two of the *Star* and page one of the *Mail*. And by Wednesday, the story is everywhere. The unexpurgated version too; how Emma set me up as the fall guy, how she covered it up and how I miraculously happened to stumble on proof of this almost entirely by accident. How I've been offered my old job back, whereas she's been let go for 'personal reasons'. The truth, the whole truth and nothing but the truth. Better than a soap opera any day. Dear God, no wonder it's such a hot story; you couldn't make it up.

My mobile hasn't stopped, so unless it's someone I know, I've taken to just ignoring it. And if anyone from the press calls me either at Channel Six or at Radio Dublin, I just politely but firmly say no comment to make and refer them back to Roger. No better man.

'Jilted Jessie Returns to Primetime!' is one banner that sticks in my mind. And I have to hand it to them, the reporting is astonishingly accurate. Facts are amazingly unblurred. But then, I've always maintained that there were more leaks at Channel Six than in a winter vegetable medley.

Anyway, come Wednesday late evening, I'm sitting in Steve's office, going through the papers to see if there are any funny stories we can use for tonight's show. Yes, inevitably once we go live on air, the phone lines jam up with callers all wanting to tell their dating horror stories, but it's no harm to have a few newsworthy anecdotes on standby to throw in, just in case the need arises.

'Trouble is,' Steve grins, 'the lead news item this week is you, Jessie Woods.'

I jokingly fling the sports section of the *Independent* across the desk at him, narrowly missing his head. Funny, but ever since I've been reinstated at Channel Six, things have been completely back to normal between us. As if we both know our days of working together six nights a week are numbered, so we're both determined to make these last, precious few weeks as much fun as possible. It's brilliant; we're right back to the way we always used to be; messing and giggling with not a shred of awkwardness between us. Or sexual tension. Which is great. Which is all I wanted. Isn't it?

'Hey,' he says, 'at least the papers all have their facts straight for once. Including Emma's sacking.'

'Yeah, madam won't like that. Not to mention that Channel Six have invoked the phrase of certain death. "Leaving for personal reasons".'

'Yeah, I know what you mean. Makes it sound like she's about to check into the Priory for a six-month detox, doesn't it?'

Come show time, he leads me down to the studio and gives me an affectionate bear hug before I step into the booth. 'Be your usual, fabulous self, Jessie Woods. And hey, remember I'm getting you disgracefully drunk this Sunday to celebrate you getting your old job back. Rat-arsed and pie-eyed and no excuses taken.'

I grin up at him gratefully. Bless him, he's probably the only boss alive good-natured enough to take you out on the tear after you hand in your notice.

Anyway, as soon as we go live on air, the phone calls start and barely stop. Poor Ian in the production booth is more like a 1940s telephonist than a producer these nights. People are all being really sweet, congratulating me on *Jessie Would* being recommissioned, then, after a bit of chit chat, launching into the real reason why they've called in.

It's barely a minute past midnight and I'm on the phone to Carole from Drimnagh who's calling in to ask if anyone out there thinks it's possible to change a man.

'Why do you ask, Carole?' I probe gently.

'Because my ex-boyfriend is back on the scene and when we broke up, he was a complete arsehole. Oops, sorry, Jessie, am I allowed to say arsehole on air?'

'Bit late now!' I say and we both laugh.

'You see, he said he wanted to "take a break" about four

months ago and I was nearly on the floor, I was that devastated. Because he was awful to me, wouldn't return my calls or anything. Anyway, I was just beginning to get my life back together again, when out of the blue he contacts me, saying that he wants to get back together. Just like that. He says that he's changed. Realises what an eejit he was in letting me go so cruelly. But my question is, Jessie, can a fella ever really change?'

'No, definitely not!' yells another caller, Jane from Rathmines. 'They'll mouth platitudes at you and tell you what you want to hear, but no man is fundamentally EVER able to change. Plus, they're like homing devices; able to sense when you're healing from them and that's when they bounce back into your life to mess it up for a second time. So take my advice and run a mile from him. Now, while you still can!'

'But, when we were together,' replies Carole, 'I was always giving out to him for never being romantic. And ever since he's started trying to get back together, overnight it's like he's turned into the Hallmark version of himself.'

'What do you mean?' I ask.

'Making all these spontaneous romantic gestures, without it being Valentine's Day or without my having to nag at him. Flowers for no reason, breakfast in bed, telling me he loves me without a gun being pointed to his head . . .'

'Well, clearly he wants to change,' I say. 'Plus, let's face it. In our love-starved society, don't these little romantic gestures go a long, long way? So I guess what I'm trying to say is, maybe you should give your ex-boyfriend the benefit of the doubt. Because if you don't, you might come to regret it and end up with a serious case of the coulda, woulda, shouldas.'

Then Tommy from Blackrock calls in to say Carole should tell her ex where to go. That in his opinion, trying to change another human being to suit your own ends amounts to little more than a human rights violation.

'And why do you say that, Tommy? Do your girlfriends ever try to change you?' I ask.

'All the time. My clothes, accent, friends, job, you name it. But the only thing I ever change is girlfriends.'

Cue an irate call from Fiona in Temple Bar. 'I am fed up with men trying to change me. All my boyfriend ever wants me to do is to dress sluttier and wear more make-up and frankly I'm sick of it . . .'

Then Susan from Cabra says, 'You know, it's a huge mistake to ever think you can change a man. Apart from their clothes and hair, that is. Because mark my words, once you start pulling at threads, the whole fabric will fall apart.'

The show skyrockets on from there, we barely even have time for music breaks, and before I have time to look at the clock, Ian gives me a hand signal to indicate that I've only time for one last caller before we wrap.

'So who have we got here on line one?' I ask.

There's a long silence. Dead time, as we say on radio, so I'm about to hang up when suddenly a man's voice says just one word. 'Woodsie?'

I know who it is instantly.

With absolute certainty.

But obviously, I don't let on . . .

'Yes, you're through to *The Midnight Hour*. Who's calling please?'

'Woodsie, it's me.'

'I'm sorry, could we have your name please?'

I think it's only delayed shock that's keeping me this calm.

That combined with utter disbelief. I mean, why would he be doing this? If he wanted to talk to me, why not just pick up the phone? Instead of ringing into a late-night talk show? When I'm working for God's sake?

'It's Sam.'

I decide to play it cool. Well, as cool as can be expected given that my bum is starting to sweat. 'And where are you calling from, Sam?'

'At the moment, from my carphone. I just wanted to say, in response to the discussion that's been going on, that yes, men can and do change.'

'What do you mean by that, Sam?'

'I want to say that, unless a man is a complete idiot, he'll change if he realises he's made a mistake.'

'Go on.'

'Because we all make mistakes. But what differentiates a winner from a loser is if you're willing to stand up and say, look, I messed up royally in one particular situation and I'm prepared to change if it means I can win back something . . . or maybe some*one* . . . that's very dear to me.'

My heart stops. For once, I can't think of a logical, coherent question to tack on. But as luck would have it, I'm saved by the bell because just then, Ian waves to tell me that we're out of time.

Nor was I dreaming or imagining things. Because the next day, Sam calls again. And again. And again. By lunchtime, he's left about five messages for me and I've yet to return a single one of his calls. Because I'm in complete freefall. For the first time in I don't know how long, I can't decide on a clear course of action. Weird to think back over all these months, when all I could do was fantasise about Sam contacting me again and now that it's happened, I'm like a rabbit in the headlamps. The thing is . . . I'm doing fine without him. Better than fine, I'm doing brilliantly. My life has finally fallen into place, like Lotto balls. I'm not Cinderella Rockefeller any more; I'm Humpty Dumpty, all put back together again. I never thought that I could function without Sam; I spent so long convincing myself that he was my split-apart soulmate and that without him, I made no sense. But, as usual, I couldn't have been more wrong.

None of this is helped by the fact that I'm completely on my own in the house. Everyone's at work, which is driving me mental; the one occasion when I really need a touchstone of sense to bounce off. I know Steve is there for me, but it just doesn't feel right somehow to discuss this with him. Like this is the one topic that would be absolutely verboten between us. If he copped onto something after a caller named Sam rang the show last night, he never mentioned it, which I was deeply grateful for. He took me home on his bike and if he did suspect that something was up, was gentlemanly enough not to ask. Or even comment on the fact that instead of all my normal high-octane chatter after a show, I barely opened my mouth the whole way back to Whitehall.

The other thing I'd forgotten about Sam is that, when he wants something, he goes after it with a kind of scorched earth policy. I know him of old, he'll basically just batter down doors until he gets what he's after, which he always, always does. So after about his twelfth attempt to call me, I eventually answer. Sitting trembling and unsure of myself at our kitchen table, with no one around to advise me or calm me down. I take a deep breath and answer the phone.

It's a short chat, brief and to the point. He wants to see

me and asks how soon can we meet? That what he wants to say isn't for over the phone. He suggests we meet at Bentleys Oyster Bar in town at seven this evening, just before I go into work.

'Woodsie? Are you still there? Does that suit you? I mean ... do you want to meet me?'

A long pause.

'I'm nodding.'

It's the only two words I've uttered for the entire conversation.

The good news is that it's a particularly busy day for me; the less time I have to think the better. Firstly, I've to run into Roger's office to go through the new *Jessie Would* contract (Sweet, gentlemanly old Roger even hands me a bouquet to congratulate me with a card that simply reads, 'Welcome back'. The aul, dote.) Then I've an appointment at Chez Pierre, my old hairdresser, to get my hair put back to blonde again. On Liz Walsh's explicit instructions it has to be said. Otherwise, I'd have been perfectly happy to stick to cheapo home colour kits for the rest of my life. Pay rise or no pay rise, the new credit crunch Jessie Woods is here to stay. OK, so I may be back in the money again, but my debts at Visa aren't going anywhere, are they? In fact, all my new 're-employed' status at Channel Six means to me financially is that I'll be finally able to repay everything I owe that bit quicker. Like maybe before I qualify for the old age pension. If I'm very lucky, that is. But, no, Liz reckons viewers won't recognise me unless I'm back to blonde, so I've no choice. By 7 p.m., I'm back to looking exactly like my old self again. The hair is almost platinum and, as I walk down to Bentleys to meet Sam, for a second I think, this was my life only a few months ago. Bouncing into

Roger's office, pricey hairdos, meeting my boyfriend at his favourite posh restaurant. It's as though nothing's changed.

Nothing except me, that is.

When I step into the Oyster Bar, Sam is sitting waiting for me in a quiet corner with a bottle of champagne chilling in an ice bucket beside him. Which, if he thinks is to celebrate my going back to him, is presumptuous and premature to say the least.

So I decide to make him work for it.

I say hi curtly and sit opposite him. As if this is a business meeting.

'Wow, you look amazing!' he starts off, x-raying me with the black eyes, the way he always used to. I just nod and let him talk.

I let him do all the talking, in fact. I use silence as a protective shield around me. His theme is clear. He's missed me and feels terrible about our last meeting, when he had to haul me out of that minging police station in Kildare. I take a tiny sip of the champagne and try to tune out that particular memory. He says over and over again how sorry he is about the way he treated me. How he just panicked and felt he needed to take time out. But that there wasn't a day that went by when he wasn't thinking about me and deeply regretting everything that happened between us.

Then he says how much he admires the way I hauled myself back up from the ground again. How he heard from Nathaniel and Eva about my flipping burgers in Smileys and actually felt proud. That I'd behaved like a winner. I didn't go under, I came out fighting. He even astonishes me by saying as soon as he read about my presenting *The Midnight Hour*, he became a regular listener, usually when he was driving home in his car after some swishy do.

For the first time since I got here, I start to feel myself melt a bit when he says, 'I just liked hearing the sound of your voice.' Then he read about the drama at Channel Six, how I was now reinstated and exonerated from any wrongdoing, and decided to get in touch. To say congratulations. It was a chance remark he heard me saying on the show that spurred him on as it happens; I'd made some comment about how little romantic gestures go a long way. So he picked up his phone and called into the show from his car. And couldn't believe it when he actually got through to me. It was like some kind of sign from above.

'And of course,' he continues, 'I wanted to see if you'd forgive me and give me another chance, give us another chance. The thing is . . . I'm useless without you, Woodsie, I need you.'

He takes a breath so deep it's almost coming from his feet up. 'I . . . I heart you.' Then he looks at me expectantly with the coal black eyes and I realise he's waiting for an answer.

That this is my cue to say, oh all right then, go on, sure let's put the past behind us and give it another go. As if it would all be that easy for him and that simple for me. But the thing is that it's not. Amazing, he's said everything that I could have wished for, absolutely everything, and all I can feel in return is, well . . . numb. I don't know what's wrong with me. This is the answer to my prayers, this is everything I possibly could have wanted out of life and yet all I can do is sit here and look back at him blankly.

'If you're really serious . . .' I eventually say.

'I've never been more serious about anything in my life. I swear.'

'Then you're going to have to accept that I'm not the same person I was. I've changed, you see.'

'Changed . . . how?'

'In a lot of ways. For one thing, I've come to realise the importance of family. They were there for me when the chips were down and I'll never forget that.'

'You mean, your two stepsisters who were with you that night in Kildare? But you always used to bitch about them! You said they were like Pattie and Selma from *The Simpsons*, only worse. You used to have to force yourself to talk to them after your dad's anniversary mass and even at that you'd only ever stick it out for ten minutes or so. Then you'd turn up at my house needing a stiff brandy.'

'Well, it turns out I was wrong. Wrong about a lot of things and about a lot of people too. So if you really do want to win me back . . .'

'It's my number one goal in life right now.'

'Then you're going to have to win them over too.'

Feck it, after everything he put me through, I'm not making this easy for him.

'Whatever you say, Woodsie.'

Hours later, when I arrive into Radio Dublin in time for the show, the first person I bump into is Steve.

'Ah, no, I don't believe it,' he shakes his head sadly, all disappointed the minute he sets eyes on me.

'What's wrong?'

'I much preferred you with the red hair.'

Chapter Twenty-One

'You have to be fecking kidding me,' is Sharon's stunned response when I fill her in the next day on the latest twist with Sam.

'Sharon, I know, I can't believe it either. But it's like he's taken a pill to make him start saying and doing all the right things.'

'Did he say he missed you?'

'Says he doesn't work without me.'

'Well to hell with him. He dumped you. He's not allowed to have feelings.'

'I've told him how important you all are to me now. And that he's got to win you round if he's to have any chance of this working again. I mean it too. I'll never forget the people who stood by me during the dark days. Even Maggie, in her own way.'

'Well unless he buys me a Porsche and pays for me to have a facelift and liposuction, he'll have a right job trying to win me over. Jeez, when will you learn to stop airbrushing history, Jess? Look at you; convincing yourself that you were just on a little break and that you're all happily reunited now.'

'Oh come on, just give him a chance, will you? That's all

I'm asking. You know, all those movies with Hugh Grant that you watch teach us one thing and one thing only: the path of true love never runs smooth. We all need obstacles to happy ever after. Well I've had my obstacle and now I want my happy ever after. What's so wrong with that?'

'Jessie, don't kid a kidder. I was there with you that night when we broke into his house. I saw for myself what a prick he was. Don't you remember? Outside the cop shop in Kildare, he dragged you away from us and was vicious to you. Swear to God, you were like a car crash victim afterwards. And then he just fecked off back to the K Club or wherever it was he was going and forgot all about you.'

'I was kind of hoping that mightn't come up. Besides, he's changed.'

'Oh yeah right. Because men always change.'

But she's wrong. He really has changed and what's more, I'll prove it to her. His average call rate to me now is about ten calls per day and all he wants to know is when he can see me next. He even offers to wait until after my show, collect me and then take me home.

Of course, by 'home' he means his mansion in Kildare, so I keep turning him down. Because I'm just not ready to hop back into bed with him again like nothing happened.

Then, even more amazingly, when I tell him that I'm looking to rent a small apartment, he offers me the use of a penthouse he owns in Temple Bar. As luck would have it, it's lying empty at the moment, as the tenant has literally just moved out.

'How much is the rent?' I ask, when he phones me up with this amazing offer.

'For you, Woodsie? Zero.'

So I say no. Because never again will I put myself in a

position where I'm under an obligation to someone with more money than me. I'm living within my budget now and there's no turning me back.

Funny, but the more I reject Sam and refuse all his generous offers, the more he ups his game. He's even picked up a bit on my habit of airbrushing history. Claiming he never liked Emma Sheridan to begin with, for one thing. That he found her insincere and always suspected that she was eaten up with jealousy of me. Utter shite of course. He was always perfectly charming to Emma whenever we were out with her and never had a bad word to say about her. But he means well, so I let it pass. More airbrushing about our break-up too: the 'time out', as he refers to it, did him the power of good. Cleared his head and made him realise how much I really meant to him all along. Which I desperately want to believe, so I do.

Next thing, he calls wanting to know my detailed plans for my next night off, which is this Sunday.

'Why do you ask?' I say, wondering what's coming next.

'Because I thought we'd do something special. To celebrate our getting back together.'

'Sam, we're not back together. We're in negotiations. That's all. Nothing more.'

'OK, well then I thought I'd take you out to celebrate absolutely nothing at all.'

'Well, as a matter of fact, I'm not free.'

Call me a bad bitch, but God I enjoyed saying that. After everything I've been through over Sam, it just feels so good to not be one hundred per cent available for him. At least, not any more.

'So, what are your plans, Woodsie?'

I fill him in about it being Maggie's big night at the

Comedy Cellar and how I've practically sworn an affidavit to her that I'll be there in the front row, laughing uproariously at gags I could say along with her at this stage.

'Well then, I'll come with you too,' he offers.

So I agree. After all, this is the one night that everyone I know will be at, and I really do mean *everyone*. If Sam is serious about getting to know my family, then there's no better occasion for him to turn up to. Maggie has half the Inland Revenue office going, Sharon's asked most of the Smiley Burger crew, even Joan is bringing along a load of her mates from the Swiss Cottage. But if he thinks I'm about to make it easy for him, boy does he have another think coming.

'You could also pick me up at Whitehall first, if you like,' I tell him. 'So everyone can meet you, up close and personal.' On home turf. In Whitehall, or 'the land of the ten-year-old Toyota' as Sam always referred to it. Because, let's face it, if he can survive being thrown to the lions like an early Christian, he can survive anything.

It's weird. I should be dancing for joy on the rooftops but instead . . . nothing. Like I'm wandering aimlessly through some kind of emotional fog and can't tap into what I really feel here.

Do I trust Sam again? Do I believe him when he says that this is really it, for good? The God's honest truth is, I haven't the first clue. Funny that I'm on the radio doling out relationship advice, yet when it comes to my own stuff, I can't see the wood for the trees. Nor is the deep confusion I'm going through helped by the fact that the two people I'd ordinarily turn to aren't around. Sharon, unsurprisingly, has written Sam off as an arch-arsehole and won't even hear his name mentioned in her presence. And as bad luck would have it, Steve, my touchstone, is away until this

Sunday, playing at a summer festival up in County Monaghan with his band.

After the show on Friday night, I treat myself to a highly extravagant cab ride home, my head spinning after yet another day and evening of call bombardment from Sam. Everyone's in bed by the time I crawl back to the house, so I slip into our deserted TV room, take out my mobile and even though it's almost 2.30 a.m., try calling Steve. Just to hear his voice. The phone rings out and eventually goes through to voicemail. But then I realise I haven't the first clue what it is that I even want to say to him, so I hang up.

Why oh why, am I such a gobshite when it comes to men?

Steve, ever the gentleman, calls me back the next morning.

'Hey, Jessie, you OK?'

'Hi,' I mumble back drowsily, still half asleep and still in bed, even though it's well after 11 a.m. So good to hear his voice though.

'I saw a missed call from you last night and got worried. Was everything OK with the show?'

'Yeah, the show was . . . emm . . . fine.'

'Hey, are you sure you're all right? You sound different. Tense. Like there's something on your mind.'

And that's when I realise I can't do it. Can't tell him about Sam torpedoing back into the calm waters of my life, at least not over the phone I can't. So, like the moral coward that I am, I settle for umming and aahing instead.

'Well, if you're sure you're OK,' says Steve, sounding unconvinced.

'Fine. Honestly. Really.'

'Then you take care. And I'll see you tomorrow.'

'Yep, till tomorrow.'

Chapter Twenty-Two

Come Sunday night and the only person NOT crowding out our tiny little TV room is Maggie, the star of the show, the lady of the hour. Crippled with nerves, she spent the day chain smoking one fag after another and counting down the hours until 8 p.m., when the contest proper starts. Either that or else bombarding me with demands like, 'The Michael Jackson gags. Final call: in or out?'

'Out,' I said firmly and for about the twentieth time. 'Overdone, tasteless and, above all, not as funny as the rest of your material.'

'But the gag about the Renaissance and the French toast should definitely stay in?'

'One hundred per cent. Trust me, it'll work.'

By 7 p.m., nerves eventually get the better of her and she decides to make her own way into the Comedy Cellar, to clear her head a bit and 'get in the zone'. Her phrase, not mine. Gas to think that she has yet to perform a single live gig and is already speaking the lingo like a pro, with a contract from the BBC tucked under her oxter. So off she goes, leaving the rest of us to follow in her wake, in time for the show.

Joan already has a little party going on in the TV room,

with her 'business partner' (swear to God, I can almost hear her talking in quotation marks every time she introduces him). Yes, none other than Jimmy Watson, who I recognise from the night I was in the Swiss Cottage with Sharon. Chunky and florid-faced with a major eye in Joan's direction, it has to be said. Anyway, between the two of them, they've invited a gang of their mates from the pub and things are just beginning to get into full swing. I don't actually recognise anyone, but they all seem to know me and keep grabbing me to say things like, 'Congratulations Jessie! Sure we never doubted but that you'd be back on telly in no time!' Everyone's here for a few drinks before we head into town for the gig, and as Joan has me on drinks duty I've the path worn down running back and forth from the kitchen to the TV room. Honest to God, every trip I make, I'm more and more laden down with trays full of Chardonnay and dips from Tesco's, all served in the good Christmas Day crystal, as per madam's explicit instructions.

Anyway, Joan's in full swing, holding court and boastfully announcing to the room that IPrayForYou.com will shortly be up and running and that they're all invited to the official launch, when yet again, the doorbell rings. Sharon's still upstairs lashing on make-up, so I go to get it. It's Matt, carrying two six-packs of Bulmers, Sharon's favourite tipple, God bless him. I hug him and tell him to go on through to the kitchen, while I race upstairs to tell Sharon he's here. No harm to keep him out of Joan's way; the form she's in, I wouldn't put it past her to introduce him to everyone as her son-in-law elect. Particularly given that whenever poor Matt's around, she has a tendency to act like Mrs Bennet from *Pride and Prejudice* on overdrive.

I hammer on the bedroom door and yell at Sharon to come downstairs, but instead of telling me she's on the way, she asks me to come inside and close the door behind me.

'What's up?' I ask.

'Tonight's the night,' she says, all firm and decisive.

I look at her blankly thinking, what exactly? That she'll sleep with him for the first time, announce she's pregnant, tell us she's engaged? What?

'The night I'm dumping Matt,' she finishes.

I slump onto the bed beside her. 'Sharon, you can't do that, he's so knickers mad about you! My God, he even arrived here with two six-packs for you and the poor guy doesn't even drink.'

'Jess, I'm very grateful to you for everything you've done, but you're not talking me out of this. He was my "in case of emergency, please break the glass box" guy but now I've my sights set on better things.'

'But he'll be devastated!'

'He bridged the gap between arsehole and Holy Grail and now it's time for me to move on.'

I barely have time to respond, because next thing Joan is screeching up the stairs that there's a visitor just arrived for me.

So he did come then. I wasn't certain if he would and frankly wouldn't have been in the least surprised if I'd got a phone call to say he couldn't make it; that some last minute 'business emergency' had come up. On a Sunday evening. But there's no mistake; by the time I get downstairs, there's Sam sitting in Maggie's armchair, the seat of honour, being fussed and preened over by Joan who looks as if she's just seen the messiah. My instinct is to race in to rescue him, but he seems to be doing perfectly fine by himself. He's introduced himself to everyone, Joan included and is now sitting back, allowing himself to be waited on hand and foot.

'And that's your Bentley parked on the road outside, is it?' a very red-faced and puffy-looking Jimmy Watson is asking him. 'Must have set you back a fair few quid.'

'Wouldn't see much change out of two hundred and eighty K,' says Sam, cool as you like, as the whole room looks suitably impressed. Then he spots me and bounds over, pecking me on the cheek. 'Jessie, you look beautiful. So how come you never invited me here before? Your stepmother is the most charming lady I've ever met. And her house is so tasteful and elegant.'

There's the tiniest edge in his voice that only I'm attuned to; a slight rise in register that Sam does whenever he's taking the piss. Joan, however, is oblivious and giggles like a schoolgirl. In fact, she's so taken with this guest of honour that I wouldn't be surprised if she made a play for him herself.

'Jessica dear?' she says in her most put-on posh voice. 'Do fetch Sam a nice Chardonnay from the fridge. And be sure to use the John Rocha crystal.' A half-wink from Sam as I go into the kitchen to do as she commands, but then the doorbell goes again, so I trot out to the hall to open it.

I don't believe this. It's Steve.

I knew he was coming to the gig tonight with his family, but I *so* did not expect him to call here first.

Ohgodohgodohgodthisisgoingtobeawkwardawkwardawkwardawkward . . .

'Hey!' he says, his face lighting up as he leans down to hug me. 'So, did you miss me? Did Radio Dublin fall apart without me?'

I barely have time to answer though, as next thing, Sam is hovering at my shoulder, right by the open hall door.

'Who's this, babe?' he asks, eyeing up Steve a bit suspiciously.

'This is Steve, a very good friend of mine,' I manage to stammer. 'And, as it happens, my boss.'

Steve stands up to his full height, immediately recognising exactly who Sam is. He's about a foot taller than him, but then Steve's about a foot taller than the rest of humanity. 'Yes, I know who you are,' says Steve, more icily than I've ever heard him before. 'In fact, I know exactly who you are. I saw you in the documentary about Jessie.'

'Oh yeah, that's right, I think I did appear in that. I was away on business when it was broadcast though, so I've never actually seen it. Besides, I'm not really someone who gets time to sit down and watch TV.'

'You used it to plug your new book.'

'Did I?' Sam laughs, then through the open hall door, suddenly he spots a gang of kids all clustered around his Bentley, noses pressed up against it.

'Jesus Christ, Jessie, look, those kids are pawing my car!'

'Well, that's kids for you,' says Steve, sounding cold. Actually cold, which is so not like him.

'Well, can we move them on or something? I'm afraid one of them might steal my satnav.'

Then, when the time comes for us all to go, once again, I'm in the gakky situation of having both Steve and Sam, one at either side of me, both offering me lifts.

Out on the road, there's the Bentley parked right beside Steve's humble bike. So what do I go for? Glass coach or pumpkin? Jaysus. Tonight hasn't even properly begun and already I'm hating every second of it.

Nor do things improve when we get to the Comedy Cellar either. I try my best to collar Steve on his own to thank him for the offer of a lift and to explain that I just didn't want to leave Sam alone when he doesn't really know anyone, which is the only reason I got into the car with him, but I don't get a chance. The place is jam-packed and so crowded that we're doing well to even get a table together.

The gang's all here: Joan is sitting beside Jimmy, although she's spending most of her time trying to get to talk to Sam, who's holding court right in the dead centre of the group, buying round after round of drinks and absolutely refusing to let anyone else put their hand in their pocket.

The gig has just started and an MC is out on stage warming up, announcing what the contest is all about, with the juicy carrot of a cash prize for the lucky winner plus getting an agent out of it too. But I'm not even focused on what he's saying. And neither is anyone else; everyone's yakking away, getting drinks down them, getting in the mood to cheer, boo or maybe even throw rotting vegetables at the acts to come.

I'm swivelling around trying to spot Steve and eventually I see him at the bar, with Hannah and her husband Paul, who've just arrived. So I go over and ask them to join us, just as Sharon arrives . . . alone.

I'm in the middle of introducing Hannah and Paul to the others when Sam interrupts me. 'So everyone, I've a surprise for you all.' He throws a meaningful glance over to me and for a second my heart stops. Not with excitement though, with worry. And I couldn't even tell you why.

'Tomorrow is a very special occasion for me,' Sam goes

on, the centre of attention, radiating bonhomie, and then suddenly everything's OK and I can breathe again. Because I do know what's coming. I remember the date all too well.

'It's my thirty-fifth birthday party and I'd like each and every one of you to come along. It's going to be held in Bentleys at eight o'clock and you're all welcome, as my personal guests. I know it's a Monday night and everything, but it would be so wonderful if you could make it. It'll be a fabulous night. And any friends of Jessie's are friends of mine.'

Gotta hand it to the guy; he really is sticking to his vow to get to know my family and friends better. The triumphant glance he shoots at me seems to say just as much. He even gets a round of applause from the assembled company. Well, from all of them bar Steve, that is. There's a chorus of 'Oh thank you so much!' and I can even hear Joan asking whether there'll be any actual celebrities there?

'Thanks for the invite, but I doubt I'll be able to make it,' says Steve quietly, flashing a subtle glance in my direction.

Then Sharon's over to him. 'No, no please you have to come!' she insists, looking pleadingly up at him. 'Couldn't you give me a lift there on your motorbike? I've always wanted a go on the back of a bike. Ah go on, Steve, please!'

He looks down kindly at her and says, well, OK then, if it means that much to her.

It's at this point that I officially can't take any more, so I work my way over to Steve and ask if I can see him in private. Now. Before Maggie goes onstage. Rude I know, but needs must. I can feel Sam's eyes boring into me, but I don't care. Gotta do this.

Steve nods and leads me to the back of the cellar, well out of earshot.

'I need to talk to you,' I begin although I scarcely know what's coming next.

'I need to talk to you too.'

'I . . . I . . . well, for starters I wanted to explain about . . . you know . . . everything. I didn't expect you to call to the house earlier you see, and I hope I wasn't rude . . .'

'Jessie,' he says quietly. 'I need to ask you something.'

'Yes?' My heart's thumping now and I don't even know why.

'Are you seeing that guy again?'

'No! No, not at all, we're just . . . well, remember that caller on the show the other night? The one right at the very end? Well, that was him.'

'I gathered. I also copped on that there was something majorly wrong with you when you barely said two words on the way home afterwards.'

'You have to understand, I was in total shock. You've no idea. Sam really put me through the wringer . . .'

'I know. My question is, and I really hope you'll be honest with me here, are you about to get back with him?'

Suddenly, I feel a wash of irritation. As if, after all the tensions of the night, I finally just snap. 'You know, I'd be perfectly entitled to tell you right now that it's really none of your business.'

'Not true and not fair. Who you go out with is my business.'

'What did you just say?'

'Because . . . look, Jessie, I never wanted to tell you this way. But it seems I've not got much choice now, do I?'

I look blankly at him, desperately trying to tune out the background noise so I can concentrate on what he's about to say. Whatever it may be.

'Because . . .' He takes a deep breath here, brushing back the floppy fair hair and suddenly I find myself having to concentrate on breathing. 'Because, Jessie Woods, I'm mad about you. Completely and utterly insanely bonkers off my head about you. I think about you day and night and . . . Jesus, listen to me, I sound like a teenager . . . But the truth is that when I'm not thinking about you, I'm counting down the hours to when I'll see you again. The only reason I never told you any of this before, is that I convinced myself you were still hurting over that smug tosser sitting there now. That the best thing I could possibly do was back off and give you time and space. I don't want to be your rebound guy. And then I come back after only being away for a few days and here he is. In his Bentley acting like he owns you. Jessie, he is NOT the guy for you. Maybe you'll tell me that I'm not either, but he most definitely isn't. Don't you see? For such a smart girl, why are you acting so stupidly? You don't hear a word out of him for months on end after the guy broke your heart and turned his back on you. Then suddenly he bounces back into your life as soon as you're officially a success again. It's not a coincidence, Jessie. Think about it. You know in your heart of hearts that I'm right.'

'Steve, please . . .' I can't even finish that sentence. Because just then the MC makes an announcement.

'Ladies and gentlemen, if I can ask you to give a warm welcome to our first comedienne tonight. Introducing *Maggie Woods!*'

I actually think there's a chance I might faint. Between trying to digest what Steve's just said and trying to concentrate on Maggie's act, my head is swimming and my breathing is coming in short sharp stabs. Like by some weird osmosis, I've now taken on all her stage fright for her.

Because Maggie is *stunning*. Not a nerve in her body. Dark. Nihilistic. And though I'm in no mood for laughing, I find myself not able to keep a straight face at some of her precision-bomb gags.

'I can't multi-task,' is her opener. 'I once had an appointment with my dentist and my gynaecologist on the same morning. I ended up lying in the wrong chair in the wrong direction. Which was very upsetting for my gay dentist.'

A huge roar of laughter and she's away, effortlessly segueing into a meticulously rehearsed routine about working in the Inland Revenue office and the cast of characters/oddballs/wackos therein. It's astonishing, but within seconds you can just feel that she has everyone in the room absolutely, one hundred per cent on her side. What can I say? A star is born.

Maggie doesn't win. To much feet-stomping and general disgruntlement, she comes runner-up, narrowly losing out to a guy with a guitar, who sings all these little ditties about how he felt when he broke up with his girlfriend and was left broken-hearted. To pick himself back up off the floor again, he decided to set up a greeting card company for guys left in his position. One of his top sellers is a simple card which reads, 'To my ex-girlfriend. At this time of year I always find myself thinking about you.' Then you open it up to read, 'Happy Halloween, you witch.' Another wildly popular card says simply, 'Will you marry me?' And inside reads, 'Ha, ha, I'm only messing, I think we should see other people.' You get the picture.

Anyway, the best and probably the only part of the

evening that I actually can look back on fondly, comes right after the gig, when everyone's clustered around a glowing Maggie, congratulating her. Even Sam gets his oar in and not only invites her to his birthday bash, but asks if she'll do a reprise of her act to entertain the guests. There'll be lots of influential people there, he tells her, who'll make wonderful contacts for her.

Looking around, I think I was the only person who found this vomit-inducingly patronising. Everyone else oohs and aahs, all looking at Sam like he's the next Simon Cowell. Next thing, a guy of about forty comes up to Maggie and hands her his business card, saying he's a comedy agent and that he'd really like to represent her. Could they possibly meet for lunch whenever she has a window? Tomorrow, possibly?

Maggie and I look at each other dumbfounded. OK, so she may not have won, but this is the best result she could ever have asked for, isn't it?

'Oh, you're Jessie Woods, hi!' the agent says, shaking my hand as he instantly recognises me. 'Are you a friend of Maggie's?'

'No,' says Maggie stoutly. Then with a fond look, she slips her arm around my shoulder and says, 'She's . . . my sister. We're family.'

It's the nicest thing that's happened the whole miserable, God-awful evening.

Hours later, Sharon and I are in our room; she's painstakingly taking off make-up, while I just lie on the bed, staring in silence at the ceiling. Desperately trying to comb some sense out of the tumult of emotions that's thundering over me.

'Four calls and six texts so far,' she says with her back to me, staring at her reflection in the mirror and playing with her mobile phone.

'Hmm?'

'From Matt. So far, since I dumped him. Says I'm making a big mistake and should give him another chance.'

'So what will you do?' My questions are all dull. Automatic. Mainly because I'm not even thinking straight.

'I told you. I've set my sights elsewhere. I've someone else on my radar now and what's more I think he's interested. All I have to do is play it cool and reel him in.'

Suddenly I sit up. 'Sharon, this new guy you've met. By any chance ... I mean, is it anyone I've already met?'

But I know the answer before she even tells me. 'Course you know him, you gobshite. It's Steve. Who else?'

Chapter Twenty-Three

Needless to say, I don't shut my eyes for the whole night. I just lie there, alternately thinking, worrying, stressing, tossing, turning, then reverting back to plain old-fashioned agonising again. And when that all gets too much for me, I keep checking to see if Sharon's awake, just in case there's any chance I could talk to her. Because I have to talk to her, there's no side-stepping this.

But what the f**k do I say? *Idon'tknowIdon'tknowIdon't knowIhaven'tthefirstclue* . . .

One thing's for certain, there's no getting away from the one inalienable truth that's staring me in the face. I am without doubt the greatest, most witless moron on the face of the earth. I mean, what in the name of Jaysus is wrong with me? All my life, I've only ever wanted two things: a television career and Sam Hughes. And now, both have been handed back to me on a plate and all I can do is obsess about Steve.

Steve. Who declared himself to me. My darling friend. God, even just thinking about life without him is like a stab to the heart. And the thing is, if I choose Sam, then that's exactly what will happen. Because I know Steve so well and I know there'll be no going back.

So what does this Cinderella Rockefeller do? Go off into the sunset with my Prince Charming? Back to a life of palatial mansions and fabulousness? Or choose Steve, who's been like a rock to me? Who I care about so, so much too. And, let's be honest, who I think I fancy a lot of the time too. Because he'd never let me down, or turn his back on me. Never.

So what's it to be? Buttons or Prince Charming?

And then there's Sharon, snoring her head off in the bed beside mine. Then a fresh worry. Suppose she and Steve are meant to be together and not him and me? Suddenly a dozen instances pop into my head of really lovely things they've both said about each other to me over the summer. I remember Sharon referring to him as Fertiliser Man because he slowly grows on you. And, what's more, I remember Steve saying over and again how well she was looking and how much softer she seemed lately. That was the exact word he used, *softer*.

There's nothing else for it. I have to come clean to Sharon and take the consequences. Trouble is, there isn't a bit of peace or privacy to be had at home next morning. Maggie has taken the day off work and is faffing around the place up to high doh on account of the comedy agent she's arranged to meet for lunch today. That, coupled with the fact that she's doing a reprise of her gig at Sam's birthday shindig tonight, has her tearing round the place, even more up to the ceiling with nerves than she was yesterday. Funny, but I thought I'd seen all incarnations of Maggie. From couch potato, to passive-aggressive put-down artist, to blossoming stand-up comedienne. But I've never in all my years seen this side of her; she's pressured, busy, motivated, buzzing around the place and . . . happy. Actually happy. Probably the only person in the shagging house who is.

Joan, who's wandering around the kitchen in one of her Barbara Cartland dressing gowns, is spewing fire because she's just heard the news about Sharon dumping Matt. 'Is that how I reared you, you ungrateful little idiot? To toss aside perfectly eligible young men?'

'We broke up, Ma. It happens,' says Sharon, munching on her breakfast of left-over pizza. 'Get over it.'

'Well you can't just dump him like that. It's . . . it's . . . illegal dumping for a start.'

'Jeez, Ma, will you cool the head?'

'What I'd very much like to know is this: what's life going to be like round here when Jessica moves out? Because if we're back to the days of you slumped night after night in front of the TV, then I'm telling you right now, young lady, you'll have me to answer to. That Matt was a perfectly acceptable fella who worshipped the ground you walked on . . .'

'Ma, we'd nothing in common, he didn't even drink or smoke, for feck's sake.'

'Well, no one's perfect. You could have broken him in gradually. But the point is, you were a different person when he was around, you were actually getting out of the house for a change, and now what? Back to watching repeats of *X Factor* ad nauseam? And you won't have Maggie for company this time, you know, madam. She has a whole new career opening up for her now.'

'I won't be doing that, Ma. As it happens, there's someone else that I've my eye on.'

At this point, I step in. 'Sharon, I need to talk to you. Can we go upstairs for a minute please?'

'NO ONE leaves the room until this row is over!' screeches Joan, as Sharon and I scarper for cover.

But my planned chat with her doesn't go as smoothly as I'd hoped.

'So, let me get this straight,' says Sharon, angrily lighting up a fag and pacing the bedroom. 'You spend months on end mooning over tufty-head Sam, then the minute he comes back to you, I'm sorry, but her ladyship now wants the only fella I've fancied, properly fancied, in ages. Are you fecking *kidding* me? What is wrong with you?'

I'm actually ready to burst into tears now. As it is, all I can do is nod mutely. Mortified and hating every second of this. Tell you something, honesty is a highly overrated virtue.

'Well, you want to know something?' snaps Sharon, more furious than I think I've ever seen her before. 'I don't care if you did snog Steve and I don't care what he said to you last night. I really think he likes me. He even offered to take me to the party on his bike tonight. So to hell with you, Jessie. Go back to Sam where you belong and stop interfering in my life!'

Sweet baby Jesus and the orphans. If tonight doesn't end up being a bloodbath, it'll be a bonus.

Sam continues with his policy of pulling out all stops imaginable, arriving in a white, chauffeur-driven stretch limo to collect the whole lot of us. The car even attracts a crowd of the local kids, all clustered around it demanding to know whether someone's getting married?

He steps out of the back, in black tie, laden down with red roses. You should see him. It's like James Bond just arrived into a council estate.

We're all present and correct, except for Sharon and Steve that is, who left about five minutes ago. I was upstairs getting ready, to a stony silence from herself, when the doorbell rang. She stuck her head out the window, didn't tell me who it was, didn't even say goodbye, just raced downstairs and was gone. I looked out the bedroom window just in time to see her zoom off on the back of Steve's motorbike.

I'm the last one into the car, mainly because I'm wearing a cheapie pair of faux-crystal sandals that cut the feet off me and which I'm practically hobbling in, hence it takes me ten minutes just to get downstairs. But I bought them anyway, a) because they were on sale in Dunnes Stores for an astonishing €8 and b) because at least they go with my dress, which is a silver, glittery strappy number, also bought in Dunnes Stores and also on sale at €24.99. I know, all Sam's pals will be head to toe in designer gear and I'll be the only discount shopper there, but Credit Crunch Jessie doesn't worry about crap like that any more.

Sam, true to form, does notice, but then he misses nothing. We're in the back of the limo and he's doling out champagne to the assembled company; Joan, her date Jimmy Watson, Maggie and myself, to toast his birthday.

'You look . . . well, OK, babe,' he says to me. 'Where did you get the outfit?'

'All from Dunnes Stores,' I say proudly, delighted with my bargains. 'Total cost: just under thirty-three Euro.'

'Do you want us to wait for you to change into something a bit more suitable?'

That sounded like a casual suggestion, but his tone was more like an order.

'No thanks, I'm happy in this. Besides, I don't have anything else.'

'But, it's from Dunnes Stores. And you can be sure the press will pick up on it too.'

'Not a problem for me,' I say firmly. 'I'm comfortable in this.' And a glare from me tells him to drop it, which he does.

Then Jimmy, already so red-faced that I'd swear he's been on the gargle for the whole afternoon, actually starts pitching the famous IPrayForYou.com idea to Sam, trying to get him on board as an investor.

'Yeah, great, whatever, call my assistant Margaret and we'll set up a meeting,' says Sam dismissively, the way he always is whenever he's trying to give people the brush-off.

Then, when we arrive at Bentleys, he says crisply to the others, 'OK. The photographers will want clear shots of Jessie and I arriving alone. So we'll get out of the car first, and if you can all just wait in here until we're well and truly inside? No offence, but we don't want to spoil all the pap shots with unknowns.'

I don't even have time to berate him for treating my family like a shower of anonymous Z-listers because next thing, he's out of the car and propelling me out alongside him. Bloody hell, you'd think we were going to an awards do instead of a shagging birthday knees-up. It's only a few paces from the limo to the door of the restaurant, but you'd swear it was the Kodak Theatre on Oscar night, between the red carpet and all the assembled press, lined up with cameras popping into our faces.

'Smile, Jessie! Over here, Sam! Can we just get a shot of the two of you together? Side by side?' is all you can hear as we both step out into what feels like an electrical storm.

'So you're back together again?' yells out another journalist and Sam and I both answer at the same time.

'Yes!' he answers back, having to shout over all the noise.

'No. I'm . . . I'm really just here for the birthday party,' I say, but no one even hears me. Impossible to in this crowd.

Then he automatically slips his arm around my waist and twirls me this way and that, beaming his mega-watt smile into whatever lens happens to be shoved into his face. It's completely surreal. There's about a dozen people roaring out questions at me and of course I can't hear them all in the cacophony of noise. So I'm acting like a mute puppet, going through the motions with Sam prodding me towards even more cameras, all while I feel I'm silently screaming inside and no one can hear.

And that's when it happens. A reporter from Channel Six, who I know of old, taps me on the arm and thrusts a mike under my nose, while a camera whirls right in front of me, almost blinding me with the overhead light. 'Hi Jessie,' she says, 'I only have one question for you, if that's OK? This big reunion with Sam Hughes. Why now after all this time? Do you think it's a coincidence that you broke up after you were fired from Channel Six, but now that you're reinstated and the cloud of suspicion over you has been lifted, suddenly Sam is back in your life again?'

Her question completely stops me in my tracks. Because

it's an exact mirror of what Steve said to me last night. The facts are right there, staring me in the face. If I were still a disgraced has been, would I ever have heard a peep from the likes of Sam ever again? Of course not, not in a million years. Suddenly I have to get away from this circus. Like, *now*. Before I know what I'm doing, I've broken away from Sam and am teetering inside on my too-tight heels, almost ready to fall over, they're that sore to walk in.

Got to find Steve. And Sharon. Got to apologise and tell them that both of them were right and I was wrong. Because Sam hasn't changed a bit, not a single bit. He thinks I'm a winner again and so I'm allowed back into his rarefied world, but that's the only reason why. I don't think he even loves me, or possibly ever did love me. I was just an asset that turned into a liability that's now miraculously transformed back to being an asset again. But before I speak to anyone else, first of all I somehow need to find the words to say this to his face.

The thing about Bentleys is that it's actually a hotel as well as a restaurant, so the party is being held on three different levels simultaneously, Sam having taken over the entire building for the evening. It takes about six goes to get his attention, mainly because every time I try to collar him, someone drags him off for a photo. The place is packed out, but it's typical of any shindig Sam organises: fifty per cent media, forty-nine per cent business contacts and the remaining one per cent are friends and well-wishers.

At one point, I manage to manoeuvre him into a corner, telling him I need to speak to him urgently. But just as he gives me his attention, a barman comes over with a trayful of drinks and asks us what we'd like. Champagne for both of us, Sam orders.

'Do you have any Bulmers?' I ask, desperately dying for a drink. Anything to get me through this.

'Bulmers? Did you just ask for Bulmers?' Sam repeats, as stunned as if I'd just asked for a pint of kitten's blood.

'Yeah, that's what I drink now.'

'Don't be so ridiculous, Woodsie. That's a knacker drink. Stop embarrassing yourself, you're in Bentleys now, you know. Not some scobie bar in Whitehall.' Then he says imperiously to the barman, 'She'll have champagne.'

I don't even get a chance to have it out with him, to say no thanks, these days cider is my drink of choice and he knows where he can shove his champagne, because just then a photographer from *Social and Personal* is over wanting a picture of him, so off he goes.

Nor can I even see any of my family, who are probably up partying in the bar at the very top of the building. Sharon and Steve included.

But one problem at a time.

God, it's like time has stood still tonight, but eventually, ages and ages, it might even be hours later, I finally do nab Sam and elbow him up against a bookcase. 'I have to talk to you,' I say, as calmly and as firmly as I can. 'Now. I've been trying to get your attention all evening and I'm sorry but this won't wait any longer.'

'It'll have to, Woodsie, some of the gang from *The Apprentice* are here and I need to schmooze them. Oil them up a bit, you know how it is.'

Oh sod this. I'll never get him alone, so I may as well just say it straight out. 'Sam, I'm sorry to do this to you, on this of all nights too. But I can't do this. I can't just slot back into the role of your girlfriend again. Because it's not what I want. I thought it was, but it isn't, not at all. And what's worse is . . . I don't even believe you really want me back either. You just . . . you like being surrounded by winners, that's all.'

Now he's looking at me furiously. 'Jesus, Woodsie, you really pick your moments, don't you? Can't we just enjoy the party and discuss this later on? Look, Nathaniel and Eva are over there and you haven't even said hello to them yet.'

'What you have to understand, Sam, is that I'm human. I made a mistake and you froze me out because of it. But suppose I make another one down the line? What then? I can't be your perfect girlfriend any more. Because I'm far from perfect. I just want to be me.'

Great speech. Shame Sam whipped out his mobile and answered a call on it before I'd even finished. Well, I said what I came to say and that's it as far as I'm concerned. With a smile and a simple, 'Goodbye Sam,' I leave him to it and walk, or rather, hobble on the shoes upstairs to find my family.

I've absolutely done the right thing. I'm certain of it, because for the first time all evening, I feel like I can breathe again. It's like a weight has been lifted from me. I inch my way up the packed stairs and from below, Eva shouts up to me, from the centre of a gang of girls all crowded around her. 'Jessie! Jessie, come down here! I want to congratulate you!'

I just wave back and keep on moving. Time to leave the past firmly where it belongs, Nathaniel and Eva included.

I was right. In the upstairs bar, I find Sharon and

Maggie at the food buffet piling up their plates, meanwhile Joan and Jimmy are sitting at a table right behind us, bending the ear off some guy who's sitting in between them.

'Where have you been all night?' Sharon and Maggie say to me, almost in unison. 'We were all looking everywhere for you.'

'Downstairs, breaking up with Sam. Sharon, I need to apologise to you,' I blurt out.

'Oh for feck's sake, Jess, there's no need.'

'There is need. Because you were right about Sam. Everything you said was completely right. But I want you to know that I've just told him that I don't want to get back with him. Not now and not ever.'

'Jeez, how did he take it?'

'Doubt he even noticed, he was on the phone.'

Then Maggie snorts laughing, 'I am so putting that in my act,' she grins, tucking into a plate of quail's eggs.

'And another thing,' I say, now that I'm on a bit of a roll, 'I'm sorry for telling you about Steve and what he said to me last night. Because he's a good guy, Sharon, and if he's the man for you, then I'd be the last person to stand in your way.'

'He's not, as it turns out,' she says, but she's smiling as she says it.

'What?'

'He's not. The whole way here on his bike, all he could talk about was you. And even since we've been here, he's been constantly looking around for you, but sure it's impossible to find anyone in this throng. Steve is knickers mad about you, Jessie, and I think you should go for it.'

'Really?' I ask, touched at her unselfishness.

'Really. And hey, if I don't get lucky with some billionaire here tonight, then I can always go back to Matt again, can't I? Funny, but now the aul' eejit is gone, I kinda miss him hanging out of me the whole time.'

I hug her and then suddenly the two of us are laughing.

'I knew it! I knew you weren't ready to let him go!'

'So,' says Maggie. 'If you're not with Donald Shagging Trump any more, then I suggest we eat all his food, drink all his drink, I'll do my act and then we can all get the feck out of here.'

'Best idea I've heard all day,' I smile back.

'Unless you'd like me to sort him out for you, that is, Jessie. 'Cos I will if you want me to. I reckon I've about two stone on him.'

My God, you should just see us. Joking and giggling together. We're like three sisters. *Proper* sisters.

'No need,' I grin at Maggie, 'but thanks for the offer all the same.'

Next thing, Joan is over to us. 'Wonderful news, girls! In a million years, you'd never guess what, so don't even try!'

The three of us just look at her blankly.

'Don't look now,' she says, dropping her voice, 'but that man sitting beside Jimmy is an entrepreneur and thinks our IPrayForYou.com idea is the canniest thing he's ever heard. Says he may even invest in it! And he's not even drunk! What do you say to that then? Your old ma's going to be rich!'

We all congratulate her and she beams as proudly as if she's already been handed a businesswoman of the year award. Then, out of nowhere, something strikes me. 'What time is it?'

'Five to midnight.'

'Already? Oh, shit, shit, shit, I've got to go.'

'But you can't go!' says Sharon. 'There are drinks present. The best kind too; free drinks.'

'I have to . . . I've a show!'

I race out of the bar and am just winding my way down the packed staircase heading for the main door, when next thing, the crystal sandals, that have been crucifying my feet all night, finally get too much for me and I stumble over. To be caught a split second later by Steve.

'Hey, I've been looking everywhere for you,' he says simply.

'I've been looking for you too. Can you give me a lift to Radio Dublin?'

'Oh come on, you can't do a show tonight! I've already called Ian and told him to put out a "Best of" tape. Stay. Enjoy your night. It's cool.'

'Steve, seeing you right now has been the best part of the night.'

Suddenly, he lights up. 'You mean that?'

And I tell him everything. That I've broken up with Sam once and for all, and that he was right about everything. About the real reason why Sam wanted me back, about everything. We've finally made our way outside onto the street now, and it's cool and deserted and for the first time all night, I finally feel calm and at peace.

'So . . .' he says, turning towards me and looking down from his ridiculous height. 'Would this have anything to do with what I said to you last night?'

'Steve, it has everything to do with what you said last night.'

I look back up at him, yearning for him to kiss me

properly. His lips on mine would explain what's going on inside me so much better than anything. But he's staring down at me instead. Taking all of me in, for what feels like an eternity; my eyes, hair, clothes, legs . . . my whole body. And I've never felt so desired in my entire life. Next thing, his arms are tight around my waist and his touch is like a bolt of electricity. Every nerve-ending in me is humming and singing and there's a watery looseness in my knees as he bends down closer and closer to me. And then his mouth is on mine, warm and velvety and very, very, sexy. Now all the intensity has moved from his eyes to his mouth as we kiss furiously, passionately.

'Let's go, baby,' he groans, breaking away gently.

'No, don't stop,' I whisper, my knees rag-doll limp. 'Not now.'

'Hey, I'm not stopping anything. I'm taking you home with me. And if you think I'm ever letting you go, then, Jessie Woods, you've another think coming.'

I look at him, drugged with pleasure, and in that exact moment, I know I'm lost. I'm his and no one else's.

Next thing, we're both on the back of his bike, zooming through the deserted streets, me hugging him tightly and rubbing up against him every chance I get. Him squeezing my hands and thighs and just about any other part of me he can grip. And we're going fast, so fast, that one of my crystal shoes slips off and clatters back onto the road, but I don't bother telling Steve to stop and go back for it.

Because I don't care. I just want to keep on going, I just want to be with him. Keep Prince Charming and give me Buttons any day.

Last thing I hear is the strappy sandal thudding and bouncing against the pavement as it falls behind us, but I ignore it and smile.

Just like Cinderella.

Read on for Claudia's

CINDERELLA GUIDE TO DATING

IS YOUR GUY A PRINCE CHARMING OR A SLIMY FROG?

1. You're out with a gang of girlfriends for a night on the town. Across a crowded bar, you suddenly lock eyes with that rare and elusive species, the DSM. (Decent, single man.) Does he . . .
   A) Mime at you that his pint glass is almost empty and that if you're going to the bar he wouldn't mind a refill. Seeing as how you're buying, that is.
   B) Saunter over to your pals, then after you've introduced them, spend the rest of the night chatting up your best friend, who also happens to be a lingerie model for Victoria's Secret.
   C) Try to impress you with his party piece; burping the national anthem.
   D) Have eyes for you and you alone; chats you up all night, charms all your friends and then insists on buying round after round of drinks for everyone.

2. It's that icky, awkward part of the night where you're exchanging phone numbers. Does he . . .

A) Scribble yours in biro on the back of his palm, then not call and when you bump into him a week later, claim that he accidentally washed the number off while saving a small child from drowning at sea, the morning after he met you. Honest.
B) Ring you a week later and apologise for the delay in getting back to you, but then explain that the FA Premiership has just started, so his life is basically on hold till cup final day. Like it or lump it.
C) Swear blind that he'll call, but five days later he still hasn't, so you actually find yourself contemplating whether to start calling the local A & E units just in case there's been some kind of horrible accident.
D) Take your mobile number, land line, email address and Facebook details and before you've even got out of the cab that night, there's a message from him just checking that you got home safely.

3. It's your all-important first date. Does he . . .
   A) Arrange to meet you in a restaurant where you're a regular and know loads of the staff, then stand you up, thereby maximising your humiliation.
   B) Take you to a pub where there's a match on, then spend the whole night absolutely glued to the big screen and occasionally shouting obscenities at the referee.
   C) Take you to an obscure Lars Von Trier movie with subtitles, then spend the rest of the night discussing the minuter points of Dogma 95 with you . . . in full detail.
   D) Take you to the swishiest restaurant in town, wine

and dine you, then say it's his absolute pleasure to take you to places like this so he can show you off properly.

4. It's Valentine's Day. Does he . . .
   A) Forget.
   B) Remember only at the very last minute and run over to the garage across the road to buy you a wilted bunch of chrysanthemums.
   C) Take you to dinner, then produce a calculator when the bill arrives, explaining that you did insist on having that side order of peas and he didn't, so it's only fair the bill be divided accordingly.
   D) Whisk you off on the Eurostar to Paris, then spend the whole evening saying that, with you, every day is Valentine's Day.

5. You're both invited to a charity black tie ball, but like all good little Cinderellas, your Nitelink bus leaves at midnight. Does he . . .
   A) Shrug when you're leaving, point you vaguely in the direction of the bus stop, then before you're barely out the door, start chatting up one of the cocktail waitresses.
   B) Faithfully promise that he'll leave when you're leaving, then when it's time to go, refuse to be dragged away from the bar, because he's just ordered a round.
   C) Escort you to the bus stop, then say he's heading back to the party as the tickets did cost a small fortune and it's a shame to let them go to waste.
   D) Let you get a bus home? Alone? Are you mental?

He insists on driving you there and back, door to door and won't take no for an answer.

6. You've invited him home to meet your stepmother and stepsisters for Sunday lunch. Does he . . .
   A) Reluctantly say he'll be there, then ring you at the last minute claiming he had a work emergency and couldn't make it. On a Sunday afternoon.
   B) Arrive late, then ask if anyone would mind if he watched the big match on Sky Sports live.
   C) Ask for a guided tour of the house then mentally calculate how much it'll sell for on the open market and consequently, how much your inheritance from it would be.
   D) Be the perfect house guest, arriving with flowers and champagne for all your family, then even offer to help with the washing up.

7. You've been dating for a while now and you've decided that his best quality is . . .
   A) None of your friends like him, so at least you never have to worry about a girlfriend running off with him.
   B) He does at least have a hobby, albeit one that involves screaming at the referee during *Match of the Day* and explaining to you, yet again, the finer points of the offside rule.
   C) He's got plenty of money. Too bad none of it gets spent on you, that's all.
   D) Where to start? He's funny, kind, sensitive, strong and adores the ground you walk on . . . so much so that you find yourself wondering if he's really too good to be true.

8. And his worst quality has to be . . .
   A) Being brutally honest with yourself it's this: you're only dating him till someone better comes along. And at this stage, you'd consider *anyone*.
   B) His obsession. Too bad it's not with you, but with Wayne Rooney and Manchester United.
   C) Ahem, there's no polite way to put this, but his very, very short arms and his very, very long pockets. Honestly, at this stage it wouldn't surprise you if he opened his wallet and a moth flew out.
   D) Worst quality? That he can't pass a homeless person on the street without buying them food, giving them cash for a hostel, chatting away to them like old pals, then calling the Simon Community and demanding to know what exactly they're doing about this. And that's his *worst* quality.

9. You've decided to take the ultimate couples test: going on holiday together. Does he . . .
   A) Let you do all the booking and organising, then the day before you're due to travel, just when you're getting a spray tan, he calls to cancel, claiming he has a work project that he just can't get out of.
   B) Suggest that you go to Paris, but not for any romantic reason; it's because there's a Six Nations match in the Stade de France that weekend. Might as well kill two birds with one stone.
   C) Insist on booking a last minute, cheap and horrible package on a charter flight that leaves at 2 a.m. and leaves you about sixty miles from your hotel. Because it's such good value.
   D) Secretly discover that you've always wanted to visit

Thailand, so he books the most fabulous hotel you both can afford and then pulls every string he can to get you both an upgrade on the flight out.

10. You take him out to meet your old childhood friend, a guy you've been pals with since you were in primary school and who's almost like Buttons to your Cinderella. Does he . . .
    A) Feel threatened that you have such a close male friend and do everything he possibly can to be rude to him.
    B) When he discovers that your pal isn't really a sports nut, he immediately tries to convince you that he's gay.
    C) Get jealous then spend the night questioning him closely and when you go to the ladies, asks him straight out if you and he ever had a drunken fling.
    D) Insist on taking you both to dinner and make a point of really getting to know your old friend. Because any mate of yours is automatically a mate of his too.

THE RESULTS
Mostly A's: Cinderella says . . . oh dear. I'm sorry to be the one to tell you but this guy is such a slimy frog that it's a wonder he doesn't catch passing flies with his tongue. Nothing to be done here but avoid, avoid, avoid and if you see him on the street, run in the opposite direction. Very fast.

Mostly B's: Cinderella says . . . hmmm. He's fanatical all right, but about Sky Sports and not you. Could possibly be worked on and sanded down over time, but is that what you really want? To invest all that time and energy into changing a guy?

You, the hot stuff reading this, can do so, so much better.

Mostly C's': Cinderella says . . . he's passable, there's no doubt about that, but being brutally honest, you're not really dating Mr Right, are you? You're dating Mr Ah Sure He'll Do. Which is an interesting way to pass the time, but supposing you miss The One in the meantime?

Mostly D's: Cinderella says . . . congratulations! You've hit the jackpot and have arrived at the dating world's Holy Grail . . . Prince Charming. Enjoy every minute of this, babe, you deserve it!

Huge thanks, as always, to my agent and dear friend Marianne Gunn O'Connor. What would any of us do without you? And to Pat Lynch . . . you are amazing!

This is my first book for HarperCollins and I can't thank the team at Avon enough for the warmth of their welcome; from day one it's been a pure joy to work with every one of you. Joining Avon feels like joining a family and believe me, I know how privileged I am to be a part of it. A very special thank you to the wonderful Kate Bradley, for all her terrific thoughts, ideas and suggestions for this book. Massive thanks also to Sammia Rafique, surely the most patient woman on the planet! And to Caroline Ridding, Claire Power, Keshini Naidoo and Charlotte Wheeler . . . somehow chatting with you ladies never, ever feels like work!

Moira Reilly, you are incredible and it's a delight to be on 'Team Moira'. Thanks also to Tony Perdue who works so hard. And a very special thank you to a very special lady who first brought me to Avon, Maxine Hitchcock.

Thanks also to my wonderful family and friends for their continued support; you know how much you mean to me and I apologise here and now for driving you all mental when I'm in the middle of writing . . . I know, I know, I'm a complete scourge and bless you all for putting up with me!

Finally, thank you to all my readers who've been kind enough to write and say nice things about my books; it means the world to me that you're enjoying them.

I'm ridiculously proud of this book and I hope you enjoy it too.

Hello from Aria

We hope you enjoyed this book! Let us know,
we'd love to hear from you.

We are Aria, a dynamic digital-first fiction imprint from award-winning independent publishers Head of Zeus. At heart, we're avid readers committed to publishing exactly the kind of books we love to read—from romance and sagas to crime, thrillers and historical adventures. Visit us online and discover a community of like-minded fiction fans!

We're also on the look out for tomorrow's superstar authors. So, if you're a budding writer looking for a publisher, we'd love to hear from you. You can submit your book online at ariafiction.com/we-want-read-your-book

You can find us at:
Email: aria@headofzeus.com
Website: www.ariafiction.com
Submissions: www.ariafiction.com/
we-want-read-your-book
Facebook: @ariafiction
Twitter: @Aria_Fiction
Instagram: @ariafiction

Printed in Great Britain
by Amazon